These Games We Play

H.R. DELANO

First Edition:
ISBN: 979-8-9928726-2-0
For permissions or inquiries, contact:
hrdelanoauthor@gmail.com
Book Cover Design by H.R. Delano

For the booktok girlies.
For the dancers and those that want too, but are too scared.
The biketok girlies.
The masktok girlies.
The horny girlies.
Yes, I'm calling you out.
Oh and the gays. Don't read if you're not chill with boys kissing boys.
And let's be honest more than that.
Let's be so for real, this book has sword crossing.
Everyone loves everyone.
This is all gas. No break.
This is smut, minimal plot.
Oh and lots of club vibes.
Also, shake some ass—you deserve it.
Check out the playlist.
It's pretty fucking lit.

I don't make the rules.
Run, Princess.

To my parents.
Please don't read this.
Thanks in advance, I'll pass away from embarrassment.
I'm serious.
Don't.
Please.
The boyfriends are boyfriends.
The girl ends up with three guys.
There's strip club lore in here.
Don't do it.
Also, if you know me personally, please don't mention it.
Booktok community be a menace.
I welcome it.
Welcome to
These Games We Play

Foreword

The club in this is fictional.
I don't even think I gave it a name to be so honest with you.
However, there is a club in Myrtle Beach, SC that has a VERY similar layout.
I have worked in multiple clubs over the last twelve years.
There are some scenes that are very much inspired by real life interactions with customers.
If you know me, there may be some dancer cameos.
Anyway, enjoy, because I had fun writing this one.
Also, to my regulars in the club — don't hate me. I promise if you can make it through the sword crossing you won't hate me.
Denny and Dwight I'm looking at you two specifically. I know you two read my books and have been there from the beginning of this journey.
My bad.
Sorry.

Content Warnings

This is book is meant for audiences 18+
Why Choose means everyone is sleeping with everyone,
do with that what you will.
Exhibitionism.
Sexually Explicit. (Open Door)
Consensual Non-monogamy/Polyamorous Relationships.
Emotional intimacy between multiple partners.
Explicit Language – I like to cuss, my bad.
Jealousy, possessiveness, and internalized shame.
Discussions of trauma and past abuse (non-graphic).
Mental health struggles, including anxiety, dissociation,
and emotional overwhelm.
Depictions of grief, fear of loss, and life-altering events.
Alcohol use (consensual, non-glorified and all of age).
Power dynamics explored with care and consent.
This story prioritizes **choice, communication, and consent**.
If any of these topics are difficult for you, please take care while reading
and know that stepping away is always valid.
The choice is yours.

Playlist

Swim Chase Atlantic
One Of Those Nights - The Weeknd, Juicy J
Lollipop - Cryjaxx, JustJokay
Talking Body - Tove Lo, The Young Professionals
BABYDOLL - Ari Abdul
Him & I - Halsey, G Eazy
My First Kiss - 3OH!3, Kesha
Get U Home - Shwayze
Faster - Cal Scruby
Bad Choices - Kode
Bleed - Chri$tian Gate$
She Got Me Like - Kode
I Like the Way You Touch Me - Bryce Savage
if u think i'm pretty - Artemas
I Wanna Be Yours - Arctic Monkeys
Softcore - The Neighbourhood
Silhouettes - Daniel Javan, Rivio
Señorita - Shawn Mendes, Camila Cabello
Curiosity - Bryce Savage
Bandz A Make Her Dance - Juicy J, Lil Wayne, 2 Chainz
Bounce It - Juicy J, Wale, Trey Songz
Low Life - Future, The Weeknd
I Like How I Look - Jesse Murph
Love You Right - Shaker, COBRA
On My Door - Gio Mkl
The Way I Are - Timbaland, Keri Hilson, D.O.E.
Pour It Up - Rihanna
So Far, So Fake - DarkLux, Xizt
Minor Tone - DarkLux
RUNRUNRUN - Dutch Melrose

Millie

"Swim - Chase Atlantic"

I was fucking cold. This club was fucking cold. Jesus Christ. Could they not keep it so fucking chilly? I swear I could see my breath in this damn ice box. Maybe that was a tiny exaggeration.

Okay, to be fair I was half naked. I had on a sparkly purple bikini, if you can call it that and Pleasers, you know the dancers heels—yeah those. I really needed to get more cover ups, so at least I wasn't completely fucking freezing when I needed to wash them or forget them on my closet floor. Leave it to me to leave every last fucking dress, body-suit and crop jacket at home on the day it's witches tits cold in here.

I looked down at my Kindle, I was about two hundred pages into a fantasy novel about fae and a main character who had been kidnapped and taken to their realm, you know whatever trending book was available right now. I typically strayed away from fantasy, I would much rather read a dark romance. On the off chance that someone asked what I was reading I could at least play dumb and say it was about fairies or some shit. The loud ass music and bass never bothered me when I was here. It hadn't bothered me for a long time, but I guess when you've been dancing for longer than a few months that's what happens.

You get used to it.

"PRINCESS!!" A loud, grating annoying voice, fuck, Theo. That I would never get used too, even if I had been working with him for almost a year and a half pretty steadily. Theo was our main DJ who also played security from time to time. I hate to say it, but he did a damn good job here.

I huffed, "If you're not paying me or making me money, leave me the fuck alone." I grumbled, turning my attention back to my book.

"Are you always this fucking mean? I'm surprised you make any money at all." He rolled his eyes, if he didn't fucking work here and could indeed fuck my entire song choices up throughout the night I'd smack him.

He sat down beside me and I decided then and there I still *might* smack him.

Who knows? The night is still young.

"Don't you have things to do? Like I don't know, shuffle your playlists or something?" I asked, scooting further from him.

"I have a friend—"

"No, you're not playing matchmaker, just because I'm a dancer doesn't mean—"

"Mils—" he started and I shot him a look, he put his hands up, "Jade, I didn't mean it like that." He opened up his phone, scrolling through his social media. "I mean I think he might be your type too."

I held my hand out, he put the phone in my hand begrudgingly, I scrolled through. He was cute. No sign of partying or any other dumb shit on his profile, a few pictures from the gym, one with his cat. A clip of him in scrubs, oh a nurse? He had curly brown hair and pretty blue eyes, I scrolled long enough to find gaming clips and another profile linked to it.

His gaming account, along with Theo's gaming account. "Didn't take you for a nerd." I grinned, handing him his phone back. "You follow me, right?"

"Uh, yeah, I do." He admitted, pulling up my profile, my dancer profile.

I'm sure my face visibly paled.

"Not that one, Jesus Christ, no..." I snatched the phone, "This one." I typed in my username, *XoMilsXo* and handed it back to him.

"You're cool with me having your personal account?" He asked, hitting follow and I saw him immediately scroll through, "Oh, so you're a nerd too?"

I grimaced, knowing damn well I had wine and books posted several times, an aesthetic shot of the library and a few book hauls posted, "Hey, no—bookworms are hot." I waved my finger at him, then picked up my book to make a point.

"I mean I'm not arguing." He side eyed me, giving me his little smirk, but whatever he was about to say he cut himself off, "Where's Iris?"

"She doesn't work Monday's." I shrugged, the last few times I'd pulled her in here on a Monday she complained the whole time. Literally all night until she found ways to entertain herself, either on stage or doing content for her socials randomly around the building.

He looked around at the nonexistent crowd, "She's smart."

"Eh, she just likes the younger crowd." I waved that comment off, Monday's were how you found regulars and retirees.

"Yeah and you know your crowd better. Like him..." Theo pointed out to the guy who just walked in, he was an older gentleman, with bags under his eyes, nice shoes and looked genuinely upset.

"Oh look, you do pay attention." I smirked, as we both watched the guy get his drink and settle down. I wouldn't be the first to approach him, there were other girls who would swoop in, I could tell he wasn't one to bite right away though.

I wasn't worried even as I watched two girls approach, they immediately got turned down, "Aren't you going to introduce yourself?" Theo asked, I looked over and he was still scrolling on my page, not that I blamed him there wasn't anything else going on in this fucking club.

"Not yet, let the man breathe." I watched as he turned his gaze to the empty stage then back to his drink, "Actually, do me a favor—put on Swim for me."

"You got it Princess." He stood up, offering me his hand.

"That's so annoying." I grumbled, as I made my way to the stage.

Theo jumped right back into DJ mode, "Let's get this party started, starting with our in house Princess, Jade."

I glared at him, but didn't flip him off this time, you know upholding the 'Princess' persona he just announced to *the entire club*. Anyway, I had a show to perform as *Swim* came through the speakers around the club, if one thing Theo did do right, it was get my music spot on, but then again I tipped even when it wasn't mandatory. If I had a request, he would play it. Full stop, even if it meant he had to download it.

I swayed my hips as I made it up the stairs, pausing at the top to lift my body off the ground, holding onto the railing and doing a few air walks until the beat dropped. I crouched down to grab the rag and alcohol bottle, taking my time cleaning the pole, and yeah, maybe it was a little suggestive.

Essentially cleaning the pole meant making it look like I was jacking it off while I went around the pole swaying my hips, it's an art, okay?

Once I was sure the pole was clean and there was no oil on it, I tossed the rag to the corner of the stage and lifted myself easily with my elbow and my other hand supporting me. I could airwalk like this, or make pretty shapes with my legs. It took a lot more strength than I'd been prepared to use, but it looked good. I held it as long as I could before going to the floor, doing a little bit of floor work, I looked over at the unnamed man and held his eye contact.

I didn't necessarily like it, but it worked every time.

Hook, line and sinker.

The man gave me a small smile and I got back up, making sure to pop my butt up and down a little before doing a full stand up motion, all the while holding his eyes. I made it through the rest of the song, flipping upside down and shaking my leg to make my ass shake to the beat, and then made my descent down the stairs as the song ended. He was the only customer here, no reason to stay up there longer if he wasn't tipping.

I caught Theo's eyes once and he grinned at me, I knew he liked watching me perform. And no, that's not cocky or a jab at Theo. Most of the employees and other girls too would watch the stage sets. If you could hold attention to the room, to the stage, everyone typically watched.

It wasn't cocky, it was performance.

He nodded to the bar, where the mystery man was still sitting, watching me walk over now. "Can I get you a drink?" He asked, "You look like you could use one after all that."

I shrugged him off, "That was light work," I gave him a warm smile, "But yeah, I'll take a drink. My name is Jade, what's yours?"

"Walter," he looked me over, "You don't look like a Jade, it's definitely a fake name."

Lord, send me the fucking patience.

"Well yeah, I don't want us to get in trouble with my real name, besides it sounds like a grannie name." I huffed, lowering my voice, "Surely you wouldn't think I was serious if I'd told you my name was Mabel..."

"Mabel?" He questioned and I ssshhhed him.

"Don't be so loud, I don't need anyone knowing that information." Of course Mabel wasn't my real name, it was the fake name I gave them when I needed them to believe it, to connect with me more.

My real name was just as bad honestly, Matilda. Who names their kid Matilda? That's why I went by Millie outside of here.

"Well, *Jade*," he said pointedly, "How long have you been here?"

"Oh you know, about a year on and off, no one stays long so I'm probably one of the few girls who's been here the longest." I shrugged, "Have you ever been here before? I'm sure I'd recognize you if you'd been here before." I reached out to lace my fingers in his.

"I haven't, I just finalized my divorce, used to hit the clubs all the time in my younger days, figured now was as good a time as any." He gave me a small smile as he flagged the bartender down. "Whatever the lady wants."

"Pineapple juice, tequila and a splash of grenadine." I said with a sweet smile, the bartender started on it, before checking his beer and silently asking if he wanted another.

"So how long were you and your wife together?"

"Twenty long wasted years." He admitted, "Actually Kiara, can you get me a double shot of tequila too?" I didn't know Kiara that well, she was new, I had actually been calling her K because I wasn't sure what her name was, we went through bartenders as fast as dancers these days. "Make that two, we're celebrating my divorce."

I looked up at Theo as I cheersed and slammed the double shot down, fuck three tequilas this close together was not my plan, I needed to sip this fucking drink. She handed me the pretty orange drink and dropped two cherries in it, Theo winked at me.

As much as I called him a bastard, he knew me, he knew me well enough to tell the bartender to drop cherries in my drink. Two for fake drinks, one for alcohol.

Bless him. Also, I really loved cherries.

"So, since you've never been here, do you want the tour? I'm sure they'll let me give you the VIP treatment since there's not much going on around here. Normally we have a manager do it, but ya know." I drug my hand across his shoulder, using my nails to give him goosebumps.

If you could get them to give you a full body response, you were in, for the night. Maybe longer honestly. "Yeah, I'd love to see the rooms."

I looked for a manager, finding none. I looked at Theo and shouted, "I'm giving a tour. If Jonah asks where I went let him know, please?"

Theo nodded, doing something on his laptop. I took his hand in mine and took him towards the back hallway, past the VIP desk, "Typically you have to call ahead for a tour," I said quietly, even if it was a lie, we could do tours whenever as long as we weren't busy. "But I'm making an exception for you, tonight we're celebrating. We're going to give you the best night of your life." His hand tightened in mine, I had it in the bag.

I felt bad, but then again I also didn't. I was a damn good time and he would be paying for my company, my presence. "First stop is our lap dance rooms, as you see they're very open and not that private, but we can still have a good time." I gave him a soft smile, before tugging him towards the champagne rooms, which was a fancy name for a room with a couch and mirrors hidden behind a curtain.

The illusion of privacy, but big brother was always watching and by big brother I meant Jonah, Theo and whatever bartender that was on rotation. The cameras were on screens behind the managers desk, the bar and the DJ booth, just in case. These cameras were so good, you could zoom in on an ingrown hair and see it.

I liked it, I liked the fact that I was safe. That nothing could happen, that they couldn't hire in girls who would try to break the rules. Or get away with it. That shit didn't belong in clubs. "Next we have our shower shows and hot tubs!"

I gestured for him to follow me down another hallway, "This is one of two shower rooms, the other is actually closer to the front, but this one is the one I default to because it's more private."

"Can I?" He asked, I nodded as he stepped into the room, a mirror lined room with double shower heads. "How do these work?"

"Well, we are still only bikini, so I have to keep this on, but you can join in and we give you swim trunks to change into, brand new and you get to keep them. You get a free drink back here and in the hot tub. Speaking of, would you like to see that?"

He nodded eagerly and I slipped my hand back in his, tugging him further down the hallway. Hot tub row, we had three of them. "These take a little bit of time to get ready, but it's an hour and you can always add in more time if you want. They get cleaned and drained after each use, then refilled. That's why they're empty right now." I ran my fingers across his back, "This way, I want to show you my favorite!" I grinned, walking to the very back. It was the bigger one, and also the only one that wasn't plain white.

"This looks nice," he admitted, "How much do these cost?"

"I can show you a price list when we get back to the front, I don't want to tell you the wrong thing." We didn't make our own prices, but we did get half of whatever it was, and some girls lied to try to make more money. That wasn't me, not when the prices were listed everywhere, the right customer would tip well.

When we got to the VIP desk, I showed him the price list, "Would you like me to get a drink order submitted for you?"

"Actually, yeah."

"What are you thinking today? I see Jade gave you the tour." Jonah said as he eyed me and then back to the customer, Walter

"I think I want to do a hot tub, with that one." He pointed at me, pulling cash out. Fuck yeah, we love a customer who pays in cash.

Jonah wrote my name down, "I'll tell you what, since you have to wait I'll cover a drink for both of you now and then once when you get back there."

Walter beamed, handing the cash over, coming back to the bar and sliding his arm around my waist as I ordered my drink again.

"I'll do an orange juice and tequila." He told her, we sat with our drinks.

In the time it took to fill up the hot tub, the back one, because Jonah knew me by now, I had learned Walter's wife had slept with his office manager. He owned several of the hotels up and down Myrtle Beach and he had a son a few years younger than me.

"She sounds like she didn't deserve you." I sighed, rubbing his back as he wiped a tear from his cheek, "You gave her everything and she took everything."

"Good news is I found out before I made her the main holder for my life insurance policies." He chuckled, "Now my son will get everything and she's left with nothing, well except for the beach house in Florida and one of the hotels in Tampa."

"Better to find out now, than way later and let her make off like a bandit, right?" I smiled, holding his eyes and trying to let him know I cared.

I mean I did care, don't get me wrong the whole situation was fucked, but in my eyes she was already making off like a bandit.

"Jade, your hot tub is almost ready if you want to change?" Jonah handed him a pair of swim trunks and pointed him to the bathroom. I kept a change of water safe outfits, because while these were technically bikini's they were hand wash only and I wasn't letting the hot tub fuck it up. They were expensive.

"I'll be right back," I whispered in his ear, drinking the rest of my drink in one go.

I changed into my dark green bikini, the one with the thong back, and ditched my heels. Loading up my *Shower Shows and Hot Tub Vibes* playlist. A decent mix between sensual and party music depending on what they were feeling.

I hoped it was party music.

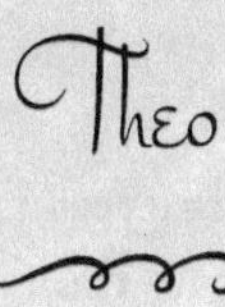

"One of Those Nights - Juicy J, The Weeknd"

Every time I saw Millie—Jade—crushing it, I was in awe. He had turned down every girl before her and somehow she'd managed to get him into that hot tub with several drinks already in his system, off of a simple tour.

And worse? She's turned off my music playing through the speakers to play her own, like I would play absolute bangers for them, but whatever. Spoiled brat, but hey she tipped well, so I wouldn't openly complain.

I glanced at the monitor, checking the camera as she led him into the hot tub area, all sass and sweetness in her movements. I could hear the faint mix of her music even from here, but she was our top earner, she could do what she wanted. We wouldn't tell her that, she didn't need the bigger ego boost, and even then I was pretty sure she knew it. Her and Iris, were always competing for the top spot, they never really competed in all seriousness, but they were always spot one and two on the dances for the month.

She was also the best tipper, we didn't even have a mandatory tip but she knew it worked out in her favor. We'd always get her music right, stash cash at the bar from fake drinks for her to pick up, and get her in with the big spenders and parties. It was unspoken between us and the girls who tipped well, they take care of us, we take care of them.

Protection was different, every girl in this building got the same amount of protection, I'd go down swinging if I had to get involved. If I was closer than security it was me and believe me I had. One thing about this industry, everyone is a threat in waiting, and no one touches our girls.

No one.

If they're in this building they're safe. Shit, even in the parking lot. If security couldn't walk them to their cars, I would.

I glanced down at the security camera, not her room, I'm not a creep. She had the big monitor by the front, Jonah was keeping an eye on her, I was however watching the parking lot and our outdoor smoking section.

I'd sent Coop her profile and no, not her dancer account, her real account. It was a mix of sunset photos, the occasional selfie, and a few sexier mirror shots. He'd appreciate it, he loved a red head. Natural or not I wasn't sure, but she was his type on paper.

She seemed to be a lot of people's type actually, maybe that was part of the reason she did so well here. Give men a perfect little red head spitfire and they cave.

I hit like on one of the most recent pictures, it was a yellow energy drink she was holding between perfectly manicured fingers against a backdrop of morning glories. I'd file that away, she liked the yellow ones.

File it away for Coop of course.

Speaking of, I looked down at the notification.

Coop: Who is she and why did you send me her profile?

I hesitated, why was I honestly?

If I was being honest, to get her to stop fucking flirting with me and maybe so I'd stop thinking about my best friend like—*like that.*

Theo: I work with her, thought you might like her.

Coop: I don't need you meddling in my love life.

Theo: Give her a chance, she plays sometimes, she's a bookworm. She was talking about playing Splitgate the other day. Just message her, she thinks you're cute.

Coop: She said I was cute... that's not a good sign.

Theo: From her it is.

I rolled my eyes, he was hopeless.

A few hours later, Jade made her way back out, giving him an unsteady hug. Fuck, how many drinks had she had, it was a fucking Monday. I didn't see her order anymore, so maybe a waitress was bringing them back there. Fuck I can't put her on stage if she's too fucking drunk. Her make up was messed up as she walked over to me and handed me a hundred dollars, "That's too much." I raised an eyebrow and handed it back.

"Shut up Theo, take the tip I did two hours in the hot tub."

"Only if you do me a big favor," I gave her my best puppy dog eyes, watch her break out into a grin at my antics, "I need you take your money that's on you right now and go lock it in your locker."

She huffed, "That's so far away, but you're right." She held up her finger, pointing at the screen. "Only if you let me choose my stage set."

"Can you even dance right now?" I couldn't help the amusement that spilled across my words.

She gasped, I couldn't tell if the offense was real or fake. "Are you challenging me right now?"

"Go, Princess." I pointed towards the dressing room.

"Yes, sir." She mockingly saluted me, but the way she said it and the way she looked at me right now? Fuck. She was in feral gremlin mode.

"And fix your make-up..for fuck's sake." I yelled, she flipped me off as she strutted to the back. I queued up the next girl's two songs as the current song ended, "Chloe, one song away."

By the time Millie came back out, her hair was basically all the way dry. She did fix her makeup, and she was now wearing the black strappy set I'd complimented her on before. She met my eyes and gestured down her body, I nodded my approval as she made her way to me.

She squinted at the computer, leaning in to swipe up on my screen, I swatted her hand. She sighed dramatically. "I want The Weeknd, Tyga, or blackbear. Give me something I can fucking kill on stage dude."

"You're only getting on stage if you don't drink anymore." I crossed my arms, looking at her stubborn ass, "I mean it."

"You're killing the vibe." She huffed, holding a finger out to me. "Two more drinks and I'll stop drinking."

I checked my phone, "It's already eleven."

"And we'll probably be here until three a.m. so fuck off." She flipped me off again, "But fine, you win this round."

"Two more drinks and I'm telling Kiara no more for you."

She groaned dramatically, "Spoil sport, put me next."

I looked at her and pointed at the playlist that was already queued up. "I already called Chloe one song away you fucking menace, wait your turn."

She crossed her arms to mirror me and I tried not to look at her cleavage that was spilling over, I redirected my attention to the group of guys that had come in. "You see that group over there, they just came in —they look like golfers, go get 'em."

She looked over as they sat down, "I'm only leaving because I'm sure their conversation will be better."

"I'm sure it'll be riveting." I smirked, shooing her away.

She scrunched her nose and sneered at me before dancing along to the music as she walked away. I couldn't hear her conversation from across the room, but I did know the song was ending. "Chloe to the stage, Chloe to the stage."

I watched the pretty blonde circle the pole, not even bothering to clean it. She was younger and didn't even bother attempting to do pole tricks, more fixated on shaking her butt, or well trying.

Maybe I could convince Millie to help run classes eventually. Most of the girls needed it. Fuck, why did my brain keep going to her? I glanced up to see her watching the girl intently, I knew she was silently judging her. She'd never say anything outside of constructive, but when she took the money from the guy's stack on the table and gave it to the dancer I couldn't stop the chuckle that came out of my mouth.

Millie resumed her animated talking, her hand resting on one of the guy's thighs as she listened to what he was saying. This girl was too fucking good. Too fucking good at this. "Jade, one song away. Jade one song away." She met my eyes and nodded. I loaded up a Juicy J song, one that had The Weeknd in it to play next.

When it started playing, she was already making her way. "Our very own Princess... Jade on stage." She did flip me off this time and yeah I knew I was pushing it doing that with a huge crowd here, but it was a fucking Monday for crying out loud.

She took her time cleaning the pole, this time keeping her eyes on the guy who she'd been all touchy feely with. She went into a pole trick, hooking her leg at the knee and sliding down to the ground.

Oh yeah, she was drunk. I had misjudged the amount she'd had. She never went straight to floorwork. She called the man over with her finger, and he sat at the stage seating. She took a dollar from him and shoved it in his shirt collar, then put another in his belt loop.

Fuck, she was reckless for that, she knew better than to come off the stage, but still no one stopped her. Probably because she'd already tipped everyone a hundred and the night wasn't over.

She put her hands on his chair and had him lean back. I knew the next move well, it was a signature on a Friday or Saturday night if she worked. She swooped down and took the one from his belt buckle with her teeth, dragging her upper body up slowly, taking the bill and tossing it behind her on stage. She did the same after a second with the one on his collar, his face went beat red and he nodded.

That little minx sold another dance I guarantee it. The song ended and the next one played, "Jasmine, one song away."

I played a remix of Lollipop, an edm vibe, to bring us into Jasmine's genre. Millie fish flopped over her shoulder perfectly, despite the copious amounts of alcohol in her system and started shaking her ass in time with the song. When she stood up, she started climbing the pole.

She better not go all the way up, I swear to God.

She did. All the way to the top, grabbed the wooden rafter pieces and shook her ass before swinging back to the pole. I hate when the girls did that, there was no fucking reason for it. None at all, other than shock value.

If you can't tell, I hate heights.

When the song ended I called Jasmine again, letting her know it was time for her to go up. Jasmine was good on stage, so I didn't feel bad about putting her on after Millie. I tried not to put girls that couldn't do pole on after her, for obvious reasons. I didn't want to fuck with someone else's money.

I was right, Millie took the guy by the hand and disappeared into VIP.

I tapped the glass separating the bartender from me, "Two cherries, no more alcohol for her. She's done."

Kiara giggled, "Yeah, kinda figured. She turns into a grade A flirt with you when she's drunk."

"She's like that with everyone, even the girls." I rolled my eyes, because honestly it wasn't just me. And if it was? I hadn't noticed, I figured that's how she was.

Millie

Oooops. I was drunk.

I had finished a thirty minute VIP, gotten a two hundred dollar tip and told a man off for trying to touch places he didn't need to be. I'd pointed at the cameras and told him if he did it again I was walking out. No refunds. I showed the offense all over my face as I asked for a tip for dealing with his bullshit. The actual audacity of men these days.

Oh and I made him sit on his damn hands.

Four hundred dollars and putting a man in his place? Fuck yeah. I'd take it. I'd been given fake drinks after I got back there, I'd been mad at Theo's meddling, but honestly he had been right.

I was indeed a little blitzed, but I can handle myself. I'd only had six tequilas, yeah six.

Wait no, *eight.*

Ooops.

Yeah, okay. We're done. *You're done*. I forced myself to get dressed. I knew better than to try to leave so I locked everything up in my locker, money included—with the exception of the extra twenties for the extra bit of tip out. I started with the floor staff, signed out with Jonah at VIP and then tipped the bartender before moving over to the DJ booth.

The lights near the booth were dimmer, pulsing with every hit of the bass that thudded through the soles of my fuzzy cow slippers. The booth always smelled like his cologne, which smelled fucking good by the way, and the faint smell of overheated equipment that had been working overtime all night. They needed to get it proper cooling or something, it always smelled like it could burn the place down if left unattended for too long.

Also Eeverything felt a little spinny. Just a little.

"You can't leave." Damn, why was he so snarky with me? What did I do to him?

"Do you see my bag, asshole?" I asked as he looked at me, a grin breaking out over his face.

"No, but I see your cow slippers and that's exactly what I needed." He laughed, checking the rotation. "Abby to the stage, Abby to the stage." He said into the microphone.

I slid the twenty into his little tip jar and he side eyed me again, "Why did you give me more?" He asked, lifting a brow as I swayed a bit, just a tiny bit I swear. Minimal sway.

I leaned against the wall of the booth and looked up at him from my lashes. "I did a thirty minute, you can take the fucking twenty." I crossed my arms, shifting my feet in my cow slippers.

"Watch your foul mouth, Princess." He grinned, clearly trying to get under my skin, "Also maybe message my friend back."

Shit, I'd forgot about that.

"Pushy, pushy." I groaned, sitting on the floor behind him. The floor was cold against the backs of my legs, grounding and dizzying at the same time. "If you wanted to hang out with me outside of work you could just ask." I surprised myself with that one.

Ooooops.

He didn't say anything to that, probably done with my bullshit. Instead, he adjusted a dial like he needed something to do with his hands. He had a weird look on his face like he didn't know why I'd said that. To be fair, neither did I.

"Don't touch anything back there." I had barely lifted my hand to mess with one of the fidget toys he had tossed on the floor. Damn he knew me too well. Why did he have them back here if I couldn't fidget with them, make it make sense.

"You're literally no fun." I grumbled, opening my phone to see a message from Coop in my DM's. I grinned despite myself. It had been way too long since I'd had any fun, gone on any dates or shit even slept with someone.

Maybe I needed this. Maybe I needed some fun. And if he knew I worked with Theo then he knew about my job and probably, probably being the keyword here, wouldn't mind the job so much. I mean maybe he didn't know... maybe that would be a selling point. Most guys didn't want anything to do with a dancer. Well, except for sex. I just couldn't do it. I wouldn't do it again.

One night stands felt yucky. Don't get me wrong, I'd had them before—but I craved connection. I wanted to know the person. I was clingy, okay? I can admit that.

Fuck, I was not sober enough for this, Coop was cute—no scratch that he was fucking hot—but Theo trying to set us up was odd. Drunk mind me was overthinking it. Way overthinking it.

CoopXPlays: I guess he thought we'd like each other.

XoMilsXo: I mean, we do both play. I don't play as much as you guys of course, actually you probably wouldn't even call me a gamer to be honest.

Shit, did that even make sense. I stared at it for a second then sent.

XoMilsXo: If that doesn't make sense, sorry. Alcohol.

CoopXPlays: How do you know the asshole I call my best friend?

XoMilsXo: I work with him. He is an asshole, he told me not to touch anything. I've been sentenced to sit on the floor behind him.

CoopXPlays: He's making you sit on the floor?

XoMilsXo: Technically, I'm using the DJ booth to hide from customers.

CoopXPlays: Ah so you're using him as cover to text me?

XoMilsXo: Kinda. I am also one too many shots deep.

I snapped a picture of Theo in DJ mode and sent it to him—blue and pink lights splashing across his face, headphones around his neck, the faint shadow of a smirk like he could sense I was talking about him..

CoopXPlays: As much as I love him, I'd rather see you.

XoMilsXo: Don't make me blush.

I turned my camera to face me, making a kissy face because smiling felt awkward right now. The flash lit my eyes up green-gold. I could feel the tips of my ears heating as I hit send.

CoopXPlays: Damn, he was right.

CoopXPlays: You are my type.

XoMilsXo: A drunk dancer?

CoopXPlays: A cute redhead, with pretty eyes and a little bit of attitude.

XoMilsXo: A little? He must not have told you, I'm a menace who expects Princess treatment.

CoopXPlays: Oh no, he told me you were a spoiled brat.

"Spoiled brat? Very on brand Theo." I mumbled, more to myself but I swore I saw him grin when he looked back at me.

XoMilsXo: Geee, great hype man there you've got.

CoopXPlays: He's my wingman, not yours.

XoMilsXo: Maybe in real life, but here he's mine. XD

CoopXPlays: You did NOT just XD

XoMilsXo: Yeah, that was cringe. My bad.

Theo looked down, checking to make sure I wasn't fucking with anything and then tried to get a look at my phone. His eyes flicked from the screen to my face, and for a split second he hesitated—just long enough for me to catch the way his gaze locked on my flushed cheeks like he was trying to figure out what was being said.

"No snooping. I could have been sending him nudes." I hid my phone, scandalized.

"One, you didn't." He said it too smoothly, too confidently, "You get paid for those when you do send them."My mouth dropped open, because how did he even know that? He leaned back in his chair, "Two, he'd show them to me."

I gasped, "No, he wouldn't."

Theo flashed me a dazzling smile, "You're right, he wouldn't. Not without your permission anyway."

"Theo!!" I giggled, because I could never actually be that bold, but my cheeks heated. "Not like you'd look anyway." I shrugged.

"I wouldn't?" He raised an eyebrow. "I don't know, I'd probably look if you wanted me too."

"NOPE. TOO DRUNK." I squealed, then quieter, "We are at work, this is harassment."

He chuckled, "Mmmhmm, that's probably the least worrisome thing we've said to each other."

I didn't miss the way he studied me for a minute before turning back to his computer. Had we said worse things? If we had, I couldn't recall it right now.

Weird as fuck honestly. Was he flirting with me? He just set me up with his friend? Weird. As. Fuck.

I'm too drunk. Let me not.

Link

I hadn't heard from the guy I'd been hooking up with for the last few months and I was on edge. Like fuck, being in a house with the girl I'd loved since middle school and having no outlet to get all this fucking tension out was really getting to me.

Until I saw *his* car pull up instead of Millie's and that he was half carrying her ass back to the house. Why the fuck was he here, with her? How did he know her? I swear to God if she got in some random guys car I'd probably beat her fucking ass.

I opened the door and met him on the porch, "She didn't listen and didn't stop drinking." His eyes met mine and he immediately tried to look away. "Fuck, okay... didn't realize you were the roommate..."

"Didn't realize you worked with her." I admitted, looking at how she seemed so at ease with him—even drunk Millie wouldn't let someone she didn't like drive her home.

"You two know each other? How the fuck is that possible?" Millie slurred as she stumbled out of his grip to me.

Oh, you know.... Just my secret hookup, but if he wasn't out about his sexuality I wasn't going to be the one to out him. "Just in passing." I glared at him.

"Yeah, it's not anything..." Theo looked hurt by that, the slightest flicker or irritation passing over his features. Fucking good, stupid asshole ghosted me. "Ummm—all of her stuff is still at the club, it's locked up. So if she asks about her money or anything it's all in her locker. She's on the schedule for tomorrow, but I doubt she'll want to come in."

"I'm right here. Geez." She looked at me, then at Theo, "Stop glaring at him Lincoln Scott, he's cool, did you know he set me up with his friend? Cooper?" Millie stumbled and both Theo and I leaned forward to catch her.

She caught herself, steadying herself on his shoulder. He looked down at her, "You good there Prin–" He cut himself off when she glared at him, but I didn't miss the way she lingered for a second longer than she should. I knew drunk Millie and drunk Millie didn't get close unless she was extremely comfortable with someone.

"I've got it from here, don't worry about her." I pulled her into me and she rolled her eyes, smacking my hands.

"I can get to my room by myself. Thanks Theo, I'll uh see you tomorrow. I 'preciate you." Millie waved awkwardly. Her cheeks reddened, as she stumbled off to her room.

Oh god, not her too.

Theo looked at the floor, "I uh, didn't realize she was your best friend."

"You hooked her up with Coop? The guy you were crying to me about? The one you said you couldn't do this anymore over? Are you fucking serious?!" I raised my voice slightly, but he shhhed me.

Fucking bastard. Shhhing me in my own house.

He stepped closer, but I stepped back. "Stop... I thought maybe if he was with someone else, someone good for him it'd be easier to move forward." Theo said with a shrug.

"And Millie looking at you like that?" I asked, blunt and to the point I guess.

He looked down the hallway to where she disappeared too. "She's drunk, she gets flirty when she's drunk, it's nothing new and definitely not something I can't handle."

I didn't have time to play games with him, "Go home Theo."

"Link...I—" He tried, I'll give him that.

I cut him off, pointing at the door. "Go home. I can't."

"You may have to get used to me being around, her and Coop hit it off tonight." His voice was so small, I wasn't used to that. Almost like he didn't want to admit it, like that made it real.

My brows pulled together, if he came in as a customer she had to be fucking careful. "He came into the club? That makes him a customer."

"No, they were texting all night. She changed and sat behind the DJ booth with me once she realized she was entirely too drunk and progressively getting more drunk." He looked up, "I did cut her off, but the night was actually pretty lively for a Monday and by time I realized she was in the back drinking a lot I cut her off at the bar."

"You didn't let her work after that did you?" I asked, my voice softening, because when it came to her nothing else mattered,

Theo nodded, "She changed by herself and then sat with me the rest of the night." He tilted his head slightly, "She's safe when I'm there, I can promise you that."

That did make me feel slightly better, I knew Theo was a good one. I knew that, but the question was why her? "And you don't think it's weird she chose to hang out with you over the other girls?"

"She only hangs out with Iris, well I mean shit what's her damn name—Grace I think. And Grace doesn't work Mondays." He chewed his lip, he probably wasn't lying about that. My girl was anti-social as fuck.

I couldn't stop the judgmental look that fell on my face, "It's weird that you're that close to her."

"It's not... we're co-workers." He stated, like he only half-believed that. "It's not like that."

"Uhuh," I sighed, "Just be careful." I warned, because when it came to her I'd start a fucking war. I'd blow everything up if it meant she was safe and happy. I'd burn the whole world down and cut every tie if she wanted me too.

"What is that supposed to mean?" He asked, studying me.

Millie popped her head out of the bathroom, "Link stop! It's Theo.... Leave the man alone, it's not like he came to stay the night. Jesus Christ. Let him go home."

"You heard her, go home." I pointed at the door.

"I'm sorry I ghosted you." He whispered and for a second I thought he might step closer to me, but he closed the door and his headlights pulled out of the driveway a few seconds later.

Millie crossed her arms over chest, "Did you have to be so mean? He drove me home."

"He wants in your pants." I fixed her with a pointed glare, she really was fucking clueless sometimes.

"Who Theo??!" She scrunched her face up in disgust, "He definitely does not. He set me up with Coop. We insult each other daily. Sure he's a little flirty, but I'm guilty of that too."

"You talk a lot for someone who couldn't drive their own car home." I fired off.

She pouted, completely unbothered by my jab. "Can we cuddle?"

I groaned, "Mils, baby girl—" Oops, that wasn't supposed to slip through, her eyes widened, she definitely heard it, "You're very drunk, probably disgustingly warm. You smell like a distillery."

"I can shower and change." She said quickly, Jesus she was a baby when she drank.

"Go get in your bed." I pointed to her room and she crossed her arms stubbornly.

Her eyes looked watery, but it was definitely fake. I'd seen her do that before. "Fine... but I'm going to cry."

Dramatic and spoiled.

I caved.

She had already stripped off most of her clothes and was now only in a super long tee shirt, it looked like one of mine. I groaned and crawled into bed with her anyway. She rolled into my chest immediately and I tried really hard not to think about how she basically pretzeled herself around me.

Maybe Theo was right, she was a damn flirt when she was drunk.

A flirt and obnoxiously cuddly.

Leave it to Theo to set me up with someone who matched my humor and sarcasm beat-for-beat. We'd been talking for days. Literally non-stop.

She was going to be a problem. I could feel it in my soul and she wanted to do a game night? Easy. Lower stakes than meeting up in person. We'd all hop into a Discord server, load up Splitgate, and if we survived that as a group... Well, nothing reveals compatibility like trying to portal-run your way out of getting killed by other players.

Theo didn't sound convinced about tonight, but he still joined my party. He was quieter than normal once Millie and her friend loaded in. We sat in the Splitgate lobby letting the awkward, pre-match silence surround us.

Millie's voice filled my headset, "Just so you both know, being able to play and being good are two very different things. I am not good. I will probably find a spot to cover you from afar."

"So, you're gonna camp?" Theo deadpanned, leave it to Theo to immediately be a fucking asshole.

"She doesn't like to call it camping," Link chimed in. "She calls it covering our asses from afar. She's a better sniper than a run-and-shoot."

"I don't have the coordination for all that." She admitted, "Also makes me sick to my stomach, I have motion sickness when I run around too much,"

"That's because you refuse to look around while running." Link huffed. "Now ready up."

"Bossy as fuck," she whispered—except she absolutely did not whisper. Theo chuckled, and I caught it immediately. Huh.

Theo cut in again, voice low and teasing. "Is the infamous sass queen taking orders?"

"I can listen. When I want to." Her tone was pure bite. Interesting.

Maybe Theo wasn't exaggerating about them not vibing. Or… whatever the hell that was.

"What's your sensitivity set at?" I asked, because that would definitely cause the dizzy effect if it was up too high.

She was quiet for a minute, "Too fucking high, Link you could have told me I could set it lower, you've just been letting me fuck shit up for no reason?"

Link laughed, "Mils, I just want you to play with me, but now I guess I've got two other people to play with."

We queued up and after a few games I could tell she wasn't half bad. Kill count nowhere near ours, sure, but she took out more enemies than she gave herself credit for. She ran through portals, followed us and did save me from afar a few times.

"Fuck!!! I've been spotted!" she yelped, diving through a portal. "Didn't die though!"

A beat later someone shredded her. "Fuuuuuck meeeee. I just got here."

"You're doing great, Princess. We've got you. Get back to a spot where you can see us." Theo's voice sounded so fucking soft.

I wish he was here right now, because I'm sure the look on my face would have shocked him into silence—Princess? Where the hell did that come from?

She groaned. "Dude—seriously? In the game too??"

Theo laughed but didn't push it, I knew that nervous fucking laugh anywhere, he'd fucked up and he knew it.

"Mils, follow me!" Link barked as his character darted around a corner.

"Fuck!" I shouted as someone surprised me and dropped me instantly. Fucking assholes.

I respawned a few seconds after Millie. She spun toward me. "Fancy seeing you here. C'mon, follow me!" I did, trailing her until I saw Link get ambushed.

"Go find somewhere to cover us, love." I told her, distracted, eyes on the kill feed.

"Ooop. Love?" Link cackled. "Already with the pet names?"

"Shut up, Lincoln," Millie grumbled, as the ambush caught up to him.

"Fuuuuuuuck, I'm down. Love is better than Princess, I guess," he snorted and it was followed by the unmistakable sound of him getting smacked in real life.

Millie groaned, then screamed, then very calmly might add, "I hate this fucking map."

The match ended with us barely scraping a win, mostly because Millie sniped the two dudes trying to go through a portal we just hopped through. "Let's gooooo!!!!" she shouted, immediately followed by, "I deserve cuddles for that."

"You deserve to not be on this map," Theo muttered.

"You deserve to mind your business," she fired back.

And that's when I knew these two were either going to murder each other or adopt each other.

No in-between.

"Queue us again," Link said. "I'm warmed up now."

"Oh, is that why you did so tragically?" Millie cackled, "You weren't warmed up?"

Link gasped. "That's rude as fuck ba–"

"Don't." Millie warned, whatever he was about to say he stopped.

I felt myself smiling like an idiot at my tv, because hearing her spill profanities at the game was fucking hilarious, but the way she really did try to cover us was pretty good, I couldn't lie.

Babygirl knew what she was doing.

We loaded into the next match and immediately all hell broke loose.

"Oh my god—WHY ARE THERE SO MANY OF THEM?" Millie shrieked as three enemies rounded the corner.

"Princess, behind you." Theo said, and I chose to ignore it.

"I SWEAR TO GOD—stop calling me that!" she said right as she spun around and fired at someone directly in the face. God damn, a headshot.

"Never mind. Keep it. You earned it. You're Princess now." I said, because god damn it, her attractive score just went up.

Link lost it laughing, I did too and something about the sound of her laughing with us made me want to latch on and never let go. None of my previous girlfriends ever entertained the thought of my gaming, let alone played with me and my friends.

Mid-match, she got pinned near a portal. “Coop, I’m stuck, help!”

I noticed Link was closer, but didn’t say anything, she’d defaulted to me. “I’ve got you.”

I flung a portal at a wall and slid through, popped the guy chasing her, then stood between her avatar and the rest of his team. “Oop—okay Knight in Shining Armor,” she teased as I shot three more players.

My cheeks actually got hot. Over gamer chat. I needed help.

“Don’t hype him up,” Theo said. “His ego can’t take it.”

“Better than yours, apparently,” she shot back.

Theo went silent.

Link whispered, “Oh she's vicious-vicious tonight.”

Millie yawned, “I’m probably not gonna be on much longer, I stayed up basically all night and all day.

“You’re tapping out already?” I asked, not wanting to stop talking to her yet.

“No,” she said, softening for a second. “I’m just getting sleepy.”

And bro—BRO—why did my chest tighten at that?

Theo cleared his throat. “We can do one more match and call it quits if you’re tired.”

“I’m fine,” she said quietly, “but... if I randomly go quiet, just assume I fell asleep or died.”

We loaded into the final round of the night, and something shifted. Less chaos. More banter, more quiet confidence between us. More of her following my lead without me asking. More of me checking on her without thinking.

And I couldn’t tell if we’d actually gotten better as a team or if we were just entering a late night flow state.

Once the game was over, Theo and Link logged off first, basically forcing her off the game.

“You want to video call?” I asked quietly, hoping she said yes.

“I’m probably going to fall asleep on the phone, but yeah, give me like five minutes.

The phone rang in three, she was wearing a hoodie and had the blanket wrapped around her entire body. “Hey beautiful.” I said, getting into my own bed. Thank God for ten foot chargers.

“Hey Coop.” She did look sleepy, not just sleepy but exhausted.

“Thank you for playing with us.”

“Sorry I suck.”

“You don’t suck.” I laughed, “You actually do better than I thought for someone who camps.”

“Now you sound like your asshole friend.” She grinned, “It’s called saving your ass from afar.”

“Whatever you say, baby girl.” I grinned, reaching down to pet my cat as he jumped up on the bed, he swiped at my hand before doing his little circle walk and laying at the foot of my bed.

Her cheeks went red, even in the dim light of her phone screen I could see it. Her lashes fluttered closed and I smiled to myself, she was fighting sleep. “Goodnight love.” I said quietly and I saw the smallest smile tug at her lips.

Millie

"Talking Body - Tove Lo, The Young Professionals"

I checked my phone, fuck, it was already midnight and Gracie—Iris here—and I were already five shots deep because we conned Phillip into drinks. Fucking Phillip, he didn't do dances, he'd occasionally tip twenty or fifty if you stayed with him long enough. He wasn't terrible company, actually we always joked he could take us to Costco with his membership and stock our house with groceries.

He talked about Costco like he was having a love affair with it, he did bring snacks from Costco too. So, we couldn't complain when he was bringing us goodies and tipping us.

He didn't do dances because he loved his wife, but he also really loved the scenery of the club. The scenery was us, he just liked attention, like most of the men who frequented these doors. Iris and I had each gotten a fifty and a drink an hour.

Other than that, the club was dead except the four construction workers who didn't speak a lick of English. Which would be fine, I have a translator app I use to talk back and forth most of the time, but these guys were here for food and a free show. It was part of the reason no one was on stage.

There was literally no point.

I rolled my eyes as Theo made it a point to nod his head to them, I stalked over to the DJ booth. "I'm not fucking with them. They don't do dances."

"Don't be a brat," his eyes raked over me, "Go say hi so, that way you're on camera doing your job, give it fifteen minutes then dip."

"I'll give it ten and then I'm out." I met his eyes, "And if I do something rash, it's not my fault."

He pinched his nose between his eyes, "For fuck's sake Mil—"

He did *NOT* just say my real name. "Theodore. Keep in mind where we are."

He ran his hand through his hair, before looking at me. "Jade. Don't push me today."

Oh he looked serious. "Okay," I put my hands up in mock surrender, "Yes sir, Daddy DJ."

His face was priceless, "Why do you insist on being like this?"

"Sorry, not sorry. Don't boss me around then." I stuck out my tongue, "Play some decent songs at the bare minimum."

I watched him inhale and look up to the ceiling, probably praying for strength to deal with me tonight. I was bored, okay? Maybe I wanted to stir the pot, although I probably shouldn't stir the pot with him. Eh, whatever, it was probably fine.

I swayed my head, feeling the music as he hit the smoke machine and fog poured from the ceiling causing a little light show with the stage lights in the background. I sat down beside one of the least familiar guys, the one who sat with a stack of ones still wrapped in a rubber band. I pointed at it and pointed at his lap. "Dance?" I asked.

He shook his head and pointed at the middle man, I turned to him, putting my hand on his leg and squeezing. "You're coming with me." I snatched the money right off the table. There were three stacks rubber banded. I could get a fifteen minute VIP and a tip with that, not a great tip, but I'd take it.

He came willing when I pulled him, I caught Theo's eyes and he eyed the money in my hand as I tugged the dude to the counter. I could see the amusement on his face, it was like he was shocked I would do that.

"Fifteen minutes. Please and thank you." I said to Jonah, putting the stacks of ones down.

Jonah grinned and ran it through the money counter and attempted to give the change to the customer. I snatched it and shoved it in my purse. I was not fucking playing tonight. With anyone—customers, dancers, management, annoying ass DJ's.

I pulled the man to one of our couch rooms and pushed him to a sitting position. He went to unbutton his pants and I smacked him. "NO." I said, loudly and then pointed at the camera.

I did the bare minimum, if he touched me I smacked him. Teach these bitches a lesson in flaunting money and never spending it. I was already making my money from this room, it didn't matter if he was happy or not.

No motherfucking refunds.

I checked myself out in the mirror, focusing on how good my hair looked today. I also needed to do my makeup better, but it was so slow I wasn't wasting any more product.

When the timer on my phone went off I pushed the curtains open and gestured for him to get out. I was met with Theo shortly after I walked towards the back. "What the fuck was that?"

"You sent me over, I told you they don't do dances and if they do they want extras. I smacked his hand and got paid." I shoved past him, going to the bar and ordering a double shot of tequila for both Gracie and myself. "Eat rocks, Theo."

"You're in a mood. You practically yeeted that man to VIP." Gracie threw her shot back and I slid two twenties to the bartender.

"He thought he was going to get extras, fucking idiot." I grimaced as I poured the shot down my throat, I adjusted how I was sitting in the seat, going to my knees so my butt was in the air as I leaned over the bar top. "Can I get a cup full of cherries?" I gave the bartender puppy dog eyes.

She chuckled and went to fill up a plastic cup of cherries. Fuck yeah, just what I needed—sugary red 40 cherries and tequila. I swayed my hips to the song, a remix of Tove Lo's Talking Body. I popped a cherry in my mouth, feeling the tequila and the vibes. Nothing was going to get me off the high of taking that man's money like that. Stupid fuckers, the audacity of some of these men.

I hated to be that dancer, but sometimes it was warranted. Fuck, this is why I had a specific type of customer. My customers didn't tend to be fucking handsy or try to pressure me or proposition me.

Theo stopped at the bar before going to the DJ booth, he leaned down and with Gracie sitting as close to me as she was I couldn't go anywhere, his voice was barely a whisper in my ear, "I walked over there to see if you were okay, but you're being a fucking brat." I turned to glare and realized how close he was to me, his face centimeters from mine. I couldn't help it, blame the tequila, but I looked at his lips.

I think he looked at mine too, but I couldn't tell. I was too busy freaking the fuck out—why had I done that? Why were his lips so fucking nice? That was unfair.

I pulled back and froze, wait he'd come to check on me? I was fine. Nothing I couldn't handle, he knew that. He took a deep breath and pushed off the bar before heading back to the DJ booth.

Why did I feel that in my lower belly? Why? No. Nope. Nope. *Nope, not going there.* This was proximity and being around him way too much. Maybe I did need to chill out. Maybe take a break from work for a while.

Fuck, okay actually that wouldn't even help anymore, he was coming to my house literally tomorrow for dinner with Coop.

I looked over at Jonah, who was giving me the *really?* look. I shrugged and considered another shot. I lifted my shot glass at the bartender and she nodded, getting both Gracie and I one. This was probably a bad idea, but it was fine.

Gracie, who had been watching that entire power play, covered her mouth with her fingers. "Ma'am are you and Theo—?"

"WHAT?! No, fuck no." I looked from her to where Theo was, now back at the booth.

"Whatever he saw on the camera, he immediately got up and went to stand in the hallway to be right there. Jonah told him you had it handled, but he stayed." Gracie said, studying me, "Are you sure? Because he doesn't act like that with anyone but you."

I shushed her, "I'm pretty positive—we don't even like each other." I said, exasperated that she even thought that.

Gracie raised an eyebrow, "So... that's why you spend your Monday's basically in the DJ booth?"

I gasped, "Who told you that? They're traitors."

She looked at me like I was dumb, turning fully in the bar chair, "Kie, do you think Theo and Jade are an item?" Gracie directed at the bartender, who quickly turned her attention to the end of the bar and started wiping things down.

I groaned, hitting my head on the bar. "For fuck's sake, we're not!"

Kie, the bartender, looked between the two of us and then at Theo who had a smirk on his face that made me want to punch him. "Actually," I licked my bottom lip, glancing at him then back to Gracie. "I'm seeing his best friend."

Gracie leaned in as I was taking a sip of my warm energy drink and whispered, "So like, you could potentially have a threesome?"

I choked, actually choked, it came out of my nose. "Jesus Christ, don't."

And Theo? Of course he fucking heard that. Just my fucking luck. I pointed at him, "Don't say a damn thing."

"Wasn't gonna, Princess." Theo said, trying and failing to school his face, but his cheeks were red.

"See!" Gracie smirked, leaning back on the stool looking pleased as fuck with herself.

I groaned.

Fuck my life.

Theo

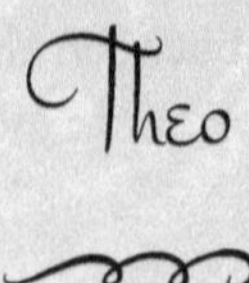

I could actually kill myself right now.

Kidding, kind of.

I don't know why Coop insisted I come with him. He can handle himself, anxiety my ass, he's been talking to her non-stop. She's already head over heels, quite literally, might I add.

Except, she looked at me—my lips—when I crowded her. And yes, I know I need to knock that shit off. Fuck, I had slept with her best friend countless times, and no not Iris—Gracie whatever—but Link.

Link and I were complicated, neither of us were technically out, which wasn't exactly something I was proud of. It was mostly my fault, I guess. I'd been the one who didn't want to date. Still holding out hope that my own fucking best friend would see that I liked him in more than the platonic way.

Don't look at me like that, I know—I know believe me. I fucking know. Why set up the literal bane of my existence with him then? Because he doesn't fucking like guys, he's so fucking straight it hurts.

Like don't get me wrong I like women too, but I can appreciate anyone regardless. If we vibe, if there's tension there I'm automatically attracted to them—fuck, fuck, forget I said that.

Millie does NOT count.

She doesn't, I swear to all the Gods.

We pulled into the driveway, I let out a breath, I didn't want to go in and have to pretend everything was fine when Link didn't want to speak to me. I didn't want to have to pretend we knew each other in passing.

But today was not about me, it was about my best friend and his ability to keep a damn girl. Or lack of I should say, but whatever he'd said to Millie she'd immediately folded.

Coop was perfect for her, and I'm not saying that as his best friend. I did genuinely like Millie, she was sweet—to most people, not to me.

She had a fiery attitude when provoked and he could be the calm to her chaos.

I knocked on the door to be greeted by Link's sandy blonde hair, the very same hair I'd had my hands locked into a few weeks ago. My cheeks felt hot, "Hi." I managed, and he rolled his eyes and side-stepped me.

"You must be Coop." Link looked him up and down, "Don't fuck with her heart or her head. I'll have to kill you."

Coop's eyes widened, "Should have expected that honestly." He looked around for Millie, "Do I have to worry about you?"

Link smirked, "You probably should."

"Oh my God, don't listen to him—he's being a protective older brother again." Millie groaned, shoving Link by the shoulder, "Stop!"

I looked at Link and then her, oh yeah, he might actually be a problem. There was no way he wasn't. The way he said that? The smirk? The way his face fell when she called him older brother? He was so far friend zoned it should be illegal.

He'd talked about his best friend before, that she lived with him, and that they'd been friends since early middle school. And that he, much like me, had been crushing for just as long. It's why we'd decided to keep it casual, nothing too much...just hooking up. That's all this was.

Fuck, we were pathetic.

The fact we were in the same situation and now those two friends were together and spending their time on video chat non-stop, wasn't lost on me.

Shit, maybe we should try again.

I had been fucking stupid to not realize that he was her bestfriend. How had I missed that? I mean I did try to keep work and outside of work activities away from each other—why had I thought introducing Coop and Millie to each other was a good idea? Worst idea of 2026 honestly. What was wrong with me?

"Theo, do you want a drink?" Millie asked, pointing at the tequila and wine on the counter.

"I'll do wine, that way at least one of us can drive back."

"I mean we have spare rooms, you could stay if it came to that." She frowned, "I wouldn't have you drive if you didn't feel comfortable."

Link was the first to speak up, "No, absolutely not."

I turned to him, walking past and quietly saying, "Real subtle." He froze, then took a sip from his glass, brushing me off. *Great, so we were completely ignoring it.*

I don't know if it was me reading into everything ten fold, but did everyone in this damn room have some kind of weird sexual tension?

I mean come on.

What the fuck did Theo drag me into?

I left Link and Theo in the living room, setting up the consoles so we could play if we wanted, and went to find Millie who was stirring a pot of red sauce. "Hope you like spaghetti because I'm a terrible cook aside from that."

"Better than eating pizza for a week straight like Theo and I." I chuckled, letting myself check her out. She was in a pair of jean shorts and a hoodie, but the sleeves were pushed up. Her hair was pulled back, but it was longer than I thought.

She looked me over, her face pulling into a bright smile. "We do a lot of pizza too, to be fair."

She went to break the spaghetti noodles and I stopped her, "Don't do that, you'll never hear the end of it from Theo, Italian bastard."

She cracked a smile, "That makes me wanna do it even more."

"DO NOT!" Theo's voice came from the living room, plus the sound of his feet coming into the kitchen. "Don't you dare break those noodles. That's offensive."

"So fucking bossy." She grumbled and I couldn't help but watch her as she put the unbroken noodles in, Theo's face visibly relaxed.

I rolled my eyes, thankful she didn't cause him to go into a spiral over fucking spaghetti. "Theo, return to whatever you were doing, you get enough of her time." I could have told him he was being dramatic about the pasta, but I didn't.

She stirred the pasta sauce, it was simmering and smelled divine. She turned to me, "I didn't even ask if either of you have any food allergies."

"We don't." I answered, stepping into her space slightly, I wanted to pull her into a kiss but didn't want to press my luck. This was so fucking new and I hadn't dated anyone in a long time, I didn't want to fuck it up.

She was fucking beautiful. Spending the past few weeks talking with her on the phone and in party chats was nothing compared to being in her presence.

"So Link and Theo know each other?" I asked, watching as she got down four plates and four wine glasses. She chewed her cheek and nodded.

She nodded, and I didn't know why she wouldn't elaborate. Instead I focused on the wine glasses. I wasn't sure about the wine with spaghetti, but she pulled out a white wine from the Dublin Winery, it was a muscadine wine, slightly chilled. A little on the sweeter side. "Can you take this all out to the table for me?"

My fingers brushed hers as I took the plates from her, sitting them around the little table before going back for the wine glasses.

Once Millie brought out the pasta, thankfully separate from the sauce, so Theo didn't have a conniption fit. She called for everyone to come get food, filling the wine glasses half way.

Link noticed the wine glasses and rolled his eyes, "Pulling out all the stops, she must like you." He met my eyes, "Normally we eat in the living room like feral raccoons."

"Shut up, Lincoln." she mumbled, as we all sat.

After a brief moment of silence and serving ourselves the food, Millie looked at me, "So have you been in the area for awhile?"

"I grew up here, same as all of us, I assume."

"I don't remember you from school."

"Because you were two grades below Theo and I."

"Makes sense, I kept to myself a lot back then. Well aside from this one." She pointed at Link, "We've been attached at the hip since sixth grade."

She took a few bites, when I couldn't come up with words—because I'm an idiot—she asked another question, "So what do you do when you're not gaming?"

"Working honestly, more recently talking to you." I admitted, meeting her eyes.

"What do you do for work?" She asked, shifting in her seat—she was adorable when she was nervous.

I smiled softly, "I'm a nurse for psych at the hospital."

She laughed, but fidgetted with her fork, "Nurses are hot, just don't psychoanalyze me—please, let's not go down that rabbithole."

"Millie, you're talking to him like he's a customer." Theo deadpanned, "Take a breath, you're fine."

"Theo... I'm nervous and no one else is having a conversation." Millie glared at him.

Link jumped in, "Okay, so let's get to it. Does everyone here smoke?"

"Well, not cigarettes." Theo grinned and I nodded, at least we all had something else in common.

"Can't smoke because of work, drug tests and all that." I frowned, "But I used to and I don't have anything against it."

"We all know Millie is a decent drinker, what is everyone's go to liquor. Also, kudos to you for picking a white wine with the spaghetti, not many people get that right." Theo winked.

Millie smiled nodding her head to Link, "Credit where credit is due, that was Link. He told me no to the red wine." I followed Theo's eyes to Link and saw how they held eye contact for a second and how Link shrugged nonchalantly.

"So..." I paused looking between the two of them, "How do you two know each other?"

"Umm," Link stuffed a fork full of spaghetti in his mouth. Theo looked down immediately too.

It was Millie that gasped, "Oh my God. Wait—"

"Princess don't." Theo warned.

I glared at him, it seemed the Princess thing was in person too. "Really, Theo? In front of Coop?" Millie squeaked and covered her face.

Oh? In front of me?

"You two have a very weird dynamic, but that's beside the point... what were you going to say?" I asked her, ignoring the protests from Theo and Link both.

Millie giggled, "Oh, it's so obvious, but if you don't see it... it needs to come from them. Not me."

I looked between Theo and Link, Theo didn't normally keep things from me. "Theodore, spit it out."

"I may have hooked up with him a few times." He said as he twirled his pasta, I tried to keep the surprise off my face at his words.

"Like recently?" I asked, because while I knew Theo was into guys too, I hadn't ever really asked about it—he didn't want to open up and that was fine. I wasn't going to push it.

"Within the last three weeks, yeah." Theo admitted, a long exhale falling from his mouth as he looked at Link.

Millie's eyes bounced from Theo, to me, back to Link. "WAIT—Link—"

"Yes, yes.. That one." Link said quickly, trying his best to cover something.

Millie's mouth opened and closed, she chewed her cheek, I had no idea what Link and her had talked about, but I really didn't want it to affect whatever this was with Millie.

"What did you tell her?" Theo whispered, but I heard it.

"I told her everything..." Link looked at Theo and he almost did look sorry.

Millie was close to finishing her plate, I shoved another bite in my mouth. She looked like she wanted to say something, but was holding back. She took several big sips of her wine.

Once we were all basically done, Millie topped off her wine glass, "Jesus, okay, ummm—why don't we smoke and watch a movie or play something." She pointed at Theo and Link, "You two are a mess, this is why we don't keep secrets. Coop? Want to help me clean up, give the heathens some space?"

I picked up some of the empty dishes and carried them to the kitchen, following behind her, as soon as I set them down she pulled me to her, her lips crashing into mine. "I don't care what they have going on." She whispered against my lips, "But you and I—we're good."

Kissing, kissing I knew how to react too. I pulled her back and kissed her again, lifting her up and sitting her on the counter. "Thank fuck, because I've been wanting to do that all night."

She giggled, lacing her fingers in my hair, nipping my bottom lip playfully.

Fuck, I might be gone for her off of one kiss, could that be possible?

Link

So, I may have fucked up and told Millie the reason my situationship had stopped was because of the guys best friend.

Yeah the one, she's currently making out with in the kitchen.

See, Theo is just as gone for Coop as I am for Millie. Which as you can see is not fucking good. Especially since he also has a weird vibe with her, calling her Princess like that in front of everyone? What the fuck was he thinking?

"What did you tell her?" Theo asked me quietly, I glanced at the dining room to make sure they couldn't see us.

"I may have mentioned you stopped seeing me because you felt bad because of a certain someone..." I rested my elbows on my knees, I didn't like that I was having this conversation with Millie and Coop two rooms away.

"And that someone is..." He pressed, but it was definitely obvious.

"In the kitchen with Millie." I sighed, "You cut complete contact with me for no fucking reason."

"Link..."

I cut him off, "No." I dropped my hands, still intertwined and sitting on my knees, "And what the fuck is that with Millie? Do you have feelings for her too? Because if so that's fucked dude."

"No! Why would I set them up if I had feelings for her?"

"Question posed for him too." I scoffed, shaking my head in disbelief.

"I thought it'd be easier if he was dating someone, our friendship is weird... he sends me mixed signals constantly. You can't tell right now, but he's normally flirting with me and it's fucking confusing."

"So you thought, oh let me just put the two biggest flirts in existence together and oooops now I'm going to be forced to see my ex-situationship on probably a daily basis." I groaned.

"Not daily, I do work."

"Yeah, with Millie. In a strip club." I huffed.

"It's a bikini bar." Theo deadpanned.

"That is so not the point."

"Oh my gods, you're so jealous right now. And I can't tell who it's towards." Theo turned slightly to look at me, a smirk playing at his lips. "Kinda hot to be honest."

Kinda hot? My spiral was fucking hot? Jesus, this was fucked.

He leaned back on his palms, staring at the ceiling like he was trying not to laugh. "You do realize we both did the dumbest possible thing, right?"

"Oh?" I scoffed. "And what exactly is the dumbest possible thing?"

"You fell for your best friend," he said softly, knocking my knee with his. "And then you fell for me a little too, it's okay you can admit it. I fell for Coop. I fell for you. And then Coop fell for Millie. And—"

"And?" I pressed, because why did he sound like he was about to say something else.

He shrugged, "And maybe it was supposed to be like this, if they don't want us maybe we're supposed to have each other."

"Is this your fucked up way of apologizing to me?" I asked with way too much shake in my voice.

"Maybe..." He said quietly, sitting up to meet my eyes.

My traitorous eyes fell to his lips, "Fuck my life." I whispered, right before his lips met mine.

Here we go again.

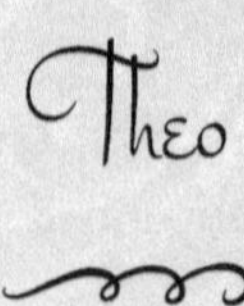

Kissing Link was easy, almost the same as breathing, I couldn't bring myself to stop. I pulled him closer, deepening the kiss. He made everything go away, he made the ache go away. I wasn't sure if that was a good thing, but right now it felt right.

When he pulled away, he looked confused and honestly? I didn't blame him. I was confused too, because I had almost said something about Millie a few minutes ago, and that was—that was not accurate.

Right? No way.

Fuck, Coop and Link were bad enough. I couldn't add her into the mix right now.

"I'm sorry." I spoke quietly, hoping he heard me.

"Me too." Link said, a frown pulling at his face.

The sound of footsteps approaching snapped both our heads toward the dining room. And fuck they looked cute together. Hand in hand. Flushed faces. I hadn't seen Coop with that big of a smile on his face in ages. And Millie? Fuck, she was glowing.

I looked over at Link, gesturing to him to scoot so we could all sit on the couch. Coop sat beside me and Millie curled into him. "Game or movie?" Link asked quietly, laying his head against the arm of the couch —away from me.

Ouch, but I guess I deserved that.

His blonde hair fell across his forehead haphazardly and I wanted to run my hands through it. *Fuck, dude, get it together.*

"Movie..." Millie said, opening her phone so she could use the remote on her phone. "Comedy?"

"Yeah, comedy. We could liven this place up."

"Glass Onion anyone?" Millie chuckled, "although I'm totally in it for Whiskey and Whiskey only."

Millie turned it on, without waiting for confirmation, then stood up and pulled a book off the bookshelf, "Are you seriously opening up a book right now? Fucking nerd."

"First of all, rude. You're always so fucking rude. Secondly, I'm going to purposely skip you in rotation now." She opened up a pre-roll pack and lit it. "No one's asthmatic right? Shit—we can go outside if we need to, sorry I didn't think... drug test."

Coop grabbed her waist and yanked her down gently onto the couch next to him. She hit it twice, then handed it to me. She blew her smoke behind her, to avoid blowing it near Coop. I hit it twice, because fuck. Fuck me.

When I handed it to Link he sat up to ash it in a little circular bowl with a crystal in it, it looked like black tourmaline. I raised my eyebrow, "Why?"

"I use it for my black salt mixture." Millie shrugged, "It's for protection."

"Theo's mom would like you." Coop chuckled and I don't know why that made my chest tighten the way it did. Coop was right, my mom would like her. My woo woo spiritual, witchy mom would take her in as her own immediately.

Link was looking at me now, I don't know why he was watching me so intently, *maybe it's because you kissed him again, you fucking idiot.* I tried to keep that thought away though. Focusing on the movie.

I looked over at Millie and Coop, he was playing with her hair, it's the red hair I'm telling you. They looked cozy, Millie was locked into a scene with Whiskey, which I knew she could appreciate a pretty woman. She did it all the time at work, but seeing her do it as Millie was something else.

I didn't realize I was staring, until Millie mouthed 'What?' at me and I felt myself give her a small smile before returning my attention back to the tv.

This somehow felt right, intimate and homey.

Maybe, just maybe, we were all where we needed to be.

When she got up to get drinks, I followed. I don't know why I thought that was a good idea.

I leaned against the kitchen counter watching her go through the fridge, "Looks like you're never getting rid of me." I half-joked, but the way she looked at me when I said that?

Her eyes roamed over me, landing on my lips before meeting mine. "Don't threaten me."

"Awww, you love it. Don't pretend you don't. 'If you wanted to hang out with me outside of work you could just ask.' That's what you said." I reminded her, the last hit from the blunt making me feel a little more loose around her.

"I take it back, you're annoying." She didn't even attempt to move away from me though, even when I shifted closer. She did however shove cans of soda into my hands and push me back away from her. "Go on, get."

I don't know what I was thinking, maybe I wanted to see what she'd do.

Millie

"BABYDOLL - Ari Abdul"

By time the movie was over, I really wanted Coop to stay, but I wasn't going to ask. He had kissed me goodnight and promised to video chat if I was still up later.

When I came out of my room for water, Link was all geared up. "Where ya going?" I asked, noticing he was grabbing his helmet.

"Out for a ride."

"Can I backpack?" He nodded, then looked down at my bare legs, I would need pants and my gloves at the minimum. "Give me a minute, I can be ready in a few minutes." I practically ran to my room, Link only took the bike out every so often, but I was always down.

I needed to get Theo out of my fucking head anyway, what better way than to wind surf? I don't know why he followed me into the kitchen, or why he'd gotten so close.

I didn't want to think about it. Or why he called me a spoiled brat to Coop. Or why he insisted on still calling me Princess.

I braided my hair up, slipped on a pair of skinny jeans and a hoodie before grabbing my gloves from my top drawer. I slid them on, the bright neon green decorating the leather glowing under my lamp light.

I gave him a warm smile, grabbing my helmet as he locked the door and let me go out first. I put the helmet on and when he grabbed it to make sure it was on properly I felt my breath hitch.

Fuck, I needed to not watch biketok so much.

He pointed for me to get on and scrunched my nose, "No sir, that is not how I get on." I pouted until he crouched down so I could get on his back. If I was going to be his backpack, I took that very literally.

"Millie...don't sir me." He grumbled, smacking my thigh, a light smack that made me bite my lip so hard I almost drew blood. Not because it hurt or anything, but because Link doing *that* had my brain questioning things I most certainly didn't need to be questioning.

"It worked though, didn't it?" I said so quietly I was surprised when he turned to look at me.

I was sure he was glaring at me through his fucking visor.

He turned and started the bike, the roar of the engine making me jump slightly, his hand immediately came back up to my thigh steadying me. "Ready?" He asked and when I wrapped my arms around his waist and leaned into him he took off out of the driveway.

He slowly picked up speed and I tapped against his chest to ask if I could let go and airplane. I loved holding my arms out and feeling the wind in my fingertips. "Let me get on the highway, pretty girl."

Pretty girl made my heart beat faster than it should have coming out of his mouth.

I flushed, thank God I was wearing a helmet.

I held onto him, my hands going lower as I relaxed, maybe I liked being his backpack a little too much sometimes. I was a very touchy feely person and there weren't many times I felt like it was appropriate to be like that with him.

But on the bike?

On the bike, closeness was safety.

Once we hit the highway, the lights blurred past us. "Trust me?" I heard his voice carry.

"Of course." I said, my left hand going up to rest on his heart.

"Lean into me and put your arms out, pretty girl." I didn't need to be told twice.

I stretched my arms out wide, as he weaved the bike down the empty stretch of highway. The way the road was lit up in sections from the streetlights, the way the road seemed to stretch forever, how Link's hand was resting on my thigh to keep me to him as I let go.

I don't know how long I stayed like that, but he finally tapped my leg twice and I snuggled back into him, wrapping my arms around his waist again. This time my hands found his thighs, squeezing on accident when he basically brake checked me. "Lincoln!"

"Your hands, Mils. Come on." I sighed and put them back around his waist. I'd get him back for that.

The revenge was served at the next red light we came up on. I grabbed his helmet and opened the visor, only to slam it back down. He groaned as my hands hung lower on his waist than necessary, so he adjusted them for me.

I frowned, normally he let me do whatever, was it because of Coop? Or had he and Theo made up? Fuck, okay, I should behave at least a little. I didn't want to make him uncomfortable, not like that. I let my left hand find his heart again, letting it rest there as my other stayed steady around his waist, his hand holding mine to his waist.

Arguably this could be worse, honestly this was a lot more intimate. I wasn't going to argue. I needed him to ground me after everything, and something told me he needed it as much as I did.

After a little while he slowed down, turning off towards Southport, we ended up at the little waterfront park, I looked at him. "Did you bring me out here to murder me?"

"What?" He asked, as he took off his helmet, the confusion clearly etched on his face.

I removed my helmet completely, smoothing down the top of my hair. "You know that two people were murdered here right? A nineteen year old and some guy named Devin."

"No, I didn't know that. How did you know that?"

"Eh, true crime podcast I listen to. They're based in Wilmington." I grinned, taking him down the sidewalk, "I think Devin was like around here somewhere, and the girl—Sarah I think—was on the pier.

"It's weird that you know that." Link smirked, plopping down on one of the swings facing the water.

"It's weird you go to clear your head where two people took their last breath, but pop off." I sat down beside him, close enough that our legs were touching. "What's bothering you?" I asked, but I already knew.

"Everything." He said, his voice breaking, "Theo... he kissed me earlier when you were in there making out with Coop." I didn't miss the way he said that either, that way he made it seem like Coop was the problem, and yeah maybe he was for Link, but Coop hadn't done anything to me.

He was sweet. He was shy and awkward. I loved it.

"And I thought that's what you wanted, right? You just told me you missed him."

"Yeah, I guess I do... but—nevermind." He said, looking up at the clouds, how the stars would peak through occasionally.

"But what?" I prodded.

"I'm never anyone's first choice." He spoke so quietly I almost didn't hear him over the crashing tide.

I leaned into his shoulder, "Link, you've been my only choice for years. Literally almost fifteen years. It's you above everyone, always."

"It's not though, not now."

"What do you mean?"

"Theo calls you Princess, Coop had his tongue down your damn throat. Theo basically ghosted me over him too, then I find out he hooks up the girl I've been—"

I didn't speak, I needed him to finish that sentence.

I needed him to finish it right now.

I poked him on the thigh to get him to keep talking, he sighed then continued. "The only girl that's been a major part of my life."

That was a damn good save, I'll give him that.

"Why did you bring up Theo calling me Princess?" I questioned.

"It bothered me, you're not his to call that."

Except, in a way I kind of was, but I wouldn't say that right now.

Shit, I don't think you could torture that out of me if I'm being honest.

Not now. Not ever.

"Theo is just Theo, there's nothing going on between us. Believe me I'd tell you." I sighed, my hand dragging across his arm.

"No, you wouldn't."

I frowned, "I told you about Coop instantly."

"Theo's different, you work with him." Link sounded...disappointed.

"Exactly, I work with him... I'm not going to risk my job for someone I don't even get along with." I looked at him, then added, "Although the sex would probably be good."

"Millie!" His eyes met mine and I hoped he could see I was joking, I was joking. Kinda.

"That was a joke, because ya know... you and him." I clarified.

"I mean, you're not wrong—he's pretty fucking good in bed." Link deadpanned and I blushed a furious shade of red.

"Link! We both agreed no sex talk, Jesus Christ. Inside thoughts." My eyes widened and he had the audacity to actually laugh at me.

"Hey, you started it." He tucked a strand of hair behind my ear and I froze. He did it often, quite often actually, but right now?

It felt charged.

I took a deep breath, staring out at the water. "You won't lose me. You're stuck with me for the next several infinities. I'll also find you, remember? In this life and the next."

And I meant that. I really did, Link was my person. I wouldn't ever do anything to make him leave and I damn sure wouldn't leave him.

If he dies, he better take me out too.

Or I'll do it myself.

I can't imagine my life without him. I didn't want to. Not now, not ever. He was my fucking person, he really was. He was the only person who knew what I'd been through with my parents, he was the only one who knew what that had done to me. His family had basically taken me in and treated me like their own kid, I was always with him. If I was there Link wasn't far behind. He'd come running every time I needed help. He'd also run off every boyfriend I had for the past eleven years.

Definitely a pattern there. I could see he was actually trying to like Cooper, but now it felt different. Why did it feel different? Fuck, I couldn't feel this right now.

The bike was supposed to help clear my head, not fuck it up more. Fucking Link.

Fuck. *What had I got myself into?*

Link

"Him & I - Halsey, G Eazy"

I pulled her helmet to me as soon as she got it on, I adjusted the strap underneath keeping her helmet up, before leaning down to tap my helmet against hers.

It was the biker equivalent of a kiss, but she probably didn't know that.

She jumped up to get on my back, a string of giggles coming out muffled from the helmet as she basically choked my ass out to get her grip. I got us situated on the bike, holding her hands steady at my waist, when she didn't attempt to move them I turned out of the parking lot.

She stayed put, most of the way, except her hand finding my heart and holding herself there.

I wondered if she could feel how fast it was beating right now.

When her hand wondered down my stomach lower, I didn't stop her, if she wanted to be close after that, fuck it, I'd let her hold me where ever she wanted.

I couldn't see myself saying no to her right now, not after the *in this life and the next* bit. She could ask me for the world and I'd find a way to give it to her.

She wasn't staying still though, her hands were roaming, raking her nails against my jeans, "Mils, babygirl, quit."

She made a sound that resembled a squeak and a gasp all in one. "Link!"

"Trust me?" I asked as we hit the highway, I searched for cops along the side of the road. They normally didn't sit here. "How fast have you been in a car?"

"Umm, maybe like a hundred, in my red car. Maybe a hundred and five, I don't know."

"Want to go faster?" I asked, "You have to hang on, I've only gotten it up to one-fifty, but it goes faster."

"I trust you."

"That's my girl." I turned, bumping her helmet again.

I wouldn't take it *that much* faster, I was comfortable riding at night, I'd gotten it up there before. I wanted to give her this.

She wrapped her arms around me tightly, I pushed the gas.

100.
110.
120.
130.
140.
150.
160.
170.

She tapped my stomach twice and I slowed it down considerably. "You know we passed a cop!" I could hear the excitement in her voice.

"Cops don't chase motorcycles, not typically anyway." I shrugged and even if they did, they wouldn't catch me.

My hand found her leg, holding her. I rubbed circles with my thumb, if she needed to be calmed that would do it. "Do I need to pull over for a minute or are you good?" I asked, I'd forever check in on her —she was my baby, whether she knew it or not.

"I'm good, that was amazing." She sighed, "Do I have enough time to do airplane again?"

I chuckled, "Go for it." I could feel her arms out, I didn't necessarily like her doing it, but with my grip on her leg she wasn't going anywhere. I wouldn't let anything happen to her. If she trusted me enough to let go, I'd show her she could trust me.

After a few minutes I tapped her leg, "Hold on." I told her as we went to turn.

Her hands immediately found my waist, holding herself tightly to me. Her hand went lower, finding the hem to my hoodie and slipping under so she could put her hand on my heart, this time without the hoodie. Her fingers brushing my skin caused goosebumps to scatter down my entire body.

Fuck, yeah, she could definitely feel my traitorous heart now. It was basically beating out of my chest between the speed and her.

"Your heart's racing." She said quietly, although I almost didn't make it out from the wind whipping around us.

"Yeah, going that fast will do that to you." I laughed, it was a good cover—mostly because it was true. "We're almost home."

I almost wanted to miss the exit, just so I could keep her this close. She pressed herself closer to me and took a deep steadying breath. I knew as soon as we got home this would end, this little bit of freedom. Both the bike and her.

She'd go to her room, probably crash immediately.

She almost always did after a late night ride.

Theo

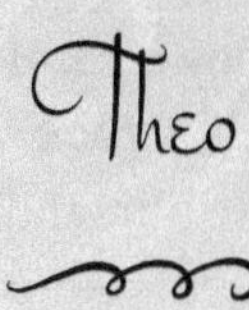

This little shit, walking in late and after missing several days of work. I'd told them she'd texted me and told me she was sick, but really she hadn't. She wasn't fucking sick.

She didn't want to come in and part of that may have been Cooper's fault, which equates to being my fault.

I texted her.

They think you were sick, miss no call no show.

Princess: Thanks for the cover XO

Theo: Just get your ass on the floor so we can get you in rotation, we have four girls.

Princess: Not my fault this place can't keep girls.

Theo: Get fucking dressed.

Within minutes she was already on the floor, her hair in two braids with little ribbon bows that matched her green outfit, she had on a green dress covering her bikini. "Iris is on the way too. We have a party of four coming in and they're getting a bottle and a hot tub. I don't like being two to four, so please keep an extra eye on us, please? I promise I'll tip you twenty percent."

"You don't have to tip me extra to do my job." I assured her, my voice going soft at the actual anxiety written on her face. Jade never showed nerves, Millie yeah, sure, but when she was in those heels it disappeared. "You okay?" I asked seriously.

"Yeah, I kinda feel weird being back after a few days, that's all."

"Did Coop say something?" I took a guess and she looked down, fuck, I was about to have to text him and give him an earful. Millie was one of the few dancers who didn't attempt to break rules in the back.

Now out front and on stage that was a different story, she'd occasionally do things like the no girl on girl shows rules, but technically they weren't doing anything illegal and they both made the club so much no one said anything. It was the way they were, her and Grac—Iris—fuck, being around Millie in real life was making that a bit harder.

"I've got you in rotation," I said gently, "Any song requests?"

"Not tonight, you know what I like." Millie stepped into the dj booth fully and leaned closer to me, under the guise of pointing at the computer. "Thank you, Theo."

"Anytime, you know that." I whispered, she was so close I knew she heard it.

Fuck, we had to stop toeing the line like this. No wonder Gracie had picked up on it so quickly, this girl was fucking flustering me. She sat on the couch right next to the booth, probably texting Coop.

I picked up my phone and texted him.

Whatever you said about her job, fucking apologize.

A text came in almost immediately.

Coop: I said I didn't like it.

Theo: You're fucking her money, she's in her head. When she's in this building she's Jade. She came in as Millie and Millie is fucking anxious. So apologize and tell her to have a fun and fantastic night. Man up, it's a job.

Coop: Fine, you win.

I watched as Iris strolled in, hair already done up in space buns, and an ungodly amount of glitter on her face. I'd have face palmed, but she's already got her night set. Buying a bottle and a hot tub usually meant more than a few hours in the hot tub.

I watched the group walk in and hated that they were younger, around my age, maybe a little older. I leaned back in my booth, “I think that’s your group.”

“Yeah, looks like it.” Millie sighed, her uncomfortableness peaking through.

“Go.” I prompted, “Greet. Do your magic, Princess.” I smirked.

She was shaking, like actually, when Grac–Iris—fuck, whatever her dancer besties name is, came over to the booth to do rotation sign up I nudged her attention to Millie, “She’s really fucking nervous tonight, she’s not in Jade mode. What song can I put you both up to that could potentially switch her out of it?”

Iris frowned, then swiped my touch screen looking for a song. “3oh!3 is her to go in the car, ooooh, do *My First Kiss,* it'll get her in a silly mood. Followed by *Get U Home* by Shwayze.” I loaded both songs. “Thank you for noticing, these guys are absolutely down to party all night. I need her game face on.”

“Yeah,” I bit my lip looking over the booth to where she was forcing a smile with one of the guys, she was so out of her element right now.

“Are you sure there’s nothing going on with you two? I won’t judge.” She asked, looking between us and then at the screen as I downloaded the songs and added them to her playlist.

I tried not to show that it affected me, there really was nothing going on. There couldn’t be. “Iris, go rescue your friend.”

“That wasn’t a no.” She squealed before practically prancing over to the guys and Millie, flinging her arms around Millie’s neck and kissing her cheek obnoxiously.

I should have said no, Gods, what is wrong with me?

“Iris and Jade to the stage. Yes, you Princess, up.” I said into the mic, she shot me a glare but when she heard *My First Kiss* she broke out into a grin.

There she fucking is.

Millie took the middle pole, we had three on the same stage, and Iris took the one in the front. In an instance, I saw Millie light up. The way she flipped a switch and instantly I saw the difference. She cleaned the bottom half of the pole, then climbed all the way to the top to clean all the way up.

Little show off.

Iris did the same thing, the each dropped the rag at the same time and I knew they were about to fuck the stage up in sync.

I wasn't wrong.

They both tucked themselves around the pole and dropped to the half way point, before flipping themselves upside down and hooking their legs. Opposite legs I noticed, so it looked more mirror-like, they popped into a superman, how—couldn't fucking tell you. Don't ask me how dancers can literally defy physics.

I sure as shit couldn't do that if I tried. They dropped into a side leg hang, don't know what it's actually called—I just work here—and let go of the pole to grab their heel and hold themselves out like that.

Fuck, they were talented.

I hope they stretched before all that.

The part that didn't surprise me is when they finally were back to standing, Millie had the biggest shit eating grin on her face, she mouthed something that looked oddly like, "*Don't you dare tell on me.*"

I saluted her as she climbed on top of Iris and kissed down her stomach. It wasn't anything real, they were very light and for show, never crossing legal lines or doing anything too much. Jonah would have stepped in for sure, just enough to get the guys throwing cash. I could tell from here that's exactly what was about to happen, and Gracie was red as a tomato. Millie laughed, looking at me and sinking her teeth into her lower lip.

Her eyes lit up as they threw stacks of ones and she squealed, doing a little shimmy to the beat, but that eye contact she should have been giving the fucking customers? Yeah, it was on me.

For someone who hates me, she sure as fuck does love my damn attention to be on her.

And I couldn't look away. I didn't want to.

Millie

"Faster - Cal Scruby"

I didn't need to go to the DJ booth, I had no reason. None.

I did it anyway.

As soon as he turned around I wrapped him in a hug, he melted into me for a second then patted my back awkwardly. "Careful, you're ruining your reputation of hating me."

I ignored his comment, "Thank you, Theo. I needed that."

"I know."

My phone buzzed, I looked down.

> Coop: I'm sorry about earlier, I hope you have fun and make all the money's.

I looked at Theo, "You texted him."

"You're damn right I did, I need Jade here, not my soft Princess."

Had he been drinking? Did he just say my soft Princess? Clearly he was drunk.

"Come again, rewind. Run it back, I'm so sober right now and I think I'm hallucinating." Also, I think I might actually have a heart attack with how fast my heart rate jumped.

He flushed, "I didn't mean it like that...I just I call you Princess and I—I'm going to need you to erase that from your memory." Theo stumbled over his words, clearly fucking flustered.

"You said *my*." I didn't step away, even though I was close enough to do something incredibly fucking stupid. My eyes fell to his lips and then quickly back up.

Nope. Nope. *Nope*.

So many reasons this was absolutely not okay, one Link loved this man even if he didn't want to admit it. And two? I was officially in deep with his best friend. That he set me up with, I inhaled and stepped back.

"I didn't." He denied, "You didn't hear it."

"Yeah, I didn't hear anything." I agreed.

"The guys are ready, they got two bottles." Iris came over, sliding her arm in mine.

I felt the panic coming back up, "Make sure to watch us please."

"I've got you, the both of you. You know that." He said, pulling up the hot tub that was filled with a bigger screen.

I followed Gracie, but I could feel his eyes on me.

Stop thinking about it. He's probably fucking testing you.

It didn't feel like a test though.

I was about to get drunk and forget about it anyway, we made our way to the dressing room to put our heels up, I shimmied out of my dress. I was already in my green bikini for the hot tub, since this was pre-planned.

I couldn't keep my fucking mind on the dancing aspect, but that was muscle memory. After several shots and about two hours into our hot tub party, I locked eyes with the camera and blew it a kiss. I saw Gracie look at me and then at the camera and her jaw could have hit the water with how low it dropped.

I looked at my texts when I went to change the song on the speaker.

Theo: Stop drinking Princess.

I looked right at the camera and smirked before taking another shot.

Fuck, I hated vodka, but fuck it. I decided it was time for a photoshoot, which was probably not a good idea. Gracie immediately picked up on it and jumped in the pictures for a few of them. The guys pointed at themselves and I laughed, snapping a few of them too.

I went almost all the way underwater and took a picture of myself. I don't know if it was a good picture, but I slapped a mermaid emoji on it. Sent to Link. Wait, Link? Probably shouldn't have sent that, oooop, those. Multiple. I sent multiple pictures. Fuck it I guess.

I put on *Faster by Cal Scruby* and started dancing with Gracie as the guys started watching. It was a vibe.

By hour three in the hot tub, we were all laying back and relaxing, honestly way too drunk to do anything else. Fuck, neither of us were gonna be able to drive. Uber was so expensive. I didn't have anything in my bank account, fuck me and my stupid cash only tendencies, fuck. I could ask Daddy DJ out there to give me a ride.

Do I trust myself right now?

Absolutely not.

I could call Coop. That would be logical right?

When the fourth hour ended, I needed food and possibly to be carried out. Speaking of that's exactly what was happening to the guys right now, they were getting helped out. Hopefully they'd stash them in a room or champagne area.

I could lay down and sleep right now. Gracie was just as fucked up as I was, *fucking ooops*, that wasn't supposed to happen. Jonah helped Gracie out, wrapping her in a towel and helping her walk to the dressing room.

Theo looked at me like I had cursed his entire family line with my drunkenness, "Theooooooo, did you come to help the Princess not drown?"

He cursed under his breath, "Fuck, you're so wasted." He exhaled, "You two are done. Get dressed and don't even attempt to get your keys from management."

I pouted at his words, why was he being so mean to me? Was it because of the shot? I'd only done—fuck, a lot.

As soon as the door shut I dried off as much as possible and unlocked my locker—it took me like six tries but it was fine. I got it. *I got this.* It was days like today I was glad Gracie and I shared a locker because she was even worse off than me.

I dug through her bag first, trying to decipher what was what. Her bag had no fucking organization, how did she know—never mind.. Found them. Sweat pants and a hoodie.

Fuck the underwear and bras right now, that was entirely too much work.

I pulled my hoodie and shorts out, I could do this. *I could do this.*

First, get this wet bikini off. I pulled the top string over my head and immediately put on my hoodie, well Coop's hoodie—or was it Link's not a fucking clue honestly.

I shimmied out of the bottoms without showing everyone everything, thank you hoodie, and pulled on my jean shorts. Looking for my shoes, fuck yeah I had thought ahead. Cow slippers.

Fuck, I loved my cow slippers.

I looked at Gracie who hadn't even attempted to undress, I forced the hoodie on her then undid her bikini top. "Work with me, woman." I pinched her and she helped. I held her sweatpants for her so she could step into them while using me for balance.

Which just barely worked, I was pretty fucked up and she tried to grab my head instead of my shoulders for support. Once I got her shoes on her, I made sure everything was locked up.

Wait. *Wait.* Money, we gotta get paid. Money goes in the locker. I blew up my cheeks like a puffer fish, trying to gain the willpower to do this.

Spoiler alert, I did not have the willpower.

They'd given us a five hundred dollar tip up front, and we should be getting around three thousand a piece from that. Four hours in the hot tub is like three thousand I think.

Eh, I'll figure it out. I waved it off, waving at the fucking mirror.

Jonah knocked on the door and then entered, "I'm going to pay you back here and make sure it goes in your locker. Tip us tomorrow, I already told everyone not to worry about it tonight."

God bless Jonah. Someone give him a raise. He needed one. Fuck, we were a problem for this man. Like the entire problem. I felt the need to apologize, but it'd probably be better to not right now, so I sat quietly as he counted it out. There was a camera too where we were.

I had planned on having Daddy DJ help me tip out. Fuck, did I trust him that much with my money? I didn't even trust Link with my money, mostly because he'd start opening investment accounts in my name with it and Link had me on his motorcycle at 170 mph.

Fuck, that was stupid and reckless. We could have died.

Jonah paid us out, yep, three thousand each. I put mine in my makeup bag. And then put Gracie's in her bag and zipped it. Locking the locker. Jonah tugged the lock to make sure it was secure before leaving.

"Leave me here to die, go getsss your man." Gracie said, lying on the counter with her arm flailing in the direction of the door.

I should have said he's not my man, but I wasn't going to argue. Instead I padded my little cow slippers down the neon lit hallway vibing to the music, doing a little jig and made my way to the DJ booth, but it took a minute because the crowd of people was a lot bigger now.

Theo was running three song stage sets I noticed. "Theo..."

He held up a finger, grabbing the mic. I pouted, like a damn lost puppy dog. "First of three, Shayla. First of three." He said, as Shayla got on stage. Shayla was really good at the pole, I could die happy watching her perform.

"What Mil-Jade? It's busy." He glanced at me, then back to the stage and then his computer.

I bounced in place, "Can you take me and Iris home?" I paused, blinking several times, "Umm–like to my house?"

He sighed, looking over at me. "I already told Coop I was taking you home."

"He's okay with it?" I asked, narrowing my eyes at him.

"Why wouldn't he be? He works at seven in the morning." He looked over at me, "You don't trust me to get your drunk ass home in one piece?"

"No it's not... that. I just—don't trust myself." I admitted, squinting when one of the lights hit me in the damn eye. Maybe I shouldn't have been that honest, bitch what are you thinking? That's Theo. Your boyfriend's best friend and him and Link have slept together... no ma'am.

He looked me up and down, his eyes landing on my cow slippers. "Go take you and your cow slippers and sit on the couch, you are too drunk for any kind of rational conversation."

I groaned, "Theo... first of all big words."

"Couch." He pointed, and I openly checked him out. I don't care, because why did he sound like that? Was he still that annoyed with me?

"Fine..." I grumbled, stumbling my way over to the couch and watching Shayla on stage. Fuck she was a goddess on the pole. Someone get this girl a Grammy or something, holy fuck. Respectfully, my jaw was dropped. I couldn't contain it.

"You're drooling." Theo smirked, looking over the booth at me.

"No, I'm not. Take it back." I was vibing, not drooling, drooling was not lady-like.

I don't know what possessed me to be a feral gremlin at work as a civilian, but fuck it. I set my phone up to film a video and climbed on the table shaking my butt and bouncing around like a crazed person. I arched my back as I leaned over the table more.

"MIL–JADE!" Theo's voice broke me out of whatever haze of dance moves I had been in, I looked over at him unimpressed. "I said couch." I let my head drop back, trying to stop the giggles from coming out.

Mr. Bossy pants over there, fine, if he wanted me on the couch I'd go. Freaking party pooper.

I did the same thing over there though, even doing a little dip showing off my arch and kicking my little cow slippers from a different angle. "Jade, you're testing me. Either sit still or go to the dressing room."

"Okay Daddy DJ." I groaned and flopped on my stomach, "Lemme know when it's time to go."

I opened up my socials and scrolled for a minute, pondering posting the video with the cow slippers right now.

Eh, better not. I could make a cute as fuck edit later, when I could actually fucking think.

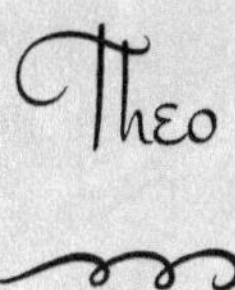

Theo

"Bad Choices - Kode"

Drunk Millie was a fucking menace, a sleeping menace now, but I don't actually think she was sleeping. More like lying there trying not to die.

I was worried about driving her home. Why did she have to say *that*?

Why did she disregard my quit drinking text? Why did she fucking smirk and look at the camera before drinking. She smelled like fucking vodka, she didn't even drink vodka. Coop was going to kick my ass. Link was going to kick my ass. Fuck... her first night back at work and she can hardly walk.

I fucking failed, I failed horribly. I watched that shit go down on the cameras, but she's an adult and I can't interfere in a damn VIP room, especially not in a hot tub. Those guys paid the club twelve thousand for just the hot tubs alone with the two of them.

I had the girl Shayla check on Iris—Gracie—a few times for me and tipped her for it, because I respect the hustle, okay? Gracie was knocked the fuck out, slumped over on the counter of the dressing room.

At the end of the night I announced, "You don't have to go home, but you can't stay here." The lights came on and most of the girls immediately scrambled. I cut the music as the last of the customers exited the building.

I crouched in front of her, gently shaking her, "Mils.. you gotta wake up."

"I am awake, it's loud in here." She mumbled, turning to look at me. "Fuck and it's bright now, what the fuck?" It wasn't even that loud, but it was pretty bright with the main lights on.

"Coop knows I'm taking you and Gracie to your house." I paused when she looked me up and down with a bright smile on her face, "It's fine, I can control myself for the both of us."

"You can control me all you want." Millie grinned, but it didn't have the same effect since she was half face down on the couch again.

I tried to compose myself, I was going to ignore that comment completely. "Mils..." I poked her, "Up."

She groaned, but pushed herself up. "Yes sir."

"Don't." I warned.

"You. Are.. no funs." She giggled, pushing at my chest a little, "Back up... you're too close."

I leaned back and met her eyes. "I'm giving you thirty minutes to lay here and rot, then you're getting up." I sighed, continuing what I should have already been doing. Shutting down the systems.

"You're pretty." She said, reaching up to ruffle my hair, the alcohol smell was radiating off of her.

This was about to be the longest fucking ride of my life.

By time everything was officially closed down and it was time to go, I got Gracie in the car first, throwing her basically unconscious ass in the backseat and buckling her in as best as possible. I had Jonah stand guard as I went back in for Millie who was talking to one of the floor guys, wrapped in her hoodie.

"Even if I don't work tomorrow I'll make sure I come back to tip. I'm sorry—" She was shaking, a cup full of cherries in her hand.

"Jade, everyone knows you and Iris are too fucked up to count money right now." I interjected, offering her my arm as she was using one of the tables to hold her weight. "Come on, Pr–." I almost called her Princess in front of security and that wouldn't bode well.

"I'll call Coop on the drive over if you want me too." I told her, catching her by the arm as she almost stumbled into a chair.

The security guy, Toby, looked at her and then me, "You sure you're okay with him driving you?" I didn't like how he said it, but I knew it was coming from a place of respect for her well-being.

"Yeah, I'm dating his best friend, he's good." Millie answered, shoving my arm slightly.

I rolled my eyes at her shove, because she immediately grabbed onto my hoodie again for balance. "She's dating Coop, he has my location and her roommate has hers. Iris is going to her house." They knew who Coop was thankfully, so it helped my credibility just a little bit.

Toby nodded and I gestured for her to go on, but she didn't make it two steps forward before I slid my arm around her waist to help her walk.

Once we were outside, I opened the car door for her and she climbed in the front passenger seat. I closed her door, fuck, fuck, *fuck*. I really wasn't in the mood to deal with drunk Millie, Gracie was in no way shape or form able to help me keep her at bay.

I took a deep breath before I climbed in the driver's seat and she immediately started messing with my bluetooth settings, adding her phone to it. Or well, trying... she'd fumbled the buttons a few times. "Mils... why?"

"I want my music, I listened to your music choice all night." She pointed at herself. "My turn." I wanted to argue that she'd technically listened to her music all night, since she'd been using the speaker in the back, but I didn't.

"First of all, rude. I have good taste in music. It's literally my job." She entered the wrong bluetooth code, not once but twice.

She fumbled with the connect button and I snatched the phone from her entering the code so it would connect. "So snatchy..." She mumbled, holding her hand back out so she could go to her Spotify.

I watched her scroll through her songs, finally finding one she deemed worthy and hit play. *Night Swim* by Sidi. "Can we puhhhleeease have the windows down?" She asked, already rolling the window down before I could answer.

I cracked mine, so that way it wouldn't make the air pressure weird. "Seatbelt, Mils." When she didn't react fast enough, I leaned across her and buckled it myself.

Her breath hitched, her eyes catching mine as I pulled away, "I'm choosing to ignore that you just buckled me in like a child." She hiccuped and put her whole arm out of the window, feeling the night air against her hand.

The other taking a cherry and popping it into her mouth, she wasn't paying me any attention, but I couldn't stop staring at her fucking mouth. She tossed the stem out the window.

"What are you doing?" I asked, watching her curiously out of the corner of my eye as we pulled onto the highway.

"Wind surfing helps clear my head." She made little wave-like motions with her hand, letting the wind carry her hand. "And cherry stems de–de–decompose really fast—so I'm not littering." She managed and for someone as fucked up as she was she could still talk pretty well.

The way she swayed in the seat a little bit to the music, I couldn't help but glance at her every so often. "Do you want me to call Coop for you?"

Please say yes, because I need a reason to not be thinking about your fucking lips.

"Nah, let him get his last little bit of sleep before work." She lolled her head to look over at me as another song played, probably whatever was next in her shuffle, but it fucked me up nonetheless.

Bad Choices by Kode.

Fuck, Millie. This is what you have in your playlist?

I was trying to hold it together, but tonight had been entirely too much, maybe I knew why she had taken days off. Maybe it wasn't just Coop after all, maybe it was because of me.

Wow, that was really egotistical. Let's not jump to conclusions. She's just a flirt when she's drunk and she's fucking wasted.

I felt my chest do the thing, the thing where it's really fucking hard to breathe. I couldn't see her like this, I couldn't. Nope. I wouldn't let myself think about her like that. It was Millie for crying out loud. Coop's girlfriend. My kinda-sorta-boyfriend's best friend. I work with her for fuck's sake.

We fight, we push each other, we joke—but it's not ever serious.

Right? It wasn't serious. *This wasn't fucking serious, I didn't see her like that.*

"You're quiet when you drive." Millie's eyes hadn't left me, but maybe she didn't have the energy to turn back towards the window.

"Just thinking..." I mumbled, it wasn't a lie. I was thinking. I was overthinking. About her.

"I'm sorry for drunk thoughts Millie... she's a different breed. She can't be stopped." Millie said quietly, hopefully her couch time out had helped her sober up a little bit.

"It's fine..." I gave her a small smile, trying very hard to tune out the song and how heated the car felt even though nothing had even happened, we hadn't done anything wrong.

"Is it though?" She looked back at Gracie, who was snoring lightly in the back, the seatbelt awkwardly holding her in place, before looking back at me.

"Yep." I popped the p.

"Theo..." Her voice sounded so small, uncertain.

I pulled up to the yellow light, stopping before it fully turned red. "Princess, please don't."

"Link said he hates when you call me that." Her eyes met mine and I couldn't help but hold the contact.

My throat felt dry, I had a feeling but I needed to ask. "Why?"

Her eyes fell to my lips again, fuck, this was not what we were supposed to be doing. She looked away momentarily before meeting my eyes again. "He said I'm not yours..."

"You are." My answer was immediate, unfortunately, so was my regret. I hadn't drunk a damn thing, I had no excuse.

"I am?" She asked, leaning forward—probably subconsciously.

"Unfortanelty, but you're going to forget I said that." I glanced at the light, it was still red.

She leaned closer and I swear to God she knew what she was doing drunk or not. "No, I'm not."

"You can't say things like that when you're wearing my hoodie." I glanced down at her, I noticed it earlier when she came to the booth and it gave me a weird feeling in my chest. How she'd gotten it? No idea.

She stuttered, "I thought it was Coop or Link's...I didn't realize it was yours..."

I chuckled, "You probably stole it from Link, last time I hung out with him I think I left it." I side-eyed her, "Although you should probably quit wearing Link's hoodies if you're dating Coop."

She waved me off, "You're not getting it back." She said after a minute, wrapping her arms around herself. "And hoodies are fair game, you leave it—I'm taking it."

"Wasn't going to ask for it back. It's yours now." I admitted, looking at the frayed strings from where I had chewed on them. Yeah, she could have it. It looked better on her anyway. "Although, maybe don't wear it in front of Coop. Might not go over well."

"Oh so you can all wear each other's hoodies, but I can't?" She frowned, then looked up at me through her lashes. "I thought I was yours." She grinned, but quickly turned it into a pouty face. "Unless you want to retract that sentence."

"Nope." I grinned, trying to keep my eyes on the road.

She perked up, "No, I'm not yours? Or no you're not retracting that sentence?"

"Millie, quit." I managed, stopping her from prolonging whatever this was.

"Fiiiiiine." She huffed, folding her arms back around herself.

Fuck, I was so screwed.

Link

I heard the car pull up, she'd drunk texted me a few times tonight. Even sent me a drunk selfie from the hot tub, she better have not driven herself home. I swear to God I'd go off on her.

Drunk or not.

I guess I should have expected Theo to bring her home, I didn't expect Gracie to be carried in by him. "You can put her in my room." Millie told him and I did notice their prolonged eye contact as she pointed towards her room.

"Get a little too fucked up?" I asked her as she stumbled to the refrigerator and picked up a chicken broth container and drank straight from the carton. I rolled my eyes, Christ, why was she like this?

She nodded and when Theo came back out, he took one look at her gremlin mode and busted out laughing, "Princess, why the fuck are you drinking chicken broth cold?"

There he goes again with the fucking Princess shit.

"I'm hungry, but making food sounds dreadful." She shrugged, drinking the rest of the carton. "Also, can you pick me up for work tomorrow? Since my car is under lock and key?"

I looked between them, fuck, they were a lot closer than I originally thought. I couldn't help the sour look I knew was on my face. Ugh, I don't know what pissed me off more—the fact that they were painstakingly obvious or the fact that he'd set her up with his best friend.

His stupid voice pulled me from my thoughts, "Yeah, I can come get both of you. Gracie is still knocked the fuck out." Theo moved to the door, but she stopped him with a hand to his chest, before pulling him into a hug. Her head resting against his heart. She nuzzled into him. I didn't take it to heart *too much*, I did know drunk Millie was a lover.

He awkwardly patted her back, his eyes meeting mine. He was

covering with that, I saw the way he pulled her closer for a split second, the way his arms pulled her into him more–wrapping around her. "Go to bed Mils, I'll see you tomorrow."

"Fine, fine. I'm going to bed." She glared at me, like *I* did something wrong. "Link play nice."

I turned my attention back to Theo as he watched her make her way to her room. "You're so fucking obvious, I wonder how Coop would feel about you two acting like that." I crossed my arms as I walked to the front door and gestured for him to go out.

He exhaled, rolling his head to the left slightly, "It's not like that Link, not with her."

'You're a really bad liar." I quipped, it most definitely was—even if they were both denying it.

"It can't be like that." He frowned, chewing his cheek. "I'll uhh, see you around I guess."

As soon as he closed the door, Millie came over to me tugging on my sleeve. "You're mad."

"I'm not mad..." I sighed, "But you do need to be honest with yourself about what's actually going on between you and basically everyone in your life, even if you can't be honest with me." Okay, so it came out as mad.

My fucking bad.

"Link—"

"I don't need or want a drunk confession, Mils, I just—I care about him—even if it seems like I don't. And I fucking care about you." I turned towards her and noticed she was in his hoodie. "You know you're literally in his hoodie, right?"

"He told me, but to be fair I stole it from you." She gave me a lopsided grin as she ruffled my hair, standing on her tip toes to do so.

I looked her up and down, "Go to bed, pretty girl."

She did a little temper tantrum stomp, a small one in her defense. "Gracie is taking up my whole bed. I might just stay up."

I groaned, fuck, *okay*, I was no better. I was about to be bold, but it didn't mean anything. I *swear* it didn't mean anything. "You can come to bed with me."

She tilted her head, giving me the cutest fucking smile ever. "And you want me to be honest with myself?"

"Nope, not anymore, I want you to go to sleep." I pushed her towards my room, "Go feral fucking gremlin, you probably made Theo's night hectic as fuck. I'm shutting it down, lay down."

"Yes sir." She mock saluted me and I had to fight the reaction to the sass, so instead I took a deep breath and climbed into bed with her, putting a respectful amount of space between us.

Which she immediately disregarded, curling into my chest, and throwing her leg over me. "You smell like vodka, I thought you didn't drink vodka." I questioned, raking my fingers through her hair. It was damp. That fucking club and their water shows.

"I did tonight." She looked up at me, a grin on her face, like she was having the time of her life.

"Millie..." Fuck, that explains her bold ass and lack of filter.

"What? I'm just laying here!" She giggled, putting her face into my chest to muffle the noise, her hands wrapped around my waist pulling me closer to her.

She trailed her fingers up and down my sides, I huffed, "You're being fucking handsy."

"I could be handsier, watch your mouth." She warned and I know this five foot nothing little shit didn't just tell me to watch my mouth.

"You're not going to or I'm moving you to the couch." I warned and she stilled for a second.

"Nope! I refuse more couch time outs. Theo already put me on the couch once tonight. No more couch." She was basically laying on top of me as she threaded her fingers in my hair.

"I can't imagine why he'd do that." Sarcasm heavily implied, if she was doing to him what she was doing to me right now then she deserved that shit.

She sat up, pointing a finger to her own chest. "Hey, I'm fun."

"You are dating Coop." I said matter-of-fact. "Now lay."

"He's the best." She agreed, immediately laying back down.

I could have said good girl, but instead I settled on, "Sleep you menace."

"Why can't it be like my books?" She said sleepily, rubbing her eyes.

"What do you mean?" I asked, looking down at her tired face.

"Why do I have to choose?" She groaned "Fuck it, I could be single and have like friends with benefits or something..."

I didn't have an answer for all that, just pressed a kiss to her forehead and hoped she would fall asleep soon, for both of our sakes.

Millie

My head was pounding. Fuck, what time was it? Who was in my bed? And why was I draped across them like this? Panic settled in my chest as I remembered absolutely nothing after my ninth shot of vodka in the hot tub.

I opened my eyes, blonde hair. Okay, so Link and I'm not in my bed. I'm in his.

Crap.

Crap. Double crap.

I drank vodka. What the fuck did I do last night?

Hopefully not my best friend.

I lifted the blanket, delighted to find I was indeed dressed, not as dressed as I normally was though, I was still in my jean shorts but no shirt or bra—just a hoodie.

Hopefully they didn't let me drive. I doubt that they would.

The big question was why the fuck was I in Link's room and not my own?

"I can feel your anxious ass, we didn't do anything, promise, but as far as whatever happened between you and Theo I couldn't tell you." Link grumbled, throwing an arm over his eyes.

My eyes widened, fuck. "Theo brought me home didn't he? Oh god what did I say?! What did I do? Why am I in here?"

"Gracie is in your bed, you were going to sleep in there, but she's hogging the entire bed." He opened his eyes to look at me, the blonde strands cascading across his forehead. "You're dumb ass knows better than to drink vodka, that was fucking dumb." Link pointed out, "Also, next time you steal a hoodie, make sure it's actually mine. You're wearing your work husband's hoodie."

"What?? Wait—work husband? Why did you call him that?"

"Millie, you hang out with him so much he calls you Princess and you hug him. You hate hugs."

"If I did that here... did he say anything about work? Oh my god. I can't go back."

"Yeah, about that... he's picking you up for work." His arm opened for me to lay on him, I didn't. "The real question is, are you worried something happened between the two of you?"

"NO!!!!"

"You sure?" Link deadpanned.

I sent him a glare before I looked around for my phone, frowning when I couldn't find it. "Do you know if I texted Coop at all?"

"Don't know, you drunk texted me a few times. Sent a few pictures over to...from the hot tub."

"I did not!"

"Oh, you so did." He pulled out his phone and showed me.

Fuck, that was a lot of cleavage to be sending to Link. My cheeks heated as I looked through the rest of the texts, "Theo put me in tim out." I read out loud. Tim. Pretty sure that was supposed to be time.

An exaggerated I love you. Link met my eyes and shook his head as I said "Linky Link" out loud.

"Oh god... the amount of spelling errors, I can't even tell what I was trying to type."

He showed me a picture of me half under the hot tub water, with the mermaid emoji.

Okay yeah, ooops, I may have overdone it.

"Alright, I'm going to my cave. Wake us up later. I can't handle the embarrassment."

I sat up, climbing over him, his hands went to my hips stopping me from getting off of him. "So you don't remember anything?"

"No, why are you looking at me like that? What did I tell you?"

"You may have asked why you had to choose?" His smirk was infuriating.

"I said no such thing."

"But you did." He scrunched his nose.

"Nope." I smacked him, "Release me you heathen."

His hands went up a little higher, finding my waist under the hoodie. "Link..." I warned, but his brown eyes were sparkling with mischief and fuck me, it was just a little bit hot. "Quit." I tried to sound stern, but it came out breathless.

"You need to talk to Coop, because this—that little reaction I just got from you? That's not best friend vibes." His eyes fell to my lips and I panicked for a second, fuck, Link...now? Of all times to be bold?

I rolled my eyes, "Maybe if three different guys weren't trying to get me to implode I'd be fine."

"Oh? So Theo is on your mind." Link shot back, his fingers tracing against my skin.

I smacked his chest, "I did NOT say that."

He let go and tapped my thigh, "Go back to bed."

I scrambled off of him, practically running to my room to find a very knocked out Gracie still hogging my bed. I looked around for Tylenol and a half empty water bottle or something laying around. That way when I told Theo later I wasn't staying at work all night I could deal with him.

I wanted to spend time with Coop, these men were fucking with my head.

Maybe I just needed to get laid. That's what this was.

I woke up to several texts from Millie and a few from Theo.

Millie's were very messy. Oh man, she must have been tore up from the floor up.

That's exactly why I didn't want her dancing, but Theo had of course torn into my ass about it. Apparently knowing what the job was, agreeing to talk to her, and then having a problem with it was frowned upon.

So yeah, I fucking apologized. That was my bad. I fucked up.

There were a few blurry pictures of her in the hot tub, with a blonde girl featured in some of them—looking equally if not more drunk.

Then the "*are you mad at me*" texts, the "*I might actually quit if you want me too.*" got me.

Fuck no, I wasn't mad at her. She didn't have to quit.

I scrolled down.

> Millie: Apparreentle I made your best frien big mad.

> Millie: He put me in time out. Couch uncomfy sne d help. Sos

> Millie: He told me he textd yuo that hes taknig me home. Sorry vodka words hard.

I snorted at the amount of fuck ups in those texts, she was normally pretty witty in her texts, but that was not. That was hardly English.

I sat my phone down, but it dinged again.

> Millie: Hahaha, delete those. Please. I don't remember last night.

Coop: Keeping them for blackmail.

Millie: I'm not staying at work tonight, just going to get my car. Can I come over?

Coop: I'm not working today, so whenever you want to come over.

Millie: I thought you worked today?

Coop: Nah, I'm off on the weekends.

I looked at Theo's messages.

Theo: Your girlfriend is wasted. I'm taking her and her friend home after work. She's safe. She wanted to message you, but she's in no shape.

Theo: I have confined her to the couch, she's in trouble, if she drunk texts you that's not on me.

Theo: She's home.

I rolled my eyes, this motherfucker, he told her I worked so she wouldn't call me to come get her.

Stop. No. He was literally already there.

It didn't stop me from texting him about it.

Coop: Did you tell her I worked today so you could take her home?

Read. No dots. I sat for a second, this mother fucker left me on read, I typed another message.

Coop: If you fucking wanted her why did you try to set her up with me?

Coop: I swear to God I can't stand you sometimes.

Theo: I was already there Cooper.

Theo: It's not like that. Don't be like that.

Coop: What happened last night?

Coop: Dude, I'm so serious. She wants to come over. I can tell her no. Just tell me.

Theo: Her car is at the club. She's supposed to work tonight.

Coop: She's going in to get her stuff then coming to my house. I'm going to take your silence as confirmation something did happen.

Theo: Nothing happened. She's not like that. She likes you.

Theo: Besides she was drunk, I'm not an asshole.

He wasn't being fucking truthful, I knew Theo. I knew his fucking tells, I knew how he was with texting. And how he avoided my fucking questions. I did know he was being honest about the drunk part though. Theo had sisters. He was the type to bark at someone for trying to get too close to someone's drink.

I clicked on her Instagram, then found Link's profile. Yes, I know how fucking crazy it fucking sounds, but look—I wanted to hear his take.

I direct messaged him.

CoopXPlays: Do you know what happened last night?

I sent it, not expecting an answer. His profile followed me back, almost instantly and then a message.

LinkInThePark: Kinda, drunk Millie shenanigans. Gave Theo hell. Came home, gave me hell and then crashed.

CoopXPlays: So… I'm not getting the vibe that there's something between her and Theo?

LinkInThePark: There is a vibe, but she swears it's not like that.

CoopXPlays: You know her better than me, what do you think?

LinkInThePark: I think this whole fucking thing is messy af. Sorry for my part in that.

CoopXPlays: Yeah, I'll talk to her tonight.

I closed my phone, because fuck me... Link was right, this was messy. Really messy. Theo had slept with Link, probably had feelings for my girlfriend—or whatever she even is to me. Link already said I had to worry about him. And fucking Millie, she was the fucking sun. It was impossible to be mad at her. Technically she hadn't done anything wrong.

I had a feeling she'd tell me if she did.

If she remembered it that is.

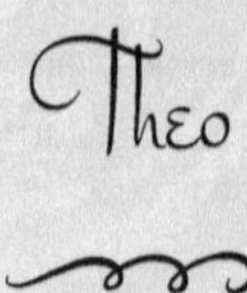

She was fucking driving me crazy, okay, maybe Gracie was driving me crazy. She wouldn't shut up. She was trying to convince Millie to work tonight, she had a group of golfers coming in today. I had no idea how the fuck she was networking to be able to pull in all these customers, but I wasn't complaining.

Millie sat in the passenger seat, arms crossed and spine stiff. She wouldn't look at me. Fucking brat. God damn. I wasn't the one who was fucking being too much last night. That was her. *All fucking her.*

Give me a fucking break.

Okay, maybe I was a little pissed about Coop calling me out and about Millie blowing off work tonight. She hadn't said a thing the entire time. Didn't stick her fucking hand out the window, didn't comment on the music taste—even unhooked her damn bluetooth.

This fucking girl.

I swear to every God and Goddess that existed. She made me wanna throttle her. Not that I would, but fuck, come on. *Come on.*

When we got to the club, an hour early since that's when I had to be there she smoothed out her skirt, adjusted her sweater and got out making sure to slam my fucking door. She didn't have to fucking slam it.

"Millie for fucks sake wait—"

"It's Jade on this property." She snapped.

She kept walking, so I grabbed her wrist and pulled her back to me. "There's literally no one here, we're not even fucking open yet."

"Don't fucking touch me." Millie growled, I don't think I've seen this version of her yet.

Gracie was watching us intently, "Iris, go inside. Please. I need to talk to her."

Gracie hesitated, looking at Millie who eventually nodded and Gracie took off in the direction of the entrance.

"Why are you acting like a fucking brat?" I asked, she flinched and I dropped her wrist, I hadn't been holding her tightly, I had only intended to stop her.

"Why are you acting like this?" Millie doubled down, throwing my own question right back at me.

I stared at her for a second, trying to calm myself, I wasn't trying to let the anger come out. I wasn't going to take it out on her. Nope. Instead I went for what I knew would work, I stepped closer, and lowered my voice. "You're acting like you can't fucking stand me. When we both know that's not fucking true."

"You don't get it. It's fucking easier, Theodore." I didn't miss how she spat my full name at me.

"How is this easier?" I didn't know how to tell her it hurt my heart, that my chest was heavy the entire fucking ride.

"Cooper is your best friend. Your best fucking friend. Link told me you're hung up on Coop." She paused, searching my eyes, "Link has a thing for you. It's all sorts of fucked up."

"Link is hung up on you too."

Oooh, fuck, that wasn't supposed to come out. Fuck, fuck, *fuck*. She was not supposed to hear that from me. God damn it, I just fucked up.

"I'm going to politely ignore that comment, since he's not here to defend himself." Millie took a deep breath in and it sounded shaky when it came out.

"Millie—" I stepped closer and she held her ground. I half expected her to step back.

"We can't fucking do this, it's messy as fuck. I won't do it to Link. And I won't let you do that to Coop. I'm taking myself off the schedule on your days. Just leave me alone." She stepped and walked away, looking back for a split second.

I let her get inside before I started to go inside, grabbing my work bag and slamming my own fucking door.

I was fuming, Millie was talking to Jonah already. She handed him a stack of twenties that was folded over. I watched her go up to security, handing them a similar stack. And then handed the bartender another.

She met my eyes and I didn't break that contact, she handed me a stack that was three times as big. I noticed at least two hundred in ones, plus some twenties. "It's twenty percent. I promised you twenty percent if you watched over me extra. You did, so...." I tried to give it back and she dropped it on the desk.

Then walked off, well she tried, I found myself being a fucking idiot. "Do you wanna know what happened last night?"

She froze, then came back over after a second. "Spill."

"You made some flirty comments, called me sir. Told me I was pretty." She flushed, probably out of embarrassment. "But for the most part, you lay right there on the couch. Nothing fucking happened."

"What about the drive home?"

"You stole my bluetooth, told me Link didn't like that I called you Princess, and why that is. I called you mine." I meant it to hit her in the feels and apparently it did, because she looked mad. I was not about to address anything else, because nothing else mattered.

"I'm not yours." But her eyes flicked to my mouth then away from me completely, *yeah—keep telling yourself that Princess.*

"Yeah." I said, blank and emotionless, I needed to shut whatever the fuck this was down now. I couldn't. She was right. I couldn't do this to Coop. Or Link. She closed her eyes for a second, then turned around and went to walk off. I couldn't help it, I had too. "Bye Princess."

She flipped me off.

I deserved it this time.

Marley was watching us curiously, another dancer, she had been listening this entire time. I swear these girls and their gossip. I think she was one of Laycee and Britt's friends though, so I knew she wouldn't say anything unless it was to them or Jonah, maybe Gracie.

I looked at the money, unfolded it, this little shit. Four hundred in twenties, and two hundred in ones? She didn't even make ones last night.

She did it to be petty.

Fucking brat.

Coop

"Bleed - Chri$tian Gate$"

Millie showed up around six thirty, she looked cute, but not sweet and innocent cute like the other night. She looked like someone who came here *specifically* to start trouble. She already had fuck-me eyes on, for crying out loud.

She had skipped off work to come hang out with me. Not the first time. Hell, she'd basically spent three days straight at my house last week. But now? Now she was curled into my side, dragging her fingers down my arm, letting me finish my run-through on the game. She was extra snuggly—clingy in this deliberate way that made my heart do stupid shit.

I hit my save point and shut it off.

I'd been dreading this conversation *all day*. I didn't want to have it. Not really and did it matter that much? She was here. She chose to be here. She chose *me* over work, but I couldn't let it sit in my chest any longer without exploding.

I took a deep breath. She shifted immediately, like she felt the worry come off me in waves. Best to spit it out and get it over with "So, I have to ask..."

"Fuck, okay, that sounds serious." She sat up a little straighter.

"Before we go any further with this... with us... I need to know if you have anything going on with Theo."

"I—" her jaw tightened, teeth catching her bottom lip. "I told them to take me off the schedule when he's there."

My stomach dropped to my ass. That wasn't an answer. That was a red flag.

"Why?" I asked and I was sure she realized how that sounded right now, "I'd rather you be there when he's there. Let's me know you're safe." She was safe with him. I knew that. "Unless of course there's other reasons you don't want to be there with him?"

"Theo and I don't get along. We're like fire and ice." She looked down, fingers brushing down her skirt, "It's not healthy."

"Did something happen between you two?" I pushed, trying to get her to say anything that would let me know if I needed to stop this before it went any further.

"No, we've never done anything. We've flirted when I'm drunk, but that's just drunk Jade, she's an idiot. She'd never actually be dumb enough to do anything though." She sat back a little, her eyes meeting mine. "But no, we haven't ever crossed those lines."

The thing was... the uncertainty in her voice killed me. He called her Princess for crying out loud, not just at work and I knew my best friend. He didn't act like that unless he really liked someone, Theo was a loner —he wouldn't hang out with anyone for long periods of time, unless it was me of course.

"Why does he call you Princess?" I couldn't help it, I needed to know the backstory.

Her answer was immediate. "To get under my skin. He does that shit when he calls me to the stage—to get a rise out of me."

I raised an eyebrow, "He does it when you're not working though."

She blinked. "Yeah, probably because we spent too much time together at work. Old habits."

"And you switched your nights to avoid him because...?" Just answer the question Millie, fuck.

She hesitated. "I'm not avoiding him..."

"That puts you at two nights a week." I paused studying her face, "Both nights he's off. That's textbook avoidance."

"Coop, you're entirely too perceptive." She chewed her cheek again, like she was nervous, like I'd caught her. "Why does it sound like you want there to be something there... I can leave–"

"Just answer the question and I'll drop it."

She took a breath. "It felt like the lines were blurring a bit. Theo and I are volatile at best. And this whole situation is messy as fuck." Her fingers slid into my hair and I didn't pull away. Couldn't. "I like you. I like you a lot."

"But you like Theo." I didn't say it like an accusation. Just a fact that her face wasn't hiding.

"Look, Theo is a fucking asshole. No offense to your choice of best friends, but I don't want to be around him... He ghosted Link and I had to deal with heartbroken, reckless Link. Do you know how hard it is to keep tabs on a biker who's triggering the speed alerts on my family app at one in the morning?"

Ahh, yes, bring it back to that, the other issue. "And Link?" I needed it out loud. I needed the whole truth.

"What about Link?" her voice went small, nervous.

I watched her hands—they wouldn't stop fidgeting. "I see the way he looks at you. He literally told me I should be worried about him."

"Link is Link..." She exhaled, breath shaky. "I don't... I don't know what to say about that. It's just how he's always been."

"So, Link likes Theo and you. Theo likes you and Link." I leaned back, looked straight at her. "So why are you here with me? When you could have both of them?"

Her head snapped toward me so fast it was almost funny. "What the fuck is that supposed to mean?"

I shrugged. "I mean logically—"

She cut me off, eyes blown wide. "Are you out of your fucking mind?"

"No, I was dead serious." I grinned. "But that reaction was funny as hell."

She looked like she might smack me—and honestly? I'd let her. Some shit just needed to be said. Fuck the consequences. "Sorry, that might've been a little out of pocket..." I admitted as I leaned in, brushing my nose against hers. She didn't pull away.

"A little?" she whispered. "I—"

I closed the gap and kissed her. Harder than I intended too. I'd wanted to do it all damn day. Maybe longer.

She melted into me instantly, hands sliding into my hair, tugging just enough to short-circuit every rational thought I had. I bit her bottom lip and she gave me the sweetest fucking sound, shifting fully, turning toward me like she was choosing me with her whole body.

And when she climbed on top of me, straddling my waist like she'd been waiting to do it all damn day? My brain just... vanished. Static. Nothing but her.

"Fuck, Mils—"

She cut me off by grabbing my jaw, tilting my head back, her mouth dragging heat down my throat while her hips rolled against mine like she knew exactly what it would do to me.

Oh. So this was how we were playing tonight.

Her skirt slid up higher, catching on my jeans, and there they were —those lacy, barely-there panties she absolutely wore here on purpose. She came over with an agenda. To distract herself. To distract *me*. And I was one second away from letting her burn down every coherent thought I had.

"Do you want to stop?" she whispered, breath brushing my ear.

I forced out a choked, "No."

God help me, I didn't want to stop. I wanted *her*.

Fuck everyone else.

I tipped her chin up so she had to look at me. "Are you doing this for me... or to forget about them?"

Her breath stuttered. Her pupils blew wide when our eyes locked. "They already get parts of me," she whispered. "Let me give you the best part." She kissed me—softly, terrifyingly, intentionally. "Even if you decide... this is all you want."

Her words hit me like a damn freight train.

Let me give you the best part. Who even says that? Who drops something that intimate, while they're sitting on your lap looking like that?

My hands went straight to her hips on instinct, thumbs brushing bare skin where her shirt had ridden up. And the second I touched her, she let out the softest little exhale—like she'd been waiting for it.

Yeah. No. I wasn't surviving this.

"You can't just..." I tried, but my voice cracked like I was going through puberty again. Nice. Real smooth. "You can't say shit like that to me."

She tilted her head, all faux-innocent, lips still swollen from kissing down my neck. "Why not?"

"Because," I breathed, tugging her a little closer, "I'll believe you."

And I would. That's the worst part. I'd take every part of her she'd give me.

Her forehead brushed mine, barely there. "Then believe me."

"Mils..." I warned, even though my hands were already sliding up her back, pulling her closer, already choosing her without any hesitation like an absolute idiot. "This isn't casual for me."

"I know," she whispered. And the way she said it? Like she wasn't scared. Like she wasn't running. Like she'd already made up her damn mind. "That's why I'm here, I don't—I don't do casual."

My pulse jumped, she didn't do casual, if she was in this—

"And if this ruins everything?" I asked, voice barely above a whisper, because it could. Theo and I had made a pact a long time ago about never letting a girl get between us.

She leaned in until her lips brushed mine without actually kissing me. Torture. Literal torture. "Then let it," she said. "I'm not scared of breaking things. I'm scared of never choosing what I actually want."

Her fingers slid into my hair. I grabbed her jaw, kissed her hard—no hesitation, no doubt, just weeks of tension snapping at once. She made this quiet sound in the back of her throat, hands gripping my shirt, pulling me closer like she needed me.

And I swear to god, every rational thought I'd ever had evaporated on the spot.

If this burned down everything? Fine.

I'd light the match myself. Fuck it all.

Her hands fumbled with my pants, pulling at the drawstring, her eyes met mine as if asking for permission. I nodded, she had it, whatever she wanted from me she had it.

Her lips pressed into the hollow of my neck, nipping lightly at my collarbone as she kissed lower, her nails dragging down my chest as she made to push my pants down.

I was hard as fuck already, leaking precum already, but I didn't have the heart to be embarrassed right now, especially when she took me into her mouth. Swirling her tongue around the head before going almost all the way down. I felt her gag just a little before pulling back up slightly.

She used her hand to jack me off while she went down again and again. Her tongue switched from laying flat when she was trying to take all of me, to doing little swirls when she pulled back up.

She found my hand with hers and I thought she wanted to hold it, but instead she guided it to her hair and when I grabbed a fistful at the nape of her neck she moaned around me, the vibrations almost sending me over the edge.

I held back, because nope, that wasn't fucking happening.

She went all the way back down, this time her nose touched me and she didn't come back up until she looked at me and tilted her head with my hand.

Oh? She liked that. Enough said, I pulled her hair and by extension her and the moan that escaped her was needy.

Fuckkkkkkk.

I used her and she let me.

Her eyes prickled with tears and I could tell she was trying not to let them fall. I pulled her off of me and looked into her eyes. "You okay, love?"

She nodded, wiping her mouth. Not good enough, a nod was not good enough, "Words, baby girl."

"I'm good, you're just bigger than I expected." I let out a huff of amusement as she licked her lips, adamant on returning to what she was doing.

"Do you want me to fuck you?" I asked, pulling her closer, this time it was my lips that marked her skin.

"Fuck, Coop–" Her head lolled to the side to give me more access, "Yes, please."

"Good fucking girl, using your words." I turned her, my grip still fisted in her hair, to kiss her again. "Face the back of the couch, I'll be right back."

Her face fell, "Wait, where are you—?"

As much as I didn't want to leave her right now, I was doing the right thing damn it. "Condom, we haven't talked about anything and I'm not letting you make any decisions during all of this."

"But—"

"You better be facing the back of the couch when I come back." I warned and the way she immediately turned around and put her elbows on the couch sent shocks through my system.

I made quick work of the condom, thankfully they were always in my top drawer, and came back out to her, I pushed her down further letting that perfect little arch of hers shine. "Fuck, you're perfect bent over for me."

She made a noise that sounded like a whine as I hiked her skirt up more, it pooled around her waist and her little see through thong? Even more see through now, fuck she was so wet it was on her thighs already. I ran my finger along her slit and she pushed herself back towards me.

"So impatient." I whispered, moving her thong to the side to push my fingers in her.

"Is this what you wanted?" I asked, expecting another nod, but she surprised me.

"I want you to fuck me."

I stepped closer to her, my dick brushing against her as I took a hold of her hair and yanked her back into me, "You sure about that?"

"Yes, please..."

I teased her folds for a second, before using my free hand to pull her thong down. When I finally pushed into her I pushed her face into the cushion to muffle the moan that escaped, gripping her hip in my other hand.

"How do you want it?" I asked, partially already knowing given her earlier actions, I turned her head to face me, still keeping her auburn hair wrapped in my hand.

What I didn't expect was for her to say, "However you want to give it to me."

I slammed my hips into her, watching her face as she took all of me, the way her eyes practically rolled to the back of her head, the way her lips parted. And fuck the little whimpers she was making, I don't think I'd ever get enough of her.

I increased my pace, burying myself deeper into her, I let go of her hair to put one hand on her lower belly, pushing lightly and using my other hand to rub slow circles right where she needed it, I pushed down just a little bit more and those whimpers turned into louder little moans.

She tightened around me, her whole body shaking, she collapsed into the back of the couch cushions, her weight going dead as I fastened my pace, determined to pull one more from her. "Coop, I can't." She whined, her mouth open slightly.

"Yes, you can, you're gonna give me one more like a good girl." I leaned forward, hitting a spot deeper in her, I could feel myself inside of her through my hand on her stomach. She clenched around me again, her body shaking against me again.

I couldn't help it this time, I followed her over the edge almost instantly.

Fuck, she was so good.

She took a deep breath, attempting to steady herself as she pulled her skirt back down and her thong back up into place. I took off the condom, tying it and tossing it in the little trashcan beside the couch. I tied my drawstring back so my sweatpants wouldn't fall off, I eyed her little skirt and sweater.

"Do you want a pair of my sweats and a hoodie?" I asked and she looked genuinely confused.

Her voice was small when it came out, "You don't want me to leave?"

"No, why would I want you to leave?" I pulled her into my side, pushing her hair out of her face. "I planned on ordering us food and cuddling you either right here or in my bed for the rest of the night." She melted into me fully, I intertwined my fingers in hers.

Had no one she'd been with ever heard of aftercare?

She smiled, "In that case, yeah, I will steal your clothes."

I leaned down to press a kiss to her lips and she deepened it immediately, I had to pull back when she pulled my lower lip in between her teeth. "We're not going to get far if you keep doing that." I teased before going to get her some of my comfy clothes.

I picked out my favorite band hoodie, a silent claim, Theo had threatened to steal it from me several times—he'd gone with me so he could have gotten a hoodie, instead he got a tee and vinyl. He couldn't have it, but Millie could.

Even if it did swallow her whole and it probably would.

I tried to dodge the orange furball from hell as he darted out of my room and took aim right at Millie, she squeaked when he flung himself onto her, "YOU HAVE A CAT!!!!" She giggled as she nuzzled into him.

"He's actually a menace and hates most people." I was mildly surprised that he was letting her manhandle him like that, he didn't even let me do that.

Traitor.

My cat was a traitor.

She looked at his name tag, her eyes lighting up with amusement. "You named your cat Crookie and expected him to not be a menace?"

I handed her the clothes and she gently moved the orange fuck head off of her, accepting a few seconds of under the chin scratches from her. "I call him Crooks."

"Men with cats are automatically hotter." She said as she passed me, "Where's your bathroom?"

I pointed to the door to the left in the hallway and when she came back out she looked like she was about to crash. I opened my arms and she plopped into me, settling almost instantly.

My orange menace stretched from his spot on the back of the couch and stepped directly onto her, laying half on her lap half on the couch. "He likes you." I chuckled.

"All cats love me." She shrugged, continuing her pets from earlier.

This girl.

She was on my couch, cuddling with my demon cat, in my clothes.

I was done for.

Yeah, she was mine.

Millie

"She Got Me Like - Kode"

I had maybe, accidentally, spent the night at Coop's for the first time. I didn't want to admit it, but he was fucking perfect.

The way he made sure I came first? The way he tucked me into his side and offered me his clothes and looked confused on why I would leave. Yeah, okay, maybe I hadn't had a real relationship in ages and hookups were far, few, and in between, but he caught me off guard.

He was sweet. Devastatingly so. And he had a cat? A cat that hates almost everyone?

Except, he immediately came to me. Orange cats were the best. He wasn't a demon like Coop said, he was adorable.

I didn't want to leave for work, but after a quick shower and a stop back at my house—where Link grilled me for not even letting him know I wouldn't be home—I finally made it to the club. I was also thirty minutes early, so I could at least have time to get ready without rushing.

I made it to the back of the club. Sunday meant no Theo, but it also meant no Gracie. I might actually need to read my kindle tonight, depending on how it goes. Toby was a decent DJ, I could get him trained in no time. I just hadn't had to recently. Working with Theo everyday, he knew my music taste. He knew what I preferred and what I hated dancing too, just because I could dance to anything, didn't mean I wanted to.

A good dancer can dance to anything and I had proved that over and over.

I was about to go in the dressing room when I walked into someone, I looked up and immediately my jaw dropped, "You're supposed to be off today, what the fuck Theo?"

"Toby switched with me." His infuriating smirk made me physically angry.

"Of course he fucking did." I went to step around him but he stepped at the same time. "Move Theo."

He didn't, instead I guess he thought stepping closer and pulling on the hoodie pocket was the move. "Nice hoodie, and uhh, might want to put some concealer on your neck." He smirked, his eyes tracking the spots on my neck from Coop. "Guess you didn't tell him the no mark rule when you have work." So much for an easy night.

I couldn't help the rage that was boiling up, why the fuck couldn't he just leave me alone? Not fucking comment. "Is that jealousy I hear?" I tilted my head as I said it, raising an eyebrow for emphasis.

The fucking nerve of him, setting me up with his friend and then acting like this.

"Not at all." He said, keeping his voice quiet, "I don't want my best friend's sloppy seconds."

Ouch. Damn, he didn't have to do me like that.

"No, you just want your best friend." I quipped, pushing past him, ignoring the rage on his face. "Sucks for you. He's mine now, sex is too good." I looked back at him, shrugging.

"I could say the same about yours." He mumbled and it shocked me he would bring Link up, but I guess if I go for a low blow I should expect it back.

He stalked off, heading back towards the front and I pushed open the door to the dressing room, making sure it slammed behind me.

He poked his head in, "Don't slam the fucking door, no one likes a fucking brat."

"Get the fuck out!" I pointed at the door, sending him a glare.

When he left I finally picked a pale purple lace set, carefully layering a second nude pair underneath the purple underwear. I didn't want to accidentally give a show. I had a cute fishnet black dress to layer over it.

I strapped up my sparkly pleasers and stopped by the VIP desk to sign in before making my way to the DJ booth. "Play whatever, you know what I like, please don't fuck with my music because you're mad."

"I'm a professional." He wouldn't even meet my eyes. Bastard. "I'll let you know when I'm about to start rotation, also watch your alcohol intake, Coop really does work tomorrow and I'll have to call Link to come get you. I'm not taking you home anymore."

"Didn't plan on drinking anyway." I grumbled, rolling my eyes as I stepped away from the DJ booth and to the far corner, there wasn't a single girl or customer in sight.

I wasn't going to drink. Not with him pretending he wasn't watching me like a damn hawk. I wasn't giving him anymore fuel, I wasn't going to be drunk around him—not now, not ever. He could fuck right off with that.

Plus, lack of customers meant minimal chances of getting drunk, I wasn't paying for drinks myself.

Not much changed throughout the night, we had a few regulars come in, I did the thing—chatted, got a glass of wine, drank like three energy drinks, and read about four chapters on my kindle before I needed to move. I had the energy drink jitters.

I went up on stage as a song was ending, hoping something good came on. Something that I could just feel. I looked at the DJ booth, Theo nodded and when the next song started it was one I knew, one I had gotten from Link's playlist a while back.

She Got Me Like by Kode.

Oh boy, here we go. I was already up here, no turning back now I guess.

I glanced at Theo, then decided to prop my phone up to film a video of me doing stage so I could send it to Coop.

I cleaned the pole, not even attempting to make a show of that right now, and immediately started a side climb all the way up the pole. Mostly because I knew it would bother Theo.

When I got to the top I dropped into a one leg hang, keeping one hand on the pole underneath me because this far of a drop would hurt like hell and I didn't want to go to the hospital, but I held the trick for a few spins, because yes the pole's spin by themselves.

Once I was certain I wouldn't fall, I hooked my foot in the crook of my other leg and tucked myself into the pole further so it would spin more, it worked and I pulled myself up to make pretty shapes with my legs, keeping one leg on it—and supporting most of my weight on it as well.

I switched my legs around so I could hold the pole between both legs and leaned back, stretching my arms out behind me so I could catch myself with my hands at the bottom. When I came down to do floor work, I didn't see Theo at the booth, but I did see a bunch of ones come down. They covered the floor. I hoped whoever did that wasn't on video, I looked up.

Theo, fuck, why did he do that?

It had to be because I gave him all the ones with my tip right?

It was just him being petty back.

I couldn't deny it would make good content.

I could post it on my dancer account and probably get more people in here.

The song wasn't quite over, so I did another climb, this time going all the way to the rafters and grabbing a hold of the wood plank to let go of the pole and shake my ass.

When I swung my legs back to get back to the pole, I let myself drop just a little bit before swinging myself out and up into an invert, hitting and holding a flawless inside leg scorpio and then adjusting so I could slide down to the floor easier.

I fish flopped across the floor to my phone, landing with my butt in view so I could give a little slow twerk before closing the video.

I went over the railing of the stage instead of down the stairs and went to get the broom so I could sweep everything up off the stage floor and into a bucket.

Once it was all swept up and put in the bucket I went to the couch by the DJ booth, because I'm a fucking addict for making bad choices I guess.

I sat the bucket on his desk and sat back down, he looked at me and shook his head, handing me the bucket back. "It's yours."

"Theodore, take the money back."

"No."

I huffed, taking the damn bucket back and started sorting it out with the faces upright. I wouldn't count money until it was facing the right way, just a superstition I guess, much like never putting your dancer shoes on the counter. You just didn't do it unless you wanted to stop your money in its tracks.

Once it was sorted, I didn't have to count it. I knew it was the two hundred I'd given him in one's the night before, so I just moved on. I watched the video back, before sending it to Coop, the money was in it —Theo thankfully was not. I opened up my dancer instagram and clipped the part where the cash came down and posted it with the location tag.

If I could get more people in here from that alone, fuck yeah I'd post it.

I was also busying myself, I took screenshots from the video to get another post out of the video, screenshotting the tricks and seeing what looked the best.

I couldn't stop myself from glancing at Theo, only to find him smirking at me.

Fuck, why were these men trying to take me out.

He could eat rocks.

Him and his stupid smirk.

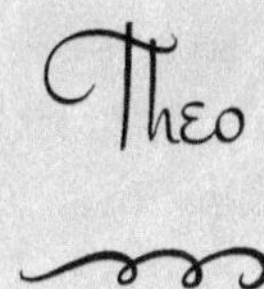

I glanced at the couch, okay, okay... I glanced at her, at how invested in the video of herself she was. My phone lit up with a notification, then another, of course it fucking dinged—loudly.

I had my damn notifications for her posts on. Only on her dancer account though, not like her personal. I swear. It was for work-related purposes. I could repost, share, whatever to get the girls more money in here.

I opened the app, immediately it opened to her pictures on the pole. I liked it, like physically, put the little heart on it, then did the same thing with the video of the money falling down on her.

Her eyes snapped to me, "Why?"

"Ummm, I'm the DJ here. That's why." I rolled my eyes, because sass wins—and pisses her off.

She stood, coming over to me, "You know you're the biggest pain in my ass."

"And you can't stay away from me." I looked her up and down, the outfit looked good on her. "That's why you only want to work when I'm not here."

"And?" She questioned and fuck, I think I may have preferred drunk and unhinged Millie instead of angry and blunt Millie.

I blinked. "And? You're not going to deny it?" I crossed my arms.

She sighed, "I'm tired, Theo." Her words did sound heavy.

"Then take a nap, I'm sure you didn't get much sleep last night." I didn't mean to sound *that* petty.

She stepped into the booth, lowering her voice. "You say you're not jealous, but you keep bringing it up."

"I am."

Fuck, didn't mean to say that out loud.

"What?" Her eyes snapped to mine and my chest felt heavy, fuck, I don't even know how to explain myself right now.

"Not in here." I said, looking over at Jonah and the bartender. I lowered my voice, looking at her, "But I meant it when I said you're mine."

She leaned against the side of the booth, her eyes were watery, "Part of me maybe, but no—I'm not yours completely. You don't get that claim over me."

"You are mine, you are my responsibility—especially here."

"I didn't ask for that." She said quietly, avoiding my gaze.

"Yeah Princess, I know." That did it, the softest smile flitted across her face just for a second. It about broke my entire composure, not that I had any left.

"Theo..." She stepped closer, she really needed to not. The way she was looking at me hurt, she really needed to go somewhere else.

"Go do something... anything... please." We had way too many eyes on us right now, sure we were talking relatively low, we'd kept our voices down—we're not stupid—but workplace relationships were frowned upon.

It wasn't *technically* a fireable offense, but I didn't want to push it.

"Theo?"

"What?"

"Eat rocks."

I really needed her away from me, before I did something to lose my job and my best friend.

Link

Why the fuck was Theo texting me at one in the morning? I thought he didn't work Sundays.

Oooof. I should not know that little detail, but whatever, he was texting me at one in the fucking morning.

Theo: Can I come over after Millie falls asleep?

This motherfucker. What was he thinking?

Link: No.

Theo: Can you come over here then?

Link: Are you booty calling me right now? Like actually? After everything.

This infuriating man. I already knew I was going to go, I knew it as soon as I opened the fucking message. It'd been too long and Theo was easy to go back too.

Theo: I might be. You can stay the night?

Theo: Please…

Theo: I'm really in my fucking head.

Theo: Millie and Coop slept together and I don't know who I'm more jealous of… and I think I just need you.

Theo: Link please, we don't have to do anything. Maybe we could go for a ride? I don't know anything…

Damn. All the double texts. Five in a row. Fuck, what happened tonight?

Link: I take it Millie has no fucking idea you're texting me.

Theo: Why would she?

Because you're obsessed with each other and won't fucking admit it. I didn't say that though, so points to me. Instead I settled on—

Link: I'm no one's secret.

Theo: You can tell her, I'll tell her. I don't care.

He'd always wanted to keep us a secret, the fact that he was open and willing to tell her? That was a big change.

Link: Fuck, okay okay, once Millie is home I'll leave. I normally wait for her. You're not coming to my house. Not with Millie here.

Theo: That's fair.

Theo: She already knows anyway… it's not that big of a deal.

Link: Yes the fuck it is.

Theo: I don't need to be near her right now anyway… I'll tell you later.

Doesn't need to be near her? Oh fuck, what the fuck did Millie do? I don't trust that little shit as far as I can throw her, which I can throw her by the way, don't ask me how I found out.

I looked back at the texts, fuck, why was I considering this?

Link: Are we really doing this again?

Theo: Do you want to?

Fuck it, I guess.

Link: Beats being alone or imploding my entire fucking life.

Fuck, okay, I'd wait for Millie to get home and then I'd leave. I wanted to make sure she was safely tucked away in bed, just because he said we could tell her doesn't mean we should.

Millie was like a bomb. She was fucking fragile and explosive when triggered and I was pretty positive Theo was one of those triggers.

But if she was moving on from us—oh my God what? Moving on from us? Us??? You're her friend. Theo is her co-worker. There was never an us. Millie is just someone who likes attention. She's always been like that. And when she feels safe with that person? It's over. The lines are always blurry. She beats herself up a lot.

I know she fucking loves me. I know it in my soul. The way she gets handsy when I take her on the bike? The way she literally acts like an overgrown koala when she lays with me?

I'm not stupid. I do know her, I know if I pushed for it she'd give in immediately. I'm just not going to. It has to come from her. It has to be her to initiate.

I thought she might kiss me yesterday, that wasn't the first time we'd gotten close to breaking all the rules we'd set.

Fuck, I should have just done it.

But that—that is messy and it's messy enough as is, plus add in an overprotective Theo in the mix, I'm surprised she hadn't had a full blown meltdown.

I sighed as I got in the shower, Theo was a problem—he understood me, he understood not being fucking chosen. He understood being in love with his best friend. He understood that hurt just as well as me.

And now?

Now I'm pretty positive he had fallen for Millie.

Don't get me wrong, I didn't fucking blame him. She's everything to me.

He had to go and bring Coop into this... Pretty sure Millie could have told Theo and I about each other and we'd have told her we can share, as long as she was cool with us being together too—but no fucking Cooper had to be drug in.

Ughh, I really didn't like Coop even more.

Okay, maybe that really wasn't fair. I did like Coop, Millie really likes Coop. Apparently enough to sleep with him. Pretty positive that's the only reason I didn't like him. He took what was mine.

Speaking of mine, I think I just heard the door.

I finished my shower, throwing on a hoodie and a pair of grey sweat pants.

Eh eh, I don't wanna hear it. I know what I'm going over to do. I can own the slut vibe just as well as anyone else, okay?

I checked my phone, it was only two thirty, why was she home so early?

"Why are you home early?" I definitely saw her eyes travel down to a place they shouldn't have.

"Why are you in your slut pants? Are you going somewhere?"

"Millie..."

"Oh no, nooooooo. You don't get to Millie me like I'm stupid. What's their name?"

I didn't say anything, which to be fair would have me jumping to conclusions if it was reversed.

"Holy fuck, you're going to Theo's aren't you?" Her jaw dropped, how the fuck did she know that?

"I might be. I mean I don't have to go if you want my slut pants to yourself, since you're openly ogling me." I don't know where the boldness came from, but the blush that broke out across her face was fucking worth it.

"I am not ogling." She countered, but I saw how her eyes tracked, I'm not blind.

"Definitely are, pretty girl." I winked, leaning against the counter next to her.

She groaned, "Go, maybe he'll chill the fuck out."

"What happened?" I asked, because I could tell it was bothering her, it was written all over her face. If there was one person who could get under her skin, it was Theo.

"A lot, he switched with Toby tonight. We... exchanged words. He said I was his. I told him I wasn't." She leaned against the back of the couch.

I narrowed my eyes, "He said that?"

Millie visibly panicked, "I—wait no forget I said that. I don't—it's not..."

I leaned closer, "Sucks you're with Coop, because I'm pretty positive Theo would have shared."

Her face went bright red, "Dude—Link—Lincoln Scott. You didn't just say that."

I chuckled, "Anyway, I'm taking the bike. I'll let you know when I get there. I'm taking your helmet, just in case he wants to ride."

"Oh, so he can be your backpack?" Her eyes narrowed.

"Why do you sound jealous?" I asked, pushing her hair out of her face.

"I'm not." She crossed her arms and moved away from me slightly.

"Oh, you so are! It's cute." I grabbed both helmets and kissed her cheek. "Have a good night. Get some sleep."

"Have fun I guess." Millie stuttered, taking off towards her room at record speed.

I shouldn't feel bad for that, but I did.

Fuck I did, but if she could fuck someone else–so could I.

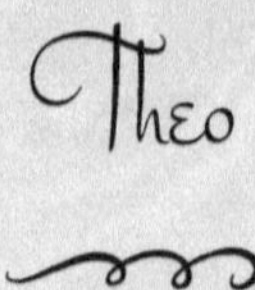

"I Like the Way You Touch Me - Bryce Savage"

We closed early, thank fuck for that, because it was so slow. Millie had left as soon as we announced closing. Throwing everyone twenty dollars for a tip, yes including me.

I had texted Link. I had caved. I'm fucking human.

I just wanted to let someone take control for once, I was fucking stressed out. I knew I sounded desperate, I didn't expect him to say yes at all.

Once his bike pulled up, I had the door open almost instantly, leaning against the door frame. I had planned to smoke with him first, talk some, but he shocked me again by immediately pulling me into a kiss. Rough and needy.

Oh okay, so we're back to this.

I wasn't sure if this is what I needed exactly, but fuck if I didn't enjoy it. The way his hands fisted my hair and his lips brushed down my jawline? Fuck...

"Did you miss me?" I ask, I meant it to come out confident, but it came out quiet and unsure.

Link's lips found mine again, this time slower and softer. "Fuck, sorry—I needed that."

I didn't even ask, I just wrapped my arms around him, I wouldn't say it, but I needed this just as much as he did. I pressed my lips to his neck and inhaled him, bergamot and eucalyptus.

Fuck, I had missed this, I had missed him.

"Okay, as much as I want to fucking devour you and as Millie put it, I wore my slut pants for you so... spill... what's going in that beautiful fucking brain of yours?" Link pulled me towards my couch and I immediately rerouted us to my room.

I tugged him down onto the bed with me. Thankful I'd washed my sheets recently, "Nothing, I'm just exhausted. Coop snapped at me about Millie, they fucked, and I don't know who to be more jealous about and that's a fucking problem."

"Are you admitting you have feelings for her?" Link asked, his fingers threading through my hair.

I relaxed into him, I forgot how fucking easy this was. "That's putting it lightly."

"She told me you called her yours." Link tugged my hair just a little bit.

"Are you mad about that?" I asked, meeting his warm brown eyes, his eyes were dilated slightly and fuck, I shouldn't have noticed that.

Link huffed out a breath, "No, I mean I was in the moment, but I get it—it's Millie." He kissed my lips gently, " She's mine too, you can share."

Was he teasing me right now?

"Yeah, if we could get Coop to share though that'd be great." The words were out before I could stop them, ooops.

Link actually laughed, like a full belly laugh. "I may have dropped that on Millie in an around the bout way."

I snorted, "You did not actually say that to her."

He shrugged, "She was appreciating the sweat pants. Of course I said something."

"What exactly did you say?" I asked, because damn, he was fucking unhinged too.

"That if she wasn't with Coop, that'd you probably share between the two of us." He said it so nonchalantly. And the fact I didn't disagree? That was a disaster.

I was questioning his sanity though, was he fucking drunk and I just couldn't tell?

"Link, did you drive over here drunk?" I deadpanned, it had to be the only explanation.

"No, I haven't drank anything in a while, but I love the confidence in me. Ten out of ten." He laughed, "Nah, I just wanted to see her face. She's down bad for you, you know that right?"

I groaned, tracing his jawline with my fingers. “I almost kissed her in the DJ booth tonight, pretty sure she would have let me.”

He drug his teeth across his bottom lip, contemplated for a second then said, “I almost kissed her the morning after you brought her home, she slept in my bed that night.”

I was quiet for a minute, “I mean we could share her.”

“But Coop.” Link pointed out, a smirk on his face.

“Right.”

Fuck me, what had I done?

I may not be able to have Coop.

But I had Link.

And I did have Millie, in our weird little way. I could have pushed for more if I wanted to.

But of course, I’m worried about fucking Cooper James and his stupid pretty face.

Link grabbed my jaw and turned me back to him, crashing his lips to mine. “I’m right here, right now. You and I. You got it? Be here with me.”

I breathed out, nodding. He was right. I needed to be present. Not spiraling about Millie and Coop. Not when Link was here, warm and solid against me, his fingers still gently gripping my jaw.

"I'm here," I whispered, closing the gap between us again.

I don't know how long we kissed, just that it felt like coming home. The familiar weight of his body against mine, the way his hands knew exactly where to touch, how to hold me. I'd forgotten how good this felt —just letting go, letting someone else take control.

When he finally pulled back, his pupils were blown wide, lips swollen. "Do you want to talk about it more, or...?"

I shook my head. "No talking. Not tonight."

He smiled, a slow, wicked thing that made heat pool in my stomach. "Good. I didn’t want to anyway.” His hands slid under my shirt, dragging up my sides with deliberate slowness. I arched into his touch, desperate for more contact. When he pulled my shirt over my head, I let him, lifting my arms to help.

"You're still so fucking pretty," he murmured against my neck, and something in my chest tightened painfully.

I pulled him closer, my fingers tangling in his hair. "Shut up and kiss me."

He laughed against my skin, but obliged, pressing me into the mattress. His weight felt good—grounding me when everything else felt like it was spinning out of control.

I don't know when my pants came off, or his. Just that suddenly there was skin against skin, his mouth hot and insistent as it moved down my body. I closed my eyes, letting myself get lost in the sensation.

When his mouth wrapped around me, I gasped, hips bucking up involuntarily. Link's hands pressed me back down, holding my hips in place as he took me deeper.

"Fuck, Link—" My voice broke as he hollowed his cheeks, the suction making my toes curl. He hummed in response, the vibration sending shivers up my spine.

I tangled my fingers in his hair, not pushing or pulling, just needing to touch him, to ground myself. He knew exactly how to take me apart, remembered every sensitive spot, every movement that made me lose my mind. It had been too long.

"I missed this," I admitted, breathless. "Missed you."

He pulled off just long enough to say, "Show me how much," before taking me back into his mouth.

I tugged at his hair, urging him up. "Come here," I whispered, and he obliged, crawling back up my body until we were face to face again.

"What do you want?" he asked, voice rough. His eyes were soft but laced with want, fuck he looked so fragile.

"You," I said simply. "All of you."

He smiled, that crooked smile that always gave me that fluttery feeling. "You've got me."

I rolled us over, pinning him beneath me. His surprise was evident, eyebrows shooting up as I straddled him. "Let me," I murmured, trailing kisses down his chest.

"Fuck," he breathed, letting his head fall back against the pillows. "Whatever you want."

I took my time with him, savoring every gasp, every twitch of muscle under my hands. It had been too long since we'd been together like this, I'd almost forgotten how responsive he was. How he'd arch into my touch, the way he'd moan my name when I kissed that spot just below his ear. The way his hands would find my hair, gripping tight enough to hurt but not enough to make me stop.

When I finally took him into my mouth, the sound he made was almost enough to undo me completely.

"Theo," he gasped, his fingers tightening in my hair. "Fuck—if you keep that up—"

I pulled back, looking up at him with a grin. "Not yet."

He groaned, tugging me back up his body. "You're a fucking tease."

"You love it." I whispered against his lips.

"I do." he admitted, and something about the way he said it made my heart skip a fucking beat.

Why the fuck had I ever given him up?

"I want you," I murmured against his mouth, my fingers trailing down his chest. "Like before."

His eyes darkened, a grin pulling at his lips. "You sure?"

I nodded, reaching for the bedside drawer. "I'm sure."

When I handed him the lube, his smile turned wicked. He flipped us over in one smooth motion, pressing me into the mattress with his weight. "Been a while," he whispered, his fingers already working me open with practiced ease. "Tell me if it's too much."

It wasn't—it was perfect, the slight burn giving way to pleasure as he stretched me, preparing me with a patience I'd forgotten he possessed. By the time he positioned himself between my legs, I was already shaking with need.

"Look at me," he commanded softly, and I did, meeting his eyes as he pushed in slowly.

Fuck, we'd never really done anything in this position, it was definitely more intimate than what I was used to with him. It didn't feel wrong though, it felt nice. It felt like love.

Fuck, I think I'm in love with him.

Not that I'd say that right now, fuck no, definitely not right now.

I gasped, the fullness was overwhelming—I gripped his shoulders, nails digging into his skin as he bottomed out, both of us gasping at the sensation.

"Fuck, Theo," he groaned, his forehead dropping to rest against mine. "I fucking missed you." His lips found mine and I kissed him back, we'd never kissed during sex before.

Not ever, but I guess that's what happens when you finally choose each other.

He started to move, slowly at first, each thrust deliberate and deep. I wrapped my legs around his waist, urging him deeper, faster. The way he filled me, the weight of him above me, the familiar scent of his skin—it was intoxicating.

"Don't stop," I whispered, my voice breaking as he hit that perfect spot inside me. "Please don't stop."

His rhythm faltered for just a moment, his eyes meeting mine with an intensity that made my breath catch. Then he was moving again, harder, faster, one hand gripping my hip while the other tangled in my hair.

"I've got you," he whispered, his voice a reverent promise against my ear. "I've always got you."

The words hit somewhere deep inside me, something raw and vulnerable that I'd been trying to ignore. I pulled him closer, crushing my mouth against his, not wanting him to see whatever I knew was written on my face.

His hand slipped between us, wrapping around me, stroking in time with his thrusts. I was close—so close—the tension building at the base of my spine, my whole body trembling with it.

"Let go for me," Link murmured against my lips. "I want to feel you."

It was too much—his words, his body, the way he looked at me like I was something precious. I came with his name on my lips, my back arching off the bed..

He followed me over the edge moments later, collapsing against me with a groan, his face buried in my neck. For a few minutes, we just breathed together, his weight anchoring me to reality when everything else felt like it might disappear..

"Fuck," he finally whispered, rolling to the side but keeping an arm draped across my chest. "That was..."

"Yeah," I agreed, not having the words either. I turned to face him, studying his features in the dim light. His hair was a mess, lips swollen, eyes soft in a way I hadn't seen in months. "You good?"

He nodded, thumb tracing lazy circles on my shoulder. "Better than good."

I should have felt guilty. About Coop, about Millie, about the whole fucked-up situation we'd created, but lying there with Link, I couldn't bring myself to regret anything.

"Are we gonna talk about the fact you booty-called me?" Link chuckled after a minute.

I groaned, "Moment of weakness."

"Is that was this is?" Link shifted, his fingers threading through my hair, "What am I to you?"

"Mine." I said simply, "I mean if you want that."

Link paused, his expression flickering with something vulnerable before he nodded slowly. "Yeah. I want that." He leaned in, pressing his forehead against mine. "So what now?"

"I don't know," I admitted, trailing my fingers down his chest. "I want you, but..."

"But there's Coop and Millie." He sighed, not pulling away. "We're a fucking mess, you know that?"

I laughed, but it sounded empty even to my own ears. "Yeah, I know."

We laid there in silence for a while, my head on his chest, his fingers tracing patterns on my back. I could hear his heartbeat, steady and strong beneath my ear. It was comforting in a way I hadn't realized I needed.

"Can I stay?" he finally asked, his voice quiet in the darkness.

"Please," I whispered, tightening my arm around him. "I want you to stay."

He nodded against my chest, his breath warm against my skin. "Good."

I didn't know what tomorrow would bring—how we'd handle Coop, or Millie, or any of it. But for tonight, I had this. I had him. And maybe that was enough.

When morning came, I woke to the sound of my phone pinging somewhere on the floor. Link was still asleep, his arm draped heavily across my chest, face peaceful in a way it rarely was when he was awake. I carefully extracted myself, trying not to wake him as I searched for my phone.

My heart sank. It was Coop. Of course it was Coop.

> Coop: You busy today? Thought we could hang.

I stared at the text, I didn't open it. I'd leave it on unread. I wanted to hang out with Link. It was easier.

It was easier than whatever this was.

"if u think i'm pretty - Artemas"

Link was still at Theo's when Coop got off work, so I did what any bored person would do and asked if I could come over, but not before turning off my family tracking app.

Link could absolutely kick rocks on my location right now.

Fucking asshole.

How was he going to drop the 'We'd share you.' shit then fucking dip, not feeling so fucking brave today, huh?

And him and Theo hooking up? Fuck, not gonna lie that was—that was hot.

Leave me alone, I am just a girl.

When I got there he was on the mic, answering the door shirtless and in slutpants—I mean sweatpants. His hair was wet and he smelled good. I dodged the headset and controller to give him a hug.

He looked at my messy bun then his eyes fell to the fact I was in his hoodie and a very short pair of shorts.

I followed him into the living room and flopped onto the couch beside him. "Who's on the mic?"

"Link and Theo." He lifted his arm so I could nuzzle into him.

I could hear the mic chatter somewhat, they were inquiring about me, "Yeah, Millie is here."

"Millie if you can hear me, turn your fucking family app on—I know your phone is active." Link's voice came through, damn, way to call me out.

He could have just texted me. I opened my family app and turned my location back on, I leaned forward so I knew he'd be able to hear me. "Happy now?"

"Yep, thanks." Link's muffled voice came out of the headset.

Coop's hand rested on my thigh and as they played, which Coop was only half playing by the way, his hand had crept up significantly higher. I looked up at him and his blue eyes met my hazel ones, I raised my eyebrow in challenge and he smirked as his hands edged closer to my shorts.

Two could play this game.

I did exactly what he did, dragging my nails against his thigh, and up higher.

He shifted and glanced at me, hitting the little button to mute us, "I'm on the mic—" I did it again, holding my ground, "with our friends."

"Then be quiet, you started it." I giggled, he had started it.

It wasn't my fault I had zero shame. It also didn't help that the two assholes on the other end knew me and knew that I simply didn't give a flying fuck. They'd both made me question myself, my relationship and all of this. If they heard, so what?

What's the worst that could happen?

They'd tease me? They already did that. Well, Theo specifically. Link would be crossfire honestly, but he had said they'd share me, so if he heard that was on him too.

Coop smirked at me as he unmuted the mic. "Sorry guys, got distracted." His fingers traced circles on my inner thigh, making my breath hitch.

I bit my lip to keep quiet, but the way his eyes darkened when I did made my heart race. This man was going to be the death of me.

"You two aren't slick," Theo's voice came through the headset, and I rolled my eyes.

"Never claimed to be," Coop replied, his voice impressively steady considering where his hands were. I decided to up the ante, sliding my fingers along the waistband of his sweatpants.

His breath caught, and I felt a surge of satisfaction. Good. Let him feel as flustered as I'd been feeling since Link dropped his little bomb last night.

I leaned forward kissing down his stomach, pushing his shirt up to kiss his hips.

“Coop, you good? You’re breathing a little heavier over there?” Theo snickered.

“Yep, perfectly fine...” Coop managed, even as I took him out of his pants.

Coop died as soon as I swirled my tongue on him."Shit!" Coop hissed, his free hand immediately tangling in my hair. I heard Link and Theo laughing through the headset as I took him deeper, watching his reactions.

"Dude, what happened?" Link asked, sounding genuinely confused.

"Nothing, just—fuck—died in the game," Coop stammered, his grip tightening in my hair as I hollowed my cheeks.

I maintained eye contact with him as I worked, enjoying the power I had in this moment. His eyes were dark, pupils blown wide, and his chest rose and fell rapidly as he tried to keep his composure.

"You sound distracted," Theo commented, and I could practically hear the smirk in his voice. "Everything okay over there?"

"All good," Coop managed, though his voice cracked slightly. He hit the mute button again, letting out a low groan that went straight through me. "Fuck, Millie—"

I pulled off him with a wet pop, smirking. "You started it," I reminded him, before taking him back into my mouth.

He gripped my hair tighter, guiding me now, and I let him take control. The fact that our friends were still talking, completely unaware of what I was doing—or at least pretending to be unaware—made it even more thrilling. And if they did hear? Well, they kinda deserved that too.

He unmuted himself again, somehow managing to keep his voice steady as he spoke. "I'm back in. Let's go."

I doubled my efforts, determined to make him lose that composure. When his hips bucked involuntarily, I knew I was winning.

Especially when he died again. I giggled around him, sending more vibrations down his shaft.

“You’ve died more times than Link, that’s not normal.” Theo was unconvinced.

Link’s exasperated voice, “Hey, that’s rude. I’m carrying us right now.”

Coop made a noise that wasn't exactly a moan, but more of a garbled muffled sound and I heard Theo's voice. "Tell Millie to stop whatever she's doing, she's fucking up your game."

"I don't think I will." I said loudly.

"Millie!!!" Coop whisper shouted, but his little breathy chuckle was enough to keep me going.

"Didn't peg you as a verbal exhibitionist." Link said his voice coming through Coop's headset. And the saltiness in his voice? I didn't miss that.

Theo laughed, "I did... she's a dancer for crying out loud."

That made my face go flush red, I pulled myself off of him, "I am not—"

Coop's sly little grin said it all, "You definitely do have a little bit of an exhibition kink."

I looked at his controller, the orange light was not on. They'd definitely just heard that. Oh?

Was he feeding into them right now?

His hand slid into my hair, clearly not done with me, and I took him back in my mouth causing a little moan to slip past his lips as I went down as far as possible and hollowing my cheeks out.

"Guys, mute the fucking mic." Theo's voice rang out and Coop snorted.

I laughed around him and he jerked—his hand tightening in my hair. His surprised gasp of my name didn't stop me. "Millie—" he bit his lip hard, trying to stay quiet.

"Good fucking girl." He whispered and I swooned, could he be more perfect?

"If you two don't fucking quit, I swear to God." Links' voice, but it sounded rougher, more gravely.

"Coop mute it, you're killing us over here." That was Theo.

Coop laughed, muting his mic, but also taking the headset off completely. "You are bad."

"You just called me a good girl, so I can't be that bad?" I looked up at him wiping my mouth.

"Come here." His blue eyes were so fucking dilated right now, fuck.

"But you didn't—" I tried to protest.

"Babygirl, come here." I got up and he pulled me into a searing kiss, his hand trailing from my waist up to my neck. "You wanna play? Take the headset, your turn."

"What??"

"Your turn, don't make noise and don't let them know. See how you like it. Only mute if you really need to."

"I'm not good at this game."

"See, that's just you trying to get out of it." He adjusted the headset onto my head, "Good luck, pretty girl."

I looked at the screen, I had thirty seconds before I had to get it together. He slid my shorts down and got behind me on the couch, pulling me into a side position.

"Wait—we didn't..."

He pulled out a condom from his pants pocket, "I'm prepared this time."

I groaned and he grinned, I didn't know how to tell him he didn't have to use it. I didn't want to ruin the moment damn it, but he was killing me with that.

As he put it on he unmuted the mic, pushing the button on the controller. "I'm taking over for Coop for a minute." I said, voice unsteady.

Link sounded distraught, "Wait, you suck at this game."

"I'll give it back in a few, he's indisposed at the current moment, you're stuck with me assho—" I bit my lip hard to stop from making any noise, because Coop wasn't playing around. He'd pushed in all the way when I was mid sentence.

I missed multiple shots, basically spraying and praying at this point —not like I was great to begin with. I shot Theo.

"Millie, you just killed me." Theo's voice rang out, but I couldn't answer because Coop's fingers were making circles now, and I was hyper aware of my breath.

"Sorry—I—my bad." I tried to get into a hidden area, as Coop fastened his pace and bit into my shoulder.

I threw a grenade, oops, Link's username appeared at the bottom. "Millie... I know you're bad—but you're not team kill bad."

"Maybe I just wanted to ruin—your—fuck—your day." My

sentence was broken and Coop hit mute for me as he pushed on my stomach and held me closer to him.

"Don't stop playing, or they'll know." He unmuted the mic—at the wrong time might I add—because the sound I made was nothing short of a whine as I pushed back against him.

Theo groaned, "Millie... that was not a sound I needed."

Link was deadly quiet.

I glared at Coop, "You did that on purpose."

"Maybe I did." He said, sliding in and out as I tried to keep my breathing even, I pushed him away for a second and looked up at him asking for permission to take it off. He muted the mic, "You sure?"

"I'm clean, I have an IUD, please..." I sounded desperate, he nodded, and I took it off. Fucking finally.

He unmuted the mic and I had to stop myself from making an ungodly noise.

It still slipped out.

"Are you two—You know what, don't answer that." Link sounded actually pained, I almost felt bad.

"Interesting you've got her listening to us as you fuck her Cooper." Theo's voice came out low and amused. "If you wanted us there you could just say so."

Coop narrowed his eyes, "Just for that I'm not muting the mic."

"That's really not helping your case Coop." I could practically hear the smirk on his face.

"Coop—I—" his hand came to my mouth as I tightened around him, I shook and went to mute it, but his other hand swatted mine.

Link and Theo groaned, "Princess... you're killing us over here."

My eyes widened because why was *that* what sent me over the edge. Coop followed, hitting the mute button immediately and the way he was looking at me right now?

I didn't know if I was in trouble or if he was going to kiss me.

I was still shaking, violently might I add, when his lips met mine I pushed back into him and couldn't even attempt to feel bad or embarrassed.

When he pulled away I sat up, looking for my shorts. Fuck... I don't know what I was thinking—that was actually insane.

Millie, what the fuck???

Why did I do that? Why did he do that?!

I pulled my shorts on as he picked up the condom I'd tossed, I refused eye contact.

Nope. I can't right now.

My hands shook as I pushed my hair back, "Umm, bathroom." I mumbled as I pushed past him. He didn't stop me, thank god.

I went pee, washed my hands, and stayed my happy ass in the bathroom for a good five minutes, maybe even ten. I sat on the edge of the bathtub, contemplating every fucking life choice that led to that.

This was not fucking good. Not at all.

I live with Link.

I work with Theo.

And they'd just heard me—I might actually throw up. Oh god.

I needed to take a fucking breath.

Why did my chest feel so tight?

What if Coop was mad? I know he heard Theo call me Princess, I know he felt what that did to me.

Shit. Shit. Shit. *Shit.*

A knock at the door startled me, I took a shaky breath and opened the door up. Coop was leaning against the doorframe, arms crossed, like he was waiting for me to say something first.

"Coop—I don't..." I had no way to explain myself, "I should go."

He cupped my cheek, his lips meeting mine, "If by go you mean back to my couch, then yes."

I chewed my cheek and swallowed down the lump in my throat, why did I feel like I was about to cry right now?

"Did you turn it off?" I asked quietly. I didn't have to say what, he knew.

He studied me, "Yeah, I just have music on now, come on, we should talk about it."

I let him take my hand and pull me towards the living room. If he noticed the tremors flowing through me right now he didn't say anything.

I sat awkwardly, pulling my knees to my chest, "I think I took that too far and I'm sorry." He reached for my hand as he spoke.

"Why are you apologizing?" I asked quietly.

He tilted his head slightly, like he was trying to figure out something, trying to gauge my reaction. "Why are you acting like I'm about to tell you to get out?"

"Aren't you—?" I asked.

He sighed, looking up and away from me, "No... I was—fuck okay, I was testing something and it was really shitty..."

"You were...testing something?" I asked, narrowing my eyes at him, what the fuck did that even mean?

He let out an unsteady breath, "I wanted to see how all three of you reacted..."

"And?" I looked down, fidgeting with my hands.

Coop grinned, but tried to mask it almost immediately. "Well, I know Theo's little Princess trick worked wonders on you."

"That's not—you—"

"I'm just saying." Coop opened his arms for me to come closer and I took a second before shifting closer to him.

He pressed a kiss to forehead, "I'm sorry I shouldn't have done that."

"That was just as much my fault, I could have stopped it." I admitted.

"But you didn't."

"Yeah..."

Coop's phone dinged, once, then twice.

He exhaled as he looked at it. I didn't miss the quiet little "Fuck."

"Theo?" I asked quietly, not wanting to glance at the phone.

"Yeah, he's chewing me out."

"Can I?" I gestured to the phone, he tilted it down so I could see.

> Theo: You two almost gave Link a damn stroke. What the fuck was that?

> Theo: Also no reason for you two to sound that hot, I am unwell.

I snorted, "That's such a Theo thing to send over." I giggled and couldn't stop.

Coop looked at me like I'd grown another head. "What?"

"Not him chewing you out and praising us at the same time." Yep, I was delusional for saying that out loud.

"Theo is so fucking gone for you." Coop said, pushing a strand of hair behind my ear.

My whole body felt hot. "He said you two. Not me. Us." Yes, get the attention off of me and make it about both of us.

To be fair, he did say '*you two*'.

Maybe I shouldn't have intentionally said that... I didn't want to out Theo to Coop. He'd never forgive me if I brought that up.

Coop's eyebrows lifted slightly, I watched as he typed,

You didn't just call us hot?

Oooop.

Theo: You are.

Coop: Theo wtf

Theo's blue dots appeared, then disappeared, then reappeared. Whatever he was about to say, he was contemplating. His little blue dots were taking forever.

Theo: It's just facts.

Theo was bold, but apparently not bold enough to completely tell on himself.

Link on the other hand, I looked at my phone—which had been placed on Do Not Disturb for the last several hours, he'd sent me ten fucking texts. And a picture of Theo lying between his legs playing the game.

They looked cozy and sweet actually. My heart did the thing, the thing where it feels like it's squeezing itself to death.

I looked at the texts,

Link: Turning off your location is fucked.

Link: And you're not even acknowledging my texts?

Link: I should have told you I was staying at Theo's. I'm sorry.

Link: whatever the fuck you're doing over there you're fucking the game.

Link: Babygirl mute the mic

Link: mute the mic you're driving me feral

Link: I see he turned off the game, need an escape? I'll come get you.

Link: I will literally pretend I didn't hear anything.

Link: Actually I'm deaf in my left eye. I didn't hear anything.

Link: Mils

I sighed, letting Coop see them. He looked mildly annoyed as he read them. "He doesn't even care that he sent these..."

"I guarantee you he'll immediately pretend he never typed any of that out." I shrugged, "He and Theo are a lot alike like that—deny, deny, deny."

"Text him back." Coop urged and I took my phone back, staring at the screen.

I didn't even know what to say. What does one say in this situation? Sorry you had to hear me getting railed. No, absolutely not.

Millie: *I'm sorry. And I'm good here. Don't worry about me.*

Coop looked at my message before I sent it. "You're perfect, you know that?"

"Really? Because I'm feeling really messy right now."

"Do you want to stay the night?" The gentleness in his voice was everything I didn't know I needed.

"You're okay with that?"

"Mils, I like you a lot. Nothing's going to change that. Even if my best friend is an absolute idiot for not just admitting his feelings for you... and your...Link...he calls you babygirl, and judging by the no reaction when you read it—he does it a lot."

My cheeks heated, I swear to God I was going to turn into a tomato at this point.

My phone vibrated, Jesus Christ Link..

Except it wasn't from Link. It was from Theo.

Theo: Princess that was fucked up. Go home, Link went home.

I EXHALED BEFORE TYPING.

Millie: No. Eat rocks.

Theo: See you say that but why was it my voice that did that to you?

Millie: NO. NOPE.

Coop looked over at the messages and laughed so hard I thought he was going to start wheezing. "If they do anything, let them... see what happens, how you feel. It's not going to bother me...much. I don't want you to just choose me because you feel bad—"

It was my turn to cut him off, "I'm choosing you. I like you. You're literally the sweetest fucking human I've ever met. You have a cat. Your cat likes me and doesn't like anyone." I paused, "Where is he anyway?"

Coop looked around, "Probably asleep under my bed, he likes to hide."

"Besides," I said after a moment, "Theo's an idiot, but he's not stupid. He wouldn't do that to you, you're too important to him."

"Theo can be unpredictable when he's hurting too." Coop admitted.

"You think he's hurting?" I asked.

"Honestly I don't know, he's kind of replaced me with Link."

"Are you jealous right now?" I asked, ruffling his hair.

"Yeah, I think I might be."

My mouth? Yeah, it fell open. "You do realize they're not just hanging out as friends right? They're sleeping together."

"I know Theo and Link are together, I just—" he trailed off, and I studied his face.

"Cooper, be honest with me—are you jealous he's spending more time with Link or are you jealous of how he's spending time with Link?" He exhaled, running his hand through his curls.

"I'm trying to figure that part out." How this man could still be soft and gentle was beyond me, I don't think I'd be so calm in this position honestly.

"Well aren't we all fucking confused." I groaned, pressing my face into Coop's chest.

Because of course none of this was easy.

Why would it be?

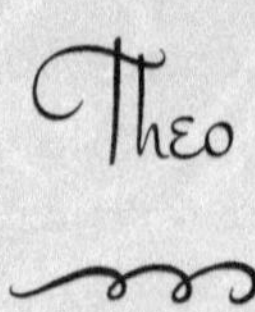

"I Wanna Be Yours - Arctic Monkeys"

Link decided to go home to see if Millie went home, I didn't want him to go—he could have stayed with me for the next week for all I care. I would have called off work if he wanted to stay.

But since he went home, I decided to go see Coop, because what the fuck was he playing at? And Millie—that little fucking shit. Eat rocks? Eat fucking rocks? After I literally listened to her fall apart after I called her Princess?

Why would he do that? Why would *they* do that?

I didn't even knock, just walked in, I had a spare key but it wasn't even locked. Which was bold considering what they'd been up to. Nothing could have prepared for me what I walked in on, it was even bad, it was annoying.

I looked between the asshole orange fluff-ball and Millie, that fucking cat wouldn't even let me get near him. Yet here she was, giving him chin scratches as he made biscuits on her stomach. "Why is Crooks in your lap?"

"What are you jealous?" Millie quipped, scratching behind his ear as the cat's purrs echoed throughout the room.

"Of the monstrosity Coop calls a cat? No." I took a step closer and the motherfucker had the audacity to hiss at me.

"He really doesn't like you." She laughed, giving him extra scratches that the fucking fur-ball leaned into. Fucking asshole cat. I rescued him and he has the audacity to be like this?

"He doesn't like anyone, he hardly tolerates Coop. He scratched me all to hell when I found him on the side of the road." He had, the thing was matted and scared and I fucking love cats, but that fucking cat did not love me.

"Theo, what are you doing here? You didn't text." Coop mumbled, coming out from the bathroom with his toothbrush hanging out of his mouth.

"We need to talk." I looked between him and Millie. Millie went pale. "You can go home Princess, Link is there—I'm sure he'll have words." At the word Princess her cheeks pinked right back up, and unfortunately so did mine.

"I was staying with Coop tonight..." She frowned, ahhh, she didn't want to face Link.

That made more sense. She should have thought about the implications of her actions before she did that with us in the party. I let out a breath, "Go home, Princess. Please."

"Theo, quit bossing around my girlfriend."

"I guarantee she likes it under different circumstances." I winked at her, just to see if it'd make her move her ass a little faster out the door, all it got me was a glare. "Besides I did say please."

She did get up though, so points to me for creativity I guess. She shoved me as she moved past me, the little shit, and the damn cat had the audacity to swipe at my ankles as he scattered past me and darted under Coop's bed.

I tried to keep my eyes from watching them as she threw her arms around Coop's neck and kissed his lips. "I'll video chat you later, text me whenever."

She looked at me like she wanted to say something, it took everything in me to not grab her and pull her closer to me. She must have felt that because she turned to me, her eyes searching mine, "Theo whatever you're about to say... just... don't."

"I'll deal with you later, I'll see you at work." I pointed at the door and she went without question.

Coop crossed his arms, "Theodore, that was fucking rude."

"Was it? Excuse me if I don't want to see the girl that got off to me calling her Princess while you were fucking her!"

"Oh, so that's what this is about?" Coop sat down, completely unbothered. "Because I saw the texts Theo, didn't sound like someone who doesn't want to see her."

“Why would you even do that?!” I asked, exasperated, because really what the fuck?

“I was testing a theory.” Coop held my gaze, he didn’t look mad—he looked like he’d been expecting this?

“Testing—testing a fucking theory??” I couldn’t help how my voice raised, I sounded fucking dramatic.

Coop's face broke into a small smile. "Yeah, a theory and I think it proved itself."

"And what theory is that, exactly?" I asked, trying to keep my voice level, but I could hear the edge in it, my barely contained frustration leaking through.

"That you're into her. That she's into you. And neither of you will admit it."

I blinked at him, momentarily lost for words. He really didn’t fucking get it. This was not the conversation I'd expected to have. "I—that's not—"

"Don't bother denying it, Theo." Coop leaned back, completely at ease. "I saw how she reacted when you called her Princess. I literally felt it. And I heard your voice when you realized what was happening."

"So what, this was some kind of fucked up test?" I ran a hand through my hair, pacing now. "What the fuck Cooper?”

“And clearly my theory was right because now you’re over here raising hell about her.”

“This is about both of you.” Fuck. Let it all out I guess. I hadn’t meant to let that slip.

“Then why did you set us up? If you wanted her, why did you set us up?” He asked, his hands clasped and his elbows on his knees, I could tell the conversation was getting to him now.

I didn’t answer for a minute, but when I did I decided it was better if I just said it, “Because I thought if you were fucking taken I wouldn’t want you anymore.”

“What?” Coop looked confused, which was rare, “What do you mean?”

"It was about you, Coop. I didn't want to want you anymore," I admitted, my voice quieter now. "But then you started dating her, and I realized I still wanted you... and now I want her too. It's about both of you."

The words hung in the air between us. I couldn't believe I'd actually said it out loud.

Coop leaned back, studying me with those piercing blue eyes. "And what about Link?"

"What about him?" I asked, even though I knew exactly what he was asking.

"Don't play dumb, he spent the night with you and you blew me off to spend time with him when we haven't hung out by ourselves in weeks."

I exhaled out of my nose, deflating slightly. "Yeah, he did stay over—because Link is easier, he's a good fucking guy who's just as fucking hurt as me." I looked at him, at the way he was studying me now. Was he jealous? That's what it fucking sounded like. I smirked, "Cooper, are you jealous I'm spending time with Link?"

"What—no—I—" He stuttered, I hardly ever heard Coop get nervous around me.

I stepped closer. "Oh my Gods, you are."

He didn't answer that, instead changing the subject entirely. "So you want all of us? Is that it?" There wasn't judgment in his voice, curiosity maybe?

"I don't fucking know, okay?" I threw my hands up. "I just—Fuck, I can't." I sat down on the couch, trying my best to avoid looking at him.

I felt sick to my stomach. No fucking way I'd said that out loud.

Every fucking touch, every time he'd played with my hair or looked at my fucking lips I fell harder. Fuck having flirty friends. Who flirts if they don't fucking like someone? Why did I have to be so painstakingly aware of my own sexuality?

"Theo..." His voice was soft, fuck I could deal with angry Coop, but soft Coop right now?

"Give me a minute, I'm trying not to fucking throw up." I stated, it wasn't a lie. I felt nauseated even thinking about this conversation.

"Theo, it's okay—" He started, his hand finding my thigh. I know he meant it to ground me. Coop had always been a physical touch kind of person, but right now it made my heart beat quicken, confusing me even more, because why? Why?

"Coop don't..." I pulled away.

"Please don't pull away from me." He whispered and this time I did look up and meet his eyes. Fuck, his eyes were so blue right now. "I'm not—I don't know how to explain what I'm feeling." He admitted and I crumbled.

This is it, this is why I didn't tell him. This kind of shit was friendship ending. You can't tell your straight best friend of over two decades that you fucking love him and not expect it to end. "I'll just—go... I'm sorry." I said, going to stand. Full intent to go home.

Coop grabbed my wrist, "Theo, I don't want you to go." he let out a sigh of relief as I slumped back into the couch. "I'm just confused right now and I need a minute too."

"I've been confused, welcome to the club." I said even as his fingers intertwined in mine.

Way to be fucking confusing Coop.

His eyes met mine and if I didn't know better I'd say his eyes fell to my lips for the briefest second. "Coop..."

"Yeah, I know..." He threw an arm over his face and I didn't even know what to do, or what to say.

So I defaulted, flopping my head sideways onto his lap. He exhaled and his hand tangled in my hair gently, pushing it away from my forehead. His touch solidified my feelings for him even more.

But he wasn't pulling away, so at least there was that.

I was disappointed to find Mille still wasn't home. Which meant she probably ran into Theo and to be honest, I wasn't sure if that was a good thing or a bad thing.

My phone pinged, *Millie arrived at home.* Yes, thanks app I *really* needed the extra anxiety from that. At least her location was back on, can't believe that little shit thought she could get away with that. We'd had each other's locations for years. The fact she turned it off to be petty wasn't lost on me.

I had no reason to feel like this. None at all, she wasn't mine. I was her friend, her best friend. For fuck's sake, I was sleeping with her boyfriend's best friend, I had no reason at all to be feeling this way towards her.

There was no reason for the pit sitting in my stomach as she opened the door, no reason for the anger I could feel bubbling up in my veins. I knew I needed to calm down before I talked to her, I knew better than to say anything...but alas I am also an impulsive idiot.

I looked up at her, "You sounded like you had fun tonight."

"I—umm—yeah about that." She sounded nervous as fuck right now, "I wasn't even going to come home tonight... figured you wouldn't want to see me." She went to walk away, but no. Not today, we were doing this. No more fucking running.

I stepped in front of her, "Nah, we should talk about it."

"Link, I'm going to bed." She stepped to the side and so did I. "You're acting like Theo, quit."

I tilted her chin up to look at me, her eyes moved to the side—trying to avoid eye contact I see. "Don't ever—ever turn your location off again."

"Okay dad." She moved her chin away from me and I exhaled trying to gain my composure. "I turned it back on anyway." She mumbled as I turned her chin back towards me.

I took a step closer, she backed up, I took another step and her back hit the kitchen counter. "You're doing too much right now." Her voice was shaky, but what did she expect from me right now? Did she not realize how I fucking felt?

How we all apparently fucking felt?

"Actually, I don't think I'm doing enough." I couldn't tell you if it was from hearing her fucking whimper over the mic or if it was everything colliding all at once. My hands caged her in, I felt myself slipping way past friend territory, I hated being out of control and right now I certainly felt it.

"Link..." She warned as I took her in, all of her, the frazzled look on her face, the messy hair, the cat fur clinging to *his* hoodie.

"You ignored my messages, you didn't mute the fucking mic, you were clearly enjoying the fact that we were listening in—"

"I—"

"No, pretty girl, you're going to listen to me." I warned, her breath hitched, but she nodded. I noticed the shift in her hips as I stepped closer, "You know the worst fucking part about it?" I didn't wait for her to respond, "Those little whimpers and moans made it impossible for me to stop thinking about you like that, but maybe it's what you wanted?"

"Lincoln!" She gasped as my hands found her hips, sealing away the last bit of distance between us.

I laughed, but it was heavy with the weight of everything the last few weeks, "What? Scared of the closeness or me calling you out? I'm gonna go with the call out because closeness has never been an issue with us, right?"

"Neither, I've just never seen you like this." She admitted, her eyes falling to my lips and staying there for a second before finding my eyes again.

"Tell me to stop," I gripped her chin between my fingers, "Tell me to stop and I'll back up immediately."

Her breath was sporadic, her chest heaved and when she looked at my lips again I caved—crashing my lips onto hers.

She squeaked, then melted into me, parting her lips to give me full access. I dropped both hands to her thighs and lifted her up on the counter. Her hands immediately went to my hair, tugging enough to make me groan against her mouth. This was happening. After all these years, this was finally happening, and I couldn't even pretend to regret it.

I pressed closer between her legs, my hands sliding up her thighs to her hips. "Tell me to stop," I murmured against her lips. I wasn't going too, not unless she told me to.

"Don't you dare," she breathed, pulling me back to her.

Fuck, *atta girl.*

I kissed down her neck, dragging my teeth against her pulse point, and she arched into me with a soft gasp. It was so much better than the sounds I'd heard through the headset. This was real. She was real, warm and pliant under my hands.

"Link," she sighed, her head falling back to give me more access.

I tugged at the hem of her—no, Coop's shirt and hesitated, I shouldn't have because she caught it and immediately panicked. I could see it on her face.

"Fuck... Link... we can't. I—Coop—" She was panicking and to be fair, yeah my bad, I took a step back. Which took some fucking mental strength to do by the way.

"Yeah, sorry... I just needed to do that."

"Link... I—" she took a deep breath, pausing for a second, "I think I need to go to bed."

My hands were shaking, with restraint or anxiety I don't know. "Mils...I'm sorry."

She stepped away from me, moving to the side, I let her.

"It's fine." She looked at me and the way she was looking at me now? I could tell whatever internal battle she was fighting, she was losing. "Just—leave me alone for a minute."

She took off down the hall and I resisted the urge to put my fist through the wall. I was not supposed to do that. More importantly, she was not supposed to react like that.

I went to my room, because the idea of seeing her right now was not a good one, and immediately texted Theo. The one person I knew would understand. The one person who could help me get whatever nervous energy out of my system.

Link: I think I fucked up.

It took a second but he replied.

Theo: Oh you too?

Alright, so we're both imploding our lives tonight apparently.

Link: What'd you do?

Theo: You first. You texted me first.

Damn it, okay. I guess I deserved that.

Link: I may have cornered Millie.

Theo: And....?

I typed, deleted, then retyped it.

Link: I may have kissed her.

There, out in the fucking open. I did it.

Theo: May have?

Link: Okay I did.

Theo: Coop saw that by the way.

Well FUCK. He didn't have the decency to fucking hide his damn phone from the one person. The one fucking person.

Link: FUCK MY LIFE.

Link: Why would you let him see that?

Link: Tell him not to be mad at her, it was me. She locked herself in her room.

Link: It's not her fault.

Theo: Chill out. He's not mad.

Why wasn't he mad? I'd be fucking mad. They literally just—you know what nevermind, I'm not even going to question it. I'll take it, whatever weird shit we all had going on I guess it was happening right now.

Link: Wait, he's not mad? What did you do? What did you say?

Theo: I told him.

Link: Told him what?

Theo: The reason I set him up with Millie.

Oooof, that was a bold choice.

Link: So you told him you're basically in love with him?

Theo: Lincoln. I swear to all the Gods. I didn't say it like that but now he saw it and he's smug about it.

Link: That's good? Isn't it?

Theo: TBD

Oh, we were so fucked.

Millie

"Softcore - The Neighbourhood"

These fucking men were ruining my life.

I mean that literally and figuratively. What the actual fuck was I supposed to do with all of this? I should have put a stop to the mic business, I should have pulled his ass to his room instead of right there in front of the damn game. On the fucking mic.

Jesus Christ, take the wheel, I feel like I might drive myself off a cliff. Kidding. Kind of. The phone dinged. I ignored that shit like the plague.

Nope. Nope. Nope.

I don't care who it is, *I don't care.*

I opened my door, looking around the house—what I could see of it anyway—there was no sign of Link, his light was on in his room. Hopefully he stayed there. I creeped to the kitchen, tip toe mode activated. I could be a ninja when I wanted too.

I wanted to drink. I opened the liquor cabinet in stealth mode. I could do tequila. Or I could do wine. Wine was probably safer. Tequila felt like a bad decision ready to happen.

Shit wine was probably also a bad idea. It is what it is, I didn't want to feel my emotions. I needed them to chill out. A bottle of wine and a book. That is what I needed.

I locked myself in the room, cracked open the bottle and drank directly from it.

My phone dinged again. I looked at it, why the fuck was Theo texting me?

Theo: You need to tell him.

Theo: Millie I'm serious, don't hide it from him.

My heart dropped. Fucking Link, that motherfucker. He would tell him. He would fucking tell him.

Millie: He told you, didn't he?

Theo: Yeah and Coop was right beside me.
So he already knows.

Millie: Greaaaaat. Fuck me.

Theo: Yeah, Coop already did that so...

Millie: Can he fucking see these?

Theo: No, he's in the kitchen.

Millie: Why are you looking out for me?

Theo: Just tell him.

I laid back on the bed, propping myself up to take another gulp of the wine. This one wasn't even that good, but let me get halfway through this bottle and it'd be fine.

I opened up my messages and looked at Coop's texts. I couldn't bring myself to do it. That wasn't me. I didn't—I don't cheat. That was so out of character.

Millie: I have something to tell you and I
don't know if it's something I need to text.

Coop: Is this about what Link texted Theo?

Millie: Fucking probably :/ He kissed me.

Coop: Baby, I told you earlier it wouldn't
bother me if you decided to just let it
happen.

Millie: You're literally the most confusing
human I've ever met.

Coop: Love you too I guess. XD

Millie: I'm going to die now. Thanks.

Coop: Don't be dramatic.

Don't be dramatic?! Is he serious right now? I took a long pull from the bottle, *fucking men*, I opened my book up and read a few pages. Taking a quick picture of the wine bottle and the book to put on my social media.

The caption? *Fictional men, because they won't make me want to drink.*

I put my phone down and settled into my book.

I realized I was a menace in both real life and the book world. Why was I reading a why choose novel right now? Because apparently I'm a whore.

Okaaaaaay, wine is working.

My phone dinged.

Gracie: Bitch, why is your post being commented on by Theo, Coop and Link right now. WHAT DID YOU DO?!

Millie: Oh god. What the fuck, let me go see.

I opened my Instagram and she was right.

LinkInThePark: Don't make me get backup.

DJTheoXXX: Princess, be fr.

CoopXPlays: That's not dramatic at all, also really @DJTheoXXX Princess online?

DJTheoXXX: She's the one posting about us.

CoopXPlays: Nah, we'll be over soon.

DJTheoXXX: We???

CoopXPlays: Shut up and come on.

LinkInThePark: Y'all coming to hang out with me?

DJTheoXXX: Absolutely.

XoMilsXo: GUYS THIS IS A PUBLIC POST

DJTheoXXX: Shut up Princess, you posted this to get on our nerves.

CoopXPlays: Can't let you drink alone.

Shit. Abort mission. I'm drunk and not prepared.

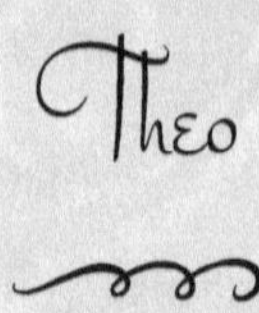

"Silhouettes - Daniel Javan, Rivio"

Coop was the king of no fucking chill. Like actually, because what do you mean we were actually going over to Link and Millie's?

"You sure about this?" I asked, uncertain on what his motives actually were.

"Theo, we're just gonna have a sleep over, drink and all that."

"You want to have a sleep over with your girlfriend, the guy she just kissed and your best friend that sees her half naked on an almost nightly basis?"

Coop glared at me, "Dude..."

"What?! You know what the fuck you're doing. I'm just being honest." I sighed.

My phone vibrated, like the menace to society I am, I read it aloud, "Millie says and I quote 'Don't you dare show up here while I'm drunk. My house is a Theo free safe zone.' Ouch."

I texted back, *'Too late Princess, we're already here.'*

Coop's phone rang, he handed it to me, "You answer I'm driving."

"Coooooop, you can't bring Theo." She looked at the screen, "Noooo, why is it your stupid face."

"Harsh, Princess. He's driving." Oh yeah, I could see the drunk disdain on her face.

She groaned and hung up.

We were about to spend the night arguing and flirting.

Although, the aspect of spending the night with Millie and Link was kind of nerve wrecking. Link was one thing, but Millie—Millie and I were strictly work—I don't know how to act around her outside of work.

I hate to say I was excited to see her in her other element. There was no denying that Millie was in her element when she was at work, but this? This was different.

Link let us in as soon as we got there, I kissed his lips gently in greeting and I did indeed notice the way Coop's eyes followed my movement.

"Good luck getting her to open the door." Link rolled his eyes, pulling down a few bottles. "But I guess since she's getting drunk, we might as well too."

"I called out tomorrow, just in case." Coop said, pouring himself a shot.

Coop never called out, so she must be important to him if he was doing that.

Coop knocked on her door. "Baby, can you come out? Or can we come in?"

There was a loud obnoxious, "UGHHH." from behind the door, but she opened it. Her eyes landed on mine, I couldn't read her face for the first time in ever.

She threw her arms around Coop's neck, hugging him tightly. Her head rested on her left arm, as he held her around her waist. The way she looked like she was a few seconds from having a breakdown right there in his arms, the way she held my gaze instead, it made my heart beat slow in my chest.

That sinking feeling in my stomach felt like it was slowly forcing its way up my throat. Fuck, I knew it was going to be hard, but this? This felt like torture. Why did that hurt so bad?

Why was she looking at me like that? Did she know I'd told Coop how I felt? About her, about him.

Fuck, this was messier than most of the work drama I avoided—fuck, now I was the work drama.

This felt like the Universe had me in one of those '*room full of everyone you've ever loved*' scenarios and I hated it.

Woah, wait, loved?

I had to take a deep inhale at that, turning to go back towards the kitchen, they needed space for a moment, they didn't need me.

Link was sipping on a glass of something, it looked like juice, but something told me it was something stronger. "You okay?" I asked quietly, nudging his foot with mine.

If I focused on him I didn't have to think about what the fuck was going on in my own head.

"I fucked up, she's never going to want to be alone with me again." He crossed his arms in his sweater, I'd only ever seen him in bike attire or dark hoodies and sweatpants so to see him in regular pajama pants and a grandpa sweater felt too intimate for what we were.

Fuck, what were we?

"Millie doesn't hold grudges with the ones she loves for long. How many times have you pissed her off or toed the line before?" I asked, prompting him to be honest about the situation. He may be in his head now, but she'd eventually move past it—or she'd accept it.

"A lot..." He admitted, swirling his cup back and forth so it sloshed up the sides.

My fidgety baby, fuck I wonder if he even realizes what he means to me. He probably didn't because I'd never told him. I was shit at ever talking about my feelings.

I was supposed to shut that shit down and not deal with it, but now it felt like my chest was physically breaking apart at the seams. Between him and Coop, fuck and her. I hated to admit it, but fuck she was mine in a weird way. I couldn't just—

Hey yo, stop spiraling.

I quickly caught myself, looking at Link who was content staring into the abyss of his kitchen corner, "How many times has she come back?"

"Every time."

I exhaled, "Exactly, you're her person Link, it's not as simple as her cutting you off and not speaking to you." I pushed his bleached ends back out of his face, "You're embedded in her life. She's not going anywhere, stop panicking—and if she doesn't completely come back from this, you have me. You know that, right?"

Link looked at me then down towards the floor, "And how are you feeling right now?"

I sighed, "I don't really want to talk about it."

He grabbed my hand and squeezed it, "You know I'm here too."

"Yeah, I do." I squeezed his hand back, this was enough, he was enough. I needed him to know that. "No matter what, you're enough."

He gave me a weak smile, "I don't believe that."

Fuck, don't break my heart Link, not right now, I can't fucking take it.

This was a test, I hated that I was pushing her like this—all of them honestly. It kind of made me feel like shit, but as we sat in her room and I took in the state she was in, red puffy eyes and all… I realized she'd been crying. I didn't want to see her cry, I didn't want to see her in pain. "If you only want to see me I can tell them to fuck off. They're fine hanging out together."

Her voice was small when she asked, "Is that what you want?"

I exhaled, because no—it wasn't what I wanted if I was being honest with myself. "I don't want to say the wrong thing, but I know Link and Theo would rather drink with us."

"Ugh, okay… we're really doing this?"

"What? Just calling it like it is. In twenty four hours my best friend admitted he loves me," and *you*, but he's gotta admit to that on his own, "Your best friend kissed you." I looked at her hands, pulling her fingers into mine. "And you? I'm keeping you. No matter what happens out there."

She met my eyes then, a small smile on her face, "That's a lot of commitment before we even see how everything plays out."

"I mean it, no matter what."

"Where's your head at?" She asked.

"Honestly, I'm trying to figure that out." I bit my lip, "Part of me really wants to kiss Theo, just for science, ya know? But I don't want to give him false hope."

"So everyone kisses everyone?" She half-laughed, half hiccuped.

"That sounds like someone who also wants to kiss Theo…" I teased and bless it, her eyes widened ever so slightly. "Unless you two already have and I'm seriously out of the loop?"

She snorted, "No, Theo and I have never—"

I interrupted her, "But you've thought about it…"

"I plead the fifth, sir, but also I need a refill and you need to catch up." She grinned, "Let me clear my bed off and you go deal with them."

"Ahhh, yes leave me with the hormone monsters."

I left her, only to find the cutest moment in probably the existence of cute moments. Theo was leaning all the way on Link on the couch, Link's fingers curled in his hair as they talked in hushed voices. "You guys coming?"

"She agreed?" Theo asked and I couldn't help but wonder why did my boy look so panicked at that?

"Yeah, said we needed to catch up though and she needs a refill."

Link pushed Theo up a little and he pouted, actually pouted. "Fine.. Fine.."

Millie waved a finger at all of us from the stairs. "Whatever happens tonight, firm boundary, everyone's clothes stay on. I swear to God I'll get stabby on all of you otherwise."

Theo was the one to bite back, "Says the one who's barely dressed."

"You've all seen me in way less. There's nothing wrong with my sleep set." Millie narrowed her eyes at him.

"By sleep set you mean a pair of tiny shorts and a baggy shirt?" Theo shot back, a grin playing on his face.

Link piped up. "My shirt, if we're counting."

"Link fuck off..." Millie groaned under her breath.

"Okay, so we're not good." He mumbled.

"I'm not drunk enough to deal with you." Millie rolled her eyes and I gestured for the guys to go up the stairs, making quick haste with grabbing the bottles off the counter. Opening their fridge and searching for juice and something of sustenance.

I found nothing.

"How about we order pizza or something?" I said, scrolling my phone as I walked into her room. "Put some food in you before you attack someone. Pepperoni?" I asked, figuring everyone liked it.

"And a barbecue with pineapple and bacon." Millie said, uncorking the tequila, I didn't miss the fact that it was Theo's favorite pizza too. Theo smirked and looked over at her from his spot on her bed.

"Why are you looking at me like that?" She asked, as she drank right from the bottle like a fucking gremlin, her back resting against the pillows against the wall.

"Because you ordered my favorite pizza, Princess." Theo interjected.

Millie coughed, wiping her mouth before she turned fully to look at him. "Why do you insist on still calling me Princess?"

I hit the favorites tab, it was labeled under Theo. I sized it up to a large and ordered a large pepperoni too. Twenty minutes.

"Pass me that." I said, gesturing to the tequila she was hoarding as I sat beside her, the bed dipping a little under all of our weight. It was a queen, but not nearly big enough for all of us.

She shrugged, passing it over almost instantly, "You need to catch up anyway, Sir."

Jesus, okay, in front of everyone? That word caught me off guard in front of Theo and Link?

Fuck, I think I was blushing.

Millie

I had meant to say it, it was just a reflex. Something I knew would fluster the fuck out of him, something I liked. What drunk me forgot to remember was that I had said that to both Link and Theo on multiple occasions.

Ooops.

It was Link who was about to spit out his juice mix, "OH?"

"What?" I asked, looking between both Link and Theo who were both looking at me weirdly, their heads turned sideways to stare at me. Just a tid bit too tipsy to tell what that expression meant.

"You called him Sir?"

"I–what? I automatically default to that."

"Like all the time? You just go around calling people sir?"

"Only people I want to fluster, or–" I held up a finger swaying slightly, "Or if I get flustered.. I don't—" It dawned on me then, why they were asking.

OH. *Oh.*

I am not the brightest crayon in the box.

"There it is." Theo said quietly, of course he saw it on my face.

Not only had I called both of them Sir, but multiple times, recently. They were definitely about to call me the fuck out. "Wait, do you do that with everyone? Or is it just certain people?" Coop asked.

"It's very unfortunately only for certain people." I wasn't gonna admit it was only these idiots. They did not need that ego boost right now.

It was Theo who leaned closer, basically leaning over Link. "It's just us, isn't it?"

I felt my heartbeat stutter in my chest as his proximity took my fucking breath. He didn't move, but his eyes fell lower than they should have before coming back to meet my eyes. I nodded, it was literally all I could do, my brain was not braining right now.

"Thought so." He leaned back, settling back into Link, Link's hand immediately went to his thigh, securing him in place.

I turned to hide my face in Coop's chest, nope, nope, *nope.* I wasn't facing this right now, literally, no face for me. Coop rubbed my back, "As long as you don't say it to anyone else, just us."

Even my wine drunk and three shots of tequila brain picked up on that. "You're all far too sober for me." I groaned.

Theo chuckled, "I mean is it a surprise for anyone when we all call her a variation of pet names? Link and Coop you both call her baby girl. I call her Princess." He wasn't even talking to me—they were freely discussing us out in the open, like I wasn't even here.

"Wait—Cooper did you just agree to letting her call us that?"

"Have I said anything about the baby girl slips in front of me, Link?"

I peaked out and Link had the audacity to look amused.

Theo put his hands up, "I swear Princess isn't meant like that."

Coop side-eyed him, "You know damn well it is."

I couldn't help myself, "Well not always, sometimes he does it to be mean. Derraaagotry." Fuck, how come I couldn't say that word right now?

"Bold of you to assume you don't get off on a little bit of degradation?" Theo held my eyes as he said it, reaching over to take the bottle from Coop and downing some of it. "Oh, that's fucking horrible, who hurt you? You drink this straight all the time?"

NOPE. My brain didn't even register the jab about tequila, why the fuck had he said that to me?

Bold of me?

BOLD OF ME?

Bold of him.

I'm actually done. I pulled the entire throw blanket over my head. I was in hiding. If they can't see me I'm not here. "Millie doesn't live here anymore."

I wasn't coming out.

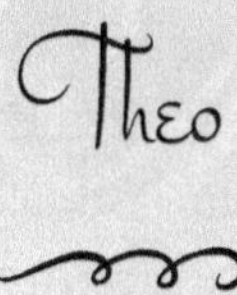

Theo

Señorita - Shawn Mendes, Camila Cabello

Ooooh, yeah, I was about to have to cut her off for her own safety. She was a giggling mess under the blanket, embarrassed or not—she couldn't hide the giggles spewing out of her.

She did eventually come out from under the blanket, once I put on music—yes yes, very DJ coded of me. It worked though and the fact that I had a lot of her songs saved from listening to the shit over and over again at work was a bonus. And when her eyes flicked up like she noticed which playlist I'd chosen? I held her gaze for a second. She gave me a small smile and I nodded, she didn't even have to say it. I knew I'd helped at least a little bit, helped her fill the silence between all of us.

Link's knee brushed mine when he shifted, on purpose, I knew it was on purpose. That man gets handsy when he's drunk, but right now he was practically draped over me like I was his emotional support stuffed animal, much like the one that sat untouched on her pillows right now.

I couldn't help but find that cute as shit.

Coop passed the tequila bottle to her and this little shit took it despite her eyes being glazed over, Coop was already several shots deeper than he needed to be too.

I couldn't really talk, I never drank at work so when I did drink my tolerance was not nearly as high. Link was also vibing beside me, I was used to touchy feely Link—but it was amplified when he was drunk. Like now, where his head kept dropping closer to my neck, and he'd catch himself at the last second, smirking like he knew exactly what he was doing.

Fuck, he was purposely trying to fluster me. It was working.

Jesus, how had these two not had an accidental night of unresolved sexual tension was beyond me. Scratch that—the air between all four of us practically crackled every time someone breathed wrong, we were seconds away from being a fucking porn video for crying out loud.

I shook my head trying to get that specific thought to get the fuck out.

Nope, wasn't doing that.

She passed the bottle to Link who took the smallest sip known to man before passing it back to me. I did the rational thing and mixed my shit with the juice Millie had brought out earlier. Water-falling the juice, then the tequila before Millie reached for the bottle and I snatched it back from her, passing it to Coop. "Hey!!"

There was the gremlin, I was right.

"Princess, one more drink and you'll be wishing you hadn't."

"Kinda regretting having you in my space right now." She crossed her arms and Coop smirked.

"You love me." I said, without thinking, yep, no rational thoughts around her and alcohol.

She stuck her tongue out and flipped me off. A Bryce Savage song started playing and heaven help me she was lip singing it—hips swaying a little, not much because there wasn't much room.

Link was watching her as he traced patterns on my thigh and I had to move his hand down a few times, fuck we're all feral apparently.

"Bryce Savage is a choice..." Link looked over at me, his eyes falling to my lips, fuck he was so fucking hot right now.

Millie, who I had said was already dangerously close to the cut off limit, looked between all three of us. "So—this is" she paused and I could see the self destructiveness in her pretty little glazed eyes "actually crazy right."

Coop snorted, but he didn't move to stop her, if it was me I'd have already redirected her, "Are we all just—I don't know like a thing?" Millie continued.

I looked at Coop, trying to gauge how he was reacting, but he was watching me.

Watching my mouth, specifically. Jesus. Okay. "Why are you looking at me like that?" I asked, I wasn't used to this much attention at once.

Coop glanced at Millie, then at me again, she must have tracked that because she sat up and looked between us. The feral look on her face said she knew more than she let on. "Don't let me stop you, I'm just here." She physically moved away from him, little shit starter, whatever was about to happen she was solely responsible for it.

She flopped down in between Link's thighs, curling around one of them. He immediately reached his hand out to play with her hair and I don't know why I was surprised she leaned into him more.

His other hand slid against her back, raking his nails up and down her spine. Drunk Millie didn't hold grudges. Maybe that's why she locked herself in her room earlier, because right now they did not look like friends.

"For science?" Millie squeaked, half giggle half fucking mouse at this point, half burying her face in Link's pajama pants.

Coop shrugged, "I mean—"

I whipped my head to him, "What does that even mean?" Why did he look nervous? Why did she move away from him? What is going on right now?

"That means he wants to kiss you, but he's afraid of the consequences." Link said, shifting so Millie could nuzzle further into him.

Coop's eyes pulled up in surprise, "I—Link! Why would you—"

"Oh for fuck's sake, just do it. Everyone kisses their best friend at some point." Link said and Millie swatted at him.

"Not everyone! I haven't kissed Gracie!" she said matter-of-fact, but she was wrong because oh yes—they had. On stage and in VIP a few times. Caught in 4k on the cameras.

Granted they got tipped for it, but still. It had happened.

"Yes you have, you're just typically drunk and getting paid for it." I pointed out and her mouth dropped open, if she did remember she definitely didn't expect me to call her out.

"I did not!" She gasped, sitting up—her hands braced on Link's thigh and turned to face me.

"Text her if you don't believe me. She's bound to remember at least one, but if not I can pull the cameras later." I waved her off, facing Coop. "Do you want to kiss me?" I asked and thank all the Gods. My voice didn't shake. It sounded bolder than I honestly felt.

He didn't even say anything, he leaned forward, grabbed my shirt in his hand and pulled me to him, so we were leaning over Link and Millie.

Damn Coop, okay, manhandle me all you want.

His lips met mine and it wasn't soft like I thought he was going to be, nope, he practically devoured me and I fucking let him. He bit my lip and when I gasped he took full advantage, his tongue finding mine. His fingers tugged at my hair and I knew right then and there if he didn't want this I'd be ruined.

Probably forever. I'd have to move, change my name and cut all contact.

I heard Millie make a noise—not a gasp, more like a choked little sound—and Link whispered "Holy shit…" under his breath.

Yeah. That didn't help.

I pulled back slightly, slowing the kiss down. When I pulled away he grabbed my jaw and pulled me back, giving me one final softer kiss. "Fuck…" Coop whispered, letting go of my shirt, "Sorry… that may have been too much…"

"It's fine," I said quietly, trying to get a read on his face. He didn't look disgusted though so I'll take it. He'd pulled me back for one last kiss and he'd used fucking tongue for crying out loud.

Link had Millie's mouth covered with his hand, "Not gonna lie, my jealousy was through the roof watching that…" He looked between Coop and I, confusion on his face.

Coop glared at him, then grinned at Millie, "Sucks for you."

Millie pulled his fingers away from her mouth, "I'm just saying. Ten out of ten—would watch again. That was hot. You two are hot."

Link looked down at her, clearly offended, she shrugged him off. "Eh, you're alright. I'm still mad at you. I'll compliment you later when I'm not mad."

"Can't be that mad if you're literally nuzzled into me and using my thigh as a pillow." He shot back.

"First of all, that's rude." Millie said, pinching his inner thigh.

This girl was fucking absurd, she was literally laying two inches from his dick, talking about *I'm mad at you*, okay Princess, think what you want.

"So..." Coop said and whatever it was, it sounded mischievous, "Link kissed Millie, I kissed Theo, I've kissed Millie, Link and Theo have kissed. Link? Come here."

Link groaned, "Eh, pass. Sorry Cooper, I like my men to be easy to boss around."

"Hey!" I flushed, because what the fuck Lincoln?! Why would you say that?

Link grinned, "Theo, babe... you're so submissive with me it hurts."

"I'm just comfortable with you." I shot back.

Link chuckled, "Uhuh, sure, baby boy."

That was once. One time. Link knew damn well I could be dominant when I wanted. Not that it was often, but still.

Millie cackled. "Did not expect you to be a bottom." Her laughter didn't stop even as her face dived into Link's chest.

I'm going to go die in a hole. I'll even dig it. "First of all, I'm a switch." I narrowed my eyes at Link, "And that asshole fucking knows it."

Millie giggled as Link flushed.

"You sure Link?" Coop asked, studying him. "Might be the only chance you get."

Link looked between all of us, sighed and then tapped Millie's side so she would move and she looked up at him like she couldn't believe he might actually do it. Link pointed at him, "No fucking tongue, Cooper."

Coop put his hands up, but he was grinning. "I won't, but if you initiate I make no promises."

Millie shifted in between Link and I. Musical chairs—bed edition I guess.

When Coop leaned in he cupped Link's face gently and gave him a slow kiss, there was no heat, but it didn't look awkward necessarily, even when Coop's hand slid into his hair and pulled him closer. If I didn't know them both as well as I did I'd say they enjoyed it, but Link didn't melt into him like he did with me. And Coop definitely didn't do what he did with me.

"Okay, so you're a good kisser, but that's all." Link did not look amused, "Never again." He huffed and I couldn't help but laugh a little, I personally think he did enjoy that.

Coop laughed, "Agreed, your lips are soft though." He looked smug, I'd never known Coop to be one to just kiss someone he didn't care about, but fuck it I guess.

They were being weird, why were they being weird? Had they felt something and just not wanted to admit it? I mean shit, we're all being fucking open about it right now anyway. A little honesty goes a long ways.

Millie was cackling like a feral gremlin. "Why are you complimenting each other back and forth, if there's no chemistry just say that!"

Link shrugged, dropping back down beside her, leaving Millie between us.

"Now there's only two people in this room who haven't kissed." He looked between us and no... No. Not gonna happen. Coop was absolutely unhinged if he thought I was crossing this line. If he thought Millie would cross this line with me. It wasn't just a Link and Coop line, it was a work line. We worked together—

It was Millie who derailed my train of thought completely, "What? No—I... Coop, it's fine." Millie said, her cheeks bright red. "We don't need to."

Oh? Was she flustered over me? Over the thought of kissing me? All ration went out the window. "What are you afraid you'll like it too much, Princess?" I asked, my eyes finding and holding hers, her breath hitched—actually hitched.

Link muttered, "Oh, she's done for." The look she gave him for that was funny as fuck, a cross between bewilderment and the 'eat rocks' face she gave me.

"I—um..." she stuttered, looking between all of us with wide eyes.

I couldn't stop myself, if I had permission from Coop I wasn't going to waste it. Fuck the consequences—I'd switch around my work schedule if needed. If this went wrong, but right now? Right now I couldn't fathom not kissing her. I turned her chin towards me, her eyes immediately went to my lips then back down, like she was trying really hard not to show how much she actively wanted me to do it.

"Look at me Mils," I tilted her chin up, "You gonna be good for me?" She made the smallest noise, almost a whine and every bit of conflict on her face melted instantly, I leaned in slightly and she met my lips before I even tried to touch hers.

Fuck, Coop's kiss was frenzied and full of want, but this? This was surrender. She let me pull her into my lap and immediately wrapped her legs around me to get closer. Her hips shifted against me and I swear I forgot we weren't alone.

Her hands went around the back of my neck and into my hair. I couldn't help but deepen the kiss. Fuck, she wanted me just as much as I wanted her. She nipped my bottom lip as my hands found her skin under her shirt.

So this is what it felt like, to finally fucking do it, all the times we stood to close or made jokes or fucking thought about it—if I was I know she was, no doubt about it.

Link cleared his throat, pulling us both out of it—her pupils were blown when she looked at me. "Sir—you can't just ask if I'm going to be good for you!" She smacked my chest, "What the fuck was that?"

Oh? Sir? In that context? Yes. Fucking. Please.

"But you were good." I was vaguely aware of Coop and Link watching us, but I couldn't help it, "Such a good fucking girl."

"Theo, you menace." She slapped my chest again and pushed off of me, this time going over to Coop, but her nails immediately went to her mouth and Link groaned, pulling her hand from her mouth.

"Don't bite your nails." He said quietly, redirecting her hand to Coop's hair.

"Well, I guess we all learned some things tonight." Coop said, holding up the bottle like a toast.

That we fucking had.

One thing for sure, friends don't know how friends taste.

Coop's phone pinged, "Shit—pizza." He disappeared downstairs and came back with the pizza's propping the boxes open on the bed.

I didn't miss the way Millie's eyes kept wandering over to me as we ate, or the way Link threw his entire body weight on me after only slice of pizza. Sleepy drunk Link was so fucking cuddly. Not that I was complaining. I liked sleeping beside Link, even if we were sleeping sideways on a small bed.

Tomorrow would be interesting. Waking up together? All of us? After *all* of that?

Not to mention Millie and I had work.

If she still wanted to go anyway.

Millie

I woke up in between Coop and Theo. Link was nowhere to be found, fuck, what time was it? My fucking throat was dry and my head was pounding. Fuck, I knew better than to mix wine and tequila.

Wait—Coop? Didn't Coop work during the week? I tapped his chest, panicking. "Don't you have work?!" He couldn't miss work because of me.

"I called out." He mumbled pulling me into him.

There was a shushing from my other side as I looked over at Theo, he looked softer in his sleepiness. "We still have work tonight, so go back to bed, Princess."

Butterflies erupted in my stomach. He said it too easily, too naturally. Coop scooted—which meant I was scooted—closer to Theo. I didn't mind necessarily, but I was super fucking close to him and hyper aware of it. Theo's warmth radiated like a goddamn furnace. "Where's Link?" I asked quietly,

Theo's breath tickled my neck when he spoke, "His dad called him —something to do with the company and if he could come into the office this morning."

A shiver went through me, his breath should *not* have that kind of effect on me at this hour. I tried my best to distract myself, "Good, the man needs to work like the rest of us. Won't hurt him to show up sometimes." I grumbled.

Link did work, he just worked from home most of the time. He was paid a decent salary—and by decent I mean probably triple or quadruple what I made dancing.

Rich little bastard.

The only tell would be his bike and his car. And maybe his obnoxious amounts of consoles and laptops he liked to hoard. Okay and maybe my book obsession, hard covers were expensive and he only bought me hardcovers.

"I should—"

Theo's arm came around my waist snuggling closer, "I said sssshhh." His hand wasn't even gripping me tightly, but my whole body went still. Warmth radiating around me as he held me still. I should not speak apparently.

I froze and Coop looked down immediately, "You okay?" He definitely felt how tense I went when Theo touched me.

Great. Amazing. *Kill me.*

I nodded and tried to relax, I was trapped now, might as well enjoy the extra warmth. I saw Coop's eyes land on Theo's arm that was pulling us all closer.

I closed my eyes for a split second and when I woke up I was laying by myself.

I know those *motherfuckers* didn't leave me.

I smelled something cooking, but it was so faint I wasn't sure if it was actually cooking or if it had been earlier. It was definitely not breakfast time, but it smelled like breakfast. My brain was foggy, I was not a morning person… scratch that I wasn't a waking up person.

I made my way downstairs, looking every bit the mess I felt—Link's shirt falling past my thighs and completely covering my shorts. My hair was a mess as I pulled it into a messy bun as I rounded the corner into the bright as fuck kitchen, seriously we needed darker curtains or something. I mixed my alcohol and now I felt like absolute fucking ass.

Theo leaned against the kitchen counter, energy drink in hand, wet hair and dressed in Link's slutpants and a hoodie. Link was sitting at the table doing something on his work laptop and Coop was indeed the one cooking.

He was so daddy it hurt. Someone get this man a fucking wedding ring.

If they don't, I will.

Damn, am I ovulating? I really need to chill.

Theo looked annoyingly good in sweatpants, but the smirk when he saw me notice said sweatpants? Criminal.

I immediately went to take some of Theo's energy drink, what? He had the big one. He immediately put it up over his head out of my reach. "Yours is in the fridge. Link picked them up."

"Oh my god," I basically ripped the fridge open like the hulk and popped the tab, downing half of it one go. I pushed Link's hair back and kissed the top of his forehead. "Thank you, I appreciate you."

His ears went faintly pink, he tried to hide it by typing faster.

"Once we eat, go get ready, we gotta leave soon." Theo smirked, what the fuck was he smirking about?

"It's literally—" I checked Coop's phone that was on the counter, "Oh, fuck it's four-thirty. Why did y'all let me sleep so long?" I looked at him and tilted my head, "Wait—we? No, you. I'm going in later."

"Yeah about that, I'm gonna take you tonight." Theo crossed his arms, like he fully expected me to argue.

Which was fair, because I did. "Why?"

"Track record of bad decisions and drinking, might as well." He said, his eyes flicking over to Link.

Yeah, I fucking saw that, "You just want to stay the night with Link and I'm your excuse."

Coop handed me a croissant as Link looked up, looked between us and laughed. "Baby girl, he knows he's welcome over here whenever, he wants to spend time with you." Link had the audacity to look amused, amused right now when I clearly didn't know up from down. I just woke up guys.

I almost dropped my fucking croissant. Literally. What do you mean wants to spend time with me? Theo? Actively wanting to spend alone time with me? My face flushed hot as I remembered that I had indeed crawled into his fucking lap and made out with him in front of not only Coop, but also Link.

Theo's face was splashed with pink as he turned around, glancing back at Link and I before rolling his head to Coop, like Coop might magically help him out. Coop snorted as he tried not to burn the eggs, but he was watching us. I was positive he knew exactly where my mind had gone. "Hey, don't look at me. I'm just here."

Link sighed as I gave him another top of the head kiss and made my way towards Coop and Theo. I kissed Coop on the lips, I had to tiptoe to reach him since he was distracting himself with food. "I'm glad you're here." I whispered, kissing his lips again.

I stepped away from Coop and turned to Theo, "Lead with that asshole." I stabbed his chest with my finger, no clue where the confidence came from right there, because I didn't feel it.

Theo's breath hitched and he put his hands up in surrender, "Well, I wasn't trying to say it."

I rolled my eyes, taking my croissant and putting it on a plate giving Coop puppy dog eyes so he gave me the first bit of eggs. "You're already cute, don't pout." He shoveled eggs onto my plate, giving me the sweetest kiss ever now that he wasn't pretending to be distracted with poultry.

I ate in silence at the table, scooting my chair closer so I could watch Link work. "Mils, it's confidential." He shifted the computer, as if I knew what the fuck it said, the fucking Scott's and they're encryption. What did they even need to hide?

I groaned, "Bruh, I can't even read it. It's literally in code because your whole family is fucking insane about encryption and shit." Instead of trying to look harder I decided I needed to eat and attempt to get myself together.

I looked around for my energy drink, fuck, it was by Theo. He must have been watching because he picked it up and stole a sip before bringing it to me. "HEY!" I pouted, "I need that..."

He took another sip, holding my eyes, but the way his eyes flicked to my lips before he handed it over? Illegal. Why was he like this?

"I'll get you two more on the way to work, chill out." He ruffled my hair, jolting my already messy bun around. I could have smacked him, or kissed him, fuck—definitely ovulating.

"She's going to go feral mode if you give her more than one." Link spoke like he couldn't be bothered with my shenanigans this morning—afternoon whatever. He was always so serious when he was working.

"Lincoln...I can handle myself." I waved him off, "It'll be fine, I normally drink more throughout the night anyway."

"Yeah, she's your problem tonight." Link deadpanned looking at Theo, "Don't even bring her home if she's gonna be loud at three in the morning."

Theo choked a little on his drink, he tried to hide it by turning his back.

These assholes. Attractive assholes, but still assholes.

"Love when you talk about me like I'm not right here." I finished my last bite of eggs and made to stand up, but Link's hand on my thigh stopped me.

My breath hitched embarrassingly loud. Jesus Christ, could we fucking not today hormones? Your fucking boyfriend is right there, he made you greasy food and bread to soak up the fucking alcohol so you could actually function.

He squeezed my thigh once and turned his face to meet my eyes, "We'll talk tomorrow baby girl, right now I have to work and you need to get ready." His voice dropped, he was so fucking calm. Controlled. So, I knew he was about to drop some out of pocket bullshit. "Now that I have your attention, stop being a brat and don't give Theo a hard time. I don't know if he can handle it."

The low-key shade was felt around the room because while Theo looked offended, Coop spit out his juice, spraying the kitchen sink. The tension between Theo and Link for half a second? Charged. Electric. Like they both knew exactly what the other meant.

"Just wait you little fucker, I'm going to get you back for that." Theo's voice was so low it even made me uncomfortable.

I stood up, "Anyway, too much testosterone in this small little kitchen..."

I walked out, intent to shower and get ready here. If I did everything here I could waste time at the bar and bother my favorite DJ.

One everything shower later, a blow dry session with a remix of Lollipop playing on full blast I had the full face going on, complete with lashes and glittery Euphoria style make-up. I did a half up, half down pig-tail style.

I wanted to snatch the hearts of men tonight to sacrifice to the Stripper Goddesses.

I tore through my closet, searching for the dark green set I hadn't worn yet. If he was going to insist on driving I was going to make it impossible for him to not notice me all night. No dress or cover up tonight. Fuck it. Ass out I guess.

I threw it in my dancer bag and I double checked everything else before heading back out to the kitchen. Coop's jaw dropped. Theo audibly groaned—not annoyed, but the kind of groan a man makes when he knows he's about to suffer.

Link grinned, eyes dragging over me like he already knew what kind of night I planned. "Yeah, good fucking luck with that. She's locked in for either money or revenge tonight."

Fuck, how did he know that?

Coop looked me up and down, "You look cute."

"Cute???" I gasped, mock offended.

"I can't take you seriously in a cat crop top. Very baby girl energy, you even did the pigtails." Coop grinned, pulling me into a hug—careful not to fuck up my make-up.

Fuck, okay… maybe he had a point.

He stopped Theo on the way out, "Take care of her tonight."

Why did that feel like it had a double meaning?

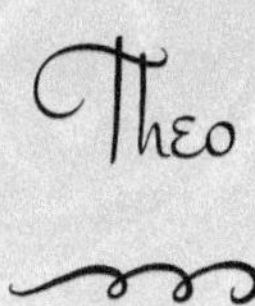

Jonah was already setting up, but the cleaning crew was still here. "Sorry, I picked up a straggler." I nodded to Millie who was already heading back to the dressing room.

Millie had been an absolute menace the entire ride, she'd chugged her second energy drink in the time it took us to get from the gas station to the fucking club. She'd added songs to my playlist for crying out loud.

"Did you forget we have a uniform?" Jonah asked, I looked down at my sweats, shit, I guess I should have stopped by my house.

"Yeah, I just didn't stay at home last night." He gave me a look and his eyes darted down the hall towards the dressing room, towards her. "Uhhhuh, don't even." I said, shutting that shit down.

"Okay, keep lying to yourself bud." Jonah laughed, logging into the point of sales system for the bar.

Fuck, okay, so we were obvious.

It was almost time to kill the big lights and I really needed to do sound check, but all of the breath left my fucking lungs when she came down the hall.

This bitch. Respectfully. My jaw was on the floor. Why was she wearing next to nothing, literally, I was pretty sure it was barely legal. And fuck, third energy drink already?

"Jade, that looks good on you." Jonas nodded his approval.

It did look fucking good, she looked like a fucking Goddess in green, she knew that too. I'd told her many times I liked her in green. I should have known when she showed up with more green in her wardrobe that she fucking liked me—even if she didn't want to admit it at that point.

"Taaanks!" Millie did a little swirl, holding her energy drink up as she did so, "And don't worry I checked it, two finger test. It's legal. I also have a double layer on the bottom, I'm not dumb. I am however about to break my weekday record."

"Love the energy, let's go." Jonas said, signing her in at the VIP desk.

"Alrighty, Daddy DJ, give me a warm up song. I'm in a Juicy J mood." Daddy DJ about took me out, I didn't know whether to be in shock at her audacity or fucking flustered.

I loaded up the songs I did have, *Bandz A Make Her Dance, Bounce it,* and then *Low Life by Future and The Weekn*d just because. I didn't expect her to stay on stage the entire time anyway. There wasn't anyone here.

"On the second song, hit the fog and light show. I'm about to get people in here." She practically bossed me around.

She took her time cleaning each of the poles. Why did she have to maintain eye contact with me when she did that? Fuck...

I opened up my phone and started a new group chat. Coop and Link.

Theo: She's doing too much, send help.

Coop: Suck it up buttercup.

Link: Told you.

She clacked her heels and it snapped my attention to her, she was watching me intently. Fuck, the dancer to customer stare, but worse. She'd only done it to me a few times and I knew why customers fell for it immediately.

Why *had* she done it to me a few times? Oh fuck, how long had this shit been going on between us? A long fucking time apparently.

She did slower movements, mostly moves I knew she did to stretch more than anything. Jonah leaned against the booth and cleared his throat, I glanced at him. "What?"

Jonah sighed, "She's intentionally trying to make you lose your head tonight, isn't she?"

I looked down at the song, it was almost over. "Fucking probably, it's Jade. You know how we are."

"Do I need to worry about you freaking out about rooms?" He asked, crossing his arms.

I flicked on the fog machine as *Bounce It* started playing, she wanted fog, I'd give her fog. "What—no, why would you?"

"Theodore, you're going to tell me there's nothing going on?" Jonah studied me.

"There's noth—"

Jonah gave me a look that clearly said *quit fucking lying*. "You two eye fuck each other every night you work together." I wanted to say we didn't, but that was a fucking lie and I knew it. Especially now, there was no fucking denying it anymore.

I watched her set up the phone and hit record, ignoring Jonah as he mumbled something under his breath. I did her little light show as requested, setting it to hit with the bass.

She went full out this time, climbing all the way to the top just to drop almost all the way down when the fog cleared, tucking her arm behind her and letting herself spin for a second before climbing back up halfway and flipping into an invert.

She held on with one leg, pulling her other foot behind her and then straightened it to shake her ass. I was respectfully staring. She brought her leg up, dropping slightly and going into an upside down split on the pole. I couldn't tell you what it was called, but it looked cool as fuck.

When she finally got back to the floor she had a bounce in her step in perfect timing to the song, she whipped out the pole pirouette followed by a perfected fan kick and into a back hook spin—I did know that one, that was a simple one.

This could not be the same girl I saw trip over her own feet at her house.

She held her back hook spin for a minute before letting it take her to the floor, her eyes met mine as she arched her back and shook her ass right in front of the camera. I hit the fog again, but for less time, so it could showcase the light show going on.

I have no idea what the fuck was wrong with me, but I couldn't help myself, I wasn't looking away. She realized that too and stuck her tongue out at me.

She side climbed up the pole and tucked her left leg under her knee so she could let go, tucking herself closer to the pole so it spun faster, so when she grabbed her heel and let her leg hang in a pretty shape she could hold it longer. She shifted into a superman pose holding it longer than I'd ever seen.

She was feeling the stage today so that was a good thing at least.

Perform your heart out, Princess, please.

I looked down at the song list as two more girls came out; Penny and Cookie. I loaded their playlists into the system and wrote down the stage set list.

By the time Millie finally got off stage I had thirteen girls already signed up. Two more and we'd need to close it off. Gracie—fuck, Iris—came up to the booth. "I saw you ogling."

"Jade? Always." I winked and her eyes got so wide I thought she might pass out.

"Good to know." Gracie flicked her long hair over her shoulder, turning to walk towards Millie.

I grinned, "You can tell her I said that too, don't care, she called me Daddy DJ before we were even open so she'll get as good as she gives tonight."

She took off to the dressing room with Millie as they talked animatedly, Millie was hyped up on energy already. Gods help us all. Please don't let it be slow.

* * *

It wasn't slow. I take it back. Please slow down.

This fucking club was packed and it was only ten at night. I could hardly see anything across the club. I caught sight of Millie and Gracie, pulling—yes, pulling—a group of guys closer to the DJ booth, they looked younger and when they sat in the bottle service I knew Millie's video had brought them in.

I hadn't even attempted to look at it. I hadn't had fucking time to look at my phone. "Marley and Laycee, one song away." We had to double up on stage with the amount of girls we had now.

I opened my phone, the group chat was going insane. Wait—this wasn't the group chat I started earlier? Nope, this was one that Millie had made and sent the video too first before posting.

Coop: Going to ignore the "I'm about to take your girl" part of the song.

Princess: Don't look at me, I didn't choose the songs. Just the Juicy J part.

Link: Jesus Christ you're trying to take me out.

Coop: I think Theo's ignoring us.

Link: Why would he look at his texts when he has that in front of him.

Princess: To be fair there's a lot of girls and a lot of people. We're slammed. He is working. Only reason I haven't bothered him. Believe me I want to. ;)

Theo: Don't let her lie, that stage set was criminal. Also, Millie sell a hot tub or something.

Princess: Send help. The guy in the yellow shirt, we went to school with him.

I looked over, fuck, I did recognize him.

Theo: Need me to get him out?

Princess: Nah, he seemed uncomfortable seeing me already so he probably won't even talk to me.

Two more stage sets had gone by, Millie was four shots deep since they got bottle service. She looked at me as she spit the shot back into a beer bottle. Oh, that was slick. Atta girl.

I felt proud of her right now. I was wondering why she had an empty beer bottle, when I knew she didn't drink beer.

I vaguely heard her say, "I have to let the DJ know we'll be gone for a bit, Iris keep him company."

When she walked into the DJ booth I had to double check the rotation and how far away the next girl was, I didn't want to leave anyone up there too long. I had six girls in VIP currently for varying times, so I was down to eight girls on rotation until further notice.

"They want to do a shower show, while we wait for the hot tub to fill. I guess take us off the rotation."

"How do you manage to sell so many hot tubs?" Seriously, how? I knew we sold back to back hot tubs a lot of the time, especially on weekends—but holy hell and every deity I'd ever worshipped how did she manage it like that?

"Fucking luck, my dude." She shrugged, "Also, you didn't repost my video. Go do that Daddy DJ."

"I don't know who you're bossing around, but it's not me." I said simply, meeting her eyes.

She rolled her eyes, fucking brat, and pulled the guys to the VIP booth.

I reposted her video.

I was still at Link and Millie's, we'd cleaned up the mess from the pizza and the empty bottles. We put on *The Quarry*, we'd played for a little bit but I was getting tired. I could tell Link was too, he yawned and stretched, looking at his phone.

I shouldn't have noticed how his sweater rode up and showed his stomach and the sandy blonde hair that cascaded down when he stretched. Or how did a little huff after a yawn, I wasn't attracted to him —not like that—but damn he was so soft-boy coded.

Link looked anxious as he checked his phone. "Neither of them have replied."

"They're probably busy. Even Millie said it was fucking packed." I shrugged.

Link groaned, "Which means she better not get fucked up and make questionable decisions with our favorite DJ."

"Theo wouldn't if she's drunk, he wouldn't let her." I knew that. I knew Theo wouldn't do that. Theo could be an absolute asshole to her sometimes, but he was raised better than that. A single mom and two sisters would do that to you.

Link chuckled, "I know, I'm more worried about her manhandling him."

I laughed, good, glad he knew who the real problem would be. The way he said it—fond, exasperated, protective—yeah. I understood why they cared about him. I was starting to get it too, he was a sweet heart and so fucking soft. I couldn't picture him any other way, seeing him here in his element.

He was absolutely fucking in love with both Millie and Theo, whether he wanted to admit the Theo part or not—I saw he looked at them. It was one and the same, it sent a pang through my chest honestly, I don't think it was jealousy?

Shit, was I jealous? Maybe I needed to schedule myself a therapy session, because this was crazy right? I wasn't entirely sure how I felt about the last twenty-four hours, but I didn't feel jealous exactly, well—I mean it kind of feels like jealousy, but not at the same time. I was fucking confused, this was all confusing.

I looked over at Link deflecting my own thoughts, "Let me guess, feeling weird about them being alone tonight?"

"Just a bit, I trust them. I love them both." He paused, *oh so he can admit it,* "Fuck, you didn't hear that. Don't you dare repeat that to Theo." He said it so fast and so sincerely that it hit me in the feels too, "I mean it." He groaned, pushing his hair back and I knew I had him figured out.

He hadn't told Theo that officially, I was sure Millie knew. This little fucker was probably the first to know everything about her too.

I tossed my paper plate and crust into the pizza box intent on cleaning up. We had finished off the last of the leftover pizza and I had just stayed. I didn't really want to leave. I knew I probably should because I did have work... and I did have a cat that wanted me home—even if he hated me.

I sighed, "I know the feeling." I admitted after a minute, because fuck, I kind of did. "This is crazy right?"

"What, that we're both seeing people who want each other? While also wanting the other person's person. Yeah, fucking wild." He paused, grinning at me, "So what are we?" Link asked, of course he'd make a joke about it.

The question caught me off guard, did he mean us as in him and I? Or like as a whole? I wasn't rising to any bait from him, he'd fuel a fire any way he could if he knew it got under my skin. But did it? Did it get under my skin? I mean I liked him enough, well beyond tolerating I guess since I'd stayed here while they went to work.

"We're all a mess." I settled on that, that was easier.

He huffed a laugh, leaning back into the couch, his hair falling a little in his face. If it was Theo I would have shoved it back out of his face, but I didn't. Something about it made him look softer and infinitely easier to read. Warmer in a sense that he was comfortable with me.

Now I was hyper aware of how I'd been with Theo and how easily those little touches and small affections turned into something bigger, what if I was the problem? Why did spending time with someone feel like this?

"How are you feeling right now?" He asked quietly, his warm chocolate brown eyes meeting mine and effectively pulling me from my thoughts.

"Like it could work if we communicated and kept it between us and us alone." I admitted, because theoretically we wouldn't be the first people in a poly-situation. I knew it could work, we'd absolutely have to communicate though. That was non-negotiable.

"I'm worried about her, I know I can handle it." I *was* worried about Millie mostly, relationships can fuck with women harder than men—I saw it in psych all the time—it wasn't the reason but it could definitely give them a push in the wrong direction.

Link sighed, crossing his arms. "I don't think any of us are going to fuck this up with her." He bit his bottom lip and I had to physically stop myself from focusing on it. "But it's a valid feeling, I'm worried about it too. I love her, I've always loved her—I'd die to protect her."

I looked over at his stupid blonde hair and his grandpa sweater. I could understand why Millie and Theo both fell for him, he was the one who'd give his all until he couldn't give anymore. I know he'd break off pieces of himself until he was gone if it meant protecting the people he loves. Zero self-preservation.

He was a campfire soul and no one ever needs to take from a fire without feeding it. I wouldn't let them. I saw him in myself and I knew right then and there I couldn't ever let it get like that. My eyes met his and I tried really hard to look away, but I saw him—really saw him, not the person he wanted to be, not the person he thought he needed to be, but him. The one who would go to war without question, the one who would find something to love about everyone he met.

Link was warmth and love embodied and it made my heart beat faster in my chest.

I didn't like that, that feeling. I needed to go. "Thanks for hanging out with me." I said as I picked up my keys off the coffee table.

"I'll let you know if he messages me, you have Millie's location?" He asked, sitting up to look at me, he almost looked upset I was going—maybe he was just lonely?

I shook my head, because I didn't. She hadn't given me that much access yet.

Link pulled out his phone and a few seconds later I got a notification asking to join their family app. I set up an account in the car before I drove off. He'd put me in the family circle. He didn't make a big deal about it either, simply including me in their life.

In their family.

Okay, so maybe I did like Link a little bit. Not in the way he liked Millie. Not in the way she liked him. Certainly not the way I liked Millie and Theo, but he was growing on me.

That terrified me more honestly, because why did it feel like that?

Millie

"I Like How I Look - Jesse Murph"

Between the shower show and the hot tub I was fucking water logged and I had to act drunk, because I'd been dumping my shots all night. If I was going to be a menace to Theo I wanted to make sure I was sober for it.

We'd managed to get four of the six guys back here. I'd cut Gracie off after her fourth shot, she'd actually been taking them.

We still had about two hours before we closed. I was going to try to pull a few more dances before we closed but I really needed to get my runny make-up off my face and I needed to warm up. I was freezing. "Iris, do you have make-up wipes?"

"Yeah, somewhere in the bag."

Oh lawd, here we go.

I had to dig through her damn mess of a bag. I found them finally, almost lost my life digging through all the sequins and lace that were thrown haphazardly, but I found them.

I quickly wiped everything off my face. Looking at my make-up bag with distaste, this took way too long to do the first time. I settled on eyeliner and mascara. My hair was sopping wet so I took it down, running a brush through it and braiding it in two braids instead.

I put the green outfit back on, but I was shivering. I didn't have a fucking hoodie, a cardigan or anything to put over top of it.

"You good?" I asked, throwing her an outfit from her bag and the makeup wipes. "Get dressed, night's not over. You're not that drunk."

"Okay mom..." Gracie groaned, fixing the make-up under her eyes.

I grabbed my purse and took off back to the VIP desk. Jonah handed me nineteen hundred and I signed the paper stating I was paid.

"I'll tip at the end of the night, because I'm planning on making more money."

"Check in at the DJ booth so he can put you back on stage." Jonah nodded towards Theo and I turned to do that, but another guy stopped me.

He looked me up and down, his eyes falling on my still dripping hair, "You look like you've had a good time tonight."

"Eh, could be better, why do you want to make it better?" I smiled, giving him my best doe eyes.

"Yeah, let's go."

Fuck, okay, that was easier than I expected.

He paid for a thirty minute VIP, I'd fucking take it. He sat down and patted the seat beside him, I sat. "What's your name?"

"Jade," I intertwined my fingers in his, "What's yours?"

"Greg, but I hate it—can I come up with a stage name too?" He laughed, squeezing my fingers in his.

I beamed, "Absolutely, but only if I can show you how to shake your ass."

"Deal, what's my stage name?" He asked, I could see the drunk glaze taking over.

"Do you want ridiculous or like normal?" I didn't have to fake a laugh when I busted out with, "Although Groovy Greg sounds dope."

"Groooovy baby!" He laughed, like a full belly laugh.

I liked this guy, "Okay, okay hear me out, what about Miles. Get it Miles Long. Or like Diesel."

"Is it because I'm bald?" He deadpanned then laughed again, "Nah, I know it's the muscle, don't flatter me Jade." He kissed his bicep and I laughed right along with him, he had a sense of humor that was hard to find here.

"Okay, so we've got some names Diesel or Miles, my vote is still Groovy Greg, but that's beside the point." I said.

He grinned, taking a swig from his beer. "Groovy Greg is nice, but I think it takes away from the stage name, don't ya think?"

"I like Miles." I stood up, pulling him to his feet, "And I think I should teach Miles how to shake his ass, don't you? You gotta watch first though." I shucked off my heels, throwing them to the side of the couch.

I put my foot on the couch and bounced my knee slightly to make my butt move and he locked in. "Like this?" He did the same thing and I shit you not, it actually did move a bit.

"YES!!! You've got it!" I clapped and he whooped like he'd just won the lottery.

"That's my new party trick for sure." He laughed, collapsing back into the couch and I started a slow little dance, starting off with shaking my butt in front of him.

My dances were chill, if I could get away with a no touch, no contact dance I would. I had a strict fifteen second lap touch rule. It wasn't industry standard, but it was Jade standard. Just like I didn't put both of my legs on the couch when I faced them, one foot on the ground helped keep some space.

After about fifteen minutes I was out of fucking breath. He patted the seat next to him, "So what made you want to dance?" He asked as I sat and draped my legs over him as he massaged my calves.

"Honestly, it's so freeing, being up on stage and getting to meet all sorts of people. I get to leave everything behind and just be the person I want to be, no holding back. No tragic backstory, just me and the music."

"That's beautiful." He said, studying my face, "Most girls just say the money."

I grinned, "That is a perk, but not the reason. I guess I like the escapism aspect. If I'm having a bad day I come here and it melts away."

"I guess it's the same for us." He agreed, "But different of course." He sighed, "You know, I'm down here on vacation—it was supposed to be my wife and I..."

"What happened?" I asked quietly, my fingers brushing the back of his hand sympathetically.

"She wants a separation, some time away." He admitted, looking down at where my fingers were dragging across his skin.

I studied him for a second, "Can I give you some advice? As a woman?"

He nodded, tears threatening to escape, he wasn't the first man I'd had cry in VIP. I had that about me, for whatever reason, I'd been deemed a club therapist since the beginning. A lot of girls couldn't do it, didn't have the mental capacity for it. They always tried to make it sexy or turn the conversations to sex. I wasn't like that, I never had been. I wanted that connection. I needed it. I enjoyed it.

I wanted to know how people worked and understand all the perspectives. This was more than just dancing to me, this was a way to connect and help. It was validating my empathy and letting me be an emotional anchor for others.

Something I had wanted all my life, yeah maybe the trauma of my childhood did show up in weird ways here and there, but honestly? If I could use that here and make other people have a better day, I would. Every time, because life is fucking hard and if this is where they wanted to come to get help honestly I didn't blame them.

Most of the time they didn't even realize they came in here needing this type of connection, but this is what I was here for. This is what made my job worth it, these men weren't all bad. Yes, we did get the questionable ones, the rude ones, the handsy ones...but most of the time this was it.

Just hurt people wanting comfort. I know, because I too wanted comfort. I looked at him, studying his face, frowning slightly for what was about to come out of my mouth.

"If my husbands first idea was to come here, to a place like this which has a bad rep I'd feel fucking heart broken, but you haven't even alluded to it at all—which thank you for that by the way, it's refreshing." I rubbed his arm sympathetically, "But it tells me you don't really get the physical or emotional intimacy from her, so maybe you're both falling short on that?"

"So, I need to try harder?" He asked, hope returning to his eyes.

"Maybe not in some grand gesture, but in small ways. Cook her favorite foods, call her or send her a good morning text. Women love to feel thought about, we love to know you're thinking of us. Maybe go pick up her favorite perfume, or find a necklace or ring with her favorite gemstone—not diamonds, like her birth stone or her favorite colors. Make her a playlist and send it to her, songs you associate with her."

He sighed, "You're better than my therapist. He told me to give her space and try to talk to her when I got back home."

"Do what feels right, if any of what I said resonated, take the advice." My phone alarm went off, "Our time is up, but can I give you a hug?"

He stood up and I pulled him into a hug, he needed that. Shit, maybe I did too.

"Thank you, I think I'm going to go back to my hotel and work on making her a playlist, she loves music." He smiled and I couldn't help the very real smile that graced my face, "I think I needed to meet you tonight, thank you." He handed me a hundred dollar bill out of his wallet before he left the room.

This? Moments like this? This was what it meant to be a dancer. This was why I came back. Helping people, easing someone's hurt for even thirty minutes, giving them hope they didn't walk in with—God, I lived for it. It made the job feel right. Like I wasn't just shaking my ass for dollars but actually doing something that mattered.

Jonah gave me a warm smile when I walked back to the VIP desk. "You always get the sad ones."

I shrugged, tucking the hundred into my purse. "I think I gave him some hope."

"This is why you're my favorite." Jonah handed me the remaining two hundred, and I signed the paper stating I'd been paid.

I pushed off from the desk and scanned the crowd. Gracie was deep in conversation at the back table, bright-eyed and tipsy in a way that said she'd be fine for another hour. Good. I needed to check in with Theo anyway.

His booth was dim, lit mostly by the glow of the mixer and the LEDs lining the edge. He looked up the second he saw me, the ghost of a smirk tugging at his mouth before he leaned in close—closer than necessary.

"Did you make that man cry?" Theo whispered, voice warm against my ear.

I swore my pulse jumped. Fuck. Too close.

"Only for good reason," I murmured, matching his tone because two can play that game. "He was really cool. Groovy Greg, but if he's ever in here again we gotta call him Miles."

The confusion on his face was *perfect*. Brows furrowed, eyes flicking over my freshly braided hair, down my shoulders, the green outfit clinging to me in places that were typically covered even in here. He clocked all of it—of course he did—but he didn't comment.

He was too busy staring.

Good. Stay confused.

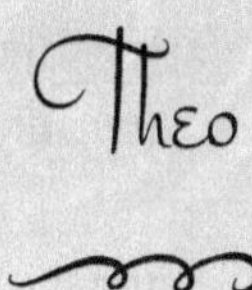

I'd been waiting all night to close this fucking place down. Millie was the first one to get changed, coming back with a two hundred dollar tip for Jonah and I, plus a hundred dollar tip for the two security guys and the bartender.

She was still shaking, so I didn't even think about how it would look, but I handed her the hoodie I was wearing. "You're cold." She put it on immediately, no hesitation. It swallowed her whole, covering her shorts. "I have to close everything down, then we can go."

She nodded, sitting down on the couch beside the booth. Scrolling on her phone, in the group chat I realized. Her message came through a few seconds later.

Princess: Sorry guys, I had a night.

Theo: She had a good night, made a man cry.

Princess: That sounds worse than it is, they were good tears. Don't go telling my secrets.

I didn't have time to reply, not when I was so close to finally having her to myself. I wanted to get this shit over with so we could leave. I went over to sign my shift paperwork so we could leave and Jonah looked at Millie, "See you say it's nothing, but she's in your hoodie."

"She was cold." I said, because she was.

"And you're taking her home?" This nosy mother fucker.

"Yeah, she's completely sober too." I added, "Jonah, can I go?"

"Yeah, you're good to go. Don't be dumb please. Not with her." He was serious.

I paused, I knew he was coming at me because Millie was the golden girl here, "I have never had a relationship with a dancer *ever*, Jade is—important to me, I wouldn't do anything to hurt her. You know me Jonah."

Fuck, he'd probably heard this same shit a thousand times over the years.

Millie picked up her bag and trotted over to us, "Ready?" She asked, looking between Jonah and I. I nodded, gesturing to the front entrance and following behind her. I unlocked the doors and opened the door for her before going to my own side. "What was that about? With Jonah?"

I tugged on the bottom of the hoodie, "He called us out."

I went to move my hand back, but she wrapped her fingers around my hand and kept it on her thigh, "I'm cold, you're warm."

She looked over at me, I could see the hesitation on her face even as she shifted. "What Mils?"

"I ummm—why does this feel so weird?"

"I don't know. I'm just taking you home." I tried to pull my hand away but she stopped me, that was a good sign I guess.

"You don't have to take me to my house..." she said quietly, shifting closer to me. "But I do require a shower and warm clothes." She snatched my phone, "And the Bluetooth."

I let her turn my Bluetooth off and connect her own once we got to the stop light. She started playing something I recognized, but I wasn't paying attention. "You look tired."

"Not gonna lie, I'm exhausted and hungry."

"Do you want something now or when we get home? I have chicken nuggets and breakfast burritos in my freezer."

"I can wait," she said quietly, her head to the side watching me as I drove. She looked so soft right now, not the menace Millie, not Jade, not drunk Millie. She looked real and sweet and nervous. So so nervous. "So, Coop is okay with us—I don't know, hanging out after work."

"He texted me," I gave her back my phone after unlocking it, "Go see for yourself."

She didn't open it, "I don't wanna go through your texts, that's personal."

"It's about you." I said, letting my eyes rove over now that I could finally do that. Her curiosity overtook her, I knew it would once I said that. I watched her read through the last few messages, it had been around eleven.

He'd told me if she was down it was fine, he wouldn't be mad. Her hands shook as she scrolled through my panic from earlier, but a small smile crept up and she looked at me with those big doe eyes, "Admit it, you kinda love me." She wrapped her arms around my arm, the one currently holding her thigh and laid her head against me.

I didn't say anything, because what was I supposed to say without sounding delusional? How was it possible to love three different people in different ways?

When we got to my little apartment, I was suddenly very aware of the cups in the sink and my gaming shit everywhere in the living room. I had to remind myself she lived with one gamer and had been at Coop's where his headsets and controllers were almost always constantly strung around.

She stopped by my DJ table, her eyes lit up, "Wait, you're like a serious DJ, not just like a club DJ."

"I'm actually offended you'd think I wouldn't have my own set up." I crossed my arms, leaning against the couch.

She frowned, "Well damn, you could have DJ'ed the private parties Gracie and I do."

"You and Gracie do private parties? Without security?" I asked, I knew she could be reckless but that was dangerous.

She shrugged, "Nah, I usually let Toby know, he does security for most of the girls outside of the club."

I tried really hard to maintain my composure, but she saw it—of course she did. Fucking Toby was playing security guard after hours and on days off? He didn't even tell me? I tried to keep myself calm, "How often do you do them?"

She saw through my facade immediately, "Oh? You don't like that I do private parties?"

"I don't care about the private parties," *that* was a bold faced lie, "but I would have been there if I knew about it."

That little smirk on her face? That meant she knew I was lying, "You're hot when you're jealous."

"I'm not jealous." I said as she stepped closer to me, leaning against me.

"You're not?" She tilted her head up to look at me and held my gaze, her eyes slowly falling to my lips. "It's okay if you are, I kind of like it when you get that look in your eyes."

Fuck. Millie, what the fuck?

I was used to bold drunk Millie, but sober bold Millie was next level. She reached her hand up to brush my jaw and I swear to all the Gods in the Universe she was going to be my undoing.

"Theo, you're overthinking it."

I was. Fuck, yeah I was. There were a million reasons this was a bad idea, a million, maybe I needed to get some air, I could make her some food while she took a shower. Anything, any reason to put some space between us.

"Go take a shower and I'll get you some clothes." Her face fell at my words and she took a step back, putting a little bit of distance between us. "You're hungry aren't you? Let me make you some food, chicken nuggets?"

"Yeah, umm... chicken nuggies are fine. Show me where your bathroom is?"

Right, she hadn't been here before.

She wasn't Coop and she wasn't Link. She was Millie and she was in my living room in a hoodie that smelled like me, asking for my shower, she'd be wearing my clothes.

I showed her where everything was in the bathroom, told her she could use whatever she needed and then went to my room to find her some clothes. I settled on a drawstring pair of pajama pants, a pair of my boxers and a shirt that would definitely go to her knees.

I busied myself with her chicken nuggets and set a timer on the stove and my phone, just in case, I loaded the dishes in the sink into the dishwasher and started wiping my counter tops with the tropical breeze smelling cleaning products, not sure why it said tropical breeze when it just smelled like orange to me but whatever, I also checked the trash. I'd just taken it out, it was fine.

My nerves were shot, my hands were shaky. Fuck, what were we doing?

I knocked on the door once I heard the shower shut off, she opened up the door with a towel wrapped around her. Her face red from the steam as she took the clothes. When she came out she was not wearing the pajama pants I gave her, just my shirt that swallowed her whole and my boxers that were barely visible.

I took her in, because fuck, that was hot. "Mils... I gave you pants."

"And I chose not to wear them, what are you going to do about it?"

Why did that sound so bratty?

Probably because she meant it too. She was not making this easy, holy shit, my heart was in my throat. I could hear it beating in my ears.

"Pants." I said and she crossed her arms.

"Nope, no pants."

My phone alarm went off, I silenced the alarm. "Come on, your food is done."

She smiled and followed me to the kitchen, her bare feet padding across the carpet. "I have ranch, ketchup, mustard—umm some other sauces if you wanna grab what you want?"

She opened my fridge, which was thankfully fully stocked, because I do know how to cook thank you very much, and I don't order fucking take-out like Link does ninety-five percent of the time.

She picked up the ranch bottle, giving me a sideways smirk, "Why is your ranch in a fancy glass bottle? You buy the boujee ranch? Link doesn't even buy boujee condiments."

"I make my own actually." I grinned, leaning back, "There's also a homemade dressing in the one next to it."

Millie looked at me fully now, a playful smile on her face. "I guess there's more to you than Daddy DJ, huh?"

"Haha, very funny." I groaned, the nickname was just as atrocious as it was endearing. "If you like the ranch I'll share my recipe."

"Why? I could just come over here for it?" She reached for a chicken nugget, but immediately dropped it with a hiss, pulling her hand back.

"I could have told you it was gonna be too hot right now." I chuckled, getting a bottle of water out of the pantry. "Water? I have room temp and cold water in the fridge."

"Room temp, only Link likes his frigid." She said, catching the water bottle I tossed at her, but she was wrong—Coop also liked ice cold water.

She gave me a look like she was about to do something she might get in trouble for—she hopped up onto the counter, struggling to do so at first. Short shit.

She kicked her feet lightly back and forth, she looked like she didn't know what to do with herself. She went to chew on her nail and I stepped in, pulling her hand away from her mouth. "Non mangiarti le unghie."

Her mouth dropped open, "Did you just tell me not to bite my nails in Italian?"

"Sorry, habit." I admitted, my cheeks felt hotter than normal.

She laughed, intertwining our fingers together, "Heard that a lot as a kid, did you?"

I nodded, stepping closer between her legs, my other hand trailing over the exposed skin of her thigh. Her breath stuttered and I took a risk of a glance up to see if she would pull away, part of me still thought she might.

We weren't drunk, we were sober. Very sober. She had agreed to come over though, so there's that I guess.

"Fuck it." My lips crashed to hers, my fingers sliding into her still wet hair at the base of her skull. My other hand pulled her closer to me, she immediately returned the favor, her teeth pulling at my bottom lip gently—playfully—before she cupped her hand to the side of my jaw and pulled me even closer.

This was better than any drunk kiss or fantasy. She was real and here, alone with me and just me. She was mine right now. That's all that mattered. I couldn't help but smile against her lips, before tracing a path down her neck, biting down on her collarbone gently.

Her hands pushed at my pants and I stopped her, intertwining both of our hands together, "You need to eat first."

She groaned, her head falling to my chest. "You're so bossy..."

As much as I'd love to fuck her on my counter tops, there would be a time for that and it wasn't right now.

She picked up a chicken nugget and dipped it into the ranch sauce, she looked at me then back at the ranch, "You made this?"

"It's easier than you think." I shrugged, stealing a nugget and dipping it in the ranch.

We ate in a charged silence, neither of us moving away from each other. She attempted to put the dishes away, but I stopped her—I'll be damned if she was cleaning up after me.

She slipped away from me and started digging through her bag, "I know I have a toothbrush in here somewhere." She started emptying the contents onto my floor— different wipes, outfits in individual zipper bags, a makeup bag, heels, and then a small pack of disposable toothbrushes. Probably for when she ate at work, but right now it definitely helped for our impromptu slumber party.

She studied me as I finished cleaning up our after work snack, carefully refilling her bag between glances at me, she wasn't sneaky about it like she normally was either, she didn't look away when I caught her staring. She smirked as she dabbed something on her wrists, then on her neck, I swear if it was that damn sweet smelling perfume she'd worn at work a few times—I might come in my fucking pants.

I took a deep breath and decided to give her some space for a minute, letting her do whatever she needed. She opened the door after a minute, "Get in here and brush your teeth so you're not kissing me with ranch lips."

I snorted, leave it to Millie to say some shit like that.

I stepped into the small space, this felt too intimate compared to anything we'd ever done. She spit in the sink and covered her mouth when she did it, quickly rinsing it down the drain with water. I rolled my eyes at her in the mirror as I brushed my teeth, when I started scrubbing my tongue she smirked.

"What?" I asked, after spitting.

She giggled, "Nothing, I just know why Link likes you so much."

I looked over at her, unscrewing the cap to the mouthwash and swishing some before handing it to her. She did the same, taking an extra long time and covering her mouth again when she spit.

"For fuck's sake, come on—bed." I pulled her by the hand to my bedroom, she took a moment to take it in all in.

I watched as her eyes took in the maps hanging on the walls, the altars in the corners and the record player that was among my little plant shelf in front of the windows. The plants liked classical music, don't ask me—it was just a weird fact I found online and it seemed to work wonders.

"Who do you practice with?" Millie asked quietly, a soft smile playing on her lips.

"No one's ever asked that before." I said, pulling my lip in between my teeth.

I turned on Apollo's light—a little sun lamp—and showed her his, "Apollo, of course..." His was closest to the window so he could get sunlight. I liked to leave the curtains pulled back for him and the plants.

"Music—that checks out." She smiled, looking at the varying trinkets and stones making sure not to touch anything.

Venus was next and I was prepared for a joke about the fact I had an altar for the Goddess of love and beauty, but none came, her pink tourmaline and rose quartz chunks glistened as I turned on the swan lamp. "I'm sure you can guess this one."

"Aphrodite, I love that." Her voice was so gentle right now, even as she looked at the other one. "And what about that one?"

"Venus, technically—but her Greek counterpart is Aphrodite." I paused, pulling her over to my personal altar, I hardly let anyone see it.

"This one is my personal altar, my tarot cards are here. This is a Cimaruta—it honors our ancestors." I pointed at the silver pendant, "I use the bell for sound energy clearing. I have a few oils, my dream journal and protective crystals that I typically keep on me go here to charge back up." There was more but it was a lot and if she was still interested I'd show her more later.

She looked around, the intrigued written all over her face. "Your space is so you and not what I expected at all."

"Guess I'm full of surprises." I whispered as I cupped her cheek and kissed her gently, so softly that if she wanted to pull away she could—not that I wanted her too. That was the last thing I wanted.

She kissed me and I slowly walked us over to my bed, breaking the kiss to pull her down on top of me, her body straddling mine as my hands gripped her waist. The feeling of her weight settling on me, it nearly made me lose my mind. She rocked against me, and I swore under my breath, my fingers digging into her hips.

"Fuck, Princess," I groaned, watching her bite her lip as she rolled her hips again.

She leaned down, her hair falling like a curtain around us as she kissed me, her tongue meeting mine. I slid my hands under the shirt I'd given her and trailed my fingers up her sides, feeling her shiver as my fingers traced her ribs, her breath catching when I brushed the underside of her breasts.

"Theo," she whispered against my mouth, my name like a prayer on her lips as she smiled against mine.

I flipped us over, pinning her beneath me, her hair splayed across my pillows like she'd always belonged there. My breath caught as I took her in—flushed cheeks, lips parted, looking up at me with those pretty hazel eyes. The green around the edges danced in the warmth of the lamp light.

"Tell me what you want," I whispered, brushing my thumb across her bottom lip.

"You," she breathed. "Just you."

I'd never wanted anyone as much as the way I wanted her right now. I tugged my shirt up her body, revealing inch by perfect inch of her skin. She lifted her arms to help me, and when I tossed it aside, I had to take a moment just to look at her, at the way she was looking at me.

"You're fucking beautiful," I murmured, trailing my fingers down her chest, between her breasts, over her stomach. She arched into my touch, a small whimper escaping her. I lowered my head to kiss her neck, her collarbone, working my way down her body. Her skin was so soft under my lips, I traced my tongue over the curve of her breast.

It earned me the smallest gasp from her lips, like she hadn't meant to let it escape. "Theo.."

She arched into me when I took her nipple in my mouth and swirled my tongue around the sensitive bud, my hand sliding up to cup her other breast, thumb circling her other nipple until she was squirming beneath me.

Her fingers tangled in my hair, tugging enough to send sparks down my spine. "Please," she whispered, and fuck, if that didn't make my heart beat faster.

I looked up at her, a smirk playing on my face as I kissed my way down her stomach, settling between her legs. Her eyes widened when she realized my intent, and I paused, holding her gaze.

"Yes?" I asked, needing her permission before I continued.

"Umm... I don't know if—" she sounded nervous, why was she nervous about this? She laid down, covering her face, "I'm just—awkward when—you can... I—yes."

I settled between her legs, pressing kisses along her inner thighs, not daring to go up any higher, if she didn't want to, I'd stop. "If you're uncomfortable, tell me to stop."

I pressed a few more kisses to her hip, then her lower stomach, "Mils, can I?" I asked, she was so fucking cute right now—her cheeks flushed, hands covering her eyes.

"Yeah, I—you can."

When my tongue found her center, she tensed, but her hips bucked up against my mouth and she tried to squirm away. I gripped her thighs, holding her in place as I tasted her, circling my tongue around her clit before sucking gently,

"Fuck," she whimpered, one hand threading itself in my hair, the other still covering her eyes. "Theo, fuck—"

I looked up at her from between her legs, watching her face as I slid one finger inside her, then another, curling them just right. Her mouth fell open slightly as she made a sound that was somewhere between a moan and a whine. She was so god damn beautiful, fuck.

I wanted to memorize every inch of her, every reaction she was giving me.

"Please," she whispered, her voice breaking as I curled my fingers inside her. "I need you."

I crawled back up her body, my lips finding hers as I positioned myself between her thighs. She reached between us, her hand wrapping around me, guiding me to her entrance.

"Fuck, Millie," I groaned against her neck as I slowly pushed inside her. The feeling was overwhelming—I had to pause halfway, my forehead dropping to her shoulder, I didn't want to hurt her, she was so fucking tight around me.

I pulled back slowly before pushing all the way in, and we both moaned at the feeling. Her eyes fluttered closed, "Look at me," I commanded softly, and her eyes opened, locking with mine as I started to move. "Don't look away."

She nodded, her hands sliding up to cup my face as I built a steady rhythm. Every thrust sent electricity through my body, every little gasp and moan from her lips pushing me closer to the edge.

"Fuck," I groaned, hooking one of her legs over my arm to change the angle. Her reaction told me everything, the way she tightened around me had me closer than I wanted.

She let her head drop to the side and I gently tilted her chin back towards me, "I said eyes on me."

She whimpered, her eyes holding mine even as I felt her trembling beneath me, her body clenching around mine as I changed the angle. The way she looked at me—eyes half-lidded, lips parted—was almost enough to send me over the edge right there.

She looked like she'd been waiting for this as long as I had.

"Theo," she gasped, her voice breaking on my name as I thrust deeper. "Holy shit, you're huge."

I smirked, but I couldn't look away from her face. The flush spreading across her chest, the way her lips formed a perfect o when I hit the right spot—it was fucking intoxicating. I wanted to memorize every detail, burn it into my memory forever.

"You're so fucking beautiful," I groaned, my rhythm faltering as she rocked her hips to meet mine.

Her fingernails dug into my shoulder. "Harder," she whispered, and fuck as if I could deny her anything right now.

I slammed into her, holding onto her tighter, I knew better than to leave marks, but I didn't fucking care right now. My lips pressed to her neck and down her collarbone, I bit lightly then sucked the skin into my mouth for a second. If she had a mark I really didn't care anymore.

Fuck it, the whole world can know she's mine.

She was shaking against me, quivering as I picked up the pace, low-key hoping I ruined her for anyone else.

Mine. She was mine right now. No one else's.

She pulled me into a kiss as I felt her break around me, it was too much and if she wanted me to pull out I needed to do that right now.

Right fucking now.

I pulled out quickly, the sticky substance splattering across her lower stomach. "Fuck, sorry." I cursed, I had expected to go way longer than that.

"Why are you sorry? I just came like three times." She looked down, her breath stuttering, "But you could get something to clean me up."

I grinned, "Aww.... But you look good covered in me."

She rolled her eyes as I handed her the discarded shirt from earlier.

Waking up naked in Theo's bed was *an experience*. His arm was wrapped around my waist, his breath steady against my back as I laid on my stomach face down on his pillow.

Fuck, we'd actually done that. This was crazy right? Absolutely insane, what was I thinking? I work with him... I—he's my boyfriend's best friend, he's my best friend's boyfriend...

Shit. Shit. Shit.

I didn't even want to move, I didn't want to wake him up, but I needed to go. I shifted slightly and his arm tightened around me. "No..." he mumbled, his lips brushing my shoulder. "Please don't."

His hand pulled me towards him, causing me to turn to my side, pressing myself into his very naked lap, he kissed my shoulder again, his fingers splaying across my lower stomach tugging me closer. Fuck, he was so sweet in the morning.

His lips found my neck, peppering kisses against my skin. Fuck it, we'd already done it once, might as well.

His hand slid between my thighs, making me gasp as his fingers found me already wet for him. "Fuck," I whispered, pressing back against him. His hardness pushed against me, making my breath hitch.

"You want me again?" He murmured against my ear, his voice rough and gravely with sleep—fuck I was done for.

"Yes," I breathed, reaching behind me to guide him better, "Please..."

He entered me slowly this time, both of us on our sides, his arm wrapped around me as he pushed deeper. I moaned, the angle hitting places that made my toes curl. His lips traveled across my shoulder, up my neck, his teeth grazing my earlobe before pressing a kiss behind it.

"Theo," I whimpered as he started to move. It was lazy, languid—nothing like last night's urgency. His fingers circled my clit as he rocked into me from behind, I took his other hand and led it to my throat.

He chuckled darkly, squeezing just enough, "You can do better than that." I teased, his grip tightening as he slammed into me causing me to shudder against him.

His grip tightened around my throat as he thrust into me harder and I felt my eyes roll back, a strangled moan escaping my lips.

"Is that what you wanted?" He asked as he did it again, I clenched around him and tried to shift my hips to take him deeper. He pushed against me, his hand finding the spot between my shoulder blades.

"Fuck, that's deep," I gasped, reaching back to grab his hip, urging him to go faster. "Don't stop."

"Wasn't planning on it, Princess," he growled, his voice rough and possessive in a way I hadn't heard before.

I arched my back more, pressing my ass harder against him, taking him deeper. His fingers worked circles over my clit, circling with just the right pressure while his other hand kept the pressure on my throat. The dual sensations were overwhelming—I couldn't think, couldn't breathe, couldn't do anything but feel him everywhere.

I tapped him lightly, I needed to breathe. He loosed just enough and slammed into me holding me against him as I felt myself let go completely—gasping for oxygen.

"Good fucking girl." His thumb caressed my pulse point as if asking for permission to tighten his hold again.

I arched into him slightly, feeling a whole lot more sleepy than I was. I nodded, giving him permission. His fingers tightened again as he increased his pace, his rhythm growing more erratic. I was already sensitive from my first orgasm and I could feel another building rapidly.

"Theo," I whimpered, barely able to get his name out with his hand at my throat. "I'm gonna—"

"Come for me again," he commanded, his breath rough against my ear. "Let me feel you come on my dick, Princess."

That was all it took. I shattered around him, clenching and trembling as waves of pleasure washed over me. He groaned, his movements becoming desperate as he chased his own release.

I pulled him to me, I didn't want him to pull out. I wanted him. He was trying to hold himself back as I felt myself shaking around him.

"Fuck, Millie, I—" He gasped as I pulled him back in, feeling his release. I let out a content sigh as he dropped his forehead to rest between my shoulder blades as we both caught our breath.

Fuck, I hadn't realized it would be like this. Fuck, he'd made me cum more times than I could fucking count last night. He had me shaking against him while he played with my hair until I fell asleep, and now?

Soft sleepy Theo was something else entirely. He was looking at me, but it felt like he was staring into my soul. "What?" I asked, trailing my nails lightly along his chest.

He exhaled slowly, his hand rubbing my arm. "I was going to pull out..." he said quietly, "That's on you, Princess."

"I wanted you to..." I admitted, "What else is going on in your head?"

"Nothing... its just—"

"Doesn't feel like nothing." I sat up slightly, chewing my cheek as I looked over his face.

"I promise it's nothing, I just—"

Fuck, was he really about to say something to make me regret this?

Nope, he doesn't get to do that. He doesn't get to shut me down first. I went to sit up more, "I should probably go, I can call Link to come get me if you want."

"What? Why?" He sounded panicked, okay—maybe I had misread.

"Was this a mistake?" I asked quietly, pulling the sheet up higher around my chest.

He looked at me like I'd insulted him, "Mils, Princess, this was not a mistake." He pushed my hair back, looking at my collarbone, "But that might be... my bad."

I looked down at the bruise forming there, "You bitch." My mouth was hanging open, I was sure, because he of all people knew fucking better.

You can't leave marks on a fucking dancer.

"I won't do it again, but fuck, it makes me fucking feral thinking about seeing you at work with it." He rolled his eyes dramatically as he laid back down, pulling me with him. "How pissed is Coop gonna be about the mark?"

Fuck, how was that not my first thought?

We hadn't really talked about all of that yet, he'd given us full permission but really we should have discussed what was acceptable and what wasn't.

"Honestly, I don't know." I laid on his chest, his heart beating so loud I could hear it on the other side. "But what were you thinking about?"

He groaned, tugging me closer, "I was thinking Link might actually kill me."

"Did he not know?" I asked, my eyes widening, and when he didn't answer? I knew I had my fucking answer, "You didn't tell him?"

"I mean he knows we've got something going on, but I think he's going to be mad he didn't get you first."

Oh. Oh. Link, my baby, my little golden retriever.

Yeah, he might be fucking pissed about that. "Oh."

"Yeah, *oh*."

"And you still did it?" I teased, smacking his chest lightly.

"Well, yeah, it's you. I—"

"What?"

"I think I've been thinking about this for longer than I want to admit."

I had to fucking ask. "How long?"

He pulled me closer, "That time you wore the really sweet smelling perfume you put on last night and helped me with inventory."

"The inventory I wasn't even supposed to be touching." I reminded him. "Seeing as I don't get paid for that. Also that checks out, it's a pheromone oil. I had a phenomenal night that night."

"I know, you were also so drunk you stumbled into the DJ booth and begged me to play Control by Bryce Savage."

"You played it if I remember correctly." I pointed out.

His hand trailed down to my wrist, wrapping my skin in goosebumps. "Yeah, after you fucked with the system and sat in my lap."

"Oops, drunk Jade has zero boundaries." I admitted, I barely remembered that night.

He chuckled, "Drunk Jade got her hand slapped and then told me harder."

I snorted, fuck, *maybe* I was the problem.

"How do you put up with me?" I asked, because honestly, why did he?

"You're pretty." He smirked, "And you tip well."

It was my turn to be offended, "I tip everyone well."

"I didn't say it was just me, but you're a fucking menace in that club and if you weren't the Pole Princess and VIP top earner Jonah would have fired your ass." He said and I couldn't tell if he was serious or baiting me.

I rolled my eyes, "Jonah would fucking never."

"Oh yes, he would." I sat up at his words, staring into his whiskey brown eyes.

I narrowed my eyes at him. "You're lucky you look like a damn Greek God."

"I'm Italian, not Greek, but I'll take the compliment." He let his eyes wander down my body, then back up, I felt exposed.

"Shut up." I grumbled, pulling the blanket around my shoulders as I laid back down, "I know you're fucking Italian. You literally never shut up about it." I propped myself up on my elbow watching him intently.

"Sdraiati, Principessa." He pulled me closer, his fingers finding my hair and brushing through the strands.

"What does that even mean?"

"I told you to lay down."

I sighed, because fuck, he could say whatever he wanted to me in Italian and I'd listen. I nuzzled into him as he pressed his lips to my head, "Fottutamente bella."

I knew bella meant beautiful, but I didn't question what the other word meant. It couldn't have been terrible if it was followed by beautiful.

At least I hoped.

Link

"Love You Right - Shaker, COBRA"

I didn't have to text her, I knew where she was—thank you family app and a shared location. It didn't make me feel better. Actually it made me feel worse, why the fuck were my two favorite people spending the night with each other?

And worse? Why the fuck didn't they tell me?

I kind of figured when she didn't come home that she was with him. It made the most sense, but not even a fucking text like hey, I'm going to go bang your boyfriend... Fuck Millie.

Oh fuck, Cooper. Cooper was in our circle now, literally on the app. I opened my texts.

Link: You good with all of this?

Cooper: Are you?

Link: I'm not gonna lie, I'm pissed dude.

Link: I'm trying really hard not to be.

Link: You never answered the question.

Cooper: I knew.

Cooper: Are you mad about Theo or Millie?

I didn't text back, because honestly I didn't know what was worse. The fact that he knew and I didn't? Or the fact that he just asked which one I was mad about?

Cooper: Or is it because you feel left out?

Fuck me, okay, I guess that was what it was.

Link: I guess I feel left out, but fuck, Theo and Millie first?

Cooper: So it is lowkey about Millie too?

Link: Yeah, probably the wrong person to be ranting too… my bad.

Cooper: You're good, dude. If you need me I'm here. I know I haven't said that, but I guess we're kinda stuck with each other right now.

Link: Same to you.

Ugh, I needed a shower. I needed to clear my head and that meant a shower, an energy drink and then a ride.

By time I got out of the shower, my phone chimed, my family app, Millie was home. Fuck, she was going to want to go on the ride and I was still mad. I didn't want to take it out on her.

I could just sneak by her, I really could, I could wait for her to go to her room—

"Link?" Her voice called out, I didn't hear Theo though, thankfully.

I slipped on my riding gear, ignoring her voice, until she knocked on my door.

I opened my door and she took a step back, "Oh, so you're afraid of a little bit of closeness now?" I asked, stepping closer, my eyes tracked down to her bruised collarbone.

She held her ground, tilting her chin to look up at me instead. "Link—"

I cut her off, "You could have told me if you just wanted Theo and Coop."

"What?" She asked, confusion marring her pretty little face.

"If you just wanted to be my friend, all you had to do was say so." I said, putting it bluntly, crossing my arms and leaning against the doorframe.

"Why are you coming off so hostile right now for no reason?"

I moved her hair the rest of the way back, skimming my fingers over the mark, "Hope you and Theo had fun." I couldn't keep the anger from bleeding into my words.

Why couldn't she have come back home when I was gone? After I'd cleared my head...

"This is why I didn't fucking tell you Link!" She snapped her voice raising, going to turn away from me.

This little shit, Millie and I didn't fight, not often anyway, but right now I could feel it. If she wanted to do this, we fucking would. All she had to do was fucking text me—better than not saying anything at all. Letting me see it on the fucking app.

My hand grabbed her wrist, pulling her back to me, closer than what we were a few seconds ago. "Nah, we're gonna talk about it now."

She looked at her wrist and then back at me, "Unhand me."

I couldn't help the rumble that started in my throat, but I let her go, I didn't want to hurt her. "Then don't walk away from me." She didn't, but her hand went to rub her wrist and I saw it. "Did I hurt you?" I asked quietly, taking another step back from her.

Fuck, that was the last thing I wanted to do. Her eyes met mine and everything I'd been holding in for what seemed like forever was starting to crack open in my chest, fuck. I hadn't meant to do that.

"No, you didn't hurt me—just surprised me." She sighed, "Please don't do that again. Use your words next time."

I bit at my bottom lip, "I'm sorry, I really didn't want you to walk away right now. I was going to go for a ride and clear my head but now you're here and I—"

She threw her hands up, exasperation dripping from her words. "Link, I was going to be ten feet from you."

"That's too far." I deadpanned.

She studied my face, a grin breaking out on hers, "You're so fucking jealous right now."

"And?"

"I like it on you, but don't you ever fucking do that again or I'll deck you." She warned, "I'm so serious. I'll get the guys to gang up on you."

I knew she would too.

I sighed, running both hands through my hair. "I'm going to go for a ride and calm down." I told her and she looked worried, why did she look worried? She's always known the bike's my reset button. Why was she acting like I was walking into a war and not a twenty-minute loop around town?

She stepped in, closer than I was ready for right now, eyes dipping to my mouth like she was deciding something she shouldn't. "Be careful," she whispered, her fingers sliding into my hair at the base of my neck—slowly, intentionally, like she was grounding *me* instead of herself—and her mouth found mine.

I swear my brain short-circuited.

I didn't have softness in me right now. I couldn't, not with my blood still boiling and my chest still impossibly tight from everything I wasn't saying out loud.

I grabbed her waist and pulled her in like she was air and I'd been drowning for hours. Kissed her like I needed it to stay upright. Is it possible to be addicted to a person? Because whatever this was, it felt like withdrawal and overdose at the same damn time. And the second I had her close, I knew the ride wasn't gonna calm me—not when she was the thing fucking me up in the first place.

"What can I say to get you to stay with me right now?" Her voice cracked—barely a whisper, barely holding it together.

I tilted her face back up with my thumb, because I needed her looking at me, needed her to see exactly what she was doing to me. I kissed her again—slowing it down this time, like I was trying to make sense of her with my mouth instead of words.

"I don't have to go," I murmured against her lips, "but I can't promise I'll be able to stop whatever this is."

She didn't even hesitate. She leaned back in, lips crashing into mine, fingers burying themselves in the fabric of my shirt like she was afraid I'd vanish if she let go. When she broke away, her breath ghosted over my mouth. "Don't want you to." she admitted and that was it.

That was the match to the gasoline in my veins. Every bit of restraint I thought I had? Gone. She wanted me and honestly? Same.

I backed her into my room, kicking the door closed behind us. I couldn't think straight with her lips on mine, her hands tugging at my shirt like she couldn't stand another second of fabric between us.

"Off," she demanded, pulling at my riding jacket. "All of it."

I shrugged it off, letting it fall to the floor. "You're bossy when you're turned on."

"And you're talking too much," she shot back, already working on my belt.

I caught her wrists, pinning them gently against the wall. "Slow down, babygirl."

Her breath hitched at the name, pupils dilating. "Link..."

"You know how long I've wanted this?" I whispered against her neck, trailing kisses down to her collarbone, careful to avoid the mark Theo had left. That still stung, but in this moment, with her beneath my hands like this, I couldn't bring myself to care. "Every time you walked around in my shirt, every time you fell asleep on my shoulder during movie nights..." I nipped at her ear. "It's been torture."

"Why didn't you say something sooner?" She gasped as my hands slid under her shirt, tracing the curve of her waist.

I laughed against her skin. "You've been driving me insane for years, Mils. I thought I was being obvious."

Her hands found my hair, tugging me back to look at her. The vulnerability in her eyes knocked the breath from my lungs.

"I need to know this isn't just jealousy," she whispered, "That this isn't because of Theo."

I pressed my forehead to hers. "Baby, I wanted you long before Theo was even in the picture, I've wanted you since fucking middle school and I thought you knew that. I have personally sabotaged every fucking relationship until now, because no one has ever deserved you." I pressed a kiss to her lips, "You're my fucking everything."

"You mean that?" she whispered, her fingers still tangled in my hair.

"Every word." I kissed her again, softer this time, trying to pour years of wanting into a single moment. "You think I buy hardcover books for just anyone?" It was half joking, half not, those books were expensive. I'd filled an entire library for her, plus what was in her room and signed copies. It was the one way I knew I could get her attention at first—then it just kept going until she was out of space.

She laughed against my mouth, a sound that sent heat straight through me. "I thought you were just being nice."

"I'm nice to everyone, Mils, but I'm only in love with you."

The words slipped out before I could stop them. Shit. Too much, too fast, but her expression didn't falter—instead, she looked like she might actually cry. Her hands cupped my face, trembling slightly, and she pulled me down to her, her breath grazing my lips.

"Lincoln," she whispered against my lips, "I've loved you for so long I don't remember what it's like not to."

Something fractured in my chest—relief, maybe, or joy so sharp it felt like pain. This was the moment I'd been waiting on forever, I kissed her like I was trying to pour every unspoken word, every longing glance, every moment I'd held back into her.

I lifted her up, her legs wrapping around my waist as I carried her to the bed. Her weight against me, her breath on my neck, the soft sounds she made when I laid her down—it was overwhelming. Real. Finally real.

I couldn't even be mad anymore.

She hesitated, "Why are you so mad about us then?" Us. I knew she was talking about Theo. I wasn't mad about Theo, not really, I loved Theo. I did, there was no denying that, but maybe Coop was right. I was feeling left out.

I groaned, shifting my weight on top of her, staring at the green waves in her hazel eyes, "I'm mad you didn't tell me. That I had to find out from your location instead of you or him."

"I'm sorry, I—should have said something. Both of us should have, you were probably worried when I didn't come home... I'm sorry." She pushed my hair back, her hand slipping down my face to cup my cheeks. "I'm sorry we didn't tell you, that wasn't cool."

I tucked a strand of auburn hair behind her ear, in the dim light it looked brown. "Just communicate with me, if this is going to work with all of us—you can't just disappear with one of us and expect the others to be okay." I kissed her lips, then her cheek, then down to her neck—the opposite side Theo had marked.

She reached for my pants and I pulled away slightly, "Are you sure?" I asked, hovering above her, searching her face for any hesitation.

She nodded, pulling me down. "I've never been more sure of anything."

"Babygirl," I whispered against her throat, "I'm going to make you regret waiting so long." The way she shuddered beneath me sent a shockwave of goosebumps down my entire body.

I pinned her wrists above her head with one hand, my other tracing down her side, mapping her body to my memory.

"Link," she gasped, as I brushed my thumb over her already hard nipple.

"Shhh," I said as I pressed my lips to her neck again, littering the side in wet kisses.

"Fine, fine." she whispered, pursing her lips in anticipation. I didn't miss her eye roll either. It made me want to bite her pretty little lips—pull it between my teeth and hear how she sounded when pain mixed with pleasure—just for the sass.

"Good girl," I murmured, and the way her eyes fluttered closed at those two simple words made me realize how much power I had over her in this moment.

Power she was willingly giving me.

Fucking finally, took her long enough.

I leaned down to kiss her again, slower this time, savoring the taste of her. When I pulled back I nipped at her bottom lip, her lips were swollen, her cheeks flushed. "Look at you," My voice sounded rough even to me. "So pretty for me."

Her breath hitched and she batted her eyelashes. "Only for you."

"You and I both know that's not completely true." I nipped at her neck, biting down so that she gasped. "But it's okay, I can share when I want to."

I felt her body tense beneath me at those words, a shiver running through her that had nothing to do with cold. I tightened my grip on her wrists, watching her pupils dilate further.

"You like that idea, don't you?" I whispered against her ear, dragging my tongue along the shell. "The thought of all of us taking turns with you?"

She whimpered, trying to arch up against me, but I kept her pinned. I wanted her to feel my control, to understand that even if I shared her, she was still mine in this moment. "Answer me, babygirl."

Her eyes darted away for a second, like she was embarrassed by her answer, "Yes," she breathed, her voice trembling. "But right now I just want you."

I smiled against her skin. "Good answer." I released her wrists but gave her a warning look, her eyes held anything but caution though, in fact she looked more like a menace than I'd ever seen.

Her hands immediately went to the hem of my shirt, tugging it upward. I caught her wrists again, this time pinning them to either side of her head on the mattress. The flash of surprise in her eyes—followed by that telltale darkening of her pupils—sent heat straight through me.

"I didn't say you could touch me yet," I said, keeping my voice deliberately low, controlled. "Did I?"

Her chest was rising and falling rapidly, she shook her head, "No, Sir."

"That's right." I leaned down, letting my lips hover above hers without making contact. I shifted both her wrists to one of my hands, keeping them firmly secured above her head.

Fuck, Millie was going to be the death of me, literally my heart was beating so fast I thought it might give out. I took a deep breath in, I didn't have time for fucking nerves right now.

"Lincoln, I fucking want you in me." She whined, and that? That was bold.

Her blunt demand sent a jolt straight through me. Something shifted in my chest—dark, possessive, hungry. I tightened my grip on her wrists, bringing my face close enough to feel her ragged breath against my lips.

"Is that how you ask for what you want?" I growled, my free hand sliding under her shirt, trailing up her ribs. "Try again."

She squirmed beneath me, those wide eyes locked on mine. "Please," she whispered, softer this time, more vulnerable. "Please, Link."

I smiled, slow and deliberate. "Better, but still not good enough."

I released her wrists, but before she could move, I gripped her jaw firmly, tilting her face up to mine. The way she immediately went pliant under my touch and it sent heat through my veins.

"If you want me inside you, baby girl, you're going to have to earn it." I finished, watching her eyes widen at the challenge.

But fuck—the way she was looking at me right now, all surrender and need, was breaking my resolve faster than I wanted to admit. I'd spent so long denying myself this, denying us this, that now I was drowning in her.

My control was slipping. I was supposed to be teaching her a lesson, making her beg, showing her exactly what she'd been missing by waiting so long. But the longer I looked at her, the more I realized I was the one who'd been missing everything.

"Please," she whispered again, her voice cracking with genuine need. "Lincoln, I want you."

That did it. That fucking broke me, all reasoning to take this slow and savor her wnet out the window, no fucking use when she was begging for me. I crashed my lips against hers, no longer able to maintain the facade of cool control. My hands were everywhere—in her hair, on her waist, slipping under her shirt. The carefully constructed wall I'd built between us over the years crumbled completely, leaving nothing but raw need.

"Fuck," I gasped against her mouth. "I can't—I had this whole thing in my head about how I'd do this."

She arched up into me, her body responding to my words like they were a physical touch. "Link, it's just me—just Millie—you've seen me at my worst. You don't need a plan with m—"

I kissed her again, it was all needed to hear, I tore at her clothes, desperate to feel her skin against mine. All that discipline, all that restraint I'd been so proud of seconds ago? Gone. Completely fucking gone. Because this was Millie—my Millie—finally in my bed, looking at me like I was everything she'd ever wanted.

How could I possibly hold back?

I stripped her shirt off, then my own, groaning at the first press of her bare skin against mine. "You're so beautiful," I breathed, taking her in completely.

"Link, fuck me." She groaned, her head dropping back in frustration. I completely lost it, the way she was looking at me—pleading, demanding, trusting—shredded whatever composure I had left.

This was Millie. My Millie. My best friend.

The girl I'd watched laugh over stupid movies while we threw popcorn at each other, who'd fallen asleep in my lap more times than I could count, she'd seen me at my absolute worst and stayed to help me pick up the pieces. She was everything I'd ever wanted.

"Fuck, I love you," I growled, yanking her shorts down her legs, dragging my mouth across her stomach as I went.

I'd spent years imagining this moment, planning how I'd take my time with her, how I'd worship every inch of her body, make her beg until she couldn't remember anyone else's name. Now that she was here, trembling beneath me, all those carefully constructed fantasies dissolved into pure need.

I needed her like fucking oxygen, I might actually die without her. She really was half my heart, I'd spent years telling myself soulmates could be platonic. I'd been content with it, I'd settled for a best friend because I didn't want to ever lose her.

My fingers hooked into the elastic of her thong, dragging it down. Her hands went to my hair, pulling me up to her. I winced slightly, but crashed my lips to hers anyway, my fingers going straight to her center.

Fuck, she was soaked already.

"Lincoln," she whimpered, her hips lifting to press against my hand. "Please don't make me wait."

The desperation in her voice shattered what little restraint I had left. I'd been holding back for years—denying myself, denying us—and I couldn't take another second. I unzipped my pants, kicking them off along with my boxers. She reached for me, her fingers wrapping around me, and I nearly came undone right there.

"Fuck," I hissed, grabbing her wrist.

She grinned up at me, all flushed cheeks and mischief. "Can't handle me, Lincoln?"

I growled, pinning her hand above her head again. "We'll see who can't handle who."

I positioned myself at her entrance, watching her eyes widen as I pushed in slowly. She gasped, her nails digging into my shoulders as I filled her completely.

"Fuck, Millie..." I groaned, stilling for a moment to let her adjust, but she was already wrapping her legs around my waist to pull me in deeper.

I started moving, trying to maintain some semblance of control, but the sight of her beneath me had trying to pull every moan and little noise out of her. Years of wanting crashed down around me, and I couldn't hold back anymore.

"Link... Can I—" She let out a breathy little whimper, "Can we switch positions?"

"Fuck, yeah, we can." Thank fucking God because I needed a second anyway.

She pulled a pillow down lower and laid on it, so her ass was in the air more. She flipped her hair to her back before looking back at me, a mischievous smile playing on her lips.

I took my time for a second, trailing my hands up her back before kissing up her spine. My right hand tangled into her hair, grabbing at the roots and pulling her back just a little bit, enough to have her arching further into me.

I picked up the pace, driving into her with everything I had. Her moans grew louder and less controlled, I let my weight fall onto my arm as I covered her mouth and nose with my left hand.

The way she tightened at that? The little flutter that gripped me more, pulling me deeper in? My girl liked breath play. Her eyes rolled back as I counted in my head. I knew my limits—I'd learned them with others—but with Millie, everything felt amplified. More intense. More real.

I released her mouth, watching her gasp for air, her pupils blown wide.

"Do that again," she whispered, voice ragged.

I growled, covering her mouth and nose once more as I drove into her harder. The way she tightened around me, the way her body tensed and trembled—it was fucking intoxicating.

When I released her again, she was practically vibrating beneath me, so close to the edge. "Link, I'm—"

"Not yet," I commanded, slowing my pace. "Look at me first." I turned her chin to me, so she was half looking at me. Her eyes locked with mine, hazy with pleasure but still so present, I moved my right hand down to circle her clit and she pushed into me, "That's my girl." I whispered, the space between us carrying my words like a live wire.

I paused, feeling my own release pulling at me, "I need to know where I can come, baby girl. Do you want me to come inside you or pull out?"

"I—" she paused, biting her lip as her eyes fluttered back. "Inside."

My heart hammered against my ribs as she said those words. The trust in them, the implication. I couldn't help the possessive growl that escaped me. "You sure?" I asked, needing to hear it one more time, even as I felt myself getting closer.

"Yes," she breathed, her fingers digging into my shoulders. "Please, Link." That was all I needed. I picked up the pace, driving into her with everything I had. The way she cried out my name, the way her body tightened around me—it was too much.

I buried my face in her neck, breathing in her scent as I came undone, spilling inside her with a groan that felt torn from deep in my chest.

I looked at her face, unable to hide my grin. "They're going to be so pissed at me."

"Doubt it," She laughed, "You all say that, but then there's all this weird sexual tension between all of you."

I rolled onto my side, she did the same so we were face to face. Her skin was still flushed, hair a mess around her face, looking more beautiful than I'd ever seen her, with the exception of the matte of hair in the back of her head—my fault, my bad.

"Theo's important to me too, but you knew that—" I trailed off, struggling to find the right words.

She grinned, "Clearly dude, you've been fucking him for months before all this shit."

I watched her eyes twinkle with mischief, and I couldn't help but laugh. "Yeah, I know, but this is different."

"How?" She asked, propping herself up on her elbow, looking at me with genuine curiosity.

I ran my fingers through her hair, trying to organize my thoughts. "With Theo, it's always been casual. We both knew what it was. But you..." I paused, struggling to find the right words. "You're not casual to either of us."

She went quiet, her eyes searching mine. I could feel my heart hammering against my ribs, wondering if I'd said too much. "So what does that mean for all of us?" She finally asked, her voice small.

"I have no fucking clue," I admitted, pulling her closer. "But I know I don't want to lose anyone."

Her head rested on my chest, "Are you okay with this? With sharing me? Sharing Theo?"

I sighed, fuck, here we go. "Coop is a good guy, I don't mind him."

"You don't mind him?" She asked, raising her head slightly to look at me, a smirk playing on her face, this little shit—of course she would assume that I'd eventually want Coop too. Maybe she was right? Maybe, I don't know… Coop was Coop.

"I don't mind sharing you," I corrected, pulling her closer to me. "He makes you happy. I can see it. And I'm not gonna lie, I kinda like the dude too."

She raised her eyebrows at me, that little smirk still playing on her lips. "Oh? Do tell."

"Don't push it," I laughed, rolling my eyes. "I just mean he's good for you. He balances you out in ways I don't."

"And Theo?" she asked, her voice softer now.

I sighed, my hand trailing up and down her back. "Theo is… complicated, but in a good way." I didn't know how to explain that Theo felt like mine in a way that was different from how Millie felt like mine.

Both intense, both real, but different wavelengths of the same feeling.

Coop

I hadn't even loaded my game fully before both Theo and Link were inviting me to the party chat.

I tugged my headset on, "What are we playing boys?"

"Apex, I'm already in," Theo's voice crackled through my headset. "Fair warning, Link's been camping with a sniper all morning."

"Oh fuck off, it's called strategic positioning," Link shot back, but I could hear the laugh in his voice.

I snorted as my screen loaded into the map. "So that's what we're calling it now?"

"Better than your run-and-gun bullshit," Link said. "You died seventeen times in our last match."

"Yeah, but I had the most kills," Theo reminded him, selecting my load out. "And you kept trying to distract me!"

"By one," Link interjected. "And you stole at least three of mine." I heard Link huff into the mic. I could practically see him rolling his eyes. It felt good—normal—to be trash-talking like nothing had changed, like we weren't all tangled up in whatever this four-way thing was becoming.

We played several rounds, Theo was indeed off his game and kept dying. He did have the highest kill count every time though, so kudos for that I guess.

I checked my phone during a snack break, Millie still hadn't texted me back. "Link, has Millie said anything to you?" I asked, trying not to break up the game flow and banter.

"She's not purposely ignoring you, I promise. She's in her room laying on a heating pad and binge reading a new series I'll no doubt have to buy the hard covers for in a few days. Last I checked she was halfway through book two, but she's probably on book three now."

"Oh? What's she reading?" I asked, maybe I could read it and we'd have something to discuss.

"God of something, don't really know. Some dark romance shit." Link sighed, "God forbid a girl have three boyfriends and still have her dark romance reads."

It gave me an idea, probably not a good one, but fuck it. "Well, I think I have our Valentine's Day plans..." I chuckled, "Y'all in?"

"Why do I feel like you're going to have us try to kidnap her?" Theo groaned, "I mean I'm sure we'd all be down—but that might be too far."

"Love the enthusiasm for that, now that we know exactly where your mind went—what are you thinking Cooper?" Link asked and I cringed at my first name and not the nickname.

"I mean, similar honestly... let me work through what we need, but I was thinking masks and all that? Girls go fucking feral for that in the book community right?" I suggested, listening to the dead silence from the other two.

"So you wanna share her together?" Link asked after a minute, his voice barely a whisper, probably to keep Millie from overhearing, "Funny you say that, because she said something about it last night."

She what? My eyes widened, "Did she now?"

"Link, what happened last night?" Theo asked, I heard his music turn down.

"Not for me to tell, ask her." Link sounded fucking smug.

My mouth dropped open, "Did you two both sleep with her yesterday?"

Theo made a choked sound, "NO! Not together, no, I mean I did... she spent the night and we woke up and—"

"Link, did you?" I cut Theo off, I already knew it was going to happen with Theo, that was unavoidable. As soon as he took her to work and he said they were going to his house after, I knew.

Link chuckled, "Ask her. She's your girlfriend."

It was Theo who spoke up, "You better be glad I'm not over there right now. I'd smack the shit out of you."

"That is domestic abuse sir." Link pointed out, not helpful in the slightest, but his voice wavered slightly.

Theo continued, his voice not cracking the slightest, "And you're acting like we're not all supposed to be communicating properly, just because you and Coop aren't sleeping together doesn't mean you can disregard him." he paused, "Now answer the question because I'm curious."

"We did, fuck Theo, possessive voice and everything. I'm impressed, baby boy." Link said, "Oh fuck, Mils—you scared me."

Millie's voice was barely audible, "Apologize right now you fucking heathen."

"I'm sorry Coop, I'm in a mood apparently."

I laughed, because leave it to Millie to call his ass out.

"Hey guys, I can smack the back of his head if you want me too?" Her voice was closer now.

"Hey!!!" Link said, there was rustling over the mic, probably dodging Millie. "Are you guys coming over tomorrow?" he asked, once the rustling stopped.

"Yeah, I'll be there." Theo's voice rang out.

"Coop you coming over too? We can play a run through of one of the interactive dark horror games I have when they go to work?"

"You know, for someone who was just the biggest pain in my ass, now you wanna hang out?"

Link laughed and Theo chuckled, "Fine, fine, I was being a smug piece of shit—my bad. Just come play the game."

"Don't let him fool you, he doesn't wanna play it alone." Millie giggled, "He wants to play them, but he's low-key afraid of the dark."

"Awwww, who's baby boy coded now?" I snorted, laughing.

"Never mind, you're not invited anymore." Link said, his voice flat.

"I'll be there you big baby." I said, because if he wanted to play a run through of the game I'd help. I didn't have anything better to do, aside from sit at home alone with my cat.

Millie

I really didn't want to go to work. I mean come on, Coop and Link were both at the house. We were all cuddle piled up on the couch, it was comfortable and warm and it was fucking cold outside. I didn't want to go. I even stomped my feet like a child throwing a temper tantrum when Theo practically pulled me off the couch.

"One more day and then we're free for two days."

"Just because I go in does not mean I'm doing anything. I'm taking my Kindle and lying on the couch." I studied his face as he gave me the most disappointed dad look ever, "And I'm bringing a blanket."

"Millie, no."

"Don't dad me right now, I want to call out."

"I'm about to fucking daddy you if you don't quit acting like a brat."

"Eat rocks Theo."

I heard him exhale loudly before closing Link's door.

Good, fucking shit head, pulling me from my nest of warmth for a cold ass club I didn't want to go to, but alas... responsibilities.

I put my hair in a bun, because even washing my hair felt like a fucking crime right now and took a quick shower, throwing on sweat pants and a hoodie. I wasn't fucking with a bra, I wasn't even going to attempt to do much makeup tonight either as I slathered on a pretty light brown eye shadow and mascara. Done. I wasn't fucking with it.

I pulled my hair down from the lopsided bun and did a half up half down pony tail, good enough, because I wasn't in the mood to curl or straighten. It was a fucking Wednesday. They probably didn't even need me.

Fire me for all I care.

I shoved my most comfortable set into the bag, a little black micro bikini and a fishnet body suit, I wasn't fucking with the pole today.

I'd do stage if I had too, by that I mean I'd lay on stage and shake my ass for three whole songs if it came down to it. Maybe just lay there and clack my heels obnoxiously loud. Whatever.

If Theo thought I was a problem when I was doing my job, he might actually hate me tonight.

He knocked on my door before opening it, taking one look at me and groaning. "Fix your fucking attitude, it's radiating off of you."

"Fix your fucking attitude." I snapped back as he took my bag from my hands.

Link and Coop were watching us carefully, "You two going to kill each other tonight?"

"Maybe." I grumbled as Theo pressed a kiss to Link's lips and then froze when Coop grabbed his arm and pulled him down to his lips as well.

Jealousy panged through me and I don't even know why, maybe it's because I was mad at Theo right now.

"Don't pout Princess, I'm sure they want kisses from you too." Theo smirked.

Link grinned between the two of us, before giving me kissy lips, he was really living up to his golden retriever vibe right now. I flung myself down onto Coop, wrapping my arms around him.

"I don't wanna go." I whined, peppering his neck with kisses, *please, please, please fight back for me.*

He kissed my lips gently, his hands cupping my cheeks gently, "One more night."

I groaned, moving to my next target. "Come here whiny." Link said, opening his arms, I slid into his embrace easily, wrapping myself around him.

"I don't wanna," my voice broke and his grip tightened on me, as he looked at Theo. "Do I have too?" I knew if any of them would agree it'd be Link. It wasn't manipulation if the thought of work really did make me want to cry.

"Theo—" Link started, but Theo crossed his arms, cutting him off with a glare.

Fuck.

"Okay... Okay..." I groaned, pressing my lips to Link's softly as he pulled me closer, intensifying the kiss.

I felt Theo smack the back of his head, "Come on, let her go. I'm going to be late."

I detangled myself from Link and pressed another kiss to Coop's lips before stomping my way out of the living room. Theo yanked open the door and waved me through.

I went to open the car door but he stopped me, turning me to face him and pushing my back against the car door with a thump. "Knock your shit off, play nice tonight. When we get home I'll treat you exactly the way you want me too, Princess." The fire in his eyes sent heat straight to my lower belly.

"Promise?"

"I know whiny bratty Millie way too well by now."

"Correction, you know bratty Jade." My gaze fell to his lips and I saw him fighting the urge to kiss me.

"One and the same if you look hard enough." His lips crashed to mine, his hand pulling me closer to him by my hips. "Fuck, I wanted to stay home to you know." His breath ghosted over my face and he kissed me again before pulling me into a hug that had me melting into his chest as he rubbed circles on my back.

"We can still call off." I suggested, hoping he'd say yes, he exhaled harshly and I almost thought he'd give in.

Instead he stepped away and opened my door, "We're already late, get in the car."

"Fine, but this better be worth it." I huffed, sliding into the seat and buckling myself in.

By the time we got to work, Jonah had his arms crossed waiting for Theo. "My fault, he picked me up." I said, aiming for damage control.

"Go get dressed, you have someone here for you already."

"We literally just opened!" There was no fucking way, what person in their right mind was coming here without messaging to see if I was even coming in tonight. There goes my book and blanket session on the back couch.

"Something about bottle service and seeing you on social media, he's the young one at the bar."

I hated the younger guys, ughhhhhh, gross. They always wanted what I wasn't willing to give. Fuck my life. I hate it here, I'm going to quit. I'm going to get a real fucking job and ditch these fucking heels.

I debated saying that, but decided that was not a decision I needed to make right now. I huffed as I headed to the dressing room, throwing on my outfit for the night. Pulling the fishnet sleeves on and adjusting it fully before sliding my heels on. I spritzed myself with perfume and walked out without even checking how I looked.

Fuck it.

After I signed in with Jonah, I slid into the barstool next to the unidentified man, who looked to be about mid-twenties. "You must be Jade." He grinned, his eyes raking over me, I didn't like how he looked at me. Which was saying something because men were men, they liked to look.

"I am and you are?" I asked, offering him my hand in greeting, trying to keep my face bright and smiley.

"Weston, but you can call me Wes if you want."

"Nice to meet you Wes, where you from?" I asked, tilting my head slightly when I looked at him, playing the naive little thing I channeled when I felt threatened. I didn't want to show fear to a man that could thrive on it.

"I'm from Florida, here on a little work trip." He attempted, holding eye contact, and while I could do that with most I didn't like the way this made me feel, so I looked down almost immediately.

"So, I take it you've never been here?" I asked, fidgeting with my hands, normally by now I would have already made more physical contact with them—either sitting my hand on their leg, holding their hand, or rubbing their arm.

"Nope, first time. You gonna show me a good time?" I definitely caught how he said that, so either this man was a cop or he was just completely unaware that this was not the place and I was not the fucking one.

"I might," I laughed, but it was fake. "You want a tour?" I asked, offering my hand.

He nodded, downing his beer in one go before standing and taking my hand. "I heard you have showers and hot tubs?"

"We do! You wanna check that out first?" I asked, sending him a wink.

"Yeah, I want to see the hot tubs." He squeezed my hand, following only slightly behind, I knew he was staring at my ass just by the distance.

I brought him to the back, ignoring Jonah almost completely, just a simple nod to the camera monitors so he'd watch more closely. I loved that he knew, loved that I didn't have to say anything.

"We have three, welcome to hot tub row." I chuckled, doing the grand gesture with my hands.

"Which one is the most private?" He asked and I felt my stomach roll a little. I'd normally try to sell the one furthest in the back, but I didn't even attempt to push for that today.

"They're all pretty far away from civilization, it's whichever they want to put us in honestly." I shrugged, his gaze flicked to me. "Sorry, I'm a little tired. I woke up super early, give me a little bit and I'm sure my energy drinks will kick in." I laughed, trying to cover by running my hand across his back.

That settled his energy, just a bit, I watched him relax. "How long do we get?"

"An hour or longer, but you pay by the hour."

"That's perfect actually." He grinned, "Do I pay you directly or the guy at the front?"

"Yeah, we gotta go by the VIP booth, I'm going to go check in with the DJ to make sure he didn't already add me to rotation." I grabbed his hand and prompted him to follow me back out. "They'll give you swim trunks to change into after the tub is filled."

When we got to the VIP desk, the man talked to Jonah, I trailed my fingers across his back, "I'll be right back, love."

I wasn't sure if Theo could see the discontent on my face or if he was just reading into it as me not wanting to be here. "What's wrong? He wants a hot tub, you'll make money."

I leaned against the booth's wall, hugging myself tightly, "Can you just make sure someone has eyes on me at all times, please?" I didn't mean for it to come out like that, I tried not to sound whiny, I wasn't sure he would take me seriously given my antics from earlier.

"You're shaking." He noted, looking over his shoulder and stepping closer to me, practically pulling me into the little booth and shielding us both from view.

"I just have a bad feeling and I don't want to be here." A tear slid down my face and yeah, maybe I was overreacting, but I couldn't stop it.

"We're not busy, there's no one here. I'll keep eyes on you at all times and let Jonah know how you feel too." He tilted my chin up to look at him, his fingers brushing over my wet cheeks. "It's going to be fine, baby."

My breath hitched, *baby?* Where had that come from?

He must have noticed, because he shook his head slightly, "I've got you, I promise. Jonah and I won't let anything happen to you. Trust us, Princess."

I didn't resist the urge to hug him, we were hidden anyway, so I quickly threw my arms around his waist and squeezed tightly before forcing myself away from him. "I trust you."

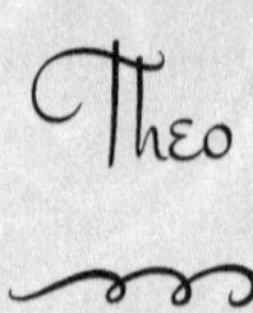

That motherfucker wasn't even back there for fifteen minutes before he fucking tried her, I know because I watched her smack his hands away. Not once, but twice. She didn't use the signal though, so she had it. At least I hoped she had it, Jonah would kick my ass if I went back there for no reason.

A girl came up and signed the sheet for stage and I just waved her off. There wasn't anyone here anyway so I wasn't worried. She locked eyes with the camera, that wasn't the signal and she knew that, I'd wait for her until I couldn't. She backed away from him, her face stern as she talked. I couldn't hear what she was saying, but he looked mad.

I looked over at Jonah, he nodded, he'd seen it. That was all I needed. I took off, Jonah still had eyes on the camera, pulling Toby over to watch the cameras as he went back with me, his footsteps echoing behind mine.

When security runs, it's never good. Just in case you were wondering.

I watched Millie shove him away from her and that's all it took. "I suggest you back up now." The way my voice sounded scared me, but I'd never seen Millie have to get physical with a customer. It rarely happened here, most people weren't stupid enough with all the cameras.

The guy looked unimpressed, slinking back to the corner, "Here's what's gonna happen, you are going to apologize to her." Jonah stated, pointing at Millie. "You're also going to tip her for being a fucking asshole, and since you ran card I'll give you the option to tip her in front of me or I'm tacking on a fee that goes straight to her anyway and you won't like that number."

Jonah looked at me, shaking his head. I knew he was telling me to keep it in check, deal with Millie, not the fucker I wanted to throttle for trying her.

"Jade, come on." I held my hand out, taking her shaking hand in mine and helping her out of the hot tub. She didn't let go as I grabbed a towel and wrapped it around her. I knocked on the dressing room door, "If there's anyone uncovered, go to the side section. I'm coming in."

Gracie took one look at us as we came in and threw on her hoodie before quickly coming over to us, "What happened?"

"Fucking handsy jackass." Millie said, tying her hair up in a bun. Only the ends were wet. "Can you get my clothes please?" she asked Gracie as she dried off, before turning her attention to me.

Millie met my eyes, "You can go, I'm getting changed and I'll just come sit with you."

Gracie gave me a small smile as she handed Millie her clothes. "I've got her Theo."

I walked out to see Jonah yelling about no refunds and learning to respect women and pointing at the door.

Fuck, I should have just let her stay home.

"Jade is getting dressed, she wants to sit with me but I'm gonna call her roommate to come get her." I let Toby and Jonah know, but Toby was watching down the hall as Millie and Gracie walked up towards us.

"You can leave if you need to." Jonah said softly, looking from me to the girls.

Oh yeah, he definitely knew.

I shook my head, "Nah, I can stay. She'll be in good hands until I can get there tonight."

Jonah nodded as the girls came up, end of discussion. I'm sure he'd bring it up again, but not right now.

Millie shifted towards me immediately, "Is he gone?"

"Yeah, had a bit of a screaming match, but he left what was left in his wallet." Jonah gave me a look that said he definitely didn't do it willingly.

Millie grinned, "Jonah, did you physically take it from him?"

He gave her a sly grin, "I might have and said I'd show the footage to cops if he said anything."

Millie held her hand out and he passed her a stack of hundreds. Her mouth dropped open, "Dude, you fucking robbed him."

“He was going to do a lot worse.” Jonah shrugged, “We’ve got you, all of you, no matter what.”

Millie flipped through it handing me, Toby and Jonah each three hundred. I took it just to appease her, but as soon as we were away from them I shoved it in her pocket. “Theo, no, this is still your job.”

“Mils, it’s fine.” I whispered, pulling her into the booth with me, wrapping an arm around her waist and tugging her close to me.

“Theo, we’re at work.” She tried to move away at the same time as I felt her lean her head back on me.

“Baby, no one can see you and I don’t care.” I started inputting the girls stage set list, just doing my job and letting her self-regulate with me. “Match my breathing, Princess.” I murmured against her hair.

Once I felt her calming down I reached for my phone, texting Link.

Theo: Come get your girl.

He took a few minutes to respond, but once he did I let Millie see it.

Link: Bike or car?

Millie shifted against me, “Bike.”

Theo: Princess says bike. Be careful, love you.

Link: THEODORE—did you just????

Even Millie looked at me wide eyed. “What he’s getting on the bike, I do love him.”

“I didn’t say anything.” She said, snuggling closer to me.

“Awww, cute but Jonah took a screenshot of you two. Just so you know.” Gracie said, writing her stage name down on the stage list. “You heading out or staying right here all snuggled up?”

“Link’s coming to get me.” Millie said softly.

“Link as in hot best friend that drives a motorcycle Link?” Gracie asked, looking at me, more specifically my arm still holding Millie to me.

“Link is our boyfriend.” I said, enjoying the shock that crossed her face, I think she expected me to be jealous or something, as if Link would ever make me jealous—she was his first.

Her eyes widened, comically wide actually, "Oh?! Link is both of your boyfriends, what happened to Coop?"

"Also our boyfriend, but not Link's boyfriend." Millie said, biting her lip and, fuck, I needed this shift to be over already.

Gracie grinned, licking her lips, "Interesting turn of events, but maybe save some dick for the rest of us." I watched her eyes flick over to the corner, but didn't think anything of it.

"Oh shut up, get on stage." Millie said, peeling my arm off of her, "I'll be right back." I didn't miss the way she squeezed my thigh as she pushed past me.

My eyes followed her as she went to the VIP booth and pulled out the three hundred she'd tried to give me. She got a bunch of ones and Gracie practically bolted to the stage.

I knew Link didn't ask her for rent, but she should really save her fucking money, but she still threw it on Gracie making it rain all over the stage. Toby was over in a flash picking it up off the floor and tossing it on stage.

I didn't miss the way he watched Gracie, I also didn't miss the wink she sent his way. Oh, so maybe we weren't the only two hiding a little secret.

When Millie came back over to me, I couldn't help but grin, "We're not the only two fucking around."

"What? What do you mean?" She asked, confusion marring her pretty little face.

"Toby and Iris, they've got something going on." I nodded my head towards the two of them.

"NO! No way, she would have told me." Millie looked at Toby who was still watching Gracie intently. "Well, shit. Maybe you're right."

I'm always right, Princess.

"On My Door - Gio Mkl"

I don't know how Coop and I had gotten in this position, but I was currently laying on his leg while we played, and he just let me. Neither of us said anything, but given how clingy Theo was most of the time something told me that Coop was used to this kind of platonic intimacy.

I had been laying on him for a good hour at this point, he had even brushed his fingers through my hair a few times during my turn to make decisions on the game, and I wasn't complaining. I was a whore for physical touch, truly it was my love language in general.

It was almost like he was grounding me, especially when he'd said he'd played this game before and he knew where the jump scares were. His fingers brushed through my hair right before it would happen, pulling on the ends slightly in warning. I wasn't going to stop it, I'm a whore for attention and head pets.

When my phone lit up we both froze. I half expected it to be Millie begging me to come get her, but seeing Theo tell me to come get her I knew she was either having a super emotional night or something happened between them.

Bike meant she wanted to clear her head, that was my fault, I'd taught her that.

Fucking oops.

Coop looked over at my phone, his hand stilling in my hair. "Millie wants you to come get her?"

"Yeah, you can stay." I gave him a small smile even as he pulled his hand away quickly, "I'm sure she'll be excited you're still here. She really didn't want to leave us earlier, but she also wants the bike so she's got some shit on her mind."

I didn't miss the way he shifted away from me when I sat up, before pulling a blanket off the back of the couch. "I'll be here."

I went to pull on my gear, making sure to grab the extra helmet.

"Link?" My eyes flicked up to meet his, he was busying himself by browsing through the guest account on Netflix, which he wasn't just browsing he was editing the guest name to Coop.

I smirked at that but didn't say anything about it, I could pretend I didn't see it. "Yeah?" I asked, pulling my gloves on.

He turned towards me fully, his blue eyes brighter in the light of the tv screen. "Be careful, get both of you back here in one piece."

"Awww, you do care about me." I shot a wink his way, to which granted me an immediate eye roll. "Don't worry, I'm always careful."

Well, except the one time we pushed the bike to see how fast we could get it, but no one else needed to know that.

I made it to the club faster than I would have liked to admit.

Yes, I was speeding. Yes, I'm aware Millie got the speed notification.

Oh, *fuck*, that means Coop did too. *Eh, he'll be fine.*

I pushed past the front entrance, letting Toby wand me down and once he realized who I was he let me in without a door fee. He knew I wasn't staying long, I'd picked up Millie before.

Jonah pointed to the DJ booth and I poked my head in to find them basically fused together, his hand on her stomach holding her to him. "You don't look like you've been fighting." If anything, they looked more intimate than I'd ever seen them before.

"We didn't." Millie said, her eyebrows furrowing slightly.

"Then why?" I asked, crossing my arms.

If they weren't fighting, why did I need to pick her up?

I locked eyes with Theo who flushed red against his olive skin and let Millie detangle from him, she kissed his cheek and he turned at the last second to meet her lips for a brief second, ahh, yeah *cameras*.

"You ready?" I asked her, thoroughly enjoying Theo in his dress pants and button down. I didn't even try to hide my wandering eyes. Fuck, I knew why Millie fell for him, seeing him like this everyday? Mouth watering. "Love you too." I said to him, holding his gaze.

Theo sighed before looking between us, "Be careful, you two are two-thirds of my heart."

Millie turned to look at him, my eyes hadn't left his as is, but he looked genuinely distraught by us leaving. "I'll be careful." I promised.

"Do the speed limit." Theo warned.

I nodded giving him a silly little salute, "Yes sir."

Millie giggled slightly at my antics as we turned to leave the building. Millie waved at the blonde I figured was Gracie and then nodded at Jonah in what looked like thanks. She didn't say anything when I crouched down to pick her up like a backpack, just climbed on my back quietly. Something had definitely happened tonight.

I weaved through the streets, she was wrapped around me tightly, but it didn't feel like she was holding on because she was scared or anything. I didn't even go five over.

"Mils, you wanna talk about it?" I reached behind to hold her leg.

"Just a handsy customer and a fragile mindset, I really didn't want to go in and then an asshole customer." I felt her helmet lean against my back. "Can we just ride?" She asked, and damn it, she sounded exhausted.

I should have pushed Theo to let her stay home.

After a few minutes and a half a dozen ruminating thoughts, we were on the backroads to the house. "He called me baby tonight... that was different."

"You finally unlocked the mushy Theo I see." I chuckled, slowing down as we pulled into the neighborhood. "Are we going to talk about the two-thirds of my heart comment?"

"I think I'm just going to bask in that actually." I could practically hear the smile on her face.

I put the bike in park and helped her off of it, she looked at Coop's car in the driveway. "Coop is still here?"

"Yeah, we were hanging out. I think he wanted to stay for when you got home." I locked up the bike, watching her yank off the helmet.

"He works tomorrow morning."

I frowned as I pulled my helmet off, taking hers from her, "He cares about you, he knew you wanted to stay home. We kinda figured we'd all pile in your room tonight."

"We? As in you too?" She gave me this look, like she was trying to figure something out

"That's the plan." I looked at her, "Do not—"

"Didn't plan on it, but thank you." Millie lips brushed mine.

Millie went in first, punching in the key code to the door pad. "Coop! You stayed." She barreled into his arms and I felt a tinge of jealousy as he wrapped her into him and held her to him.

"Yeah, I figured I'd stay since you looked like you were about to cry earlier." Coop said, kissing her temple.

"Can we all go lay down? I'll tell you what happened?" Millie looked between us, "I'm honestly exhausted."

I followed them to her room, plopping down on the side closest to the wall, all the way over so if Theo came over after work he could fit. Millie laid in between us.

"This guy was giving me the fucking ick from the moment I saw him, but he wanted a hot tub. I kinda broke down and cried in front of Theo, told him I needed him and Jonah to watch us because I was scared." She paused, lying on Coop's chest. I wrapped myself around her, my fingers brushing Coop's side. "He got too handsy, I didn't even have to signal and Theo and Jonah were already there. Theo saw me shove him off of me after I'd smacked his hand several times already. I thought Theo was going to murder him."

I took a deep breath, I knew she was in a safe space but still, it made me uncomfortable with how fast something bad could happen to her. "When I got there they were snuggled up in the DJ booth, he was holding her to his chest." I grinned over at Coop.

"Hey! He helped me breathe." She chuckled, "He also called me baby instead of Princess, which was cute as fuck." She sighed, her hand coming up to Coop's neck to tangle in his hair. "OH!!! Jonah stole all the money from his wallet and gave it to me, then threatened to show the cops the footage if he said anything." Her voice sounded sleepy, like she was finally letting herself relax.

"I fucking love Jonah." I laughed and she jumped slightly. I pressed a gentle kiss to her shoulder in apology.

"Someone text Theo the door code." Millie sighed as I watched her eyes close against Coop's chest.

"He's already got it babygirl."

"Make sure he knows to come lay with us." Coop met my eyes,

holding my gaze for a second, I couldn't figure out what he was thinking. "Goodnight golden retriever." He reached his hand to pat my head like I was a damn dog.

"I think I'm more of an orange cat, but okay—goodnight to you too I guess."

"I have an orange cat, you are not an orange cat."

"Why are you two so awkward around each other? Did you two have like a moment or something?" Millie asked quietly, when we didn't answer she lifted her head up to look at both of us. "Wait—did you?"

Coop pulled her back down onto his chest, "No, we didn't. Now lay down."

Liar.

He'd played with my damn hair while I laid on him, it may have not been a romantic moment, but it was definitely out of the norm for us.

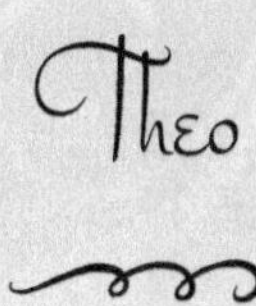

Thank fuck we closed early, once two rolled around and we only had a handful of customers left in the building Jonah called that shit immediately. We were closed thirty minutes later.

When I got to their house, I typed in the code and quietly shut the door behind me. Link told me to climb into bed with them but I really needed different clothes, so naturally I rummaged through Link's closet pulling on one of his shirts and a pair of sweatpants.

When I cracked open the door, Millie looked up from her spot on Coop's chest. She gave me a warm smile, she looked cozy between the two of them. I tracked Coop's arm that was thrown back over the pillow to Link's hair and my breath caught in my chest, because that I hadn't expected. Both of them were knocked out though, and Link was pressed right up against Millie, his arm wrapped around her waist. Which meant he was touching Coop too.

I tried not to think about the fact that Coop had stayed with Link while we went to work, there wasn't anything between them—just two guys thrown into a weird situation. Right?

I slid into the bed beside Coop, we hadn't talked about anything as far as this, but there really wasn't too much space so I turned on my side facing Millie.

Coop's arm immediately pulled me in closer and I felt myself relax into him, Millie watched the interaction sleepily brushing my hair back, "Thank you for tonight." She whispered, her hand cradling my face.

"Get some sleep, Princess." I breathed, just barely above a whisper. I nuzzled into Coop's warmth, the cold from the outside had soaked into my bones in the short walk from the car to the house.

He felt fucking good and sleep hit me like a train.

* * *

Waking up still tangled in everyone I tried to look at my phone to see what time it was, still pretty fucking early, why did I wake up?

Coop's alarm was going off. That's why. I poked his chest, "Dude, you gotta get up."

He pulled me closer, eyes still closed. "I'm staying right here."

Millie woke up slowly, rubbing her eyes and yawning, "Coop, you have to get up."

He groaned, attempting to turn and suffocate himself in the pillow. "You two are warm."

Millie pushed up, trying to detangle from Link's arm, he pulled her in tighter. His "Noooooo" was muffled though, because he was covered by her hair.

"We gotta let Coop up, Theo up." Millie shoved me slightly and I narrowed my eyes at her. I felt like death warmed over, why did he have to leave so early? I'd only gotten two hours of sleep max.

"Fine, fine." I basically rolled out of the bed so Coop could get up.

"Sorry, I have to go feed my hell cat and go to work." He said, pulling on his jeans and a hoodie.

Fuck, I forgot about Crooks. Yeah, okay, valid reason to leave early.

I crawled back into the bed, surprised when he leaned down to kiss my lips gently. "I'll be back later if you're still here." Then leaned across me to kiss Millie on the lips, she was already half back asleep.

Link stirred slightly, "That's rude. No good morning kiss for me?"

Coop rolled his eyes, ruffling Link's hair, "Not a chance, Ponyboy."

I snorted, leave it to Coop to drop a literary nickname on the golden boy.

I barely had enough time to change into my work scrubs and feed Crooks, that asshole had torn up the toilet paper and killed a mouse in the time I'd been gone.

My fault for leaving him here alone I guess.

I disposed of the mouse, left the toilet paper shreds everywhere because fuck it, I'd deal with it later. Dramatic ass fucking cat. Literally, why did Theo bring me this little shit fuck? If I knew Link wouldn't fucking kill me, I'd give Millie the cat since he very obviously likes her more.

Fucking unruly beast.

I put down a can of wet food into his little fish bowl and he rubbed against my legs as I scraped the rest of it in, checking his water fountain filter and the dry food stash before I refilled the treat ball for while I was gone. Then I turned on the TV and put on a twelve hour long bird video. There, that should keep him happy.

Don't say anything. He's still the king of the damn house.

I checked the time, fuck, I was going to be late. Not by much, probably not even five minutes, but still.

I got back in my car, which was thankfully still warm, the warning light coming on for *low outdoor temperature*, yeah—I couldn't fucking tell. I'm fucking freezing.

I made the trip to New Hanover, grabbing my badge that was hanging up, as soon as I walked in it was chaos, how the fuck seven in the morning was chaos was beyond me. Jesus, Mary and Joseph. What the fuck?

"We're short staffed, you're late." Jenna, the older blonde woman, probably older than my mom, I'd worked with her for years.

I scoffed, "Jenna, don't do me like that, I'm five minutes late, it's not even seven in the morning."

"You're never late, who is she?" She took one look at me, her grin widening.

"What?" I asked, fixing my hair out of habit.

Jenna typed something into the computer, "The girl?"

I flushed, logging into my station. "It's a guy actually."

Maybe that would keep the other nurses away from me, Jenna wasn't a problem but there were several others always trying to get me to take them out or come over.

"Oh. I didn't realize." She tried to hide her wide eyes, good that's what she gets for being nosy.

I sighed, looking around, "Come on, we've got huddle."

She wasn't lying when she said we were short staffed today, holy shit, why were there only five of us—we normally had twelve of us.

Fuck. My. Life.

I didn't have time to text the group chat back, I hardly had time to breathe.

Between deescalating multiple situations, meds, and listening to the last patient rap about his dog—even nine patients it hadn't been a bad day. When you work in psych you learn to roll with the punches, these people weren't crazy—at least not all of them. They were normal people who were having a hard time. Life doesn't all deal us the same cards and honestly, that's why I landed here.

I wanted to be able to help, when I first started at the hospital I was floated around, mostly ED until I was able to help a psych patient from a complete crash out, then they wanted to see if I would do well over there.

I did.

I knew then I wanted to switch the rest of my schooling to focus on the psychiatric parts as well. The nurses were glad to have a male on their side, I doubled as security most of the time.

My stomach growled and I realized I didn't even take lunch today, I was starving. I pulled up at Millie and Link's house and was immediately met with the smell of baked chicken.

Link sat up when he saw me, "Thank fuck, I'm starving."

I shot a look at Millie, choosing to ignore Link, because I might actually snap. I know he's a snacker and has probably eaten all damn day.

Millie checked her phone timer, "It's almost done, I wanted it to be fresh for you. It's just chicken and rice with carrots, but when you don't text all day I assume you probably didn't take lunch."

She was a fucking angel.

I stepped in towards her, lifting her chin up and kissing her lips lightly. She melted into me easily, throwing her arms around my neck and pulling me closer as the timer went off.

"Aww, cute. Millie food." Link said getting plates down, I shot him a glare.

I pulled away from Millie with another quick kiss to her lips, "Lincoln, do we have a problem?" I couldn't help it, it slipped out.

He rolled his eyes, why was he being so bratty—okay, maybe wrong word choice, we'll go with pain in my ass.

"Nope," he popped the p, "No problem."

"Are you jealous right now?" Millie asked, double checking the chicken, "Link, we cuddled all day."

I leaned against the counter, "Oh, he definitely is." I let my eyes roam over him, not that I was checking him out or anything... nope, definitely not that.

"Fuck off, Cooper." Link huffed, sitting the plates by Millie on the side of the stove.

Millie grabbed Link by the shirt, pressing a quick kiss to his lips, "Chill out, go sit down, annoy Theo or something."

Yeah, where was that fucker at anyway? How was he supposed to be my boyfriend and not greet me when I got home?

"Theo's asleep." He whined, looking between Millie and I, I could tell he just wanted attention.

I almost caved, but figured that would be weird, he didn't really want my attention anyway, right? I looked him over, taking in his bleach blonde hair and how warm his eyes looked in this lighting. "Then go wake him up."

Link grimaced, crossing his arms, studying me, "Have you ever woken his ass up? He's grouchy."

"Wasn't grouchy for me." Millie shot him a smirk over her shoulder as she messed with the food and even my mouth dropped open at her boldness.

"If he likes you, he's not that grouchy." I shrugged.

"Hey! He does like me!" Link gasped, clutching his heart dramatically, "I guess I've just seen him at his worst."

"Doubt that, I dealt with hungover Theo during our college years." I smirked, "And that was a crisis. He used to throw things at people."

"I heard that. All of that." Theo's voice filtered through the hallway before he leaned against the doorway to the kitchen, he pushed his hair back and blinked a few times. "I wasn't that bad Cooper James."

Fuck, he was adorable when he was sleepy.

Millie

The way both boys were watching Theo right now, honestly same, he was adorable. “Why are you all looking at me like that?” Theo asked, running his hand through his hair.

He really didn’t know, he was beautiful. I looked over at Coop, catching the redness to his cheeks at being called out. Link was the one who spoke up, “Because you’re cute as fuck right now.”

I couldn’t help the smile that broke across my face. I’m sure anyone else would be jealous as hell in my position, but seeing them like this? All of them? The way I could see the admiration in the way they looked at each other, it made my heart flutter with warmth.

I started dishing out food on the plates, handing them out one by one. I’d made enough to feed a small army—making sure they could each get more if they wanted. Coop kissed me as he took his plate, “Table or living room?”

“Wherever you want.” I said as I handed my starving golden retriever his plate, he also stole a quick kiss.

“I appreciate you.” he whispered, joining Coop at the table.

Alright, so table it was tonight.

I gave my sleepy boy his plate next and he lingered for a second, also pressing his lips to mine. He surprised me by taking my plate off the counter and sitting it down for me.

We ate in a comfortable silence, my eyes fell on Coop who looked even more tired than normal. “Long day?” I asked.

“Short staffed, psych ward chronicles. Story of my life.” He sighed, finishing up the last bit of food on his plate.

Theo ruffled his hair, “You need a break.”

Coop smiled, “I get three days off in a row.”

I looked between all of them, Link tapped my foot with his under the table. "So, I was thinking if we're going to have more nights like last night we should probably get Millie a bigger bed."

I practically spit out my rice. "Link, please tell me you didn't."

"No, I didn't." He gave me an unimpressed look, "I wanted you to pick the bed frame and mattress."

"Link, you can't just buy me a new bed!"

He held his hands up in mock surrender, "Hey, it benefits all of us."

Theo shrugged, Coop was smirking, "If I didn't know better, I'd say you liked sleeping in the same bed with me." Coop winked and Link looked taken aback by that.

"Puh–lease, you wish." Link crossed his arms, kicking my foot again.

"Alright, stand down Ponyboy." Coop laughed.

I looked between the two of them, they had been spending more time together recently. Maybe there was something there.

"What?" I mouthed as Link kicked me again.

He smiled, looking up at me with the softest fucking expression on his face. "Yeah, we're going tomorrow and we can move your bed to one of the guest rooms." He looked at Theo, then Coop. "I actually was going to offer the guest rooms to you two, you're here enough and we have space. I mean one of them is Millie's library, the other is my office —but I don't use it."

"Millie, this man built you a library and you thought he was just your friend?" Coop looked exasperated and exhausted all in one go.

"And stocked said library." Link smirked, "I'd give her the world even if she didn't want me like that." His face softened as he looked at me.

I feigned innocence. Nope, not looking into that right now. Link and I had been friends since we were kids, literally pre-puberty kids. Maybe I'd just gotten used to him and how he was, the whole damn family actually, his mom had taken me school shopping multiple times. At the good stores too, she'd pick me up from my house in the middle of the night if I needed a quick escape and once Link was old enough to drive he'd pick me up. As soon as I turned sixteen, his mom had practically handed us the keys to the second home on the property. I knew she was aware of my home life. Who wasn't? CPS had been involved a few times over the years, but there was never enough evidence to fully take me out of the home.

They'd always taken care of me when my family wouldn't. That's just how Link was, I didn't think twice about it. Damn, maybe I was fucking stupid. If I couldn't see it all those years.

"Are you spiraling right now?" Theo asked quietly, but there was a small smirk on his face, I chewed my inner cheek unsure how to answer that. Why did he seem so smug right now?

Yes. No. *Maybe.* It seemed like a stupid thing to spiral over. I felt Link's foot connect with mine again, softer this time. "Come here, I know where your head went."

Coop and Theo looked confused, but Link was already up and pulling me into a hug, "I'm sorry I didn't realize..." His fingers buried in my hair, his other arm pulling me closer.

"You had a lot going on, love." I sighed into him at his words, for fuck's sake I'd been out of my parents house for ten years, I should have realized it between now and then.

"I've lived with you for ten years dude, come on." I grumbled, pulling away slightly.

He studied my face, then back to where Theo and Coop were, "Mils, I'd have waited an eternity if it meant I kept you around."

"I'm glad you didn't."

"You two are cute, you sure you want us around?" Theo's voice said from behind us, I turned to give him an unamused look. I couldn't tell if he was joking or serious.

I tested my luck with the joking, "Are you jealous?"

He shrugged, "A little bit Princess, but it's fine."

My gaze shifted from Theo to Coop, raising my eyebrows to silently ask if he was okay, he grinned, "Considering Ponyboy here just asked if we were moving in I think we're all good."

"Stop calling me Ponyboy, for crying out loud." Link huffed, but I didn't miss the way Link looked at him, I looked over at Theo—mostly to see if he was clocking this tension between them too or if I was crazy.

Coop grinned and picked up the rest of the plates, "Why? You're the youngest of us guys, you're the dreamer golden boy."

Link glared daggers at the back of his head, even though I definitely saw Coop rinsing off his dish too and shoving it in the dishwasher. Link rolled his eyes, "Aww, look at you doing my dishes."

"Shut up, blondie."

Theo leaned against the door frame watching them, before he looked over at me dropping his voice, "Bets on how long it takes them to make-out?"

I snorted, which caused both Coop and Link to look at us. I tried to school my face, I really did. Coop glared at us, "I heard that, absolutely not." He closed the dishwasher, but I didn't miss the way he quickly glanced at Link.

Uh huh, that wasn't—you know what never mind—we'll let that play out. I looked at Theo who mouthed, "Told ya."

I rolled my eyes, "You good with staying with Link tonight?" I asked, hoping he'd say yes, because whether I wanted to admit it or not—my queen size bed was definitely not big enough.

"Yes, yes, you and Coop can have some alone time." Theo leaned down to kiss my lips gently.

Thank fuck. One boyfriend was hard enough, why did I think this was a good idea?

Millie

It was fucking cold, did this place not know heat? February was our coldest fucking month. Hell, our house was set to seventy-six right now, much to Coop's distaste. I was later than normal, but the club was still empty.

I could have stayed at home in my abnormally large bed that Link insisted on paying an arm and a leg for, but it worked. We all fit comfortably when the guys did stay over—which was more and more frequently, Coop had quit calling Link Ponyboy, but had moved to Blondie permanently.

For two people who swore it was nothing, they'd certainly gotten closer, which to be fair Theo and I did leave them alone at night. A lot. Sometimes Link would be in his own bed and Coop in mine, on rare occasions I'd find them on opposite ends of my bed so Theo and I could crash in between them when we got home.

I made quick work of getting ready, stamping on my eyeliner and dusting my cheek bones with a light pink highlighter and dotting some on the inner corner of my eyelids. I live for sparkles.

I wasn't even on the floor for fucking ten minutes before Theo stalked his ass up to me, oh shit here we go, I already knew what this was about. "Why are you on the schedule for the fourteenth?"

I groaned, loudly, because fuck my life. I hated Valentine's Day and it was a good day for the club. Lots of lonely men. "Theodore, it's a good night."

I wasn't going to mention that it was my least favorite holiday, granted I had never actually had anything more than a casual hookup on Valentine's Day. "Nope, absolutely not. I took it off, even Coop took the day off."

Coop took the day off? They had something planned, sneaky

bastards. "I have Galentine's with Iris, we have brunch and we get drunk. We splurge on red and pink outfits and heels and we do heart make-up that looks absolutely ridiculous. Then we come in and we make banks. No." I had half a hope he would drop it, he knew money was the goal.

He narrowed his eyes at me, "Princess..."

"We'll talk about it later." I cut him off, because people were coming in.

I would treat my guys after the fact.

Theo bit his lip, "How much do you normally make on Valentine's Day?"

I exhaled, "I don't know it varies, minimum a thousand, last year I made fifteen hundred, why?" It wasn't a lie, I'd made more in previous years, but it really did vary. Some years were better than others, just depended on who came in and how lonely they were.

"No reason," He shrugged, but the way he looked right now? Oh, there was a fucking reason.

I chose to ignore it, going to greet the guys who were at the bar. I hung back for a minute, letting them get drinks first and look around. "Hey guys!" I plastered on a half fake smile, I noticed one of our regulars mixed in with the group, "AHHHHH, it's you!!!!" I gave him a quick hug.

He flushed, "Hey Jade baby, how are you?"

"Better now that you're here." I mused, "Introduce me to your friends, love." I prompted, raking my eyes over each other, "Or I could guess, but if I give you stage names that's what you go by all night—no if's and's or but's."

His friends laughed, but he deadpanned, "No, she's serious. This is Scotty," he gestured to the man in the checkered shirt, he was an older man—arguably the oldest. "This is Ethan." It was a younger guy, probably a couple years older than me, he had blonde hair that reminded me of Link's. He pointed to the last guy, "And this is—"

"No, wait, let the pretty lady give me a stage name!" He grinned, yep, bingo he was the one. A blue. Blue's love to have fun, this would be easy.

Hook, line, and sinker.

I looked at him, tilting my head with a smirk. He was so stereotypical blue coded, he had little flamingos on his button down. He was wearing fucking shutter shades on his DTF hat for crying out loud. "Alright, I'm going to give you two names, then once you choose I'll give you the full stage name. Neil or Mike, pick your poison."

"Something tells me to pick Mike, but for shits and giggles I'll choose Neil."

I giggled, I had hoped he'd choose that one. "Neil Down."

"Clever girl, whatever you say Princess." He sank to his knees, my eyes widened and I couldn't help but flick my eyes over to Theo. We were close enough he definitely heard us.

"Save it for the back, buttercup. We'll go have some fun in a little bit, I don't want to steal you from your friends immediately."

"Is that a promise?" He asked, standing up and dusting off his pants.

"No, it's a threat." I said grabbing his hand and tugging him to the couches beside the DJ booth, it was my comfort spot, okay?

"Okay, so Paul, tell me why you brought in stragglers, hot stragglers, but stragglers." I winked at Neil who flushed as he took a drink of his rather large orange juice looking drink.

"It's Scotty's birthday!"

I grinned wickedly, "OH!! A birthday boy! Fortieth birthday? If it's not you're lying to me, you probably still get carded."

"Sixty-seventh actually."

"No fucking way!" I said, my mouth dropping open, "You're lying."

He pulled out his wallet and then his ID, showing me his birthday. I'll be fucking damned, 1959. "Well, holy shit. You don't look a day over forty, I hope my genetics are as good as yours."

"What are you like nineteen?"

I put my hand to my chest, widening my eyes into my perfected doe eyes, "No sir, but thanks for the compliment. That was seven years ago." I scrunched my nose, "I look better now, for sure. By the way, I have a friend getting ready in the back, she's a little blonde barbie doll and I'm sure she'd love to spend some time with the birthday boy!"

"Is my babydoll here?" Paul asked, looking around for Iris.

"Yeah, Iris should be out in a minute, you know how she is. She likes her outfits strappy and sultry." Slutty is more like it, but pop off queen, love that for her.

I knew Iris would appreciate a birthday boy, she liked to pull them to the stage, if they didn't want to she'd casually suggest a hot tub or the sky box. By the time Gracie came out, I was two shots in. Theo hadn't looked over once, his head down and a soft glow on it. No doubt texting the guys.

Gracie introduced herself, as Iris of course, and I couldn't help it. "Iris! Guess the birthday boy's age, I guarantee you're going to get it wrong!"

She sat down, crossing her legs, her knee pointing towards him before grabbing his hand in both of hers, "I"m going to say max forty-five."

"Add twenty two years to that, babydoll." Scotty said and I giggled at the use of babydoll, that was what Paul had called her.

"No way!"

I grinned, "Oh yeah, I saw his ID. Fucking amazing genetics right?"

"You two are the best, I'll take the two of you for my birthday."

Gracie stuck her tongue out, "That can be arranged, a little party here and there. We have options, we have a sky box—it's private, we can see out. They can't see in." She winked, "And it'll fit all of us."

"We also have shower rooms and hot tubs if you feel like getting wet and wild." I interjected, my hand tracing patterns into Neil's thigh, dragging my nails up and down.

"Can we see them?" Scotty asked, his friend groaned—fuck what was his name? Ethan maybe?

"I see you're the reluctant one?" I asked, giving his knee a gentle squeeze.

"Not my scene." He admitted quietly.

"Can I?" I asked Neil, "I'll be right back, guard this with your life." I handed him my purse, there was nothing but lipgloss in it, I really just wanted to see what he did. He immediately tucked it into his lap and folded both hands over it.

I walked behind Ethan and leaned down in his ear, "Don't worry, if you don't want anyone touching you I'll let Iris know to chill. If you see a girl you like, just let me know and I'll get her. If not, I'll keep them off of you. This is a safe place for everyone, okay?" When he nodded, I patted his chest and then went back to my seat, immediately resuming my teasing touches on Neil.

"Princess Jade and Babydoll Iris to the stage please." Theo's amused voice cracked out over the music, oh that fucker had definitely been listening this entire time.

I handed Neil my purse, "You're on sparkly bag duty." I blew him a kiss as Gracie and I made our way up to the stage as *The Way I Are* started blaring.

"That's how we're playing tonight, Theo?" I all but yelled towards the DJ booth, as both Gracie and I started pulling out all the fun moves as we stretched and cleaned the poles, I did a few pole walks around and then pirouetted, moving my hips and shoulders to the beat, turning around to put my back on the pole and flailed my arms for a second, Gracie realized I wasn't trying to be eloquent and did the same thing.

I chanced at glance at Theo and he was grinning, his head bobbing in time with the beat. He hit the fog, our sign to climb to the top and start the trick sequence.

I nodded at Gracie as we both started climbing the same pole. "Pencil, to remi sit?" I asked, holding myself out as she did too, busting into the trick easily. Once we were in the sit we let go with our hands and leaned back. It wasn't as hard as it looked, it just took more trust in the other person than I'd like to admit—but if one of us falls the other falls.

Once we untangled we took to our own separate poles, busting out a few cutesy spins, a few aerials, a simple little back hook, stepping down to sway my hips playfully before doing a pole walk into a carousel spin.

The second song started, *Pour It Up* blared out of the speakers, Theo hit the fog again and then the light show. I made my way to Gracie, "Surf board?" I grinned, "I can bottom." I nodded for her to go up, she sat pretty tucking the pole behind her arm and folding over while she waited for me to get into my superman.

I hooked my right knee, letting myself spin like that for a minute before climbing up using my side climb and opening my legs up and dropping my hips slightly so I could get into the trick. Once I was sure I had my grip, I stuck my fist out in front of me. Superman pose perfected and it was also our signal for Gracie to stand on me.

She put the top of her heel on me, careful not to put the actual heel on me and held most of her weight on the pole. She carefully twerked, throwing her ass in the perfect circle, her fucking ass was amazing. I watched us in the mirror, we looked fucking good, this was one of our party tricks. Everyone loved it.

You know what else I saw in the mirror though? A biker helmet and fuck ton of money coming down on us. I whipped my head around to Theo as Gracie sat on me and did the lasso thing as we made our way to the floor.

The helmet guy didn't stop, he undid two more bands and tossed them on the stage. I knew it wasn't a hundred because they used regular rubber bands for a hundred, blue for five hundred and red for a thousand. This motherfucker, I'd recognize that helmet anywhere.

The guys we were sitting with had disappeared, only to reappear with their own stacks of ones. I didn't get a look at how much it was, but there was easily a couple thousand on this stage right now.

I locked eyes with Link, even though he was behind his visor and he did a little salute into a peace sign and left the building. Theo had planned that shit. This was him trying to pay me off to get me to take off for Valentine's Day.

The song came to a close, "Patience, one song away." Theo said into the mic as he and Toby both came over with buckets and the sweeper brooms.

I glared at Theo, "You had him come here didn't you."

"I have no idea what you're talking about, Princess, but your guys also bought a hot tub with you two. Booked out for two hours." He looked me up and down, "Go get em."

Once the buckets were full and yes it took five. Gracie and I went to the dressing room, apologizing to the guys and saying we'd be right back.

"That was Link wasn't it?" Gracie asked as soon as we got to the back.

"Yes, that was my biker." I admitted, counting out the money evenly between us. I was going to throw these fucking singles on him in his fucking sleep.

"He can come in whenever he wants, my rent just got paid in one night."

Touché, touché.

Maybe I needed to bring the guys in on days when I wasn't working, let Gracie make a quick bag. I knew Link would let me throw money if I really wanted to.

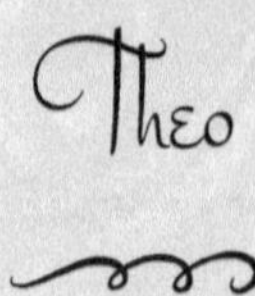

When I texted Link, I didn't expect him to throw that much, I knew he had money, but holy shit, that was a lot. Even for Link. I wasn't surprised she missed him coming in, I had to tell Jonah to let him through and he lifted his visor and once they realized it was Link it was easy going from there.

He even used the ATM which had a hell of a charge on it. Absolutely insane.

I also knew from the look on her face we were in a lot of trouble. She'd been even happier to know I got all the money raining down on her on video and had already sent it to her.

Have some content Principessa.

She can be mad at me, she was fucking hot when she was mad.

Besides those guys taking them off the floor for a hot tub meant I only had three other dancers. I texted Link back once I saw he was home on the family app.

Theo: Bro, that was a bit overkill.

Link: I've never seen her on stage, worth it.

Theo: Glad you made it home safe, I love you.

Link: I'm always safe.

Link: Wait, an actual I love you?? OVER TEXT?!

Theo: Shut up blondie.

Link: Nah, not you too...

Theo: Sorry, you want a Sir or Baby Boy or something? I'll change your contact right now.

DELIVERED. READ.

Theo: Damn, leave me on delivered. Okay.

The next two hours passed, I watched Millie and Gracie both dump their shots, then one of the guys said no more and the bartender brought them all water. I knew they were in good hands, but I kept watch in between stage rotation. Besides, Toby was watching the camera too.

Whatever he and Gracie had going on, it was just as transparent as Millie and I. The guys hugged the girls and once they were dressed Jonah helped them call for a taxi.

Within a few minutes Millie was back out, hair still slightly wet at the ends. "You told Link to come in to pay me off for Valentine's day didn't you?"

"I may have suggested you were worried about the money aspect." I grinned, looking at the dark blue scraps of lace she threw on quickly.

She crossed her arms over her chest, I had to resist pulling her arms away so I could keep looking. "Stop ogling, we're at work and I don't ask Link for money."

"You didn't and he was exactly where he wanted to be." I did move her arm, because I needed to see what she was wearing was even legal. "You need pasties with that." I pointed out, "Don't want to catch a charge."

She looked down, "Fucking Gracie. This is one of hers."

"I figured, I've never seen it on you before." I let my eyes wander down, she was wearing a second thong under the lace bottoms though, good girl, that's not for show.

As if she could read my mind, she frowned, "I always wear two, sometimes three depending on the outfit."

"Go get some pasties from Jonah or change."

"I have my own pasties, what am I an amateur?" She rolled her eyes and turned on her heel before walking back to the dressing room.

Toby came over to me, he looked like he wanted to say something, but also didn't want the backlash. "Spit it out dude." I huffed, loading up the next few songs for rotation.

"Sooooo... you and Jade?"

I side-eyed him, "Sooooo..." I drew it out the same way he had, "You and Iris?"

His eyes went wide, "Yeah, that's what I thought." I chuckled.

He made himself busy, pretending to go help with the outside crowd, which to be fair there was a line of at least ten people outside. When the girls came back out the club was livelier than before.

People were drinking, standing around the bar since all the stools were now taken, time to get this party started.

Link

"So Far, So Fake - DarkLux, Xizt"

Millie was about to be pissed at me, she probably already was if I was being honest. She told me I wasn't ever allowed in the club, but I've seen her completely naked now. I've literally heard her moan my name and took her breath away. I think I've earned a club trip even if it was just for a stage set.

I know better than to start anything in the club, she lets Theo see her all the time. And yes... maybe I'm jealous about that. I can't believe all that time we were fucking around he was literally working with Millie and apparently harboring some feelings for his co-worker too.

Huh, small fucking world.

But hey, if I could have them both fuck it. I'd take it. Even if Coop was hot and cold with me. I swear to God he's thought about it, or maybe I just associate touch with love. That's a me problem though, I wasn't fucking with that can of worms, perfectly fine with Millie and Theo.

Is that why I climbed into Millie's bed where Coop was currently laying down? Nope. Sure as hell was not.

"What did you do?" Coop asked, turning to face me.

"Millie scheduled herself for Valentine's Day, worried about missing money." I grinned, "So I may have doubled what she made last year and threw it on stage at her and Gracie."

"I would have contributed." He frowned.

Why did he look upset? Should I have included him in our plans? Fuck, I hadn't meant to leave him out. "I had it, it's fine." I looked at him, "Are you still getting up extra early to go feed your cat?"

Distract. Distract. Distract.

He grimaced, but I could see how tired he actually was. "Yeah, the beast still needs his wet food and treat balls filled daily."

I exhaled, looking anywhere but at him, "You could just bring him over here, I'm sure Millie would love that. I feel bad you're spending so much time away from him."

"That's like the final step of moving in with you." His eyes searched mine and my stupid stomach did the butterfly thing, Jesus, not right now.

Not Cooper.

"Moving in with Millie you mean." I corrected, trying to change the subject, even just the slightest shift.

He chuckled, his eyes lingering lower than they should have. "You live here too, blondie." Why did he keep looking at me like that? I wasn't fucking crazy I knew what tension felt like, and this? We were fucking tip toeing this line.

I flopped back onto the pillow, adjusting the blanket over me, trying to figure out what to do when he was looking at me like that. "Fair enough, but I'm just saying I could help you move stuff over if you want."

"My lease is over at the end of March. We'll see where we're at then." Coop shrugged, pulling Millie's blanket over his head as he turned back around.

I closed my eyes and the next time I opened them Millie was straddling me with Theo's hand over her mouth. "Don't you dare wake up Cooper." he whispered in her ear, "You can be mad tomorrow, lay your ass down."

Ooooh, Theo's dominant voice always did things to me, as long as he didn't direct that energy at me we'd be fine. There wasn't a submissive bone in my body, I mean unless Millie wanted to boss me around—then fair game I guess.

Millie turned over into Coop, pulling her arm around his waist. Theo's lips met mine, "Thank you for that, she took herself off the schedule."

I smiled, part one of the mission accomplished.

"Did you and Millie really take bets on Coop and I?" I barely breathed.

Theo's eyes shot to mine, "Should we have?"

I shook my head slightly, "Maybe we're just spending too much time together."

Yeah, that's all this was.

Coop didn't like me like that, he'd even said it himself, but why had he looked at me like that?

What was that?

"You sure?" Theo whispered, nuzzling into me, "I mean I see the appeal—on both sides."

"Oh shut up." I half mumbled, falling into the warmth of them all.

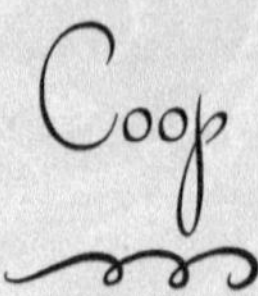

Coop

I'm going to pretend that whatever that was with Link, was not *that.* Yeah, no, I already had a boyfriend—honestly don't even know what the hell to do with him. The kissing is nice, but I'm fucking terrified to take it any further. It's kind of why I'm terrified of this whole plan we have for Valentine's Day.

I don't know what the hell I was thinking, combing through her Goodreads and library like some weirdo, but all of her books had common themes. Masked men, bikers, chase scenes—our girl was into predator and prey whether she liked it or not. My submissive sweet girl.

You'd never fucking know it, until you got to know her of course. Link had helped me order the gear and cosplay outfits. He said he wanted us all dressed the same so she didn't know who she'd be getting—that is if we didn't talk.

Considering we were all different heights, Link being the shortest of us all and Theo being only an inch taller than me, it wasn't that likely she wouldn't figure it out, but if we covered the windows with black out curtains and cut the power, we might have a chance.

I left earlier this morning than I had been, I did miss my cranky ass cat. He must have missed me too because he rubbed against my legs. He still had dry food in his auto-feeder, but I moved to check the filter on his water fountain and once I refilled it to the water line, I went searching for the treat balls.

After successfully fishing one out from under my couch and finding the other in the bathroom and filled it with treats from the canister. He really loved the expensive ones, but I was running low so I threw in the regular ones too. Tossing them on the floor in the living room, I also went searching for his laser robot toy. He hardly played with it, but I hadn't been home and he looked like he was gaining some weight.

I scraped a gravy packet into the little bowl and mixed in the shredded wet cat food. He head-butted my hand and I scooped him up, he sounded like a motor. "Did you miss me boy?" I scratched behind his ear, nuzzling into him.

I'd need to take a lint roller to my scrub top, but it was fine.

Fuck, I missed my cat.

Maybe bringing him over to Link and Millie's wasn't such a bad idea.

I made it through my work day unscathed, which wasn't that common, especially when you're the muscle of the unit and the bad guy wrangler if a patient is making one of the female staff uncomfortable.

I checked the family app, seeing if they were home and no—they were at my house? Theo was the only one with a key. When I walked in, I was met with a Crooks sleeping on Link, Millie giving both Link and Crooks head scratches.

And Theo was in my kitchen, his voice ringing out. "I'm glad we stopped to get food to cook, because dude you had nothing."

"I haven't been home, other than to check on my fur-ball. Who seems to be fucking content with Lincoln right now." I grumbled.

"You seemed worried about him, so we figured he could use some company." Link gave me a small smile, smoothing Crook's fur down.

He'd actually listened to me the other night, it wasn't hard to see why Theo and Millie loved him—he really was a sweetheart—*not in that sense, I mean come on he's cuddling my fucking cat.*

The cat that hates almost everyone.

I stepped into the small kitchen, not sure how to respond to seeing Theo wearing my cat apron that he'd gotten me as a gag gift last Christmas—well Yule for Theo. His family celebrated Yule. "I see you dug out my apron."

"I"d much rather see it on you, shirtless preferably." Theo snickered.

"Cooking shirtless is not practical."

"He's flirting with you, dipshit." Link called from the living room, "Oww, you fucker!" Crooks darted into the kitchen winding in between my legs. I bent down to give him pets, only to be met with forced kitty head-butts.

Millie groaned so loud I could hear it in here, "Way to go Lincoln! You made him move!"

"Don't Lincoln me! He scratched me, not you!"

Theo laughed, messing with the food, I peaked over, "Is that—?"

"Yes, I'm making my mom's favorite dish." Parmesan risotto, fuck yeah. I watched him mix the broth and just enough white wine. "It's not done yet, but should be soon."

I looked at the counter, cat toys and treats, including the pouches. "Did you get those?"

Theo bit his lip, glancing at the doorway, lowering his voice. "I helped pick out the ones I knew he liked, but it was Link's idea and money. He told me not to tell you, so don't say anything."

Fuck Link, why?

Why must you be so you?

I propped myself up on the cabinet, watching Theo stir the rice, "And why did he tell you that?"

"Said you'd be weirded out by it, because it came from him." Theo admitted, not even able to meet my eyes.

"Not weirded out by it, it's Link. Gift giving is his love language, he's constantly taking care of others." I brushed my hair back out of my face, looking for something to do with my hands.

"Sounds like someone else I know." Theo mumbled giving me some major side eye, I stepped closer, it was still weird—this dynamic between us. I threaded my fingers in his hair, yanking slightly—just enough to lean his head towards me so I could kiss him. "Thank you for cooking and coming over here." I said in between kisses, he nipped at my bottom lip before pulling away, a smirk playing at his face.

"Might want to pick a different way to thank Link, since it was his idea." Theo raised an eyebrow, "But feel free to do that too, he might fight you if you grab his hair though." He joked, licking his lips, before taking a swig out of his wine glass.

"It's not like that with us and you know it." I grumbled, but was it?

No? Right?

No, it was not.

"Keep telling yourself that, bud." Theo shrugged, returning his attention to the food.

Fuck.

I'm going to blame it on proximity.

Proximity, *that's all this was.*

Link

"Minor Tone - DarkLux"

I was trying to distract myself, the cat had been a good distraction, but now that he'd taken off I felt out of place.

Theo had spilled the beans on the fucking treats and NO I wasn't listening, Theo is just not a soft whisperer. I swear he has hearing loss from the club sometimes. So that's great, cool, it wasn't a big deal anyway. So what? The dude missed his cat and he's been at my house more than a few times a week. It was the least I could do.

And his face when he saw the orange fluff-ball asleep on me? It looked like someone smacked him. Hey, don't blame me, animals love me.

I'd already decided I'd take off after dinner, that's why I brought the bike—Coop staying at our house was one thing, but me staying here overnight was totally different. I could give him time with Millie and Theo, it didn't bother me to be alone.

"What ya thinking about?" Millie asked me quietly, her fingers brushing my hair back as she tilted her head slightly to look at me, my breath hitched as her pupils dilated when our eyes met.

"Nothing" I yawned, leaning into her fingers that were still tangled in my hair. I mean what was there to say?

Theo's cooking was always fucking perfection, even if he flat out refused most of the time, I could smell it when they brought it in the living room. Theo handed me my bowl and coop handed Millie hers before they both crowded into the couch forcing us all to shift slightly.

Coop looked tired honestly, like bone deep exhausted, he ate faster than I'd seen him eat in a long time. Millie handed me her bowl, "Hold this."

She took his bowl without question and disappeared into the

kitchen for a minute, bringing out a full bowl and handing him another. "Thanks love."

Millie took her bowl from me, leaning into Coop's side slightly as they ate. I knew she missed him when he worked, she was like that with all of us. She always wanted to be close to one of us, not complaining, I liked that about her. When she found someone to attach to she stayed, almost always—even if it was bad for her. Not saying this was, but shit I've known the girl my whole life, when she falls she swan dives.

That's just Millie.

Once everyone was done I took the bowls and figured I'd tidy up the kitchen while I was at it. He had a dishwasher thankfully, I took the time to rinse everything out before stacking it neatly in. It wasn't full so I figured I'd let him start it later if he wanted. Millie and I would slam ours full before we ran it.

It was Theo who came in, probably to make sure I'd put the food away—which I had, after looking through all the cabinets for Tupperware. He was so unorganized it made me anxious, I wanted to organize the fuck out of his kitchen. Not that I was going too.

It did need it though.

"You cleaned up by yourself?"

"Well yeah, you cooked. Coop worked literally all day, he looked exhausted, and Millie looked cute all snuggled up to him." I wiped the counter tops off, noting that the cat treats were moved to see through glass containers now. "I figured it's the least I could do before I leave."

Theo looked like he was going to say something but the orange ball of fluff came darting into the kitchen, followed by a confused Coop, "Wait, you're leaving?"

I bent down to pet the cat who was now brushing up against my leg, he head-butted my palm—violently asking for pets. "Well, yeah, I kinda figured you'd want some alone time with Theo and Millie you get the least amount of time with them—"

"You can stay." He cut me off quickly.

Theo leaned against the counter, his gaze falling between the two of us, I held up my finger in Theo's direction. "Don't say it."

"I wasn't gonna—," Theo put his hands up, a smirk playing on his smug face, "but now I feel like I should."

Coop shot him a death glare and Theo laughed, "It's funny you think that works on me." Theo winked, "You're hot when you're pretending to be mad."

"Who's hot when they're pretending to be mad?"

"Cooper." Theo grinned, watching as Millie came into the kitchen in just a long shirt.

When the fuck had she changed?

That was criminal. Jesus take the wheel.

"Oh, yeah he is. He does that stern death glare thing and it gives *Get On Your Knees* vibes." Millie chuckled, turning towards Coop. "But you sir, need to get a shower and sleep."

She pulled him towards his room, entirely too comfortable with his house—with him. "Are you two coming or not?"

Theo checked the doors to make sure they were locked, "If our girl says come on, we come on."

"I'm going home." I stated, making a point to gesture to my helmet and riding gear, "You guys need alone time too."

Theo looked me up and down, crossing his arms. "He likes you, Link."

"No, he doesn't. He tolerates me for you and Millie." I raised an eyebrow in challenge as I picked up my gloves.

He put his hand on the door, preventing me from opening it. "Dude... I'm telling you it's fine."

"Theodore...." I groaned, even as he stepped closer and his finger went around the back of my neck to tug me closer to him, pulling me into him for a quick kiss. I gave in, chasing his lips as he pulled away.

"Millllllllllliiiiieeeee! Come get the golden retriever. He's trying to leave." Theo practically yelled.

"Traitor!" I hissed as the auburn haired goblin made her way towards us.

"Why are you leaving? Coop said you were staying?"

I dropped my gloves back beside my helmet and looked between the two of them. "Fine, but I'm sleeping by Millie." I grumbled, letting her pull me into the hallway and into his room.

His room was clean, but definitely unorganized. He was like the less messy male version of Millie, books scattered around the room. Notebooks left open and cat toys everywhere. When Coop came out of the bathroom he had on a pair of plaid pajama pants that were hanging very low on his waist and he was towel drying his hair.

"I know y'all aren't tired, we can put on a movie or something. I'll still pass out." He tossed Millie the remote and then turned to throw Theo and I pajama pants. "Get comfortable." Coop turned around when I didn't make a move to get undressed like Theo did.

I tugged on the pajama pants and flopped onto the bed, to the right of Millie and the edge. Coop settled in, Millie curling into him immediately. Theo pulled the blanket up and over all of us before he snuggled into Coop too. I turned to throw my arm around Millie who immediately thought it was a good idea to wiggle in my lap. At first I thought she was just getting comfortable, but she was not.

"Mils," I breathed out, "Quit it."

She giggled, "Sorry..." but she did it again.

"Baby girl, quit." I tightened my hold, holding her steadier so she couldn't move as much.

"Mils, are you being a tyrant?" Coop asked.

"Nope, I'm behaving." She nuzzled further into Coop, causing my arm to press against him.

I chuckled, loosening my hold ever so slightly. "Yeah, now that I've basically restrained you."

"You didn't have to." she quipped, but as soon as I gave her some leeway she did it again.

"If you don't quit..." I warned, tightening my grip on her waist.

"Make me."

Theo laughed, his eyes meeting mine. "You heard her, make her."

"Wait—" Millie's eyes widened, "You wouldn't."

"Keep pushing him." Coop grinned, quickly hiding his smile in her hair as he pressed a kiss to it. "We already know you're a little bit of a voyeur."

"I am not!" she hissed, but the way her hips rolled into mine? She definitely was.

This was insanity, were they telling me to do that? In front of them? In the same bed?

Absolutely not.

She shifted against me again, and you know what? Fuck it. She wanted to play? I'd show her what happens when I stop giving a shit.

My hand went into her hair, tangling in the strands at the base of her neck and pulling her back. "You sure about this?"

I watched her nod slightly, "Words, babygirl."

"Yes, yes, I'm sure."

I looked between Coop and Theo, needing their permission too before taking this further. Coop was watching me carefully and he nodded, but I couldn't tell what was going on in his head. Millie's hand found my pants, I knew she could feel how hard I was already.

I pulled her closer, whispering in her ear. "You want to do this? In front of everyone?"

She whimpered, that's all I needed. Except this was about to be a group activity, I guided her head down towards Coop's pants and heard his breath hitch as she looked up at him through her lashes. His raspy little "Please." sent shivers down my entire body.

I wasn't going to think too much into that right now, I pulled down her lacy strap of underwear, that couldn't have been comfortable at all. Looks like I took care of that problem for her.

I pushed myself through her folds, fuck she was already wet, well fuck, maybe he was right—our girl did enjoy being watched. Theo didn't move from his spot next to Coop, but he watched as Millie took Coop out of his pants and pumped him a few times with her hand before dragging her tongue against him from base to tip.

I didn't dare push into her yet, teasing her slowly enough that she was trying to push back onto me, shifting her hips so I would abandon what I was doing. Not going to happen, I slid through her wetness as she took Coop fully into her mouth. I shoved her head down just enough before finally sliding into her, controlling her movements with my hand.

Coop groaned as he watched my hand grip her hair and push her down further and faster matching the same pace I was giving her. "Tap Coop's thigh if you need a minute." I exhaled shakily as her eyes started watering when I shoved her down all the way at the same time I shifted her to go in deeper.

"Fuck, Link slow down." Coop managed his hands gripping the sheets as Millie did something with her tongue.

I listened, because he was just as much a participant in this as we were, if he needed a minute I'd honor that. I pulled Millie off, she looked wrecked.

Theo wiped her cheeks and then her chin, "Look at you, a fucking mess for them." Millie whimpered as Theo shoved his fingers in her mouth, immediately sucking on them. "Good fucking girl, sucking on my fingers while he fucks you."

My hips stuttered at that, fuck meeeeee. I laced my fingers into her hair again, massaging gently for a second, before meeting his eyes. "Hold her hair this time."

I went to push her back down, but she looked panicked. "Wait—"

"Color?" I asked.

"Yellow... Just for a second. Who am I tapping if I need air? That's a lot of hands."

"Tap me, since I have your hair" Theo answered her almost instantly, he turned to me, "Link if she taps, chill out and give her a second. No argument."

"You good Coop?" I asked quietly, noticing how he was watching us.

"Yeah, I just—consent is fucking hot and you're all hot and I'm having bi-panic or something." Or something caught my attention and bi-panic? Bi-panic was weeks ago.

"Or something?" I asked, feeling my hand move as Millie started going down on Coop again, this time on her own accord.

He let his head drop back to the pillow, refusing to acknowledge that and I gestured for Theo to take her hair so I could pull her against me more, my other hand gripping her hip harder than probably necessary.

I was practically seeing stars as I felt Millie tighten around me, her body responding to my rougher handling. Theo was controlling her movements with his hand in her hair, the sight of them working together while I was buried inside her was almost too much.

"Fuck," I groaned, tightening my grip on her hip. "You like this, don't you, babygirl? Being used from both ends while he watches?"

She moaned around Coop, the vibration making him curse and buck up into her mouth. His eyes met mine over her body, and there was something there I couldn't quite place—hunger, definitely, but something else too. Something that made my heart race even faster.

"She's close," I told them, feeling her start to flutter around me. "Aren't you, Mils?"

Theo tugged her hair, pulling her up just enough that she could gasp for air, her eyes watering. "Answer him," Theo commanded, his voice low and rough.

"Yes," she panted, "I'm so close. Please don't stop."

Theo looked up at Coop, "Coop—can I?" His voice was quiet, and I almost missed what he was even asking to do, but Coop nodded and I felt Millie clinch harder around me as Coop slipped his fingers into her mouth instead.

Theo shifted and took Coop in his mouth, I shouldn't have watched—the moment not necessarily for me anymore—but I couldn't stop.

I picked up my pace, driving into her harder as Millie now guided him back down onto Coop. The sight of her taking that little bit of control with Coop's fingers in her mouth still so eager and desperate, pushed me right to the edge.

"Fuck, I'm gonna—" Coop's warning was cut short as his body tensed. Millie held Theo's head down, making him take all of him as he came.

Fuck, okay, that should not have been as hot as it was.

That was it for me. Watching him swallow around him while her body squeezed mine like a vice—I lost it completely, slamming into her one final time as I came harder than I could remember.

Millie pulled Theo up off of Coop by his hair, I didn't look I swear. Okay, maybe just a little, but fuck, that was hot. Theo crashed his lips to hers, hungrily devouring her mouth.

Fuck, that was even hotter.

When he pulled away he patted her cheek, "Thanks for sharing." He grinned as Millie flushed red as an incoherent string of giggles came from her mouth.

"Why was that so hot? Holy shit." She managed after a moment.

Coop groaned, putting an arm over his face, his muffled words coming out embarrassingly low. "Theo, I don't know what to do with that right now."

I chuckled, pulling out of Millie slowly, she whined at the loss of contact and I pulled her into a kiss. Tasting Coop and Theo on her didn't bother me, I thought I'd feel some kind of jealousy with sharing her with Coop, really this was a test for myself to see what I could handle.

I wasn't jealous. If anything, it kind of made me wonder why the fuck Cooper was being weird towards me. If he was fine with this, with sharing her and Theo, what was so bad about me?

He'd let Theo do it, why wouldn't he let me?

Millie climbed over us, heading to his bathroom. Coop laid there for a second before he lolled his head to look at me, "What was *that*?"

"You were right there, she was being a brat—but if you're not cool with group activities we may want to rethink our plans." I said quietly, glancing to the door of the bathroom.

"I meant—fuck—that's not what I meant." Coop looked over at Theo, "And you—"

Theo ducked under the blanket, "Nope, I'm not—"

Coop huffed, "I'm not mad, Theo."

Theo pushed his head out of the blanket slowly, "Thank fuck, because I enjoyed that."

I tucked my arm under Coop's pillow, antagonizing him just a bit, slight antagonization, minimal. "Are you flustered right now?"

Millie opened the bathroom door, glaring at me. "Link, leave him alone."

"Fine, fine..." I groaned before scooting back over, "You two win this time, but next time I fluster Coop—"

He cut me off, "You didn't fluster me."

"Whatever you say." I chuckled as Millie padded across the room.

"Would you two quit?" Millie crawled over Theo and Coop, "Jesus...I'm gonna make you two sleep next to each other if you can't get along."

I pulled her into me, letting her wrap herself around Coop too.

Sleep pulled me under faster than I wanted to admit, I didn't even remember it.

I woke up to Coop's alarm. I was cuddled into Link's chest now, Coop's arm slung around me and his hand resting on Link's stomach. Theo was lying on his side, facing the opposite direction of everyone else.

Coop groaned, "I'm not kicking you guys out, you can stay. Play with Crooks for me." He stretched, trying not to wake Theo, who was knocked the hell out.

He climbed over him and Theo grabbed his leg, "Wait—"

The dim lighting caught Coop's face, he looked softer and slightly blurry—mostly because my eyes were hazy with sleep—he leaned down and kissed Theo on the lips gently, "Go back to sleep, keep our girl warm."

I shifted from Link to Theo, Link was still passed out so he didn't even budge. I took the opportunity to stretch out ever so slightly, just enough to make my back feel better. "Come here, Princess." Theo mumbled, pulling me all but on top of him.

I never really slept next to Theo, so sinking into him was nice. I'm pretty sure I actually sighed in contentment. I was in and out of sleep as Coop got ready for work. He looked fucking hot in his scrubs, I was sure he saw me ogling him a few times.

When he shoved his keys and wallet in his scrub top I whined, loudly. He ssshhhed me, then whispered. "Don't wake them up, I wouldn't leave without a kiss."

His lips met mine and my heart jumped slightly, this was good. This was everything. Sleepy brain overload. "I love you, be careful." I let slip, not even carrying I'd just blurted it out.

He looked caught off guard, his eyebrows pulling closer together for a split second. “I love you too. Be good, no more extracurricular activities in my bed without me.”

I giggled and Theo pulled me closer, “Don’t tempt me, Cooper.”

“Okay, Theodore...” Coop’s morning voice was fucking hot. Jesus Christ.

“Don’t ever say my name like that... it’s too hot...” Link mumbled and I stifled a laugh, because what the fuck Link.

“What was that Lincoln? Care to repeat?” Coop asked as he went to walk out the door, Crooks winding around his feet and then jumping on the bed.

“Nope... you heard me.” Link mumbled, turning to cuddle into my back again.

I giggled, loudly, trying to hide it by shoving the blanket over my face. He’d done the voice with his full first name too, I wish I had enough composure to see Link’s face.

Crooks made his way between mine and Link’s legs, “Traitor...” Coop huffed as he walked out.

“The cat has chosen me, I am the favorite.” Link said, shifting so he could pet Crooks.

Yep, we weren’t going anywhere.

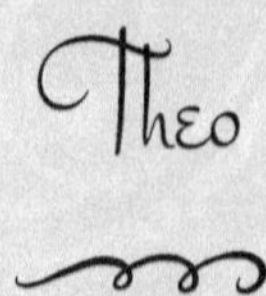

I can't explain it, but the way Link and Coop had been interacting recently was anything but platonic, it was charged. Ask me how I know? I was the same with Coop, the little touches—the looks and little things?

Oh yeah, there was definitely something there even if they didn't realize it. Yet.

We were also two days out from Valentine's and I was fucking nervous. I'd downloaded some of Millie's books and read some when I could, but being over at their house or at work with her hadn't given me much time to prepare for all of that.

We had a solid plan, Link had bought everything. Literally everything. Comms, outfits, black out curtains.

Link was going to send her with extra money to treat Gracie to Galentine's brunch, a little shopping spree while we set everything up. Coop was going to be the one to approach her, Link would hit the breaker.

It was like a big pre-planned manhunt, Coop would tell her to run and hide. We'd give her a head start, let her get hidden, then we'd start our little hunt.

Hide and Seek with a spicy twist.

If we find you, we fuck you.

Coop had been the one to think of it, he'd seen her reading a book with a masked chase scene—she'd tried to hide it. Of course she did, little feral bookworm. I knew she was reading that shit at work too.

I'd seen her read worse, way worse, right there at the bar. Completely oblivious to everything and everyone. Completely unaware that I was reading over her shoulder a few times.

She'd said no to work tonight, thank God, they'd called her and she'd said no. She was giving up a few days of work this week and I had a feeling she'd be giving up a few more after Valentine's Day.

The goal was to tire her out, if she couldn't walk for a few days... fuck it.

Link and I had been moving things around at the house for the past few days, he'd broken down Millie's library and rebuilt it in the sunroom. Even though one of the shelves was now in her room, she'd added all of her personal favorites to the one in there and had the rest in the sunroom.

He'd also added new shades to the room so she could make it darker or lighter in the room. Hung her lights up, bought her a new fluffy rug, since there was no carpet in here.

The library room was basically cleaned out, he wanted me to move in. I immediately said yes, I was on a month to month lease anyway so it worked.

His 'office' which was basically just a desk and one bookshelf was moved to his room. Coop wouldn't move in until March or April, if he decided to do that—something told me he would. Millie's old bed was in there currently, it was basically brand new too. I'd probably throw my bed out and take this one for the random nights she got sick of me.

Which was beginning to get increasingly more, because as it turns out working with someone and being around them all the time was probably not a good thing.

Especially since we already clashed a little bit, but it made the sex better in my opinion.

Crooks darted out from Millie's room, yes, she'd convinced him to move over the damn cat early since he was over here most of the time.

For some reason, she loved that fucking beast. Link had installed a catio off the sunroom for him, cat door and everything so he could come and go as he pleased.

I peaked into her room, she was reading on her tablet. "Mils?"

She flipped me off, "I'm reading."

I entered anyway, ignoring Link's "Bad idea dude."

I laid on the bed beside her, watching her facial expressions as she read, her nose scrunched. "That's weird. Stop."

"You're pretty when you do that." I said softly, my tongue wetting my bottom lip slightly before I could stop it.

She sighed, pointing to the door. "Theo, for fuck's sake out."

I rolled my eyes, pouting. "Fine."

Link had his arms crossed in the hallway, "Told you so."

I looked at Link's room, then at him, he grabbed my hand and pulled me in.

I knew I'd get cuddles one way or another.

It was freezing, but if Gracie wanted to sit on the rooftop bar and eat steaming hot chocolate for breakfast I'd happily join in. I stabbed an entire strawberry and coated it in chocolate. "Pretty sure the guys have planned something today, they've been keeping it under wraps whatever it is," I said, stabbing a piece of pineapple. "What do you and Toby have planned?"

She sputtered on her drink, her eyes comically wide. "WHAT?"

"You two are not slick, how long have you been seeing each other?"

Gracie flushed, swiping her long hair behind her as she fiddled with the edible flower. "We've been sleeping together for a while, we're not serious."

"Does he know that?" I quipped, raising my eyebrow.

"Well, yeah, we can't exactly just date out in the open."

"That's a lie and you know it. Jonah and Laycee have been dating for years, don't even get me started on her ring tan line." I rolled my eyes.

Gracie frowned, "Yeah, but Lace has been dancing for a while, like a long while, I think they were dating before she came over to us."

"Point is, it can work."

"You and Theo are close..." She pried, trying to get the attention off of her.

"He moved in with us and Coop moved his cat over. He's tied into his lease for another month, but he's slowly moving his entire apartment over."

"What's it like living with and working with Theo?"

"He pisses me off, like always, but it's nice having him around." I admitted.

"Is he good in bed?" Gracie asked.

I looked up at her, "I'm literally sharing a bed with all three of them nightly."

"You know that's not what I meant." She rolled her eyes, downing her second drink of the morning.

"He is very—yeah, he's good." I flushed, my cheeks burning.

"I figured he would be, but I didn't want to push it because of the way he looks at you girl. I'd paid to see that go down." Gracie winked, "So if you do ever film it—let me know, I'll be the first to subscribe."

"GRACIE!" I shrieked, stabbing a grape that had rolled away from me twice now. "Anyway, Link gave me his credit card and told me to treat both of us for new work outfits." I grinned, "Literally told us to go fucking wild."

Gracie basically inhaled her entire portion of the tray, I finished the remainder of my pineapple and strawberries, I wasn't fucking with the grapes.

We left a decent tip on the table before making our exit. I'd only had one drink, and I'd sipped it between sips of orange juice so I was fine with the fifteen minute drive it took us to get to the sex shop.

This one was my favorite, there was more selection than the other stores.

I browsed, grabbing several thongs in multiple colors for each of us. Gracie shyly picked up a few things giving me puppy dog eyes and I laughed, "He said for both of us. Pick what you want."

I ended up picking up a few different colored dresses, a few baby-dolls, a few fishnet dresses and several new teddy's because I was sure he'd freak out if I came back empty handed. I was browsing the shoes, because why not. I found a pair of ankle boots and a pair of clear heels I'd been needing for the nights I wanted to wear brighter colors. Gracie found a pair of rhinestoned heels in her size and I immediately agreed.

By the time we left, I'd also grabbed two different pheromone sprays. Some edible body lotions, not for work clearly, since you know no lotion on the pole.

Between the two of us, we'd spent well over a thousand dollars. "Fuck, is he going to be mad?" Gracie whispered as I entered the pin.

"Honey, this wasn't even a dent. Besides, we used the dancer discount." I smiled at the clerk, "Thank you! Have a great day!"

Gracie didn't look convinced, I shrugged, "We could go to the mall and Windsor if we wanted, although I should let him know if we do that." I clicked open my phone on the way out of the store.

Millie: Going to Windsor and possibly another lingerie store.

Link: No worries babygirl, splurge.

Millie: I planned on it.

I drove us to Windsor, so we could pick out some nice little cover up dresses for when we felt like feeling fancier. Gracie picked out quite a few sparkly dresses and I found a few velvet dresses I really liked and even tried on a few of the sparkly dark green and blue ones I found. We both settled on four each. I had one that I was saving for the guys and the guys only.

Gracie had stayed true to the theme and gotten pinks and reds, I'm glad she could pull it off. My red hair didn't exactly look the best with those colors.

I dropped Gracie off at home, and texted the group chat.

Millie: I'm on my way.

Coop: It's just me at the house right now.

Millie: Where'd they go?

Coop: Don't text and drive baby. See you when you get here.

"RUNRUNRUN - Dutch Melrose"

Everything was in place, we'd triple checked. I'd lied when I said they weren't here. Theo and Link had moved the car and bike to the garage, something they apparently never used so she wouldn't think about it. They'd even turned off their locations down the road so Millie would be thrown off, probably thinking they were doing something for her surprise.

We'd hung black out curtains, turned off the lights to check that it darkened the room enough—it did. It was basically pitch black. The bluetooth headphones Link had gotten were an over the ear piece, we had our server set up already so we could talk over it.

Link was near the breaker so he could turn it off as soon as I sent out the signal. Theo was upstairs in the hallway bathroom, that way he had an element of surprise if he needed it.

I looked down at my tactical pants, which were basically black cargo pants. We had on black tee shirts, and balaclava masks. If she got close enough she'd realize who was who. Especially me, since I had the lightest eyes of the three of us, but it was the fantasy of it. And in the dark? Good fucking luck, babygirl.

I checked her location, she was almost home. It was almost go time.

Why was I so nervous?

My app dinged with a notification, *Millie arrived at home.*

I sat down at the table, the floor lamp the only light on in the kitchen. When she opened the door she looked around, "Why is it so fucking dark in here? It's the middle of the day."

"Because we're going to play a game." I said, grinning when she jumped. She hadn't noticed me.

"Why are you dressed like that?"

"It might be part of the game." I shrugged.

Her eyes widened, "What game?"

"Run." I stated.

"Run?" Her eyes widened and she took a step back, studying my face.

"Yeah, I'll give you a head start." I smirked under the mask.

"And if you catch me?" Was that brattiness coming through? I fucking hoped so.

"Oh I think you know." I hit my comm under the balaclava, "Target acquired."

You better hide, we're coming for you.

The lights went out and all I heard was Millie's feet take off and a mumbled *shit* as she tried to make her way through the hallway leading to the stairs.

Fuck it was dark, what did he do to get it this dark? It had to be black out curtains. Had to fucking be, there wasn't an ounce of sunlight in this fucking house. I had no clue where the fuck the breakers were in this house, that had been Link's job.

Fuck, fuck, fuck. Okay, but if he wasn't here? Was his bike here? I fumbled with my phone, looking for a location and saw his and Theo's locations were off.

Those bastards. They tricked me. No doubt about it, they had to be here right?

"Babygirl, did he not explain the rules? No cell phones." Link's voice came from behind me, I spun around and he plucked the phone right out of my hand. I immediately pulled back, letting him take it.

My heartbeat thudded in my ears loudly, I knew I was safe with them but fuck, this was actually terrifying in a way.

"So you are here. Three against one isn't exactly fair." I took a step back, looking for an escape plan. I could get under him and go upstairs but then I'd actually be trapped.

"Three? It's just me and you right now." He took a step closer, looking menacing and nothing like I'd seen on him before. It almost made me want to see what he would do.

Almost.

I ducked under his arm, "See ya suckaaaaa." I threw up a peace sign and sprinted up the stairs.

I could hear his footsteps behind me, he wasn't even attempting to run after me. I looked back to see him touch his ear under the balaclava and say "Target is going upstairs."

I giggled, but when I turned around I smacked right into Theo, "Easy there, Princess." His hand went over my mouth, "You got away from Link too easily... you won't get away that easily this time."

I stuck my tongue out to lick his hand but he didn't budge, "Matilda, now now..."

I squirmed at the use of my real name and he tightened his hold around my waist and yanked me into a room. It was so dark I couldn't tell whose it was.

I bucked back, trying to get him off and he paused, "Color?"

"Green." I said quietly, before stepping further away from him.

He took a step closer to me, his eyes lit up like they did when he would do his stupid little smirk thing. I darted behind him, half getting the door open only to be met with Link and Coop in masks.

I chuckled nervously, "This isn't fair and you know it." I looked at Coop, who was just a bit taller than Link, "You lied to me, said they weren't here."

"Yeah, my bad." He laughed, but it sounded darker than normal. "Is that a problem?"

I took a step back, only to step into Theo who immediately grabbed my wrists and pinned them behind me. I squealed and pulled away, but even I couldn't deny this was fucking hot.

Coop stepped into my space, "I said is it a problem?"

My chest heaved slightly, "N-No..."

"No, what?" Theo's voice asked in my ear, sending goosebumps down my spine and arms.

"No, sir." I corrected, but my knees felt weak as I said it.

"Good girl, give me a color." Coop's voice was normal for a split second.

"Green." I whispered, I felt a hand tug my chin towards them.

"You wanted to be shared, right baby girl?" Link's voice, I could just barely make out his eyes and a slight spot of blonde hair peaking through at the top of the mask.

I nodded, but it was Theo who spoke up this time. "We need words, Princess."

"Yes, yes I want to be shared. I'm yours." I felt someone's hand in my hair tighten, "Fuck, I'm all of yours." The hand didn't relax at all.

"Good, then let's have some fun." Coop's voice sounded smug.

Theo's hands let go momentarily as they pushed me into the hallway and I broke out of the grip on my hair, it wasn't as hard as I thought it would be. I took off full force, but it didn't last long. One of them grabbed me around the waist and yanked me to them, "You really thought that'd work?" Coop's voice.

Damn, maybe I should have thought about the fact he was used to people running in psych. I had zero chance of one upping them.

"I hoped..." I grumbled, but I wasn't mad, not really.

His grip tightened on me, and I could feel his breath hot against my neck. "Did you really think we wouldn't have planned for that? That's cute."

I struggled against him half-heartedly. My heart was racing, and I couldn't deny the heat pooling between my legs. This was so much better than I could have imagined. It was like they'd plucked the fantasy right out of my head.

"Take her to the bedroom," I heard Link's voice command from somewhere in the hallway.

Coop spun me around, lifting me over his shoulder in one smooth motion. I yelped, my hands instinctively grabbing onto his shirt.

"You guys are really committed to this, huh?" I tried to sound casual, but my voice betrayed me with a slight tremble.

"You have no idea," Theo's voice came from behind us as Coop carried me to the bedroom. I could tell from the layout it was my room, with the new king-sized bed that would finally be put to good use.

He tossed me onto the mattress, and I bounced slightly, my hands instinctively going out to catch myself. Before I could scramble away, Link was there, grabbing my wrists and pinning them above my head.

"Where do you think you're going?" he asked, his voice low and dangerous in a way I'd never heard before. It sent shivers down my spine.

I tugged at my wrists, testing his grip. It was firm but not painful. "Nowhere, apparently."

Theo chuckled from somewhere in the darkness. "Smart girl."

I felt the bed dip as Coop climbed on, his weight settling beside me. I could just make out his silhouette in the darkness, looming over me.

"You know what happens to girls who try to run from us, don't you?" he asked, his voice thick with promise.

I bit my lip, my breath catching. "No, what happens?"

"They get exactly what they wanted all along," Theo's voice came from the foot of the bed. I felt his hands on my ankles, sliding up my calves with deliberate slowness. "And they don't get to decide how."

Link's grip on my wrists tightened slightly. "Color?" he whispered against my ear. Leave it to Link to check in like that.

"Green," I breathed. "I promise I'll say it if I need to."

"Atta girl." Link chuckled, pulling his mask up over his mouth so he could kiss my neck.

I felt hands at the hem of my shirt, pushing it up my stomach. I couldn't tell whose they were in the darkness. I arched my back slightly, my body betraying my eagerness even as I tried to maintain the pretense of resistance.

"Look at you," Coop's voice came from my right. "Already so ready for us."

I felt the cool air hit my skin as my shirt was pulled over my head, Link momentarily releasing my wrists before capturing them again. Someone's hands—Theo's, I thought—were at the button of my jeans now, deftly unfastening them.

"You've been thinking about this, haven't you?" Theo asked, his voice husky as he tugged my jeans down my legs. "About all of us taking you at once."

I bit my lip, not wanting to admit how close to the truth he was. How many times had I fantasized about exactly this scenario?

"Answer him," Link commanded, his lips at my ear.

"Yes," I gasped as someone's hands—Coop's, I thought—cupped my breasts through my bra. "I've thought about it a lot."

"Tell us what you've imagined," Theo commanded, his fingers hooking into the waistband of my underwear.

My cheeks burned hot in the darkness. Even with everything we'd done together, saying my fantasies out loud felt more vulnerable than being nearly naked beneath them.

"I—" I started, but my words were cut off by a soft moan as Link's teeth grazed my neck.

"We're waiting," Coop reminded me, his thumb brushing over my nipple through the thin fabric.

"I imagined being caught between you," I admitted, my voice barely above a whisper. "Being surrounded, not knowing whose hands are where, all of you taking what you want."

I felt rather than saw them exchange glances in the darkness. The atmosphere shifted, their playful dominance taking on a heavier edge.

"Seems like our girl knows exactly what she wants," Theo said, his voice thick with approval.

My underwear slid down my legs, leaving me in just my bra. I shivered, but not from cold. Link's grip on my wrists loosened slightly as he leaned down to whisper in my ear.

"Which one of us do you want first?" he asked, his breath hot against my skin.

Before I could answer, Coop's hand slid between my thighs, finding me already embarrassingly wet. "I don't think she gets to choose," he said, his finger circling my entrance teasingly.

I gasped, my hips bucking up involuntarily. "Please," I whimpered, not even sure what I was asking for. “I want—”

Link paused for a second, I could see he removed his mask completely now. “What do you want? You don’t have to be embarrassed with us.”

“I don’t want you to take turns.” I said quietly, my whole body felt warm at the admission.

“Mils, baby—are you asking for all of us at the same time?” Theo sounded amused and that made it worse.

“Nevermin—” That was definitely an embarrassing ask.

"Don't you dare," Coop cut me off, his voice firm as he shifted on the bed. "Never be embarrassed about what you want with us."

I felt my cheeks burning even in the darkness. "I just thought maybe it was too much."

"Nothing is too much if we all agree," Theo said, his hand sliding up my thigh. "And I think we're all very interested in what you're suggesting."

Link's thumb brushed across my wrist where he still held me. "Tell us exactly what you want, babygirl. No holding back."

I took a deep breath. "I want all of you. At once." My voice was barely a whisper, but I knew they heard me from the way the atmosphere in the room suddenly intensified.

"Color?" Link asked, his voice tighter than before.

"Green," I breathed, "Actually yellow, Lincoln can you at least turn the breaker on."

"Yeah, hold on," Link said, releasing my wrists. "Don't move." He warned, still very much in his dom-mode.

I heard him slip off the bed and fumble his way to the door. A few moments later, there was a distant click, and dim light flooded the room. Not bright, but enough that I could see them all clearly now.

They'd removed their masks, and the sight of all three of them looking down at me with such intensity made my breath catch. Theo's eyes were dark with desire, Coop looked almost predatory, and Link's face was flushed as he returned to the bed.

"Better?" he asked, crawling back onto the mattress.

I nodded, suddenly feeling exposed under their gazes in the new light. "Yes, thank you."

Coop's hand slid up my thigh, reclaiming his position. "Now, where were we?"

Theo leaned down and kissed me, his lips hungry against mine as Coop's fingers teased my entrance. I moaned into Theo's mouth, my back arching off the bed.

"You want all of us?" Theo whispered against my lips. "You're sure about this?"

"Yes," I breathed, looking between them. "I've thought about it... a lot."

Link's hand replaced Theo's on my wrists, pinning me down again as Theo moved lower on the bed. I felt him settle between my legs, his breath hot against my core.

"Who goes where?" Coop asked, his voice husky as he watched Theo's head dip between my thighs.

I gasped as Theo's tongue found me, my hips bucking involuntarily. Link tightened his grip on my wrists, but his thumb traced circles into my skin.

I met Link's eyes, I already knew I wanted him to be the one to do anal, I knew he wouldn't hurt me. Not that the others would, but Link would be extra careful, I knew that and he knew that.

"She's made up her mind already about at least one of them." Theo grinned up at me, "You're just trying to figure out if Coop is comfortable enough with Link for all that."

I flushed, looking away because damn it, how had he known?

Theo shifted, swiping through my folds one last time before he moved up towards where Link was. "Coop lay down." Link said, his voice gentle but slightly commanding.

"This is the one and only time you get to use that voice on me." Coop warned and I stifled a laugh, because I doubted that.

I climbed on top of Coop and sank down onto him, Theo was doing something and then disappeared for a moment before coming back in and tossing Link a bottle. Lube I realized.

I tried to keep down the nervousness as Link pushed me down onto Coop's chest, his fingers brushing across my back for a second urging me to relax. Coop put an arm around me as he rocked up into me, causing me to gasp.

The lube was cold, "Sorry, I would have had it warmed up—but didn't realize we'd need it..." Link apologized, I didn't know that was a thing, but given Link's bougie ass it probably was.

He inserted a finger and I stiffened, he stopped, "Mils, you have to relax. If you need Coop to stop for a second, just tell him."

I forced myself to relax fully into Coop, grinding myself further down onto him and letting him do the work for a second. Link added in another finger, but this time it was Coop who made a noise. "Fuck, okay, that's why you needed to know if I was comfortable with it..."

Link flushed, "I can switch for Theo..."

I looked at him and Theo shook his head, "Nope, if anything I'm switching with Coop. She picked you."

At least he understood.

Coop sighed, "It's fine, no one has to switch. I'm fine with Link. I promise."

I pushed back into Link more when he added the third finger and he pushed me back down, "I don't want to hurt you, let me do this the right way."

I groaned, but listened. Coop fastened his pace, enough to keep me happy while Link worked me open. I tugged at Theo's boxers and pulled them down, immediately taking him in my mouth. His hand laced itself into my hair, grabbing at the base of my head, “Fuck, look at you taking us all so well.”

I grabbed Theo’s hips and pulled him closer as Coop thrusted into me harder, I heard the cap of the lube bottle again and Theo lifted my head off of him. “You ready?” He asked, and I felt Link slide himself in slowly.

I fell into Coop for a second, letting my body get used to the feeling of both of them. “Fuck... Link...” Coop’s voice sounded broken and slightly ashamed.

Link chuckled into my hair, “Can you feel him?” I asked quietly.

Coop nodded, trying to match Link’s pace. “Words Cooper.” Link spoke softly, like he was testing something.

“You both feel so fucking good.” Coop said as he rocked into me, I felt the way Link faltered at that ever-so-slightly.

Oh yeah, they were definitely into each other and didn’t want to admit it.

Theo shifted closer to my face, sliding his tip against my lips. "I didn't forget about this pretty mouth of yours," he said, his voice husky as he guided himself past my lips, tapping my cheek lightly.

I moaned around him as Link and Coop established a rhythm, each thrust sending waves of pleasure through me. It was overwhelming in the best possible way—being completely filled, surrounded by them, exactly as I'd fantasized.

"Fuck, you feel so good," Coop groaned beneath me, his hands gripping my hips tightly.

I felt Link's hand smooth down my spine. "You're taking us so well, babygirl," he praised, his voice strained with the effort of maintaining control. "Color?"

I hummed around Theo, unable to speak with my mouth full.

"Tap his leg once for green, twice for yellow, three for red," Link instructed, I tapped once.

I felt myself tighten around Coop as Link went in deeper this time, I almost choked on Theo as I went all the way down. He pulled me up for a second, letting me catch my breath. “You’re doing so good.”

I added a hand to Theo along with my mouth as I stroked him, “Shit, you’re trying to make me come faster aren’t you?”

My giggle turned into a loud muffled moan as both Coop and Link fastened their pace, "Fuck, I can't..." Link groaned and I felt the way he twitched inside of me as he came.

"Shit," Coop cursed and I felt him come too.

I increased my pace with Theo, intent on getting him off too. He fisted my hair and forced my head down lower, I swirled my tongue on him and fondled his balls and felt his legs lock up just before he shot his release down my throat.

I swallowed it, because I am a good girl.

Link pulled out of me slowly and when I looked at him he looked smugger than ever, "Whatever you're about to say, do not." I said, but he was looking at Coop now.

"You definitely came with me."

I snorted and even Theo chuckled. "Link, leave the man alone."

"What? It's just an observation." He shrugged, then rolled his head over to me, "You need to go to the bathroom."

I pouted, because honestly? I didn't know if I could.

Theo's the one who caught onto that. "Princess, do you need me to help?"

I felt like something was sitting on my chest. I wanted a shower but I also wanted to stay right here with them. I felt like I was going to cry if I got up.

I shook my head, "Nah, I got this." I climbed off of Coop, pressing a kiss to his lips. "I'll be right back."

I didn't have it in me for a full shower, so I bird bathed it after I used the bathroom. I ran the water until it was hot and cleaned myself up. I was unsteady and shaking. I splashed water on my face, fuck why was I crying? There was no reason to be fucking cry.

Someone knocked on the door, I ignored it. I wanted to lock the door until I could control my emotions, I didn't for the record. Which is why when Theo opened the door I turned to hide the tears that were falling down my face. "I thought so," he pulled me into a hug and I melted into it. My body shook against his as held me close, "You're dropping. Come on." He scooped me up and carried me back to the bed.

Link kissed my lips as he went to the bathroom to clean up too. "I'll be right back, love." He reassured me.

I cuddled into Theo and Coop, Coop at my back and practically laid on top of Theo as he held me tightly. "We've got you, it's okay."

"I don't know why I'm crying..." I admitted, as Theo wiped my cheeks.

"You just did a big scene, we chased you through the house in the dark. You just did something your body isn't used to. It's normal, it's a drop." Theo kissed my hair and I felt Coop's fingers drawing patterns on my stomach.

"How did you know?" I asked quietly.

"I dropped a lot after Link and I did things."

"Wait, you never told me that." Link looked hurt as he came back into the room, a frown settling on his face.

"We weren't serious, it wasn't your responsibility." Theo shrugged, Link got into the bed behind Coop, lying on his back so they weren't touching.

"It was my responsibility though...I'm sorry." He spoke quietly, like he was upset with himself.

I lifted up slightly so I could turn to see Link. I knew he didn't do well with things like that. I reached my hand over Coop to touch Link, to help ground him too.

Coop's blue eyes found mine, "You okay?" I asked, needing to check in with all of them after that.

Coop had been quiet, like eerily quiet, even for him. "I'm okay, baby, I'm okay."

I pressed a kiss to his lips, that sinking feeling in my chest still there. I hoped I hadn't ruined everything by asking for that, they must think the worst of me.

I mean who wouldn't?

My eyes watered again, Coop saw it this time. "Hey...no, no, I'm not in my head about you, come here."

Fuck, I'd just gotten myself to stop shaking and that tremble now felt bone deep. I shifted to cuddle into Coop, my face in his neck as I took a deep breath in.

"I'm—I'm going to go get us all some water." Link said, shifting slightly on the bed. I reached my hand out to stop him, my silent little plea to get him to stay. “In this life and the next Mils, I’ll be right back.” He promised, kissing my hand.

Once Link was down the hall, footsteps barely there anymore, Coop brushed my hair back gently. “He loves you more than you can imagine.”

“That’s where you’re wrong, he loves all of us more than you can imagine. Link has never just tolerated people, he either loves you or he doesn’t.”

Theo nodded behind me, “I believe that.”

I traced Coop’s stubble with my fingers, “I think you might be a part of that too, ya know?”

He chewed his cheek, I felt him pull at it. “I’ve never really thought about ending up with multiple people, but it’s feeling like that more and more.”

Link knocked, like actually knocked on my door frame. “Sorry I didn't mean to interrupt, I have brought back hydration though.” He sat on the bed, not making a move to lay back down.

“I can lay next to Theo if you want me too.” he whispered and Coop shook his head, moving over more so Link had more room if he wanted it.

I watched the two of them closely, ughh, my heart.

“I love you,” I admitted, “All of you.” I made sure to meet each of their eyes.

Link laid next to Coop and I saw the way he looked at him, he could deny it all he wanted but I knew that look.

It was the same way he used to look at me before I was his.

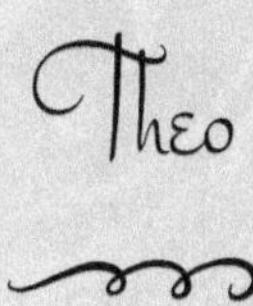

We'd skipped off work for three days after the fact, Jonah was pissed—more about me than Millie. So the fourth day we begrudgingly decided we should go back in, Millie was not into it.

I knew she wouldn't be, but a few energy drinks and a shit ton of candy later she wasn't as miserable. She did however spend a whole stage set basically stretching until a man came up to talk to her.

I saw the switch flip almost instantly, she turned into Jade without hesitation. She was a fucking beast honestly, I wasn't sure I could do that.

If I had to switch personalities for each customer, I'd fail. Immensely. Sure, her real personality came out sometimes here—especially with the sweeter guys, the ones she knew needed that. I tried to school my jealousy when it came to that, it was just Millie being the sun. She would give what she could when she could.

This guy however was very touchy feely, even on stage, Millie did a few pole tricks then exited the stage and led him to the VIP booth, she took him the champagne room, so she'd be back there for at least thirty minutes.

I looked down at the camera every so often, it wasn't that I was necessarily jealous, but things had shifted. With all of us. It was more serious now.

When her time ran out, he paid for more time. She'd conned him into rubbing her feet while she played with his hair and I could feel my mood turning sour.

I tried to remember this was literally her job, she got paid for this. I busied myself getting the playlists together for the other girls.

Gracie was the first to call me out. "Are you and Millie fighting?"

"What makes you ask?" I questioned, trying to school my face.

"Nothing. No reason, I just haven't seen you look this angry in months." She wrote her name on the stage paper and headed towards Toby who was talking to Jonah.

I fiddled with the lights as Britt stepped on stage and clicked her playlist. She started her little warm up stretches and eventually went into her normal tricks, I wasn't paying attention.

I kept my eyes on the room Millie was in, she wasn't breaking any rules but I was mad. I had no fucking reason to be. Absolutely none.

When her room was done, she sat at the bar with the man.

All night.

He slid her a twenty every hour, I didn't blame her for staying. What really fucked with me was when she saved his number and texted him.

She fucking texted him.

At the bar.

Right in front of me. Right in front of the cameras, was she dumb? I knew some of the girls did that shit, but Millie? My Millie?

She must have seen my face, because she mouthed "What?"

I shook my head. Nope. Not going there right now.

This was the one thing I wouldn't do, I wouldn't fucking deal with this shit at work—regardless of if it happened at work.

"I'll be right back, gotta go check in with the DJ to make sure I'm on rotation." She said sweetly, rubbing his back.

When she came up to me she looked confused, "What's wrong? What happened?"

"We'll talk in the car." I said, barely looking up at her.

"Theo—" Her face fell, great, now she was going to be mad at me, but we really couldn't talk about it here.

"I said we'll talk in the car." I repeated, this time meeting her eyes, I was serious.

Not here.

"Fine." She grumbled, stalking off back towards the bar, mouthing "Eat rocks."

Great, that's where we were tonight.

Fan-fucking-tastic.

Theo slammed the car door, "What the fuck was that?"

"What ever do you mean?" I glared at him.

"You gave that man your number? At the fucking bar?!"

I scoffed, I'd given that man my fake number and got paid for it. I had an app with a second number, it was encrypted and safe. He was overreacting. "Theo, you're overreacting—it wasn't even my number!"

"So you didn't give that man a phone number to contact you?" He deadpanned, his fingers thrumming against the steering wheel.

I looked down, "I mean I did..."

"And you didn't think about that?"

I had thought about it, it's literally how I get and keep regulars. He was out of his mind if he thought it was anything else. I didn't do outcalls, he knew that—he knew I only went to work and when I wasn't at work I was with one of them.

"Theodore, are you asking as my boyfriend or as my co-worker right now?"

He glanced at me, then back at the road.

"Ah, so boyfriend. It's not like that... I'm telling you it's not like that."

"Do you think Coop would see it like that? Or Link? Because I know the fucking game, I know the industry."

I looked at him, "Link wouldn't. Link knows the game, he knows my game. It's how you get regulars, how you keep them." I sighed, "This is actually sounding a lot more like Jonah territory, so why do you just go ahead and message him then if you think it's such a problem. Every fucking girl does it."

Theo looked down at his phone, "So Coop doesn't know."

I huffed, rolling my eyes. "It never came up, fuck, I'll tell him, just stop with your bullshit tonight."

"Stop with my bullshit??" He exhaled deeply, "Millie, that guy was looking at you like he wanted you."

I cackled, "News flash, they all want me."

"And you entertained it." He snapped, trying to keep his eyes on the road, the speedometer creeping up slightly.

"Theo, I'm literally an entertainer. Why are you—?"

He cut me off, "You didn't talk to me all night, you were all over him, you didn't smack his hand the first time he got handsy."

"He had a black card Theo! Again I wanted a repeat customer and I still told him no." I turned towards him again, my arms crossed, "Oh my God, you're so fucking jealous right now. You're picking a fight with me because you're fucking jealous?" I glanced at his speedometer, "You need to slow down before Link calls one of us."

"Oh yeah, bring Link into it to calm the situation down." He hissed, his eyes glancing over to me then down, hardly slowing down.

"Pull over." I snapped, I was fucking done. If he wanted to be fucking childish, I was getting out.

He glanced over at me, "No, you're not fucking walking right now."

I grabbed the handle of the door and unbuckled, "Pull the fuck over, Theodore."

"Fine." He threw his arm out in front of me and stomped the break, throwing me into his arm harder than necessary.

"Eat fucking rocks, you asshole." I grumbled, shoving his arm away from me and opening the door.

He shrugged, following me out of the car, "Hey, you took off your seatbelt, I could have let you hit the dash." I pulled out my phone as it was ringing, called it—Link. "Y'all went from eighty to a full stop. Are y'all good?"

"We're having a disagreement, can you come get me? I'm not getting back in his car tonight." I glanced over at Theo who was leaned against his car with his arms crossed watching me pace.

"You want a ride?" Link asked, concern layered in his voice.

"Please, if you're awake enough." I didn't want him driving at all, car or bike if he was tired.

"I'm good to drive, I've been awake. Took a nap earlier so I could wait up for the two of you."

"Okay, I love you—I'll see you when you get here." I said softly before clicking end call.

Theo stepped towards me, "Millie, if you get on his bike and don't finish this conversation—"

"You'll what? Never forgive me? Break up with me?" I threw my hands up, standing my ground. "Fucking say whatever it is you need to say. I won't apologize when I haven't done anything wrong, I'm sorry if I made you feel that way but I didn't do anything wrong."

He pushed his hands through his hair, "The fact you don't fucking see it is insane, you know that?"

When Link pulled up, he could see the tension radiating between us, he crossed his arms. "Nuhuh, make up. You're not getting on this bike until you do."

"I said my peace." I shrugged, tugging on the spare helmet. "He can do what he wants."

Link hesitated, "Mils..."

"I'm tired Link, please." He adjusted my helmet, making sure it was snug, and I hugged my arms around him, making sure to lean with him as we took off.

He didn't push the speed today, just letting us enjoy the cool night air. I looked behind us, of course he was following behind, probably stewing in his own head, I don't think he expected me to hold my ground on it, but I'll be fucking damned if he was going to get mad about a customer, he knew me better than that.

Regulars and having fall back money made it so I didn't have to go in as often, I could just call them and come in whenever they wanted to see me. It was smart.

Especially since I was considering leaving the industry more and more.

Theo

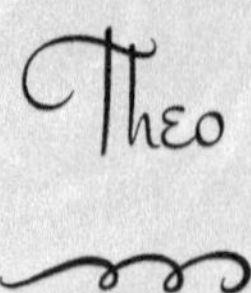

It happened faster than I could comprehend. Link had waited, he'd checked everything. The car flew through the intersection, fuck, fuck, *fuck*.

No. This wasn't real life, right?

I didn't see which person took the blunt of it, I know Link flew off the bike. I'd seen that and I knew I'd probably relive that for the rest of my life. I swallowed in air fast, probably too fast, as I pulled my car to the side of the road and hit my hazards.

"Please, please, please be alive." I begged, my throat tightening around my words, Gods please, do me a favor just this once.

Millie was on the side of the road, the car had kept going. Straight through, running the bike over completely and then plowed into the tree line. There was no one else on the streets. Millie groaned, picking herself up from the grass.

"Lay back down, I've got him. Don't fucking move." I ran past her, sinking to the concrete. My hands shook as I felt for a pulse, it was there but barely—just barely.

"Please don't right now, I'm fine." She tugged her helmet off, limping her way to Link. She looked around her eyes scanning for her phone, but the screen was shattered and half the glass was missing when she found it.

"My phone is shattered, I need your phone." Millie sank to her knees as I handed her my phone, Link's blood on the back of it from my hands.

"Call 911, right now."I said, she dialed, her hands shaking, her teeth were clattering so hard and she was pale.

"Don't you dare pass out on me, Mils." I looked her over as I kept my hands on Link, I couldn't even tell where the blood was coming from—there was so much.

"Our app already notified to a crash." She stuttered out, "I need an ambulance, maybe fire and rescue. I don't know, umm, maybe two ambulances. He hit our motorcycle. I was a passenger—I uhh..."

I took the phone. "Stay with him, I'm going to check the other car," I directed at her, as she swayed a little on her knees. "I witnessed it, I'm going to go check the other car. The driver of the motorcycle is not good, pulse is weak. Please hurry." My voice broke as my sobs broke through.

The car was wrapped around the tree, god how fucking fast was he going? "This car doesn't look good. Only one passenger that I can see. He's moving."

I didn't want to leave them alone, help would be here soon enough —if they were moving they were fine. At least that's what I told myself, I had to, as sirens approached in the background.

Millie was sobbing, she looked even worse than I thought, I pulled her into me as I sank beside her. "Don't move him." I said as she went to move his neck, "You could hurt him more, baby look at me, look at me." She was hyperventilating, if she has a concussion she needed to breathe.

"Link, please, if you can hear me please don't die on us, please." I checked his pulse again and Millie crawled into the grass away from us. I tried to call out to her, to stop her, but my voice wasn't working.

I felt sick, I was in shock, I'd never been in shock before. I could hear Millie throwing up between sobs. I really needed to check on her, but she was alive, she was up. I couldn't leave him.

I couldn't leave his side.

Please don't die. Please don't die. Please don't die.

A four am alert, a speed alert.

Another alert not even fifteen minutes later? Crash alert?

Fuck. Oh fuck. I checked the locations, all of them? All of them??

How could they all be right there? I threw on the closest pairs of pants, Link's sweat pants and a hoodie, slipping on a pair of slides. I didn't know who they belonged to but it was easy.

I pushed it to the intersection, pulling up to the lights. A helicopter was on the highway, no, life flight was serious. Life flight meant someone was about to die. Fire trucks, ems, police cars. Theo was up and talking to a cop.

I parked my car by his and ran to the scene, well I tried. A cop stopped me, "What happened? Who's in the helicopter? That's my family."

Theo said something to the cop who ushered me over, "You're the fiancé?" The cop questioned.

"Yes, yes."

"Your fiancée was on a motorcycle, she's in that ambulance. She's going to New Hanover."

Theo had red eyes, "Link's being airlifted, he's stable but hardly... it doesn't look good."

"Why was Millie on the bike? I thought she was with you?"

"Can we do this later please?" Theo inhaled, tears rolling down his face as the helicopter lifted and started to fly off.

I looked down and noticed another car, "What about that car?"

"That's the one that hit them, blew through a red light. Ran over the bike and kept going into the trees. He was awake when I checked on him." Theo said, sitting down on the curb and crumbling into his hands.

He wasn't telling me something.

The cop came over to me, "He shouldn't drive in this state, but can you move the car to the side. I'll tag it so no other cop does. Just come get it tomorrow."

I took Theo's keys and moved it into the grass. Making sure to lock the doors. I lifted him up, pulling him to his feet. "Come on, I'll get us in. I work there remember."

Theo fell into the passenger seat, "It's my fault. It's my fault. Millie and I were fighting. She called Link to come get her because I was speeding... if I'd have just shut up—"

"Hey, he's stable right?"

"Stable as in not dead yet, yeah."

"Don't.. don't say it like that."

Fuck, not Link.

My heart hurt. Millie was by herself, Link was by himself. I pushed the gas, ignoring the police behind us. Trying to catch up with the ambulance. We blew through two red lights with the ambulance.

I know I got two traffic light picture violations at least, but it was fine. I didn't care. I could pay them.

When we got there and parked, we basically ran to the ER side, I pulled Theo to the desk. "My fiancée and his boyfriend just arrived, a motorcycle accident. Matilda Adams and Lincoln Scott."

"Lincoln Scott is in surgery. They just took him back. We can bring you to Matilda. Cooper James?"

I gave her a barely there smile, it was all I could manage, "Hey Mrs. Trixie, probably going to need to call out this morning aren't I?"

She gave me a nod and made a call to psych, I knew that extension number immediately. "Hey, Amanda. One of your guys just came in. His partners were involved in a motorcycle accident. Might want to take this as a call off, add it as paid day off since he's in here anyway."

"How did you—?" I questioned.

"I follow you on social media, you're always cozied up with these three." She pointed towards the waiting area, "I know you know your way around. You can both go back when they let you know. Don't wander off looking for them please."

I pulled Theo into me, wrapping my arms around him. "Millie is fine, Theo. Link is going to be okay. He has to be."

I felt the tears coming down my face, Theo had blood on his hands I noticed. I pulled him up, not saying anything, and tugged him into the bathroom.

I ran his hands under water as he sobbed, I had never seen him crumble. I'd never seen him cry like this, but I guess seeing someone you love like that, that would do it.

Once it was off of him I pulled him into a hug, letting him collapse on me. "Come on, we gotta go out there so we can know when they call us back."

Millie

If these damn nurses didn't let me see him I was going to freak the fuck out, I was going to rip this fucking IV out of my arm and start walking until I found someone who could help.

There was a knock on my door, it slid open, Coop. Thank fucking God. "Coop!" I went to get up and he narrowed his eyes at me, then at the nurse.

Theo appeared behind him and I couldn't even bring myself to be mad, if I wouldn't have called Link he wouldn't look like that. "Theo..." I said, voice breaking as he made his way to me.

"I'm sorry... I'm sorry... I'm so sorry." He pulled me into a hug, basically crawling into the bed with me. I scooted to make room for him. Wincing as he touched my hip.

"We had to pop her hip back in place," the nurse clearly knew Coop, knew him enough to just give my medical information freely. Not that I was complaining.

"Which of you is the fiancé?"

I probably looked really confused, "We're all together."

"All of you?"

"All of us, including Lincoln, but if you need it for records— Coop is my emergency contact. Theo is Link's, it's in his phone. If you have it I can unlock it." I said quietly, "Fuck, I need to call his parents."

"We can do that." The nurse said, "Just give us the numbers."

"No, this woman is basically my mom, she'll answer my call." I said, fumbling with my shattered phone.

The nurse excused herself, leaving a folder on the table, which Coop picked up.

I hit call on Link's mom, "Mom, Link and I are at the hospital, New Hanover... I—I need you. Link needs you."

"How bad is it?"

I felt my chest seize up as I remembered the blood on the concrete, as I felt for his pulse and found a weak one. As I prayed to every God or Goddess that would listen. I couldn't tell her that. A sob broke through, sending pain rippling through my body,

Coop took the phone, "Mrs. Scott's this is Cooper. I'm a friend of Millie and Link's. They were in a motorcycle accident. We know just as much as you do, he's in surgery right now. He was life-flighted here, Millie came in by ambulance."

I couldn't tell what she was saying, and Coop's responses seemed far away. My head fucking hurt, my tears fell faster.

Surgery meant he would be okay? Right? That they'd do what they could? New Hanover was a trauma center, they were equipped for this, right?

I felt sick. My best friend was going to die and it was my fault. I knew the fucking statistics. I knew most motorcycle accidents result in death.

I tapped Theo to get off, he sat up, looking at me with sad puppy dog eyes. I grabbed the IV pole and wheeled it to the bathroom, the warm feeling in my throat bubbling up.

I was going to throw up and if I was going to do it, no one was going to see it.

I was right, it came up seconds later.

And of course, of course Coop came in looking concerned. "You have a concussion..."

"I know, I hit the concrete before I rolled into the grass." I grumbled, trying to ignore the pain in my entire body.

"Mils, baby girl." Coop pulled my hair back.

"Do not baby girl me right now. Not when Link is—" my voice broke as another sob ripped through me.

I meant what I said, I can't do this without him. I don't want to. If he dies... if he dies... if he dies—I can't. *I won't.*

"Hey, no... he's in the best hands. His mom is on the way." I looked up at him, his eyes were red, he had tear stains on his face too.

"You're trying really hard to keep it together right now aren't you?" I asked quietly, the guilt hitting me ten times harder seeing him holding it all back for my sake.

Coop pulled me up, pulling me into a hug—careful to avoid the IV. "I'm scared... as a nurse I'm scared, okay. I'm going to lose someone I love, and I'm going to watch the other two blame themselves."

My chest stuttered, the sob catching in my throat. "Coop—"

He said he loved Link. Oh my god, he said he loved Link.

"Come on, you need Theo as much as Theo needs us right now. I'm going to go see if I can get some more information. I gave his mom your room number."

I've never had an out of body experience before. Maybe I needed to think a little more seriously on Theo's metaphysical bullshit, maybe he wasn't so wrong.

I could see the monitors, I could see the blood being fed into my body. I could see them trying to stop whatever was bleeding in me.

Those bastards better not—

And there goes the hair.

What the fuck.

What are they putting in my fucking head?

Oh great. I probably have brain damage or something.

Perfect love that for me. *Brain damage and bald*. I wonder if I can walk down these halls? Float? Whatever.

If I were a trauma where would I go? I wanted to find Millie. I hope Theo and Coop were here with her.

Shit, I hope someone called my parents.

God forbid a man die without everyone here crying over him.

I felt a tug, *oh nope*, back to the operating room I go. I guess.

Well, hey I always did want to see surgeons in action.

Theo

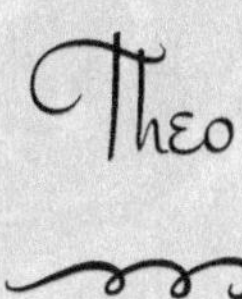

I had actually cried myself to sleep. Millie had tucked me into her bed, they were keeping her on observation. I had woke briefly to someone coming in and causing a fuss, but Coop shut it down immediately. They had listened, whoever it was.

Millie was playing with my hair, Coop hadn't sat down once. I'd heard the door open a few times, but I was so tired.

"How is she?" I heard a woman whisper.

"She has a concussion, they had to pop her hip back in place. She has a few fractures. Other than that, she's okay. Some mild road rash on her arm I think."

God's Coop, you're not even the nurse. You're a nurse, not her nurse.

"He's out of surgery, but I don't want to wake her until we know more. He's in a medically induced coma, we won't know more until he wakes up. He has a TBI, internal bleeding they were able to fix during surgery. He lost a lot of blood, but he's alive."

Coop sniffled, the woman—I'm assuming Link's mom—continued, "And something tells me you know more than you're letting on."

"I'm a nurse, I'm not a trauma nurse, I work in psych..." a sob came from him, his voice broken. "but I know medical terms."

"They said there's a good chance..." his mom said quietly.

"It's a good hospital and Link is stubborn."

"What are you to him?" she asked.

Coop hesitated, "Umm, I love him. Just like I love Millie and Theo."

Just like he loves us? I knew it.

I sat up blurry eyed and looked at them, "He's out of surgery?"

"You must be Theo, Link told me about you." There was no doubt this woman was his mom, they had the same eyes and freckles. Although her hair was the sandy blonde Link liked to hide under his bleach blonde highlights.

"Hopefully good things." I gave her a small smile, "Sorry we're meeting under the worst possible circumstances."

"Just wondering why we haven't met your mother yet." She raised an eyebrow.

Oh. Oh? Link had told her about us like that?

"He never asked." I admitted.

"Mom?" Millie spoke quietly, squinting towards the sound.

I got up to make room for them, "Oh hunny, I'm so glad you're okay."

Link's mom immediately pulled her into a hug. Embracing her like her own child. And I guess she kind of was at this point. Millie immediately broke down.

"Let's give them a minute." Coop tugged on my arm, "Go get some food. Some juice for Millie. She's going to be extremely unhappy about the no energy drink rule. I'll mix it with ginger ale and hope it satisfies her."

Coop

When I get my hands on that boy.

I'm going to strangle him for making me care so much. Well, maybe once he's healed and good. If he dies on me? I'm buying an ouija board and cussing him the fuck out.

I can't. I can't deal with it.

He can't die.

My fucking cat loves him for crying out loud.

Millie needs him like oxygen. I wasn't sure what would happen if he died, I didn't want her to become a shell of herself, and I didn't want to have to be the one to call for an involuntary hold if she tried to hurt herself.

He's Theo's person even if he doesn't realize he is and fuck maybe he was becoming that for me too. Insane little shit. I told him I didn't like the bike, I'd seen too much shit come through the emergency room.

It's exactly why I switched to psych, I couldn't handle it. I have no idea what the scene looked like before I got there, but Theo seeing it happen?

Fuck, my boy was going to have fucking C-PTSD for life at this point.

Fuck and Millie? She would probably never get on another bike ever again.

If Link—no, when Link survives this, I'm taking all his fucking gear and burning it. He won't be getting another one. Ever. Theo and Millie would never have peace if he did.

"Coop!"

I narrowed my eyes at Theo, "What? Why are you yelling at me?"

"I've been trying to get your attention for like ten minutes now." he said, softer now, his eyes puffy and red.

"Sorry, I'm just in my head." I admitted, lacing my fingers into his.

"Aren't we all." Theo sighed, "He's going to wake up, right?"

"I don't know..." I shrugged, I wasn't fate, I couldn't decide that. It was up to whatever higher power and Link's will to stay here. To come back to us.

"Should I ask him to marry me?"

My head whipped to him so fast, "You're serious?"

"Sirius Bl–" he smiled weakly, but cut himself off when he realized he was making a funny at a time like this.

"Maybe get him a ring first." I suggested, grabbing his hand and pulling him closer.

"You wouldn't be mad?" he asked, looking at me now, like I would be mad about that?

"Theo. I love you." I paused, "I love Millie and fuck I think I love him. I wouldn't be mad. You're my family, you all are." I admitted, squeezing his hand in my own.

Millie

"So you and Theo seem pretty close too?" Mom, well Link's mom, asked.

"Umm, yeah about that." I frowned, "It's complicated. The guys and I—were all together. Well except Link and Coop. They're more like best friends."

"I don't think so..." Mom said, her eyes darting to the door, "Coop seemed more like a concerned boyfriend for all of you."

"He's the dad of the group for sure." I laughed quietly, leaning into her shoulder.

"When are you two finally going to give me grand-babies?" she asked, grinning at me like she'd been waiting ages to finally say that.

My eyes widened, shock probably written all over my face. "Mom!"

"What?" She shrugged, "It's a valid question, you just said you're all together. So grand-babies, I'm not getting any younger."

"We'll see." I rolled my eyes at her antics.

She'd probably *had* wanted to ask that question for years.

The door opened and instead of the guys it was a nurse. "If you want to see him, we cleared you to go in, both of you. I have to warn you, it's not pretty."

I looped my arm in hers, knowing she needed me just as much. "Where's dad?"

"He's on his way. He had to book an emergency flight this morning. He's in Florida." *Fuck, Florida?* That was a good twelve hours or longer by car.

The nurse pulled us into the ICU room and my heart dropped. He was bandaged up pretty well, he had his head wrapped in gauze as well. So much for his helmet being top of the line.

He'd said he loved me right before he sped up. He knew it would hit me or him and he'd made a choice. He took the most damage. He should have let it hit me.

It was my fault he was even here. Tubes down his throat, machines beeping in tandem.

Damn it Link.

He was alive. He was alive and that's all that mattered right now.

I didn't follow the nurse as well as I'd have liked, I wished Coop was here to translate the medical garble.

Mom sat to the right of him, her hand lying over his. I couldn't bring myself to pull my chair to his side. I wanted to, but fuck seeing him like this scared me. What if he never came back? What if he did and he wasn't Link anymore? What if he didn't want anything to do with me or Theo?

I tried to shake it off, pulling up a chair to his other side and slipping my hand in his. "Dude, you can't leave us like this. You're supposed to go out jumping out of a plane with me. Or cliff jumping. Or something equally terrifying. Not like this." I dropped my head to his hand—pressing a light kiss to his fingers. "Your mom wants a little Link Millie hybrid running around eventually." I said quietly.

Obviously, we'd never discussed kids, ever. I wasn't even sure I wanted them, but if he woke up right now and asked for a baby I'd probably give him one.

Shit, I'd probably pray to whatever God or Goddess I could everyday if that meant he walked away from this how he was before.

Okay, maybe I'm trying to bargain. Definitely.

"You think it's your fault don't you?" Mom asked, studying me.

I wiped the tears with my hand. "It kind of is."

"Millie, baby, the man that hit you had a 0.29 BAC. It wasn't your fault. Traffic cams are being pulled, but Theo said Link checked the intersection before going and had a green light. This isn't your fault."

"I called him to come get me, I shouldn't have done that." I choked on a sob, folding my hands in my lap nervously.

She sighed, "He shouldn't have defaulted to his bike on a weekend at four in the morning."

"He'll always find a reason for the bike." I chuckled, because he would.

"Not anymore, his bike is totaled. Completely. And as his mom, if he gets another one you tell me because I'm going to steal it." she narrowed her eyes, "Don't let my son get another bike."

"He's going to have to fight all of us if he wants another one." I told her, squeezing his hand.

For a second it felt like he squeezed back, just the softest pressure. "I think he just squeezed my hand."

I squeezed his hand again, hoping for another sign—another squeeze—anything for him to let me know he was there.

It didn't come.

"Fuck Link..." I dropped my head to his bed, trying my best to keep it together. Shit, if his mom was keeping it together, I could.

Mom stood up, squeezing his hand one last time before brushing my hair back. "I'm going to call his dad, I think his flight just landed—do you want me to find the boys?"

"Please..."

This felt like defeat. Like he might not ever make it out of this fucking hospital, maybe I'd imagined him squeezing my hand. Maybe I just wanted him too.

If he doesn't make it... I don't know if I will. It's always been him and I. The two goofy kids who understood each other. But this? This I didn't fucking understand. Why did he speed up? Why did he let me take the full force of it?

Why did it have to be him?

Why did I call him? Because I'm stubborn as fuck and Theo was being an ass. We never even talked it out. I needed to apologize but it didn't feel right, not right now.

Right now it was forgotten, not important. I shifted in the seat, pain shooting through my side. Oh yeah, fuck, that hurt.

My face was wet, I was crying openly on his sheets and I didn't care.

"Mils...I think your nurse is looking for you." Coop's voice rang out, I lifted my head slowly.

A nurse peered in, "If you can come with me, I'm gonna do one last check over and get you discharged."

"I don't have clothes..." I whispered, pulling the sleeves of Theo's hoodie over my hands.

Mom looked over at me, "I can go see what the gift shop has." Her eyes darted to Theo and Coop, "Stay with my boy, please."

I begrudgingly followed the nurse back to my room.

We'd all taken shifts with Link's parents, the hospital allowing three of us in instead. I'd go home and check on my cat, come back and force Theo and Millie to eat something.

Sitting in the waiting room with one of them, this was day four. Day four and no change. I knew what that meant, his parents had been told. I was just waiting for someone to say something, maybe I needed to bring it up.

I wasn't sure.

I don't know how to do this.

This is why I did psych, I didn't have to deal with death often. Not like this.

How can I tell them? How could I be the one to fucking tell the two people I love that they are about to lose the person they're both in love with? They could deny it all they want, but that was the truth.

For fuck's sakes, Theo asked if he should marry him. How can I—I can't. I'm not fucking strong enough for this. I can't do it.

This is where a social worker comes in, our chaplain. Someone. Anyone but me. Link is not my patient—he's my—fuck what even were we? What are we?

Maybe I just needed to get them home for a night, get them a decent night's sleep. Ease them into him not being there. In his house. Fuck, what happens when Millie doesn't have him anymore?

When *we* don't have him anymore?

I pushed open the door, his mother was shifting through paperwork, her eyes rimmed red.

"Thank Gosh it's you, I can't—I can't look at Millie and tell her..."

"He's not coming back is he?" I asked quietly, but I knew. I fucking knew already.

Fuck. Fuck. *FUCK*.

"They don't think so." She shifted her papers, before putting them down on the windowsill. "Did you know he left everything he owns to you three?"

"What? Three?"

"Yeah, he specified that a third of it go to Cooper James so his cat can continue to enjoy the fancy treats and robotic laser toys. And for any and all future vet bills. Also, to buy Millie hardcovers and special editions on her birthday or if she ever misses me."

"He knew he'd die on that fucking bike didn't he?"

"Seemed like he knew there was a chance, yeah."

I looked down at him, at the different monitors and tubes. "Link, man, come on. Don't do this to us." I paused, my voice shaking, "Don't do this to Millie. Or Theo. Fuck, I need you to come back. I need you to fucking fight. I love you and they love you. Your parents love you." I took his hand in both of mine, "I'll never call you blondie again." I let out a watery laugh, "Or Ponyboy."

I sat there for seconds that felt like hours, willing something to change, please anything.

I can't do it, I didn't want to. Not just for how I knew this would wreck Theo and how I knew Millie would never come back from this, but because we had things to talk about. We needed to know what we were, because we weren't just friends.

His mom could see that. He'd told her about us, about me. He put me in his fucking will.

His hand squeezed mine, actually squeezed.

I thought I'd fucking imagined it, false hope and all that.

I looked at him, studying his face. His eyes opened slightly after a few seconds, "Hey, hey.. don't... don't talk. Don't move. It's me, it's Coop." I looked at his mom, my voice hurried, "Go get a nurse, if he tries to fight this vent it's not going to be great."

His mom practically ran from the room, I brushed his cheek gently. "You came back, thank you. Fuck, thank you." I lifted his hand up to press a kiss to it and his heart rate monitor kicked up, not enough to be anything to worry about.

But enough for me to understand.

He was here. He was alive. And I fucking loved him.

Theo

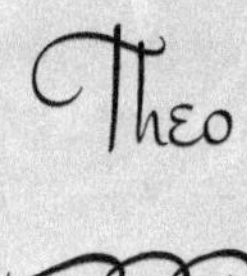

"Is Millie with you?" Coop's voice came out fast and rushed, which meant one of two things. He was gone or he would be gone soon. There was the slightest chance he'd woken up, but not enough to hold onto.

I knew it, Coop knew it, hell even Millie knew it.

My mind was spiraling.

No, please tell me he's not about to tell me he's gone. He can't be gone.

We didn't get to say goodbye.

Was he going to make me tell her?

Was this my punishment?

I cleared my throat, trying to manage words when I felt like dying myself. "Yeah, she's finally eating. I think her phone is on DND. Too many messages from everyone." I paused, "Please tell me—"

"He's awake."

"What?" My brain didn't catch up in time. "He's awake?"

Millie perked up, "He's awake?!"

I jammed the speaker so fast, Coop let out a laugh that sounded more like relief than anything, "He's in a lot of pain, they just removed the vent and had to clean him up. I didn't want Millie here for that."

Millie rolled her eyes, the first little bit of her coming back through. Finally, *finally*.

"His mom and dad?" I asked.

Coop's voice came through, "They're both here."

My chest felt so much fucking lighter, thank the Gods.

Millie abandoned her food, grabbing the juice and ginger ale mix I'd been pumping into her for days now. She'd finally eaten more than a few bites, she'd managed at least half the bowl of soup this time.

I had to basically jog to keep up with her, she was a woman on a mission. When she got to his room she took a deep breath and opened the door slowly, pushing her way in. I stood awkwardly in the doorway, the room was already crowded enough.

Link's dad pushed past us, giving my shoulder a light squeeze before exiting the room. I didn't need to see it to know Millie had thrown herself around him, well maybe not thrown because she was in pain too. "Fuck, I thought I lost you."

"I'm right here, babygirl." Link mumbled, pulling her closer even though he winced slightly. "I'm so sorry, I didn't see him and it was you or me."

Link's mom looked between the four of us, "We're gonna run and get some coffee, he's in good hands here." She took another long look at her son, "We'll be back soon sweets."

I heard Millie mumble something that sounded like "Don't you ever do that to us again."

As soon as his mom was gone, Link grabbed her chin and tilted her face up. "I love you so much, Mils." His lips brushed hers and she wiped her tears on the hoodie she was wearing.

Coop had gone back and gotten a few of Link's hoodies, we'd all practically lived in them the last two days.

Even Coop.

I took a step forward, unable to hold myself back anymore, Millie immediately made room, shifting towards Coop who wrapped an arm around her waist and tugged her in closer.

"Link, baby..." I exhaled as a tear slid down my cheek. "I thought—"

Link immediately kissed me, wincing as he brought his arm up higher than he should have.

I sat down, carefully embracing him. I let myself cry, because crying in relief that I had him, that he was here and not going anywhere felt a whole lot better than thinking I was going to lose him.

After a moment, Link grinned, shifting in the bed. "So you're not going to call me blondie anymore? I kind of liked it."

I looked at him confused, but he was looking at Coop. Coop who was now a very bright shade of pink. "You heard all that, huh?" Hh said quietly, his voice betraying the nervousness I hadn't seen in him in years.

"All of it." Link confirmed, and I didn't miss the way Link looked disappointed, like he was expecting something else.

Coop untangled from Millie, who looked just as confused, whatever they were talking about, we hadn't been around for it. I watched as Coop cupped his cheek tenderly, "I love you." Coop whispered, like he just wanted Link to hear, just between them.

"I love you too, Coop." Link's voice was hoarse, but I could still feel it, Link didn't say that unless he meant it.

He meant that.

When their lips met, neither pulled away and Millie's mouth fell open in a little 'O' shape that was half shock, half love.

"About damn time." I whispered.

Because honestly, it took them long enough.

Link

I was getting sick and fucking tired of this house.

I was craving open roads, *uhuh, don't look at me like that. I'm not.*

I'm not getting another bike.

Everyone threatened me; my parents, Millie, Theo, and Coop. Millie wouldn't even let me go see the bike in impound, which was bullshit.

Theo did show me pictures though and that shit was crazy. My hair was growing back, not much I might add and Millie had Gracie come over to fix it the right way, so I was at least growing it in evenly now. I guess maybe the era of bleach blonde was gone, replaced by my mom's sandy blonde color.

Coop had been attached to my hip since I got home, even taking an extra day off during the week so he could be here. He was currently laying in my lap, flicking through different tv show recommendations. We'd binge watched everything he'd cycled through so far.

Crooks laid beside me, he really had chosen me. He was such a sweet cat, spoiled but sweet, Theo was also just a little jealous that Crooks loved me so much. He wouldn't say it, but I could see it.

Theo and Millie had worked out whatever it was. She'd sat down after and said she wasn't going back, I'd gotten her to tell me what it was about. She'd given a customer her fake number, the encrypted one I'd helped her set up and Theo had seen it. He reacted exactly how either of us would have honestly.

I'd bought her a pole for her library shortly after that combination. I'd also taken her money from the accident and set her up multiple accounts. She didn't even argue this time. Just let me.

Theo looked like he wanted to say something, Millie was lying on him. "So are we all gonna get married or—?" He tried, I'm sure meant it to sound like a question, but it came out uncertain as fuck.

Millie's eyes widened, "How would that work?"

I grinned, "Well, I mean—you and Coop. He already called you his fiancee at the hospital, and then I can marry Theo." I shrugged, "It'd work better that way anyway, because finances. You'd all be set up for life either way."

Coop tensed, I knew he was told about the will. He knew he was in it. Those bastards thought I was done fighting for them? My own mother—Jesus, I had to come back out of spite.

No way were they unplugging my ass.

"What about like kids?" Millie asked quietly, her eyes falling downward. "I–um—mom mentioned grandkids and I haven't been able to stop thinking about it."

"Mils, do you have baby fever right now?" I asked, threading my fingers through Coop's hair.

"I—" She paused, "I almost lost you, of course I had that what-if."

"We'll come back to that." I couldn't help the smile on my face as she flushed.

"I'm just saying three kids might be a lot." Coop looked up at me, "But if you want three kids, we gotta get on that." He chuckled, bringing his hand up to touch my jaw gently. Coop being lovey dovey with me was still not something I was completely used to, but fuck I loved it.

Millie blinked, "Three?"

"I think he means one from each of us." Theo spoke as his hand fell lower on her stomach. "But we can discuss all of that later on, don't even worry about it Princess. Not right now."

"Gracie is going to kill me for quitting with absolutely no notice." She groaned, her fingers hovering over her phone screen.

"Oh!! Toby and Gracie are officially together, Jonah knows now too." Theo laughed, raking his fingers through her hair.

"About damn time." She huffed, "Also Theo did you just fucking propose without rings?"

I pursed my lips, I had them. I'd had them ordered from the day I got home. They were sitting upstairs in my room. "Not technically he didn't...I'll be right back."

I stood up, limping slightly still. Fuck, this was bullshit.

I told them no to extra pain meds, but the pain hadn't really gone away. I made my way up the stairs, waving off Coop's attempt at helping me. He sighed, sitting back down. I could have sworn he mumbled, "Stubborn ass." I wasn't going to even acknowledge that.

I grabbed the four rings, all of ours matched. Intricate silver, moss agate and diamonds woven into the bands, and Millie's had a moss agate marquise cut with diamonds surrounding it. They were all in their own boxes, inside of a bag.

When I finally made it downstairs I gave each of them their own box, opening my own afterwards. "If you want them of course, we may need to resize."

Coop looked at his, "How long have you had these?"

"I bought them right after I got out of the hospital." I admitted, "I didn't know when to ask, but I figured we were all in this, ya know?"

Millie put hers on her finger, I knew hers would fit. She was admiring it, Theo slid his on to, no questions. I looked at Coop and he leaned over to kiss me, his lips soft against mine. "I'm in it, with you and them."

He slid the ring on his finger, it was only a half size too big, but I could get it resized no problem.

I exhaled, this is everything I didn't know I wanted.

This is why I had to come back.

They were my people.

In this life and the next.

www.ingramcontent.com/pod-product-compliance
Lightning Source LLC
LaVergne TN
LVHW090553110826
845146LV00001B/112

* 9 7 9 8 9 9 2 8 7 2 6 2 0 *